"BLOOD.

Arno Volek's words were barely understandable. He turned from the window, and young Samara Volek swallowed a gasp. His face wasn't Arno's. It was changing, growing a muzzle. The snouted beast that had been Arno raised its muzzle to sniff the air. Its glowing golden eyes fixed on the closet where Samara and her brother hid, and it flexed taloned paws. Fangs gleamed when the mouth opened. A long, drawn-out howl chilled Samara's very bones.

"He's coming after us," Samara warned. "He's trying to get into the closet. What if he breaks through?" she asked fearfully.

"Don't worry. Grandfather's coming. Grandmother, too," her brother said.

If Samara hadn't seen the beast, his words might have reassured her. But how could *anyone* challenge the beast—and live?

If you and/or a friend would like to receive the *ROC Advance*, a bimonthly newsletter featuring all the newest and hottest ROC books and authors, on a complimentary basis, please fill out this form and return it to:

ROC Books/Penguin USA
375 Hudson Street
New York, NY 10014

Your Address

Name _____

Street _____ Apt. # _____

City _____ State _____ Zip _____

Friend's Address

Name _____

Street _____ Apt. # _____

City _____ State _____ Zip _____

Moonrunner #2:

GATHERING DARKNESS

Jane Toombs

A ROC BOOK

With special thanks to Jacqueline Lichtenburg

ROC
Published by the Penguin Group
Penguin Books USA Inc., 375 Hudson Street,
New York, New York 10014, U.S.A.
Penguin Books Ltd, 27 Wrights Lane, London W8 5TZ, England
Penguin Books Australia Ltd, Ringwood, Victoria, Australia
Penguin Books Canada Ltd, 10 Alcorn Avenue,
Toronto, Ontario, Canada M4V 3B2
Penguin Books (N.Z.) Ltd, 182–190 Wairau Road,
Auckland 10, New Zealand

Penguin Books Ltd, Registered Offices:
Harmondsworth, Middlesex, England

First published by Roc, an imprint of New American Library,
a division of Penguin Books USA Inc.

First Printing, April, 1993
10 9 8 7 6 5 4 3 2 1

Chapter 1

After making certain the door to her tower room was still barred, Liisi lifted her sable pouch from a wooden chest. She crossed to the round blue silk rug positioned in the exact center of the room and sat cross-legged on it.

One of the old tapestries behind her stirred as Liisi readied the stones for casting, a movement she felt rather than saw. The scene on the tapestry was an old Finnish folk tale, one of those chanted by rune singers—the maiden Aino fleeing from the shaman Vainamoinen, about to cast herself in the lake to avoid becoming his bride.

Aino didn't drown; she became a magic fish and thus escaped. No one died in the old songs; they merely changed.

In the past, Liisi had sometimes regretted not having Aino's ability to avoid her fate. From the first moment she'd seen him in that fearful summer of 1850, she'd known Sergei Volek was dangerous. She'd also known they were so irrevocably linked that only death could break the bond. In these thirty years since they'd met, they'd been apart more often than together, but the link still held.

Caressing the soft sable fur, she sighed, remembering those early days when Liisi Waisenen had come very close to dying instead of becoming Liisi Volek. Since then, Sergei had brushed against death too many times here in the United States and in Russia.

Yet they'd both survived. She'd built her castle in this beautiful California valley, and Sergei had made it into a fortress to shelter them and those of their blood.

Volek blood was tainted by darkness—but a darkness that could be controlled, as she'd proven.

Sergei had sworn that, for the safety of the clan, no outsiders would ever live in Volek House. Why would he violate his own vow within a week of making it? Never mind that Guy Kellogg was an old and valued friend. As soon as she'd met the three Kelloggs—husband, wife, and daughter—Liisi had felt in her bones that along with the Kelloggs Sergei admitted danger and death.

She hoped the stones would show her the way to rid Volek House of them once and for all.

Removing the quail egg–sized stones from the pouch, Liisi slid the ruby ring onto her left forefinger, then breathed on the other eight stones: granite for eliminating errant energy, crystal to focus the summoned energy, agate to stabilize, amethyst to promote foreseeing, coral for wisdom, obsidian for strength of purpose, turquoise to protect, and malachite for strength of will.

She dropped all but the ring into her lap, closed her eyes, and chanted each stone's origin. As she finished the last words, the stones flew from her skirt onto the blue carpet. Opening her eyes, she bent over to determine how they'd fallen. Despite the dimness of the round room, illuminated only by the pale light from four high and narrow slitted windows, the ominous pattern was clear.

Malachite lay atop both turquoise and granite. "A strong will overcomes protection," she murmured. Whose will? One of the Kelloggs, she feared. Also, the ability of the granite to keep out unwanted energy was blocked—a warning that her own *noita* spells might be bypassed by another.

Amethyst, coral, and agate circled crystal, as though in protection, but as she passed the ruby over the stones, the crystal and amethyst grew opaque, unreadable. Definite outside interference. She was being prevented from seeing ahead.

Liisi stroked the ruby absently. It must be the presence of the Kelloggs. Guy had tracked down Sergei in desperation, claiming that finding him was his last hope for his wife, Annette. Though she had little hope of solving Mrs. Kellogg's problem, Liisi knew she must try. Otherwise Sergei would insist on his friend remaining at Volek House.

She muttered under her breath as she gathered the stones back into the pouch. Sergei's devotion to his friends had led him into danger all too often. He was the first to insist the family came first—why couldn't he hold to that?

More troubled than she'd been since the time of the night howling, Liisi put the pouch away. It had been years since she'd ventured on that dreadful journey between the worlds. The Maiden knew she'd hoped never to go again.

Reluctantly, she removed the deerskin drum from the chest and set it reverently on the floor. She stripped to the skin. Bells tinkled and iron charms jangled as she donned the shaman's long deerhide shirt.

As she began to dance in a circle in time to the beat of the drum, she banished the thought that this time she might never return from Tuonela's deadly realm.

Wolf Volek stood on the tower balcony staring into the cold gray tule fog shrouding the valley. A similar miasma had clouded the interior of Volek House for over two weeks—from the moment his grandfather had unlocked the gates to three night travelers and invited them in as guests.

Guy Kellogg, Grandfather claimed, was an old friend from New Orleans by way of France. The other two guests were women—Guy's wife, Annette, and his daughter Cecelia.

Grandmother Liisi hadn't welcomed the guests.

Death, she insisted forbiddingly, stalked Annette. A death that would doom them all.

Once he saw Cecelia, Wolf hadn't paid much attention to the elder Kelloggs. Cecelia was so pretty that the sight of her stole his breath from his chest. Mima had scolded him about how his eyes followed every move Cecelia made, but he didn't feel guilty. The bond between him and Mima wasn't in the least weakened by the excitement that thrummed through him on those all too few occasions when Cecelia's green eyes chanced to meet his.

A sound warned him that the door to the tower was opening, and for an instant his heart leaped in hope. Could it possibly be Cecelia?

"Hello, Wolf," Guy Kellogg said as he stepped onto the balcony. "Still foggy, I see."

Wolf, concealing his disappointment, nodded.

"Fog in New Orleans is whiter," Guy said. "Mistier. And it doesn't last for days on end."

After a moment of silence, the reticent Wolf reminded himself that it was polite to speak when spoken to. "I've never been to New Orleans."

"That's where your grandfather and I met."

Wolf nodded again.

Guy smiled. "You remind me of him when he was young—he wasn't much of a talker, either. He was twenty then, as I was. How old are you?"

"Sixteen."

"You look older. Seem older." Guy leaned on the iron balcony rail and faced Wolf. "Sherman told me—" He paused and ran a hand through his graying hair. "I have trouble remembering to call your grandfather by his real name. You see, I knew him as Sherman Oso, not Sergei Volek. How long ago that seems—over thirty years. We were both young, Sergei and I. That sense of secret darkness within him fascinated me from the first. But art was my life, and so I sailed off to Paris, leaving him with Papa."

Wolf's interest was caught. Grandfather had never spoken of his early life in much detail. He did know that Guy's father, a doctor, had uncovered Sergei's dark secret.

"My father never wrote me what he knew about Sergei," Guy said. "Until I came back to New Orleans from France, after my father's death, I had no notion my friend was any different from myself. Not until Francois, one of our old servants—he'd been a slave before the War Between the States—told me what he'd witnessed under a full moon one fateful night."

When Guy didn't immediately go on, Wolf prompted him. "What did he see?"

Guy lowered his voice, at the same time intensifying its timbre. "Speaking of that night, even all those years later, made Francois tremble. His voice quivered as he told me how Gauthier, the master of the neighboring plantation, a murdering devil of a man, drove his horse at the unmounted Sergei, meaning to kill him. 'Your friend, he change,' Francois told me. 'He is no longer a man—he is a beast.' It was the beast who tore out Gauthier's throat, putting an end to that bastard once and for all. *Loup-garous,* we Creoles call men who change."

Wolf knew the French word meant wolf-men, but it wasn't true that Grandfather's shifting turned him into a wolf. He changed into something else entirely.

"Which is why your name interests me," Guy went on. "You're called Wolf, yet Sergei insists you don't inherit his problem."

"Grandfather didn't choose my name."

Guy shrugged. "In any case, Sergei fled New Orleans to save himself from exposure as a *loup-garou,* using the name my father gave him—Nick DePlacer—and set up as a doctor in Michigan. He still suffered from amnesia, as he had ever since he was eighteen when he woke up, naked and injured, on a beach in California. Sherman or Nick, he had no idea who he really was or why he bore the curse of shapeshifting."

"Mima went with him to Michigan," Wolf put in.

"Yes, Francois told me that Sergei saved Mima—a slave girl of nine at the time—from that devil Gau-

thier's lust.'' Guy sighed. ''I missed all the excitement—and here I was so sure Paris would be far more
interesting than New Orleans. If only Sergei had
trusted me enough to confide in me before I sailed for
France. I wish he had. For many reasons.''

Wolf said nothing, well aware shapeshifting was not
a secret a man willingly shared. He still carried the
memory of that terrible moonlit night three years ago
when the posse of ranchers roamed the hills beyond
the valley hunting the mysterious beast who'd abducted
Mima. The beast had been a shifter, though the men
who shot him never discovered that. The posse had
almost killed Grandfather, too.

''I'm glad Sergei found a woman like Liisi to help
him,'' Guy said. ''When I knew him, he vowed never
to marry or father children.''

Friend he might be, but it was none of Guy's business that having the twins was Liisi's idea and Grandfather had known nothing of them until he returned to
California from Russia. Unexpectedly coming face-to-
face with his twin sons had driven Sergei into a dangerous state of uncontrolled shifting. It had been days
before he returned to himself and was reconciled to
the twins and Liisi.

''I know Ivan and Arno are Sergei and Liisi's twin
sons,'' Guy went on, ''but I'm not quite clear on how
the other children at Volek House are related to Sergei.
You're his grandson, the son of a child he fathered on
a Kamchadal women before he fled Russian in 1848—
am I right?''

Wolf nodded.

''Remarkable how Sergei recovered his memory on
that Russian-bound ship so many years later,'' Guy
added. ''He told me that he befriended me in the first
place because I reminded him of someone—and it
turned out to be his dead twin, killed in Kamchatka
when he and Sergei fled for their lives.''

Wolf shivered. Not from the chill of the November
fog but from the memory of himself as a child among
his people, the Kamchadals, caged and treated as an

animal. Grandfather's rescue had come just in time—
Wolf knew he couldn't have survived naked through a
Siberian winter.

"Did your mother have unusual abilities?" Guy
asked.

Wolf hardly remembered his mother, but he knew
that the fact she was a shaman's daughter had enabled
her to protect him from the rest of the tribe until she
died. He didn't care to discuss her with Guy, so he
merely shook his head again.

"And you?" Guy persisted.

Wolf shrugged. "None." He wasn't a shifter like
Grandfather nor a *noita* like Grandmother Liisi. He
had no talent for seeing what was to come like Mima.
He and Cousin Natasha were ordinary, and he was just
as glad.

"This second set of twins—the boy and girl—Sergei
told me they were also his grandchildren," Guy said.

"Yes." Samara and Stefan had been sired by the
dead shifter; their Miwok mother had delivered them
the same night the posse shot their father. Grandfather
had decided the shifter had been a son he fathered
before he left California for New Orleans; a son he
hadn't known existed.

Wolf said none of this.

"And then there's his grandniece, little Tanya," Guy
went on. "The small baby, I understand, is your
daughter?"

"Druse is mine. Mine and Mima's."

Guy didn't comment, though Wolf thought he raised
his left eyebrow slightly.

Why? Because I'm sixteen and Mima's thirty-nine?
Wolf scowled.

"I suppose it's too early to tell about abilities the
little ones might inherit," Guy said.

It was and it wasn't. In the Volek line, shapeshifters
were limited to one of identical twin sons, the shifting
first occurring when the boy became a man. Though
he couldn't explain how he could tell, Wolf knew the
shifter, in the years to come, would be Arno. So maybe

he did have a sort of talent, after all—though this had yet to be proven, since Ivan and Arno were only six.

The rest of the Volek children weren't identical twins, so they wouldn't be shifters. Time would tell about other talents.

Guy changed position to stare, as Wolf was, into the shifting grayness of the fog. "I feel we're safe here," he said, so softly he might have been talking to himself. "Safe. For the first time in years."

Volek House, even though built of stone to resemble a castle, was by no means a fortress like some castles Wolf had seen in Russia. Still, high adobe walls topped with iron spikes enclosed the grounds, and locked iron gates shut out trespassers.

"This California valley is a perfect place," Guy went on. "Beautiful, isolated, fertile. Endless fogs seem to be its only drawback."

"They always lift."

"Unlike mine." Guy looked at Wolf. "Did Sergei tell you why I brought my family here?"

As a small child, Wolf had been taught by his mother that it was impolite to look others in the eye. After she'd died and he'd been seized and penned by the men of the tribe, he'd been afraid to. But once Grandfather rescued him and took him away from Siberia, he'd noticed other people didn't behave like the Kamchadals. Still, he found it difficult to gaze directly at anyone when he spoke, and so he stared over Guy's head. "I know your wife has an illness you hope my grandfather can cure."

It was Mima who'd told him. "Me," Mima had added, "I think the Kellogg woman's got something no one's going to heal. You watch yourself around that girl of theirs—like mother, like daughter."

"You might call it an illness," Guy said to Wolf, "but it's not the kind doctors can treat. Sergei is the only one in the world who can possibly find a way for Annette to control her affliction."

Control. The word echoed in Wolf's mind. Was Mrs. Kellogg a shapeshifter? Surely not, or Grandfather would have told him. Wouldn't he? Unlike Grandfather, Wolf couldn't see auras, so he had no ability to identify adult shifters.

As if reading Wolf's thoughts, Guy said, "Sergei's learned to control his shifting, hasn't he? I'm happy he's survived against the odds, that he's thrived and prospered. I'm glad he's built a safe haven for himself and his family. Because of my wife's problem, the three of us aren't safe. Without his help, we will never be safe. Is help too much to ask of him?"

Wolf shuffled his feet uneasily. What could he say? "Grandmother Liisi fears you bring danger," he blurted finally, immediately unhappy with what he'd revealed.

Guy shook his head. "I pray we don't. I'm sorry to distress her. Is that why she's shut herself in her tower room?"

"Not exactly. In her own way, she's trying to help." Grandmother Liisi was a *noita,* a Finnish wizard, a spell-maker. She was the one who'd taught Grandfather how to control his shifting. While she couldn't see into the future as well as Mima, Liisi could sense trouble before it happened. With her silver eyes seeming to probe his very thoughts, Wolf was never entirely at ease around her.

Aware that Guy had been silent for a long time, he glanced sideways and found him making bold black strokes on a white pad of paper. Moments later, Guy tore off a sheet and handed it to Wolf.

Wolf stared in fascination at the sketch of himself standing at the rail. Is that really how he looked—dark and glowering? He glanced again at Guy and met his gaze by accident.

"I can see my drawing's unsettled you," Guy said. "Perhaps you don't think of yourself as dour. But do you know I've never seen you smile? You should learn how. All our lives we—you, me, everyone—teeter precariously on the brink of a dark void. What can we do about it? Nothing. Except smile because the darkness hasn't swallowed us yet.

"Sketching you reminds me of when Sergei and I were young in New Orleans and how I upset him with my drawings. Though at the time I knew nothing about his shifting, I once painted him crossing the grounds at Lac Belle at night under a full moon. To my surprise and his consternation, he emerged as a sinister monster. That painting, believe it or not, turned out to be my masterpiece. Today it hangs in a Paris museum. You Californians may never have heard of me, but I confess that my name is not unknown on the Continent, even though I haven't painted in years."

He smiled sadly at Sergei. "Ah, but the young care little for museums or for the ramblings of an aging artist, *n'est ce pas?*"

Seeing a chance to learn more about Cecelia, Wolf gathered his courage. "How old is your daughter, sir?"

"Ah yes, Cecelia. Though she's not quite eighteen, my little girl fancies herself a woman of the world. You must try to excuse her if she snubs you, as I'm afraid she will. At present, she insists that any male under the age of twenty-five is a mere boy. I fear we've spoiled her, Annette and I. We've certainly protected her, perhaps too much. Cecelia has no notion how serious her mother's affliction really is."

Guy held his hands out as though caressing the fog. "In truth I welcome *la belle brume,* the beautiful fog, because tonight its gray cloak will cover the valley and hide us from the full moon's silver rays. It's hard to recall how I once loved to walk in the moonlight."

Grandfather, too, avoided the full moon. "Though I control it," he'd once told Wolf, "the temptation is always there—the pulsing of blood lust, the urge to shift and run free."

"Wolf?" Natasha called from the doorway. Her voice, like everything else about her, was hesitant. She'd never fully recovered from what the soldiers had done to her in the czar's palace in St. Petersburg.

"I don't mean to interrupt." Natasha spoke in Russian—she understood some English but rarely tried to speak it. She'd also been taught the French tongue as a child, but she avoided that, too.

Guy greeted her in French, and she smiled nervously at him. Natasha remained afraid of all men. Except Grandfather.

"Would you come and try to quiet Samara?" Natasha asked Wolf. "She's screaming again, and Uncle Sergei is nowhere to be found."

Though the twin's widowed mother, Morning Quail, lived at Volek House, she left much of the care of three-year-old Samara and Stefan to Natasha or Mima. Stefan was no more trouble than any little boy, but Samara had inexplicable crying spells that disturbed everyone. At those times, Morning Quail fled, seemingly afraid of her little daughter.

"I'll come," Wolf told Natasha, remembering only when he reached the door to excuse his departure to Guy.

Samara huddled in a corner of the second-floor nursery, her eyes tightly shut, sobbing piteously. Tears squeezed past her closed lids, dribbling down her cheeks, and her nose ran. She was a picture of misery.

Wolf strode to the corner and hunched down beside her. He didn't gather her into his arms as his grandfather would have. Instead, without speaking, he laid his right hand gently on her head, feeling the softness of her dark hair under his palm.

After a moment, the intensity of Samara's crying diminished. Without opening her eyes, she reached up with both hands and grasped Wolf's wrist, clutching hard. With the child clinging to his arm, he eased to his feet, bringing Samara to hers. Only then did he lift her into his arms.

He sensed her fear ebb as her sobs gave way to sniffles, sensed it not in his mind but more with his entire body. If he'd had to explain the feeling, he wouldn't know where to start. Though not the same, the feeling reminded him of the bond between himself and Mima. Something connected him and this child who shared the Volek blood. And, young as she was, Samara understood this.

Unexpectedly, an image flashed into his mind. *Huge trees. Under them, a dark and menacing figure. Waiting.* Before he could make sense of it, the image faded and was gone.

Though this had never happened between them before, he knew the mind picture came from Samara, knew that she'd shown him what frightened her. But he had no idea what the image meant. It had been nightmarish—the trees more gigantic than real trees, the dark figure a monster. As he dried her tears and wiped her nose, he wondered what he should do.

Questioning her wouldn't help. Once the spell was over, Samara never remembered what set off her terrified weeping.

He'd share the nightmare image with Mima. He shared everything with her. Except a confession of the strange allure Cecelia had cast over him. How could he share that? After all, Mima was the mother of his child.

He cuddled Samara in his arms, murmuring soothing words. Stefan, who'd run out of the room as he always did when his twin began screaming, peeked in the nursery door, then raced inside and flung himself at Wolf, holding onto his leg. Wolf reached down with his free hand and patted the boy's head.

An instant later, his hand jerked back. Shifter! his special sense warned. He'd touched a shifter!

Startled, he stared down at Stefan, who scowled up at him. "My turn," the little boy said. "You always pick *her* up. It's my turn!"

He'd touched the boy before. Why did he only now see what Stefan was to become? He glanced at Samara. Could she be providing a linkage? He didn't know. The only things he was sure of were that he was right about Stefan, and he had to warn Grandfather there wasn't only one Volek boy but two who'd shift when they reached manhood. Arno and Stefan.

Morning Quail came and took the protesting Stefan

away, but Samara refused to leave the sanctuary of Wolf's arms, so he carried her with him while he went in search of Mima. If Natasha hadn't been able to find Grandfather, chances were he was outside. Wolf would look for him later.

Descending the stairs, he heard music and, curious, detoured to see who was playing the piano. Pausing at the open door of the music room, he caught his breath. In time to the pulsating rhythm of her mother's playing, Cecelia, dressed in a gauzy, floating gown, twirled past him, the bright red of the dress accenting her dark beauty.

The passion of her dancing transfixed Wolf. He'd never seen anyone move so gracefully, yet with a fire that sizzled through the space between them, heating his blood. He was conscious of nothing but Cecelia. Her arms reached out in an invitation that drew him toward her.

Come to me, her dancing urged. *Come to the flame and burn!*

Unaware of what he did, he glided into the room, following her as she spun away from him. With a sudden turn, she changed direction and whirled into his arms. Or would have, if he hadn't been carrying Samara.

He clutched the child with one arm while with the other he supported Cecelia. She clung to him to keep her footing. Her scent was spicy, arousing. But before he had time to enjoy their accidental embrace, a radically different message shot through him.

Shifter!

He let go of Cecelia so quickly she stumbled.

"What a nerve!" she exclaimed in French, turning her back and stalking to the piano. "*Maman,* this clumsy boy has quite ruined everything. Make him behave!"

Wolf was hardly conscious of her scolding or of Mrs. Kellogg trying to smooth things over. Overcome, he all but staggered from the room.

What was wrong with him that he sensed a shifter

every time he touched someone? Cecelia couldn't be
a shifter! Could she?

He found himself in the kitchen, Samara still in his
arms, without being certain how he got there. Mima,
stirring a pan on the stove, took one look at him,
shoved the pan to one side and hurried to him.

"Upstairs!" she ordered, and all but pushed him
toward the back stairs. He climbed them dazedly.

Mima had touched him and he hadn't sensed that
she was a shifter. Why would he? She wasn't.

Mima urged him into her room and shut the door
firmly. "Let that poor child go," she scolded. "You're
squeezing her so tight she can't breathe."

He tried to set Samara on the bed, but she wouldn't
let loose her grasp of his shirt, so he sat down with
her on his lap.

"That's some better," Mima said. "Now, tell me
what's the matter. But keep your voice down—Druse
is asleep."

Their daughter slept in a cradle on the far side of
the bed. Hearing Druse's name, Samara scrambled off
Wolf's lap and across the bed to peer down at the baby.
She began crooning a wordless song, presumably to
the sleeping Druse. Ordinarily, Wolf would have hung
over the cradle, too. The tiny perfection of his daughter thrilled and moved him. But he was too upset.

He gestured with his head toward Samara. "She had
a spell. Natasha fetched me and I quieted her. But this
time Samara showed me what scared her." He rose,
crossed to where Mima sat on the chaise longue, and
dropped to the floor at her feet. Speaking low, so Samara couldn't hear, he told Mima about the nightmare
picture.

"Nothing to show if what she saw was inside or
outside the gates?" Mima asked after a moment.

Wolf stared at her. "I didn't think of the trees or
the monster as being real, more of a bad dream."

"Something might be lurking around; how do you
know there isn't?"

A memory of the stalker in the spruce grove near

St. Petersburg came to Wolf. Grandfather, who could sense all humans and animals by their auras, couldn't sense the stalker—a man with no aura at all. But Wolf had known something lurked in the grove. Even though he'd been able to warn Grandfather, the stalker had stabbed Sergei with a silver knife, poisoning him. Grandfather had nearly died.

"Samara." Mima's voice was low but commanding. The child turned to look at her.

"Come to Mima."

Samara did.

Mima took the child on her lap. Cupping the girl's head in her hands, she looked deeply into Samara's light brown eyes. Stefan's, Wolf thought, were more yellow than Samara's. Like Arno and Ivan's eyes. Golden Volek eyes. Cecelia's were green. But Cecelia wasn't a Volek.

She couldn't be a shifter. Cecelia was already a woman; she wasn't a little girl. She should have shifted by now, if she was a shapeshifter. Wolf shook his head, confused. He lacked Grandfather's talent for reading auras—at one glance Grandfather could spot a shifter. That is, if the person was an adult and had already shifted at least once. Children lacked the telltale shifter aura.

Whatever it was Wolf sensed in Arno had nothing to do with auras. When he touched the child, he simply knew this was a potential shifter. Never before today had he sensed it in Stefan. As for Cecelia, if she'd changed shape even once, he'd no longer be able to tell she was a shifter any more than he could tell that Grandfather was. That meant it hadn't happened to her yet. He grimaced unhappily. If he was right, some night, under a full moon, she'd change.

He couldn't be right.

Still, hadn't Guy hinted than Cecelia's mother was a shifter?

He must talk to Grandfather!

"She has a talent," Mima announced, startling him. He stared blankly at her and Samara.

"This child," Mima insisted, "shines. It's too early to tell what her ability is. We'll watch and wait." She frowned at Wolf. "Whether you can sense anything out there or not, you'd best look around the grounds—at least inside the fence. How do we know Samara didn't have a true foreseeing?"

The fog closed around Wolf the moment he stepped through the front door. Surrounded by the dense gray blanket, he walked down the steps and circled the house, finding nothing unusual.

What now? No landmarks were visible through the fog. He didn't fear getting lost—his sense of direction had never failed him. But he could see only a foot or two ahead. Until the fog lifted, wasn't a search futile?

He thought of the Russian stalker, that ordinary looking man who had no aura, rendering him invisible to Grandfather's special sense. Thanks to Wolf's warning, Grandfather had been alerted, and he'd killed the man. Did other stalkers exist in America?

I'd feel the danger if a stalker were near, Wolf assured himself, at the same time wondering what unusual talents a stalker might have besides the lack of an aura.

He glanced uneasily at the fog shrouding everything familiar and wished he could give up and go back inside. Knowing he couldn't, not yet, he took a deep breath and walked away from the house into the cold gray unknown.

Chapter 2

This damn fog could smother a man, Wolf told himself. He'd followed the inside of the adobe wall surrounding the grounds for its entire circumference and was now making random sorties through the trees and bushes. So far he hadn't sensed any lurkers on the property but, because he couldn't see more than a foot in front of himself, he remained on edge.

When a building loomed ahead of him, he stopped. The barn. He caught the murmur of a man's voice and tensed. Had Jose come to work this morning? Not likely, with the fog this thick. Belinda and Rosa, the cook and maid, hadn't arrived. Listening carefully, he realized the man spoke Russian. Jose didn't.

Grandfather? Wolf couldn't be sure. He advanced cautiously.

"I could use some help, Wolf," Grandfather called, and Wolf smiled in relief. No one could creep up on Sergei Volek.

Except a stalker with no aura for Sergei to read. Involuntarily, Wolf glanced behind himself. Nothing but fog. Between Grandfather's special sense and his own sensitivity, he was all but positive no trespasser lurked inside the walls.

He trotted around and into the barn, where he found Grandfather on a stool, milking one of the cows. Without speaking, Wolf found another milking stool and a clean pail and started on the next cow. For a time, there were no sounds except the streams of milk hitting the pails, the snuffle or stomp of a cow, and the clucking of hens in the coop at the far end of the barn.

There wasn't a cat in sight. Wolf knew cats lived in the barn because he'd seen them come around for their daily quota of milk when he helped Jose. Cats never came near Grandfather. Though all animals feared him after he'd shifted, when he was himself they'd do anything Grandfather wanted. Except for cats. Somehow they sensed his underlying darkness.

"Much as I dislike the idea, I suppose it's time to think about hiring a man to live in," Grandfather said at last. "I wouldn't have him in the house—we'd build a cottage near the stables. The stock plus the grounds are too much for Jose to handle alone."

"I like helping him," Wolf said.

"After your tutor arrives, you'll be too busy."

"Tutor?" Wolf knew what the word meant, but he didn't see how it applied to him.

"You can't expect to enter a university without schooling," Grandfather said.

Wolf's grasp on the cow's teats loosened as he gaped at Sergei. The university! Him? His milking rhythm faltered, and the cow stomped impatiently, flicking her tail at him.

"At the same time we build the cottage," Grandfather went on, apparently oblivious to Wolf's bemusement, "we'll put up a school for the little ones."

"I didn't know you meant for me to go to the university," Wolf said haltingly. "You didn't go to one and you know everything."

Sergei chuckled. "Not quite. But Vlad and I did have almost the equivalent of a university education from our Cossack tutor. He was a tough taskmaster."

Until the beast killed him, Wolf thought, and then felt guilty. The beast and Grandfather were one and yet not one. Grandfather had no control over and no knowledge of what he did in his shifted state. But if the beast hadn't acted quickly, the Cossack tutor would have carried out his orders from the Volek family and killed Sergei after the first shifting.

"I wish you could have known Vlad." Grandfather sighed. "Vlad died in my place. He was no shifter— the Kamchadals killed the wrong twin."

Reminded of what he'd meant to tell Grandfather, Wolf blurted, "Stefan's not an identical twin, but he's going to be a shifter."

Grandfather stared at him. "What do you mean?"

Wolf did his best to explain what had happened with Samara. "I was holding her, and I believe I was able to feel the darkness inside Stefan when I touched him because I was bonded to Samara," he finished.

"I know you share a bond with Samara. But my father assured me the Voleks have never produced a shifter except in identical twin sons."

"Maybe boy and girl twins were never born into the family before."

"I suppose that's possible." Sergei's voice held reservations. "We'll keep an eye on Stefan."

"That's not all," Wolf added. "Samara wouldn't let me put her down, so I was still carrying her when—" He paused, trying to find an easy way to tell his grandfather what occurred in the music room without mentioning embarrassing details. "I accidentally touched Cecelia Kellogg," he said finally, "and I felt the same shifter darkness within her. It—it startled me."

Grandfather was silent for a long time, long enough to finish stripping the cow's teats and slide the stool over to the next cow. "How much do you know about the Kelloggs?" he asked at last.

"I know that Mrs. Kellogg has some affliction that makes her husband fear the full moon; something he believes only you can help her control."

Grandfather sighed. "There's no reason not to tell you all the facts. Annette was a famous French dancer when Guy met her. He's always been attracted to what he calls a 'feral mystery' in people, and she fascinated him from the first. His discovery that she disappeared from Paris for five days every month, days that coincided with the full moon, made him all the more determined to make her his. Desperate to keep her secret, Annette resisted marrying him for years.

"At last Guy found a way to follow her when the moon was full, watched his beloved Annette change in the moonlight into a half-woman, half-beast, and fled when she attacked him. But Guy, as brave and remarkable a man as his father was, returned in the morning, vowed he still loved her, and insisted they marry so he could protect her." Grandfather shook his head. "A brave man. Would you have had the courage to do the same?"

Wolf didn't answer. Grandfather was a shifter—he loved Grandfather; he'd give his life for him. But marry a woman who might change to a beast even as you made love to her?

Grandfather's smile was touched with sadness. "I see my question troubles you. In any case, marry they did. Annette's shifting has never been complete, and Guy manages her by tying her to the bed in a locked room on the nights she's dangerous. Unfortunately, she got loose last year, escaped from the house, and seriously injured a man in a Paris park. Guy caught up with her in time to keep anyone from discovering what she was, and later the French newspapers reported a wild panther was loose in the city. It was after this that he decided to bring his family home to New Orleans."

And in New Orleans, Wolf knew, Guy had heard from a servant that the man he'd known as Sherman Oso was a *loup-garou*. So he'd searched for Grandfather, hoping to find help.

"Can you help her?" Wolf asked.

"I can't, but I hope Liisi can. She's locked in her tower room, searching for a way. God grant she finds one." Sergei shook his head. "Liisi tells me she was able to teach me control because of the bond between us—a binding neither of us had any choice but to accept. Such bonds are not forged by will or by spells but in some inexplicable fashion."

"Like mine with Mima," Wolf put in.

"Exactly. Two strangers with no blood ties. Liisi

has no such bonding with Annette.'' He shrugged.
''We'll have to wait and see if any of Liisi's *noita*
spells are effective.''

''Does Annette Kellogg's aura show you she's a
shifter?''

''She doesn't have a normal human aura. Guy and
Cecelia do. Guy tells me Annette's first shifting was
at the time of her first woman's bleeding. My observation of Cecelia tells me she's well past her first shedding of blood. Are you sure about what you sensed in
her?''

Wolf, flustered by the discussion of women's bleeding, finished his milking before he responded. ''I'm
sure.''

''I can't say whether you're right or wrong because
I don't know. Only time and a first shifting will prove
your ability. Until then, you'll tell no one else what
you suspect about Stefan and Cecelia.'' He fixed Wolf
with a stern glance. ''Do you understand?''

Wolf nodded. He hadn't intended to tell anyone except Grandfather anyway.

''As for the image Samara showed you—I don't
know what the trees and the monster mean,'' Grandfather went on. ''If you're right about Stefan, she could
possibly be seeing into the future, seeing him shifted.
There's no way to tell. I'll speak to Liisi about it.
Come on, let's finish up the chores before lunch.''

Grandfather was right—how could anyone know
what Samara's distorted vision meant? Wolf was relieved to think the child might be a foreseer and had
been viewing the future instead of the present. At the
same time, he was disturbed by what Grandfather had
said about a tutor.

He was no scholar; he didn't want to go to the university. He winced at the thought of being shut in a
building all day poring over books or listening to pro-
fessors lecture. Outdoors was where he belonged, but
how was he to convince Grandfather?

Grandfather expected him to become the head of the
family—and he would if he had to. At six, Arno and

Ivan were obviously too young to assume any responsibility. Given Grandfather's good health, though, chances were the twins stood an excellent chance of becoming men before anything happened to Grandfather. In that case, they could take their rightful place as heads of the Volek family—and welcome to it.

If he could live any life he wanted, Wolf knew he'd choose to be a wanderer. He'd avoid cities and seek the woods, the fields, the mountains.

Like Morning Quail. She'd confessed to him that she didn't like living in Volek House.

"My people—poor," she'd said in her halting English. "No money. Little food. Live in mountains like quail, like bear, like deer. Free. Is good."

But Sergei insisted Stefan and Samara stay at Volek House, and Morning Quail didn't want to leave her children. Someday, Wolf vowed, he'd take her back to her people.

By noon, as Sergei and Wolf walked from the outbuildings toward the house, the fog was thinning.

"Clear by tonight," Sergei predicted, smiling.

Wolf knew the heaviness inside the house wouldn't lift with the fog. He hoped Grandmother Liisi's *noita* knowledge would solve the Kelloggs' problem soon, so they'd leave and Volek House would return to normal. So *he'd* return to normal. Cecelia's presence was as much a torment as a delight. He'd be glad when she was gone. When all the Kelloggs were gone. Everyone would be glad.

"Liisi tells me we should put in more orange trees," Grandfather said. "What do you think?"

"Yes." Wolf had no idea whether a larger grove was good or not, but if Grandmother Liisi said to plant more orange trees, that was enough. She was never wrong.

"I'll talk to Paul," Grandfather said.

Paul McQuade, their closest neighbor, was Grandfather's partner in McDee Enterprises. They'd started small—canning fruit and vegetables in Thompsonville in an old barn. Now they owned a packing plant in

Thompsonville as well as a large canning factory in Sacramento. Grandfather always said Liisi's foresight and advice had built the business.

Lately Grandfather had been buying railroad stock and spoke of opening an office in San Francisco. Wolf was willing to work hard at anything outdoors, but he wanted no other part of running the Volek businesses. So far he'd lacked the courage to say so.

Just before opening the back door, Grandfather looked up. Following his glance, Wolf noted the pale outline of the sun behind a high curtain of fog.

"We've a good chance of seeing the moon tonight." Grandfather's voice was grim.

But, though the fog lifted, it didn't entirely dissipate. By evening the gray mist once more enclosed Volek House in its damp, depressing shroud, hiding the moon and the stars.

Because Liisi was still locked in her tower room, Wolf helped Mima put Arno and Ivan to bed. Natasha came into their bedroom after singing Tanya to sleep and told the twins a bedtime story.

"This is how the brave Dobrynya," she began in Russian, "saved Prince Vladimir's favorite niece, Zabava, from the dragon's lair. . . ."

Wolf listened as eagerly as Ivan and Arno. Vladimir had also been the name of Grandfather's twin, killed by the Kamchadals as he and Sergei sought to reach the Petropavlovsk harbor and the safety of an outbound ship. Sergei had survived only because the moon was full, so he'd shifted and fought his way clear.

"So," Natasha went on, "Dobrynya's mother bade him saddle the horse that had been his grandfather's and then his father's, the magic horse that had been waiting in the stables for him these fifteen years. And she gave to him a silken whip from the Caucasus Mountains—a whip with secret powers. . . ."

If only *he* had some secret power, Wolf thought. He wouldn't care to be a shifter, but he wouldn't mind having Dobrynya's strength and bravery. If he did, he could keep Volek House safe from any threat. Cecelia would be impressed and stare at him admiringly instead of calling him a clumsy boy.

"Because the earth would not soak up the evil dragon's blood," Natasha continued, "Dobrynya found himself stranded in the middle of a huge bloody lake. Again the voice from heaven spoke to him and Dobrynya obeyed. Striking his lance through the blood to the ground, he commanded, 'Open, moist Mother Earth and swallow up the blood of the dragon. . . .' "

And so Dobrynya rescued the beautiful Zabava. Wolf wasn't quite sure if dragons had ever existed, but he knew there were none anymore. If all the dragons had been slain many, many years ago, what was left for him to rescue Cecelia from?

He longed to prove himself to her somehow. Perhaps his chance would come if he secretly watched over her and saved her from harm on that unlucky day when she finally shifted for the first time.

Grandfather warned that first time shiftings were the most dangerous because they were unpredictable. If seen by normal humans, the shifter could be hunted and killed by the frightened men. Especially if they used a silver weapon.

Shifting was always painful, and once begun, it was all but impossible to stop the change and revert to human form. Even worse, when he woke up naked as a man again, the shifter didn't realize how the beast had howled for blood under the moon. Whatever the beast did while shifted remained unknown to the man.

I'll protect Cecelia, no matter what, Wolf vowed.

"Tomorrow I'll be the dragon," Arno announced, half his words Russian, half English. "Ivan can be Dobrynya. But *my* dragon won't die."

"Hush," Natasha murmured, and began to sing a Russian lullaby about the moon shining on a baby's cradle.

It was then Wolf noticed that a silver sliver of light had slipped through a slit where the window draperies failed to meet. He walked to the window and peered at the sky.

Only a sheer veil of mist covered the full moon, riding high in the heavens. Concerned, he hurried from the twins' room and ran along the hall toward the Kelloggs' suite.

Before he reached the door, he heard Liisi chanting inside and paused. His grandmother must have conjured up a charm for Annette Kellogg.

"Dark spirit," she intoned, "do not ride the silver moonlight. Remain in Tuonela's depths where you belong. Evil one, seek not the light. You of the dark, remain in darkness. . . ."

On and on she chanted, her voice raising the hair on the nape of Wolf's neck. Just so had the Kamchadal shaman chanted when he plucked Wolf away from his dead mother's side and thrust him into the animal pen, calling him an evil spirit from the darkness between the worlds.

Yet the boy he was then hadn't been evil. That boy hadn't contained a dark spirit any more than Wolf did now. Was it possible Grandmother Liisi, like the shaman, could make a mistake? He tried to erase the frightening thought from his mind, but it clung, as sharp and prickly as a goathead seed.

The melancholy five-toned notes of his grandmother's kantele wove through her chant. Her instrument was made of bone. "Like Vainamoinen's," she'd told him. "Vainamoinen, the greatest Finnish *noita*—he lives forever, somewhere between the worlds."

Wolf waited outside the door, chilled by the music and the words. He didn't believe his grandmother would fail to control Annette's beast, but he wanted to be sure. He had his baby daughter to protect as well as the other children.

He was leaning against the wall when the chanting finally stopped. Wolf straightened as the door eased open. Grandfather ushered Grandmother Liisi from the room, nodding approval when he saw Wolf.

"Annette's asleep," Sergei said softly. "Liisi's spell seemed to work, but for safety's sake, Guy tied his wife to her bed. He'll stay with her—no need to stand guard any longer.''

Dismissed, Wolf ambled along the hall and around the corner to his room. He wished he could go to Mima instead. He hadn't slept in Mima's bed since Druse was born, though sometimes he had to fight the urge to go to her. But he'd promised Grandfather that he and Mima wouldn't have any more babies, and while there were ways to avoid creating a child, Mima had told him no method was altogether certain.

Tonight he needed Mima's warmth and comfort as much as anything else. But if he went to her, one thing would lead to another.

In his room, Wolf stripped off his clothes and slid beneath the covers. It had taken him some time to grow accustomed to sleeping in a bed. He'd never gotten used to nightshirts; he slept naked.

Reassured by his grandfather's words, he allowed himself to be sucked down sleep's dark tunnel into the world of dreams.

And nightmares.

He ran along a street, the paving cracked and rubble-strewn, toward a forest of greenery. Among the trees and bushes death waited. The metallic taste of fear fouled his mouth, terror clouded his mind, but he ran on.

Ahead, the dark spirit hidden in the greenery screamed a challenge: a caterwauling cry more chilling than any cougar's. He longed to stop, to turn back. He could not. All he could do was race toward his doom. . . .

Wolf sprang from his bed, heart pounding, the cry echoing in his head. As he grabbed his trousers and pulled them on, he assured himself the cry must have come from his evil dream. Unconvinced, he padded to the door, opened it, and looked into the hall. In the brass wall sconces, oil-fed flames flickered behind their protective chimneys as he listened.

The caterwaul came again, rising and falling in an eerie pitch that brought gooseflesh to his arms. A man shouted. A heavy object thudded to the floor. Glass shattered. A door crashed open. A woman screamed.

Wolf ran along the hall toward the commotion, driven by his fear for the children. As he rounded the corner, he stopped short. Something half-human, half-beast thrashed furiously in the grasp of Guy and Sergei, yowling as it fought to get away. Farther along the hall, a white-garbed figure flitted down the front stairs, disappearing from view.

Forcing himself on, Wolf hurried to help Guy and Grandfather as they dragged the snarling, spitting half-beast back into the Kelloggs' room, where moonlight streamed through open draperies. Wolf jerked them closed.

As Guy and Grandfather forced the half-beast onto the mattress, Wolf wrapped rope around its taloned hands and its human feet and tied it, spread-eagle, to the bed frame. The half-beast continued to struggle, yowling. Knowing this had to be Annette Kellogg, Wolf took only one appalled look before averting his eyes.

As Guy had told Grandfather, her shifting wasn't complete. She wasn't really a beast, but fangs, a coarsely feline cast to her features, and black patches of fur on her torso separated her from being human. And her abnormal strength—it had taken the three of them to pull her into the room and onto the bed.

"I'd hoped Liisi's *noita* charm would prevent this," Guy said wearily, "so I'm afraid I nodded off. I promise I won't let her get loose again."

"I'll sit up with you until morning," Grandfather told him.

Realizing they didn't need him any longer, Wolf made for the door.

"Thank you for your help, Wolf," Guy said. "I'm sorry you had to witness this."

Wolf mumbled that he was glad to help and fled. About to return to his room, he recalled the figure in white who'd flitted down the stairs. He was sure it had been a woman. He couldn't imagine Natasha leaving the safety of her room, and he knew Mima would stay with Druse. Liisi would have come to help, rather than fleeing. That left Cecelia.

Was she all right? Was she in danger of shifting? Wolf ran down the stairs.

When he reached the bottom, he heard the plink of a single note on the piano. Heart pounding more from anticipation than fear, he padded toward the music room. Though the wall sconces in the entry were lit, the music room was dark except for the silver glow of moonlight slanting in through the open draperies.

Wolf paused in the doorway and drew in his breath. Illuminated by the moon, Cecelia, in a white night-gown of some gauzy fabric, stood by the piano picking out a plaintive melody with one finger. He watched her for long moments, certain he'd never see a woman more beautiful or desirable.

She turned away from the piano and drifted to the window, where she stood with her back to him, the silver moonlight showing her woman's curves through the thin gown. Unable to wait any longer, he crossed the room to her, his bare feet silent on the floor and on the carpet.

"Cecelia," he breathed when he stood behind her.

She gasped, whirling to face him. "How you frightened me!" she cried.

"I'm sorry. I only wanted to—" He paused, unable to find words to tell her she aroused him. She smelled of some mysterious flower—a tropical flower that bloomed only at night, he decided—and of herself, infinitely alluring.

"Are you all right?" he finished.

"No." Her head dropped. "I'm frightened."

"Of me?"

"Why should I be afraid of you? I heard a terrible noise and I saw—" She broke off. "Never mind."

"I know what you heard, what you saw," he said.

"You do not!" She stamped her foot.

Wolf thought he understood. She was afraid to admit to him that she suspected her mother was the half-beast that had frightened her.

"Cecelia," he said gently, thinking her name was like the sound made by a mountain stream. "I do know because I helped your father and my grandfather tonight. Your father came here in the hope Grandfather had a cure for your mother."

"There's nothing wrong with my mother!"

Longing to touch her, he rested a tentative hand on her shoulder. "I don't mean to upset you."

She shrugged free of him. "Then go away. I don't want you here."

But he couldn't make himself go away. She was far too fascinating. Besides, she needed to be warned about what lay ahead for her. Even without Samara, his touch just then had confirmed what he'd felt in her earlier. She was a potential shifter.

"Cecelia, it's dangerous to close your eyes to the truth," he said at last. "There are such things as shapeshifters."

She turned away from him and started for the door. He caught her arm.

"Listen to me!" he ordered. "Never mind your mother's affliction—this is about you. I can sense shifters before they change. I have to warn you—you're one. You're a shapeshifter."

Cecelia raised her hand and slapped him hard across the face. Startled, he released her.

"Liar!" she sobbed, tears streaming down her face. "There's nothing wrong with me. Nothing. Do you hear, you stupid boy? I hate you! I'll hate you forever!"

Chapter 3

Still smarting from his grandfather's stern words, Wolf let himself out the back door and loped toward the barn. A chill wind from the north had blown away the last vestige of fog and today the sun shone. But Wolf was in no mood to appreciate the fine weather.

Jose had already driven the cows into the field, and Wolf hurried through the still open rear gate. He circled back along the outside of the wall, on his way to the pine grove west of the grounds. He preferred being outdoors even during the best of times, and when he was upset, his craving for being under the sky and among the trees surpassed all bounds.

Today was not the best of times. Early this morning, Cecelia had sailed past him on the stairs with her head held high, not sparing him a single glance. Guy, following her, had greeted Wolf coldly. He'd more or less expected such treatment from the Kelloggs but Grandfather's subsequent tongue-lashing was a surprise.

"I told you to keep your mouth shut," Sergei had begun. "Why did you defy me?"

Wolf tried to explain his feeling that Annette must be warned of what she was to become, but Sergei cut him off. "None of us, including you, know for certain you have the power to sense potential shifters. What if you're mistaken? You may have ruined Cecelia's life because you presumed to 'warn' her of something that may never occur."

Wolf hung his head. He hadn't thought about being wrong, and he was forced to admit it was possible.

"You will apologize to her," Grandfather ordered. "And to her father."

"Yes, sir."

And then Grandfather said the words that cut to the bone. "I'm deeply disappointed that you've betrayed my trust in you."

Tears stung Wolf's eyes at the memory of that moment. He blinked them back. He was too old to cry. Besides, his hurt went too deep for tears, too deep for anyone to heal. Even if he wanted to turn to Mima for comfort, her parting remark to him when he left the house would have turned him away.

"Didn't I warn you to stay clear of that French girl?" she'd said.

I won't go home tonight, Wolf told himself as he approached the grove. He wished he didn't have to go home at all.

I did what I thought best, he told himself sullenly. They may not believe me, but I could be right, couldn't I? Why does everybody blame me?

As the pines closed around him, a squawking blue jay flew ahead of him into the grove, warning of his coming. If Wolf had been feeling better, he might have smiled—he'd always admired the feisty jays, the sentinels of the woods.

He wandered aimlessly among the trees, breathing in the fragrance of the evergreens. Brown needles crunched under his feet, and the wind whispered to him from the overhead boughs. At times, he thought he was on the verge of understanding the wind's message but not today. He was too disturbed to let himself drift into the spirit of the grove.

A pine cone plunked onto the ground in front of him, followed by the angry chirr of the squirrel who'd been harvesting the cone. Just as Wolf glanced up at the squirrel, something moaned. He froze.

No animal or bird he knew moaned in such a way. Only humans did. Humans in pain.

The sound came again. Ahead of him to the left. He eased toward it cautiously.

"Please . . ." A woman's voice, her plea no louder than a sigh.

Abandoning caution, Wolf strode forward only to stop, staring, when he saw her. She was as out of place in this pine grove as he would be in the czar's court. A young woman sat propped against the trunk of a pine, her fair hair tumbled over her shoulders, her pine green riding costume rumpled and soiled.

Evidently hearing him, she turned her head. "Thank God!" she cried when she saw him.

Wolf knelt beside her. "Where are you hurt?" he asked.

"My—my ankle," she faltered, raising her riding skirt to show her left foot.

Uncertain if he should touch her, Wolf tentatively reached for her foot. When she didn't object, he lifted it gently. She wore a short black riding boot, coming just to the ankle. The silk stocking above the boot was torn, and he couldn't help savoring the warmth of her bare skin against his fingers.

"I don't think your ankle's broken," he said after a careful examination. He was no doctor, but he'd treated broken bones in animals.

"Merely twisted, would you say?" she asked, her eyes wide and trusting, eyes as brown as sable.

"Probably." He released her foot with great reluctance.

She was very pretty with her blond hair, brown eyes, and trim figure. She'd opened the front of her jacket, and it was an effort to keep his glance from the soft rise and fall of her breasts under the white shirtwaist she wore.

"What shall I do?" she asked plaintively.

He hadn't really paid attention to the difference in her speech until now. Though she spoke English well, she had a faint, charming accent.

"Don't worry, I'll help you," he assured her. "My

name's Wolf Volek—I live near here. What happened
to you?''

She put a hand to her cheek. "Oh, it's too embarrassing. My friends will scold me when they discover
how foolish I've been."

"*I* won't scold you."

She smiled at him, a flashing, brilliant smile, like
the sudden appearance of the sun. Wolf blinked, dazzled.

"You are a wonderful man! What would I have done
if you hadn't found me?" She shivered. "When night
came, I might have been killed and eaten by wolves
or bears! But you don't want to hear about my fears;
you wish to know how I came to be here. It's very
simple—my horse bolted and threw me. You didn't
happen to see a dappled gray, did you?"

Wolf shook his head.

"I dragged myself into the trees here and collapsed," she went on. "Perhaps it *was* foolish of me
to venture to ride from Thompsonville on my own, but
I was so tired of being shut in because of that awful
fog and today was so lovely and clear. . . ."

"You're staying with friends in Thompsonville?"

"Not exactly. I'm staying in that charming inn in
the town, waiting for my friends to arrive from San
Francisco. Alas, they've been delayed."

"I'll be happy to escort you to the inn, Miss—?"

"Wainwright. Linden Wainwright."

Linden. The name was as lovely as she was.

"I do hate to be such a bother, Mr. Volek. I've been
enjoying every minute of my visit to your most interesting country—until that unpleasant animal bolted. If
they ever manage to arrive, my friends are planning to
take me on a camping trip into the mountains so I
won't be homesick for Switzerland. They've assured
me the Sierras are the American Alps. I rode out alone
today to try and see for myself if they were right."
She smiled again. "I confess to being a goose."

Wolf was only vaguely aware that Switzerland was
in Europe, and he was still more uncertain about the

Alps. His lack of education bothered him as it never had before.

"Let's see if you can stand up," he said.

Linden Wainwright, leaning heavily on him, found she could hobble slowly if she didn't put too much weight on her injured ankle. As he helped her along, her dependence and trust warmed Wolf's heart—and her softness pressing against him created an entirely different sensation in another location. She smelled of roses and of horse, an earthy scent that aroused him. The trip home couldn't be too long for him—he never wanted to let her go.

When they came in sight of the wall, Linden slumped against him. "I—I'm afraid I can't go on," she admitted, biting her lip. "The pain—"

"I'll carry you." Without waiting for her to agree, he scooped her up into his arms.

"I'm imposing dreadfully," she said softly as he strode on.

He couldn't tell her how wonderful she felt in his arms, but carried away by his emotions, he blurted, "I'd do anything to help you."

Though she didn't reply, he thought she nestled closer against him. He hoped it wasn't his imagination.

Because he knew the rear gate would be open, he brought her into the grounds that way, entering the house through the back door into the kitchen where Mima was talking to Belinda, the cook. Both women stared at him. Mima frowned.

"Miss Wainwright's hurt her left ankle," Wolf said.

Within minutes, Mima had Linden settled into a chair with her boot off and was kneeling beside her, examining the injured ankle.

"No bones broken," Mima muttered as she manipulated the ankle. "No swelling, so it can't be sprained." She looked up at Linden. "You say your horse threw you?"

Linden nodded.

"I can't see where you're hurt much at all." Mima's words were a challenge.

"My ankle does feel better," Linden said, reaching for her boot. She glanced at Wolf. "I'm sorry to have caused trouble."

Puzzled and angry at Mima's attitude, he leaped to Linden's defense. "Miss Wainwright obviously twisted her ankle," he told Mima. "I'm taking her into Thompsonville in the buggy."

Mima shrugged and rose to her feet. "The sooner the better." She walked away without another word.

Twenty minutes later, Wolf and Linden sat side by side in the buggy on their way to town. Linden, who hadn't spoken since he'd helped her from the house, laid a hand on his sleeve.

"I'm so very grateful to you," she said.

It was as well he held the reins in both hands, tempted as he was to cover her hand with his. He wished the ride into Thompsonville were longer; he couldn't bear to think of their time together ending.

"I've never met a man quite like you," she went on.

"You're like no one else!" he told her.

Her smile and the warmth of her hand through his sleeve encouraged him to go on. "I want to—I mean, I wish I could see you again."

"Ah, but that might prove to be a problem. You understand that it's not proper for me to invite you to visit me at the inn and, as for your house . . ." She allowed her words to trail off.

Wolf's heart sank. He couldn't invite her to Volek House. Not with his grandfather's prohibition about admitting strangers. He was already in enough trouble with Grandfather.

"Don't look so downcast," Linden told him. "We'll find a way to meet."

He turned to her. "But how?"

She shrugged. "I can ride, can't I? I assume the stupid horse came back to the livery stable, and I'll make certain to request a more trustworthy mount next time.''

Next time. The words thrummed in his blood.

''There's always the pine grove,'' she murmured, soft as the wind in the boughs. ''We met there once, why not again? To give my ankle a chance to heal, we'll make it in two days' time.'' She leaned closer and touched her lips to his cheek in a fleeting caress. ''That's for your brave rescue.''

Though she didn't come as close to him again for the rest of the ride, Wolf floated on air. He knew she must be older than he—at least in her twenties—and he suspected she was acquainted with far more polished men. But Linden liked him; she wanted to see him again.

Unlike those at Volek House, here was a pretty and exciting woman who didn't scold him or snub him. The way she looked at him and her praise made him feel ten feet tall. And she'd kissed him. Only on the cheek, but one kiss could lead to another. Especially in the pine grove, where they'd be alone.

Wolf didn't know how he'd manage to get through the hours until he saw her again.

When he returned home, he half expected another lecture from his grandfather—this time about bringing a stranger into their midst. He meant to defend himself—Linden had been lost and injured, after all. Grandfather, though, wasn't waiting for him.

''I didn't tell Sergei,'' Mima advised Wolf later, ''but bring that woman here again and I surely will. If you ask me, she was putting on a show of being hurt for just that reason—to get inside Volek House.''

How could she say such a thing about poor Linden? Annoyed as Mima made him, Wolf held his tongue, not wanting to argue with her.

''I suppose you didn't even notice how she talks,'' Mima went on. ''She's a foreigner.''

''Visiting from Switzerland,'' Wolf said in triumph. Mima seemed to think he was still a know-nothing ten-year-old.

Thinking it over when he was alone, Wolf decided he'd confess to Grandfather that he'd found an injured woman in the woods and given her a ride back to Thompsonville in the buggy. There was no need to mention she'd actually been inside the house—what difference did that make?

When he got around to making his confession, Wolf thought that Grandfather seemed distracted, giving only half an ear to what he said.

"—and so I left her at the inn," Wolf finished.

His grandfather nodded. "That should be the end of the matter, then."

It wasn't a question, but guilt roiled inside Wolf because he had no intention of admitting he'd arranged to meet Linden again in the pine grove. He hated to keep secrets from Grandfather, but it was his own business who he associated with off the grounds.

Relieved that he hadn't upset Grandfather, Wolf hugged his secret to himself. The fact that he'd soon be seeing Linden enabled him to endure Cecelia's pointed snubs and Guy's chilliness without difficulty. What did he care how they acted? Spending most of the next day out of the house helping Jose or wandering into the woods meant he was mostly alone anyway.

When the morning of their meeting day dawned, Wolf remembered they'd set no time. Not that it mattered—he meant to go to the grove early and wait. He wished he could take enough food along for a picnic, but if he did, Mima was certain to find out and ask questions. He didn't want to arouse any suspicions.

After leaving the house, he detoured through the orange grove, admiring, as always, the contrast of the bright orange fruit against the glossy green of the leaves. He picked a couple of ripe oranges from one of the trees, and as he left the grove and strode toward the pines, he practiced different ways of presenting the oranges to her.

"I wish they were made of gold."

Much as he meant it, the words sounded foolish in his own ears.

"My heart goes with them."

Even worse.

Wolf finally decided he'd simply hand the fruit to her without comment.

If she came.

When he'd begun to doubt she might not come, he didn't know. True, Linden had praised him—even kissed him. And she was the one who'd suggested the pine grove. But what if her friends had arrived? Would she remember she was to meet him? Would she care whether or not she did?

The morning, fair and bracing, stretched on endlessly. A dozen times he told himself he was going to leave, all the while knowing he'd stay until dark before giving up.

It was past noon when he heard a horse's hooves. Wolf, sprawled under a pine, sprang to his feet. A handsome bay appeared between the trees with Linden riding sidesaddle. Wolf drew in his breath as he saw her. He thought of the two oranges and winced inwardly. They were far too humble a gift for the elegantly garbed woman who rode toward him.

"Mr. Volek!" she cried as she reined in the bay. "I feared you might not be here!"

She dismounted by sliding off into his arms. "You smell of roses," he said involuntarily, holding her a moment longer than necessary.

Linden wrinkled her nose. "And horse, too, I've no doubt."

"But I like the scent of horses!"

She smiled and patted him on the cheek with her gloved fingers. "I've brought a surprise in the saddle-bags," she said.

Her surprise was a striped blanket to sit on and a small picnic hamper crammed with food. As he spread the blanket, Linden noticed his oranges underneath the pine and exclaimed over them.

"I adore oranges! How wonderfully thoughtful."

"Picked ripe from our grove," he said, pleased that she appreciated his simple gift.

He tethered the bay and stood watching her as she knelt on the blanket setting out the food. He wasn't one to notice women's clothes in detail, but she looked so pretty in hers that he paid more attention than usual. Today her riding habit was golden-brown, and the jacket was trimmed with a darker brown velvet collar and cuffs. She wore a soft felt hat with a moderate brim. Yellow roses decorated the band.

"Come sit beside me," she suggested, patting the blanket.

He obeyed eagerly. Linden peeled off her gloves, revealing soft white hands. She removed her hat and set it aside with the gloves.

"I've even brought wine," she said, holding up a green bottle. "And, yes, I remembered a corkscrew. Would you like to open it?"

Wolf, who'd never opened a bottle of wine in his life, said, "I'd rather watch you do it. I like to watch you."

Actually, he'd never drank more than a glass or two of wine—and that recently. Grandfather didn't drink anything intoxicating himself—as a shifter he didn't dare—and hadn't had wine served with meals until the Kelloggs arrived.

"You'll quite turn my head," Linden protested.

After she'd opened the bottle and poured a small amount of the fine white wine into one of two small stemmed glasses, she offered the glass to Wolf. Recalling how Guy sniffed before he tasted his first glass of wine with dinner, Wolf imitated the actions.

"A good year," he said, copying Guy's words. At least Linden wouldn't think he knew nothing at all.

She smiled and poured herself a glass, then offered Wolf a plate of sliced cheese. He took some of everything she offered, hardly aware of what it was or how it tasted, so intent was he on Linden herself. Though he didn't remember drinking it, by the time they'd finished eating, the wine bottle was empty. Linden cleared the blanket of picnic remnants.

He felt wonderful, better than he'd ever felt before.

"Linden," he said. "Linden. Your name is beautiful. Like you."

"I shall take that as an invitation to call you Wolf," she said, edging closer to him and taking his hand. She held it between both of hers. "You're so strong," she murmured, looking up at him with admiring brown eyes. "So much stronger than I. I adore strong men."

Bemused, he lowered his head until their lips met. Then she was in his arms, clinging to him, returning his kisses, arousing him beyond his ability to control himself. Though he wasn't clear how it happened, eventually she lay on the blanket, undressed to the waist, while he caressed her bared breasts.

"Oh, Wolf," she whispered, her breath warm in his ear, "I want all of you."

God knows he wanted her! But when he tried to raise her skirts, she pushed away his hand.

"Not here," she murmured. "It's not right, out in the open like this. I can't. I won't."

"No one will see us," he said hoarsely, urgently, afire with need.

"I'm afraid," she said piteously. "If we were in your room, in your bed . . ." Her words trailed off as she inched her fingers along his thigh until they touched his rock hard prick, inflaming him. "Oh, Wolf, Wolf," she whispered. "How desperately I want you to take me. But not here. Properly. In your bed."

"Linden, please—"

"No." She pulled free of him, sitting up and turning her back as she put her clothes in order.

He tried to find a more comfortable position, but his continuing need made it difficult. "Your room at the inn?" he suggested.

She glanced over her shoulder at him. "Never! Everyone would know! This is our secret, yours and mine. I couldn't bear it if the whole world discovered what we mean to one another."

Exactly what he'd told himself. It was their secret. He had to have her—but how? Was it possible to smuggle her into Volek House? He started to shake his head, then paused. Not in the daylight, no. But at night?

"I've never felt for any man what I feel for you," she said softly, turning to him. "More than anything, I want to show you how much you mean to me."

More than anything, he wanted her to show him.

"I can't ask you into the house," he said slowly. "My grandfather forbids visitors. He'd know if I broke his rule. I'd have to—" Wolf paused, looking at her. Even for Linden, did he dare defy Grandfather's taboo?

"You'd have to what?" she prompted, stroking his arm with her soft fingers.

"I'd have to sneak you in at night," he blurted, afraid she'd take offense.

She looked at him solemnly. "I'm not used to being unwelcome. I'd thought to be invited to your house as a guest."

"I'm sorry. Maybe if Grandfather knew you—" Wolf stopped again. Whether his grandfather met her or not, she was still a stranger. "I can't explain," he said finally.

"Poor darling Wolf. I should be angry with you, but how can I be?" She brushed her lips over his, pulling back before he could put his arms around her. "I can't help feeling insulted, though. Why, I've been a guest in some of the finest homes in Switzerland!" She sighed. "Perhaps we just weren't meant to belong to one another."

"We were, we are!" Wolf spoke fervently. "Please don't give up. You don't know how badly I need you in my bed tonight."

She pouted. "But so clandestine!"

Wolf grasped her hands in his. "That'll make it all the more exciting."

"Do you think so?" She still seemed doubtful.

He brought her hands to his lips, aching to hold her, to kiss her mouth instead of her hands, but knowing she wouldn't let him. Tonight, in his bed, she would.

She'd let him do anything he wanted then. If he could get her there.

"You're very convincing," she murmured. "How can I resist you?"

"Don't. Just trust me."

"I suppose I must."

His heart leaped. He'd demolished the first barrier. Now all he had to do was perfect a plan to slip her into the grounds, into the house, and into his bed without anyone discovering what he was doing. Then, of course, out again before morning. Naturally, he'd see her safely to the Thompsonville inn afterwards. But why concern himself with the afterwards when he hadn't yet possessed her? His need to make her his mounted by the minute.

"I'm not at all certain I should go along with this," she said.

Wolf stood, drew her up, and held her loosely in his arms. "*I'm* certain."

She gazed into his eyes. "I want you to know I've never done anything remotely like this in my entire life."

He believed her. Not an elegant lady like Linden. He only hoped she wouldn't change her mind and ride off before nightfall.

"I think you've cast some sort of spell over me," she murmured.

If only he could! As it was, he considered himself the luckiest man in the world.

"I've never before met a man who lived in a castle," she told him, easing from his arms. "Your house must have hundreds of rooms."

"Not *that* many."

"We have so long to wait until it's dark. So very long. Since we must pass the time somehow, I'd like to close my eyes and picture your room before I see it. In anticipation." She leaned against the pine trunk, her eyelids drooping shut. "I imagine the bedrooms are on the second floor?"

Amused and touched, he told her she was right.

"Describe how we get to your room," she went on.

He did, naming, when she asked, who was behind the closed doors they'd pass. He hesitated when he came to the Kelloggs but, realizing their name would mean nothing to her, he said it.

"Ah, now I have my picture," she said, opening her eyes. "Except for what is inside your room. Will you tell me, or do you wish to surprise me?"

"It's very plain."

"By your choice, I think. You're not a man for frills. Am I right? The rest of the house must have all those frills you don't care for, though."

"Yes," he admitted, amazed at how well she understood him. Encouraged by her interest, he described the downstairs rooms and their furnishings.

"Someday I would like to live in a castle," she said. "A castle with a tower like yours."

"The tower is really my grandmother's; the castle is hers and Grandfather's."

"But one day it will be yours."

"In a way."

"By then I'll be far away over the ocean, back in Switzerland, and you'll have forgotten all about me."

He took her hand and drew her closer. "I'll *never* forget you!"

She gazed at him for long moments before saying, with a one-sided smile, "Perhaps you won't, at that."

Chapter 4

He'd done it! Wolf closed the door to his room, and in the darkness illuminated only by moonlight from the window, reached for Linden.

She evaded him. "I've lost my oranges," she whispered. "I wanted to eat them with you when we got to your room."

"Later," he murmured. "I'll get oranges later."

Linden submitted to his kiss but then pulled back. "Please find the oranges," she begged, touching his mouth with her fingers. "I'll undress while you're gone. Then you can take your clothes off, and we'll peel the oranges and eat them, section by section while we—love one another."

His breath caught at the picture she painted—the two of them naked, lying flesh to flesh while she passed an orange segment from her lips to his. He could almost taste the sweet juice.

"You will do it for me, won't you?" she whispered, her warm breath teasing his ear.

He'd do anything for her.

Wolf eased through the door and padded barefoot along the hall. He had no idea where she'd lost the oranges he'd given her, but a bowl of fruit was always kept on the dining room table—he'd find oranges there.

He'd been incredibly lucky so far. Jose had almost caught them at dusk, when they'd crept through the rear gate with the cows coming in to the barn. But Wolf, leading the unsaddled bay, had been able to distract Jose by announcing he'd found a stray horse and asking the man to tether the animal in the barn for the night. While he transferred the reins to Jose, Linden had slipped past unseen and hid in the shrubbery.

Wolf joined her later and led her away from the house into the cluster of valley oaks near the wall. There they'd waited, she telling him stories about life in Switzerland, until Wolf was sure Jose, Belinda, and Rosa had left the grounds and the children had been put to bed. He'd brought Linden to the back door, went in alone to scout, found the coast clear, and whisked her up the back stairs to his room.

No one had seen her. The only possible chance of discovery was if Grandfather chanced to count every aura he sensed inside the house and found one too many. Wolf thought that unlikely because Sergei was too distracted by Liisi's failure to control Annette Kellogg. The moon was only just past full, so his grandfather would be busy helping Guy cope with Annette's shifting.

In the dining room, Wolf lifted two oranges from the fruit bowl and hurried back upstairs. To his consternation, he saw Linden walking along the hall. Running to her, he grasped her by the arm and pulled her with him into his room.

"Where were you going?" he demanded, forgetting to keep his voice down.

"Ssh," she cautioned. "Someone will hear. I wanted to wash and I was looking for the linen closet to find a clean towel."

"You must stay in this room! What if someone had seen you? There should be clean towels by the wash basin—didn't you find one there?"

"Never mind the towel." She reached for his hands and brought them to her breasts. "Since you're back so soon, would you like to undress me?"

The feel of her soft breasts under his hands made him forget everything else. He peeled off her jacket and was fumbling with the tiny buttons of her shirt-waist when a shriek shattered the night's quiet.

Wolf held, listening to the wavering crescendo of terrified screams. Samara. From experience he knew she'd go on until either he or Sergei quieted her. Sergei would be too busy.

"What in heaven's name—?" Linden began.

"My little cousin has these spells. I'll be back in a few minutes. Don't go out of this room!"

He hated to leave Linden, but Samara gave him no choice. Before he reached the nursery, he passed Morning Quail, fleeing toward the front stairs with Stefan in her arms. She wouldn't return, he knew, until Samara was quiet. In the main nursery, Ivan and Arno sat up in their beds, blinking at him.

He found Samara huddled in a corner of her crib in the small bedroom off the nursery that Morning Quail shared with her twins. In the light slanting in through the open door from the hall sconces, he saw Samara's eyes were squeezed shut. Rather than startle her by picking her up, he laid his hand on her hair to let her know he was there.

She seemed to understand who he was, for without opening her eyes, she immediately sprang up and flung her arms around his neck. Wolf lifted her from the crib.

"I'm here," he murmured into her ear. "You're safe."

As Samara clung to him, wailing, a monstrous dark figure loomed in his mind, a figure he knew came from Samara's terror. Despite this realization, he had to fight to control his own surge of fear.

Grandmother Liisi's sudden appearance in the doorway startled him. "Get Samara out of here!" she cried. "Flee the house. Hide! Death is loose in Volek House."

She yanked Ivan and Arno from their beds and, pulling her twins with her, ran down the hall shouting, "Listen, everyone! Save the children. Grab a child and run from the house. Hurry!"

Doors slammed. Men shouted. A woman screamed. Linden! Was she all right? With the sobbing Samara

clinging to him, Wolf raced back to his room. His
door was open. Linden was gone.

Where was she? Somewhere along the hall a gun
cracked once, twice. Who was shooting? Why? Had
Annette shifted and gotten away from Guy and Sergei?
He thought of Druse and prayed that Mima had heard
Liisi's warning and fled to safety with their daughter.

As he tried to decide what to do, he heard Grandfather's hoarse cry.

"Stalker!"

The word broke Wolf's paralysis. With Samara in
his arms, he ran toward the sound of his grandfather's
voice. The gun roared again.

Wolf plunged through the open door to the Kelloggs' suite and stumbled over the sprawled body of
his grandfather. He regained his footing to find himself staring into the muzzle of a small revolver.

"Linden!" The word jolted from him.

She stood over two bleeding bodies—Guy's and Annette's. Her smile froze the blood in his veins.

"A nest of shifters," she spat at him, aiming the
pistol. "Shifters breeding shifters."

As her finger tightened on the trigger, he tried to
leap aside, knowing he was too late. Someone darted
in front of him as Linden fired. Mima. She dropped
at his feet.

Linden laughed harshly. "There's another bullet left
for you, Wolf. One for two—you and that Volek spawn
you hold."

Samara stiffened in his arms. Linden gave an inar-
ticulate cry, then stood transfixed. The revolver
dropped from her hand; Wolf tried to lunge for the
gun and found he couldn't move a muscle.

He stared in horrified disbelief as Mima, blood
staining her white nightgown, raised up on one elbow
and reached for the fallen gun. Grasping it in a shaking hand, she forced herself to her feet and staggered
to the unmoving Linden. Slowly, painfully, she lifted
the gun until the muzzle rested against Linden's temple. Steadying the pistol with both hands, she pulled

the trigger. A tremor convulsed her as the gun fired. She collapsed onto Annette's dead body.

Samara relaxed in Wolf's arms. Linden started to lift a hand to her head, groaned, and crumpled to the floor. Wolf, the child still hanging around his neck, knelt beside Mima, calling her name.

Mima opened her eyes. "Liisi has Druse," she whispered. Before she could say anything more, blood welled from her mouth and her eyes glazed over.

At the same time, something inside Wolf seemed to shatter and he knew she was dead. "Mima, no!" he cried.

The whimpering Samara kept him from cradling Mima's head in his lap. He stumbled to his feet and found himself standing in a pool of blood.

A lake of blood.

But he was no hero, no knight saving a good and virtuous maiden from evil. Instead, he'd brought an evil maiden into the center of his family. Brought them death. He'd betrayed them all by inviting a stalker into Volek House.

Knowing he had to make certain she was dead, Wolf forced himself to kneel beside Linden's body and feel for a heartbeat. He found none. He stared into her vacant brown eyes for a long moment.

A stalker. How could he have been so blind?

He discovered Guy and Annette were dead, too, both shot through the heart. Numbness crept over him. Who else besides himself and Samara was alive?

Behind him someone groaned.

Wolf whirled. His grandfather, blood trickling down his left cheek from a gory furrow along his scalp, was struggling to rise. Wolf hurried to help him. Sergei stared at him, seemingly without recognition.

"It's Wolf, Grandfather. Lin—the stalker's dead."

Grandfather, holding to Wolf for support, put a hand to his head, winced, then gazed uncomprehendingly at the blood on his fingers.

"A bullet must have creased your skull," Wolf told him.

"Silver." Grandfather's voice was hoarse and slurred, but Wolf understood.

Silver bullets. Linden, like the Petersburg stalker, knew silver poisoned shifters. Ordinarily Grandfather's wound would already be healing because shifters healed fast. But not when the wound was from a silver bullet.

Grandfather looked around the room. "Mima," he said sadly. "Guy. Annette." He let go of Wolf and staggered across to stare down at Linden's body. He knelt and picked up the small revolver, and Wolf noticed for the first time that the top of the barrel and the plate above the grip were embossed with gold. A lady's gun.

"Holds five bullets," Sergei said. "Four dead. One wounded. Was the stalker alone?"

Wolf looked away as he answered, unable to meet his grandfather's eyes. "She was alone."

"Is everyone else all right?" Grandfather asked.

Wolf admitted he didn't know.

Without another word, Grandfather, his head still bleeding, stumbled from the room. Feeling as though he were in a trance, Wolf followed, scarcely aware of Samara's warm presence.

They found Natasha dead on the threshold of her room, a silver dagger embedded in her chest. Frightened sobbing from inside the closed mahogany wardrobe led them to Natasha's daughter, five-year-old Tanya, terrified but unharmed.

Carrying Tanya in one arm and Samara in the other, Wolf trailed after Sergei. They found no one else, living or dead, in the house.

"Liisi warned everyone to take the children outside," Wolf said, finally remembering.

Grandfather clutched the frame of the back door. "Can't go any farther," he muttered. "You search. Try the barn first. Leave Tanya and Samara with me."

Free of the two children, Wolf sprinted across the moonlit grounds to the barn. "Grandmother Liisi?" he called when he reached the closed doors, not wanting to frighten her. "Grandmother, it's Wolf. The stalker's dead."

He heard the scrape of the bar. Liisi opened one door a crack and peered out.

"Sergei?" she asked.

"He's alive but hurt. Samara and Tanya are with him."

Liisi opened the door wider and motioned him to enter. As he did, he saw she carried Grandfather's Winchester.

"How badly hurt?" she demanded.

"A bullet creased his head. A silver bullet."

Liisi shuddered. "Help bring the children to the house," she ordered, and hurried away without waiting for him to say anything more.

By the light of the lantern Liisi left behind, he found Morning Quail huddled in the hayloft holding Druse, with Stefan cuddled close to her side. Ivan and Arno, clinging to one another rather than to Morning Quail, stared wide-eyed at Wolf.

"Is the bad monster dead?" Arno asked.

Wolf had to swallow twice before he could speak. "Yes, she—it's dead. We're going back to the house now."

"No." Morning Quail spoke softly but firmly. "No go in house. When sun rise, I go to my people."

Though he tried to persuade her that there was no longer any danger, she kept shaking her head.

"What about Stefan and Samara?" he asked finally.

In answer, she pushed Stefan at him. "You take."

"But they're your children!"

Again she shook her head. "*His* children. I no bring trouble to my people."

Knowing that Stefan would become a shifter like his father, Wolf didn't argue. Stefan was better off at Volek House. Possibly Samara would be, too. In any case, he was sure Morning Quail had made up her mind as to what she meant to do and wouldn't change her decision.

"I'll bring your belongings to you at sunrise," he told her finally.

She nodded her thanks and held out Druse for him to take. Morning Quail helped the other three children down the loft ladder but went no farther than the door with them. Holding Druse in one arm, Wolf scooped Stefan into the other, ordered Arno and Ivan to hold onto his belt, and headed for the house without Morning Quail.

Liisi, he found, had turned the morning room into a makeshift bedroom, with the kitchen cradle for Druse and blankets on the floor for the other children. Sergei was propped on the settee, eyes closed, his face and hands no longer blood-stained. Liisi had obviously tended to his head wound.

"So you couldn't change Morning Quail's mind," Liisi said as she helped Wolf settle the children into the blankets and quilts.

"She said she was leaving at sunrise," Wolf told her.

Liisi nodded. "Perhaps it's best. She was never happy here. Her twins stay, of course."

"Yes."

"Wolf." Grandfather's voice made Wolf start.

"Sit by me," Sergei ordered.

Up close, Wolf noticed Sergei's head wound still gaped open with no sign of healing. Blood no longer oozed from it, but he knew that might be due to one of Liisi's spells. Blood-stopping was a *noita* skill.

"You let her in," Grandfather said.

Wolf sank to the floor beside the settee, head hanging. "Yes." He remembered how Sergei had scolded him after Druse was born, saying how he regretted that young men were foolish enough to let their pricks rule their heads.

God knows he'd made the same mistake again. For the last time. But that was small consolation for the dead. For Mima. For Natasha. For the Kelloggs. Suddenly he realized he didn't know what had happened to Cecelia. She hadn't been in the barn; she wasn't here. Was she dead, too?

He braced himself for Grandfather's harsh words. Words he deserved. In fact, he should be dead rather than Mima, who'd died in his place. Tears welled into his eyes. Mima had been his friend, his foster mother, his teacher, his lover, and the mother of his daughter. His lust for another woman had killed her.

"You've already suffered the consequences of your rashness," Grandfather said, and lapsed into silence.

After a time Wolf looked up at him. Was this all the punishment his grandfather meant to deliver? "Was—was Cecelia killed, too?" he asked at last.

Liisi answered. "She says she locked herself in her room after the first shot. When I spoke to her, she refused to come out. You can hardly blame her."

"What's going to happen?" Wolf asked.

Again it was Liisi who spoke. "Sergei's a friend of the sheriff. We'll work it out."

"I heard her," Sergei said without opening his eyes. "I was sleeping in the dressing room off the Kelloggs' bedroom because Guy and I were taking turns watching over Annette. Samara's screams woke me, then I heard voices.

" 'I followed you from France, Annette Kellogg,' the stalker said. 'Death to all shifters!' I leaped up, but she shot them both before I could stop her. Then she shot at me, and that was the last I knew."

Wolf found nothing to say. There was no excuse for what he'd done. Bemused by her caresses, he'd answered all the questions Linden had asked about the house and told her who was in which bedroom. He'd provided a map for her as well as letting her into the house. He'd done everything but pull the trigger of the gun for her. How could he have been so foolish?

"Searching for the Kelloggs, the stalker must have opened Natasha's door by mistake," Liisi said.

Recalling how loudly he'd spoken when he chided Linden for going into the hall, Wolf wondered if his voice might not have roused Natasha. Perhaps she'd come out of her room and listened to them. Hearing a woman's voice in his room would have alarmed the fearful Natasha. Had she rushed back and hidden Tanya in the wardrobe for safety, planning to warn Sergei that a stranger was inside Volek House?

When Linden crept out for the second time, she'd have silenced anyone who might have interfered with her plan to kill Annette Kellogg. If she'd seen Natasha coming from her room . . .

The bitter taste of bile flooded Wolf's mouth. He'd not only caused the death of Mima, the woman who meant more to him than anyone except Grandfather, he'd also as good as killed poor Cousin Natasha. Plus the two Kelloggs. Whatever their problems, they didn't deserve to die.

"Samara knew the stalker was in the house," he said when the silence grew threatening. "That's why she screamed."

"She *sees*." Liisi's voice was sad. "I don't envy her that talent, but I'll help her adjust to it, if I can."

Wolf wondered how many of the children lay awake in their blankets on the floor, listening. But there was no way to keep the night's horror from them. Sooner or later, each of them would have to face whatever their Volek blood brought them. Face it and learn to live with the consequences.

"I wish—" he said and stopped. What good did it do to say he wished he'd never met Linden? That he wished he hadn't been so brainless as to be taken in by her?

"I knew death followed the Kelloggs," Liisi said. "And I'd heard Sergei's tale of his near-fatal encounter with the Russian stalker, but unfortunately I didn't put the two together. I didn't think of a stalker."

Grandmother Liisi mustn't blame herself!

"It's all my fault," Wolf insisted.

Nobody disagreed.

Suddenly unable to bear being in the house, Wolf rose from the floor and strode from the room. At the back door he hesitated. He'd promised to gather Morn-

ing Quail's belongings. Turning, he climbed the back
stairs. Liisi had closed all the doors, but the stench of
death hung in the corridor, turning his stomach.

After he'd made a bundle of Morning Quail's sur-
prisingly meager effects, Wolf stood for a long moment with the bundle in his hand, thinking. At last he
nodded.

When he opened the door to his room, he smelled
roses. Linden's scent. He gagged, retching until sour
fluid filled his mouth. He spat it into the slop jar.
Yanking a blanket from his bed, he flung a few clothes
and other belongings into it and rolled the blanket into
a bundle. As he started to turn away from the bed, he
noticed the dim light gleam on metal peeking from
under his pillow. Puzzled, he reached underneath.

He drew out a small silver dirk with a needle-sharp
point. Hers! As he stared at the deadly little weapon,
it occurred to him why she'd hidden it under his pillow. She'd meant to kill him first. While he made love
to her. He closed his eyes, shuddering.

When he recovered, he quelled his impulse to fling
the dagger as far from him as he could. Instead, he
thrust it into the holster that sheathed the Colt Grandfather had given him. He wouldn't leave this reminder
of her to taint Volek House.

Easing quietly down the front stairs with the two
bundles, he thought of Druse asleep in the cradle, and
a lump came into his throat. He hesitated, then shook
his head. Like Morning Quail's twins, his daughter
was safer here than anywhere else.

And, like the rest of the Voleks, better off without
him.

Chapter 5

Was he making a mistake? Sergei asked himself as their horse-drawn cab passed yet another streetcar. Market Street had grown into a jungle of streetcars, wagons, buggies, and people. The tangle of wires overhead defied belief. Cecelia Kellogg gazed entranced at the bustle around them—obviously cities were her milieu just as surely as they were not his.

He didn't doubt her ability to cope with the city and the people of San Francisco, what worried him was that Wolf might have been right. If Cecelia *was* a latent shifter, leaving her here in San Francisco would be a terrible mistake. But he didn't know what the hell else he could have done with her.

He couldn't keep her locked away at Volek House forever. For one thing, there was no proof she'd ever shift—five full moons had passed, and she'd showed no inclination to change shape. For another, if he didn't try to help her realize her dream of dancing, eventually she'd run off and try on her own because she hated living in the country. God knows the world was not a safe place for an orphaned young girl of eighteen.

The excitement of the trip had lifted Cecelia's gloom, and he realized how much prettier she was when her expression became animated. For six months she'd been drooping about, interested in nothing and of not much use in the household. He hadn't expected her to recover quickly from the death of her parents, but since she'd locked herself in her room at the first sign of trouble, she'd been spared the worst of that terrible night.

Wolf and Morning Quail had fled Volek House without so much as a farewell, leaving Liisi and him to reassure the frightened children and take care of the dead. The task fell mostly to Liisi, since his head wound took weeks to heal and he'd run a fever much of the time. Cecelia, who might have helped, didn't lift a hand.

A crime of passion, the sheriff had called the murders—with a bit of encouragement from Liisi. She'd concocted a dramatic tale of a discarded woman traveling halfway around the world to extract revenge by killing her lover and his wife. Mima, Natasha, and Sergei, Liisi said sorrowfully, had been accidental victims because they'd tried to stop the deranged woman from carrying out her dreadful deed.

Sergei had tried to soften the truth when he explained to Cecelia what had happened by saying that the killer had been an enemy of her parents. He didn't know what he might have told her if she'd asked questions, but she didn't. Nor would she discuss Guy and Annette at all. It was as though they'd never existed.

"She won't face what happened," Liisi had said to him, "because she can't admit to herself that her mother was a shifter."

Sergei knew Liisi was right. He could only hope Wolf was wrong and Cecelia hadn't inherited the trait. She not only refused to discuss it with him, she burst into tears and fled if he brought up the subject. When and if she ever decided to marry, he'd have to make her listen.

"Why, the hotel truly is as big as a palace!" Cecelia exclaimed, recalling him to the present.

Their cab, on Montgomery Street now, turned in and passed under an arch into Grant Court—the Palace Hotel's seven stories were built around the court.

Though nothing in America, according to Cecelia, came close to the perfection of Paris, Sergei thought she'd have to admit that the 800-room, lavishly furnished Palace surpassed anything Paris had to offer. Every room in the hotel boasted a fireplace, closet, and a private toilet.

Cecelia was delighted by the ornate lobby and their ride in one of the hotel's five elevators to the top floor where he'd reserved a suite—two bedrooms separated by a sitting room.

The oriel windows faced the bay, and he pointed out Shot Tower and the spire of the Masonic Temple. Still, she remained silent.

"I imagine you'd like to freshen up," he said.

Cecelia nodded, started to turn toward her bedroom, and paused. "You've been very patient with me, Mr. Volek. I *am* grateful."

Sergei watched her walk away before turning back to the windows. She moved gracefully—a born dancer's gait, Liisi called it. Cecelia had never mentioned gratitude before. What he'd heard from her at Volek House were complaints.

"In Paris," she'd say dramatically, "I took lessons from the finest dance instructor in all of Europe. She told me that one day I'd be a famous dancer. But now it's hopeless. Hopeless."

He'd finally written to Fred Douglas, a business acquaintance in San Francisco, inquiring about reputable dance instructors. The letter had led to a correspondence, the upshot being that tonight he and Cecelia were to have dinner with the Douglases in their rococo mansion on Taylor Street, an address Mrs. Douglas claimed was "smarter" than Nob Hill.

The Douglases had, at his request, found a respectable apartment for Cecelia to live in, and Ada Douglas planned "to keep an eye on her" while Cecelia took dance instruction from a Madame DuJour, said to be from Paris.

Sergei hoped the arrangements would work out. To tell the truth, he'd be glad to have the girl gone from Volek House. Not only was she unhappy there, but she was a constant reminder to Sergei that he'd failed his old friend Guy.

He blamed himself more than he blamed poor Wolf, trapped by a woman's wiles. The boy should have known better, but after all, Wolf *had* told him about the pretty young woman he'd rescued when her horse bolted and threw her.

If I'd thought to ask a few questions, Sergei told himself, the massacre might never have happened.

He'd lost Wolf just as surely as if the stalker had killed him, too. Until Wolf was gone, Sergei had never realized how much he'd come to depend on his grandson for companionship. He loved Liisi, but she didn't fill the gap. *Noitas,* he suspected, never made good companions, being a bit too other-worldly.

Paul McQuade, his neighbor and business partner, was the closest he came to having a friend, but a shifter didn't dare encourage closeness with humans.

McQuade hadn't the slightest idea he was anything but human. He doubted Paul would call Sergei Volek friend if it was discovered what he really was. Wolf, though, knew. Wolf had seen him shift, had faced the beast without fear and still loved him.

Damn, but he missed the boy. His twins, Arno and Ivan, were only seven—too young to take Wolf's place. If only the silver bullet hadn't made him so sick. If he'd been well, he'd have realized Wolf planned to leave and would have convinced him that he was not only wanted but needed at Volek House.

Wolf understood in a way no one else did. Liisi couldn't grasp why President Garfield's assassination in March had upset him so. "But you never met the man," she'd said.

He could have told his grandson how the President's death made him relive Lincoln's assassination all those years before—Lincoln, the greatest President of them all. Wolf would have listened and nodded solemnly. Damn it, he'd *know* how Sergei sorrowed.

He'd searched for Wolf in vain. He could only pray

that the boy was all right, and that time would heal him and bring him back home.

Sergei sighed, turned away from the window, and began to get ready for the evening's dinner.

Two days later, he was alone, strolling down Kearney Street toward Clay, looking for a present to bring home to Liisi. Cecelia was off his hands and settled for the time being. She'd seemed excited by the idea of living in the city, and he hoped the illusion of being on her own plus the dancing lessons would speed her recovery from her parents' death. He'd arranged for her to receive a generous monthly allowance through his bank so she'd have no financial problems. He could well afford it—business had never been better. Hell, they were rich.

Rich because of Liisi. He'd mention a possible investment to her, and she'd disappear into her tower room for an hour or two and, later, tell him yes or no. She'd never yet been wrong. What could he buy her today that would show her how much she meant to him? Jewelry? She seldom wore any. He wished Liisi was here, walking with him. If she were by his side, he wouldn't mind the city quite so much. His special sense was no use in crowds—with so many people around he couldn't separate one aura from another, and that made him uneasy.

He assured himself that as far as stalkers were concerned, he was at no more of a disadvantage in San Francisco than he'd be anywhere else. If a stalker tracked him, city or country, crowds or lonely wilderness made no difference because stalkers had no aura at all—at least none his special sense could read.

He'd heard the woman stalker tell the Kelloggs she'd trailed them from France. In six months, he'd seen no evidence she'd had any companions, but he couldn't relax. The Voleks must never forget the danger of attracting a stalker, as Annette had evidently done when she'd hunted in her shifted state in a Paris park. He no longer felt entirely safe anywhere.

The day was overcast. Though the sun had shone earlier, by noon high fog had drifted in to settle over the twin peaks at the upper reaches of Market. Typical San Francisco weather. He preferred his own valley. As he walked, he was continually on the alert, watching for any sign he was under observation or anything else unusual.

He noticed a Chinese vegetable vendor coming toward him, carrying his huge baskets on either end of a long flexible pole over his shoulders and, because of the crowded streets and sidewalks, having difficulty maneuvering. The man was dressed in the usual blue cotton tunic and pants, with padded shoes and a round, brimless cap. Chinatown was down around Dupont, so it was odd to see a Chinese in this neighborhood.

No sooner had he thought this than a whistle blew, men shouted, and the Chinaman flung down his pole and bolted. As he fled past, his hat flew off and Sergei saw he wasn't a man but a boy of maybe twelve or thirteen, his face distorted by terror. Sergei also got a fleeting impression of a violet-tinged aura rather than the normal human reddish one. An aura similar to Wolf's. Intrigued, he picked up the hat, black with a wide red silk stripe at the bottom, and hurried after the boy.

Behind him other pursuers shouted, "Stop the Chink!"

Sergei glanced over his shoulder and saw, half a block behind, a heavyset man pushing through the shoppers, brandishing a Colt. Two younger men ran with him. When Sergei faced forward again he didn't see the boy at first, but then he caught a glimpse of telltale blue disappearing into a barrel sitting on end just inside the entrance to an alley.

He hurried to the barrel and said softly, "Don't move; I'll help you." He tossed the hat into the barrel, then leaned against it.

While he waited, he wondered if the boy understood any English and also if he'd been too impulsive in trying to help him. Violet-tinged aura or not, for all he knew the boy might be a member of one of the deadly Chinatown tongs.

The three pursuers came even with Sergei and paused to glance down the alley. "Seen a Chink?" the heavyset man asked.

Sergei pointed across the street. "One ran between those two stores."

When the men disappeared into the narrow opening between the buildings, Sergei turned, reached into the barrel, yanked the boy out and, pulling him along, sprinted down the alley, trying every door he came to until the knob of one turned under his fingers. He pushed it open, stepped inside, shut the door, locked it, and looked quickly around.

A storeroom. The floor was littered with straw from half-unpacked crates of dishes and glassware. Before he could decide what to do, a man dressed in a dark blue pinstriped suit with a lighter blue vest, stepped through the drapery blocking the back room from the rest of the store and stopped, staring.

Deciding he was a clerk, Sergei reached in his pocket and pulled out a roll of bills. He peeled off four and set them on top of an unopened crate.

"I want you to deliver a crate to the Ferry Building," he said to the man. "Above and beyond that, I wish to order a twenty-four place setting of your finest china, with all the extra pieces thrown in—to be sent to an address in Thompsonville. Payment, of course, in advance."

The clerk closed his mouth and blinked. "Yes, sir," he said finally.

"How much will it cost?" Sergei asked. "Hurry, I haven't much time."

"But—but I don't know what pattern you desire," the clerk said.

"Anything with flowers. My wife likes flowers. You choose."

"Yes, all right. That will come to—" He pulled a pad and pencil from his pocket and began figuring.

The boy hadn't said a word through all of this. Sergei hunched down and looked him in the eye. "Do you understand English?" he asked.

"Little," the boy whispered.

Sergei pointed to one of the empty crates, all stamped FRAGILE, stacked along the wall. "I'll put you in a crate. That man—" he gestured at the clerk "—will send you, inside the crate, on a wagon to the Ferry Building. I'll be there to let you out and then you'll be free to go home. All right?"

"Two hundred and fifty dollars, sir," the clerk said. "Including the shipping fee."

Sergei rose, peeled off more bills, and handed them over. "Now, for the money I've laid out on that crate, here's what I want you to do."

When he finished telling the clerk essentially what he'd said to the boy, the clerk glanced at the fifty dollars and nodded.

"Yes, sir. I'll be glad to arrange for a wagon."

Sergei bent down again. "You understand what will happen?" he asked the boy.

The boy swallowed. "No got home," he whispered. "Men burn."

"Where's your mother? Your father?"

"No got."

Sergei eyed him, considering. What was he to do with this waif he'd impulsively rescued? He could think of only one solution. "Will you come home with me?" he asked finally.

The boy's slanted dark eyes looked fearfully into Sergei's for a long moment. "I come," he said at last.

"Good. My name's Sergei Volek—what's yours?"

"Loi Fui Chung."

"Okay, Chung, into the crate you go. Get set for a bumpy ride—it can't be helped."

As the clerk assisted him in nailing the boy into the crate, Sergei wondered what Liisi would say when he arrived home accompanied by a stranger—one he'd invited to live at Volek House.

* * *

Early in June, in the late afternoon, Wolf sat morosely on top of a granite boulder staring not at the breathtaking mountain valley below but at the few crumbs that remained of the food he'd brought with him from the Miwok village.

Though he'd been invited to stay with Morning Quail and her people in their foothills village, he found himself uncomfortable among them. The men were generally friendly, especially after he proved quick to master their tongue. Even Bear Claw, their shaman, seemed to accept him, but Wolf rested uneasily at night, waiting for an attack that never came.

He'd tried to tell himself the Miwoks were not the same as the Kamchadals, who'd caged him like an animal. This tribe was poor and not warlike, everyone was kept busy hunting for food in order to survive. But he didn't convince himself. After six months, he could no longer endure waiting for the ax to fall. Though he and Morning Quail had become friends, he wasn't surprised when she decided to remain with her people.

He'd climbed, heading farther into the mountains, away from any vestige of civilization. Now here he was, hungry and tired, without any idea of where he'd find his next meal. Or see another person. Hunger he'd expected, but not loneliness.

The thought that he might be the only human for hundreds of miles around daunted him rather than giving him the sense of exhilaration he'd expected to experience. He'd never felt so alone since he was a naked and filthy nine-year-old penned like an animal in Kamchatka.

After Grandfather rescued him, he'd become part of a family. He missed every one of them, but especially Sergei.

A growl of thunder startled him, and he glanced up to see dark clouds obscuring the sun. He'd been warned by Morning Quail that storms in the mountains were dangerous.

''The thunder spirit grows angry with any man who

challenges him,'' she'd said in Miwok. ''Thunder shoots his arrows of flame at that man. Death arrows.''

Wolf stood up, searching for shelter. He settled on a small stand of pines with odd-looking trunks of coarse brown bark. He'd seen lightning hit tall trees, so he kept away from the center of the grove where the tallest pines grew.

The rain began before he reached the trees, spattering him with cool drops. By the time he was under the fragrant branches of the coarse-barked pines, the wind was whipping through the boughs, singing a storm song. Lightning illuminated the dark sky; thunder cracked all around him. Rain drove through the boughs, soaking him.

Wolf, more stimulated than frightened by the storm, ran between the trees. He shouted each time the thunder rumbled to show his disbelief in thunder spirits.

As the storm's fury began to ebb, Wolf suddenly felt the hair raise on his nape. Something watched him. Animal? He knew cougars roamed the mountains, and that they laid on low branches in wait for prey. He quickly slid over against a thick trunk and scanned the branches above him.

Movement! He grabbed the handle of his holstered Colt, aware he had only two bullets left.

''You're not thinking to shoot *me,* are you, laddie?'' a man's voice asked from overhead.

Wolf gaped at the bewhiskered face staring down at him. The man slid from the branch, dropping to the ground beside Wolf.

''John Muir,'' he said, holding out his hand.

''Wolf Volek.'' He grasped the hand and had his shaken heartily.

''Nothing I like better than a man who knows how to enjoy a storm,'' Muir told him.

Tall and lean, Muir wore rough clothes, carried a small knapsack, and packed no gun. His keen blue eyes peered through a tangle—his hair, long and untrimmed, was as ragged and wild as his beard. The

creases in the tanned skin around his eyes told Wolf
he was middle-aged.

"Magnificent!" Muir cried, turning his face up to
the rain. "Think what those who huddle in houses are
missing." He looked again at Wolf. "When I woke
this morning, something told me I'd meet a friend today. The Scots are known for their second sight; I'm
not sure I believe I have it, but I do get hunches. And
I've learned to act on them."

Wolf had never met anyone quite like this wild man
of the mountains. With growing interest, he listened
to Muir speak of the glory of the storm and the beauty
of their surroundings.

"I've never seen pines like these lower down,"
he volunteered when at last Muir fell silent.

"The Jeffreys? A noble sight they are, indeed. The
bark smells like vanilla, I've always thought." He
glanced up. "The storm's passing us by—time to move
on." He glanced at Wolf. "If you're on your own,
shall we team up?"

The notion appealed to Wolf and he nodded.

The sun came out as they left the Jeffrey pine grove,
and Muir pointed to the southwest where a rainbow
spread its brilliant colors across the sky. "Good luck,
us meeting—that's what the rainbow says."

As they hiked through the rugged country, Muir told
Wolf the names of the trees and plants. He talked back
to the Douglas squirrels who chattered at them, halted
Wolf with a hand on his arm while two mule deer
sprang from cover ahead of them, and left crumbs for
a tiny chipmunk that darted across their path.

"A man's never alone in the mountains," Muir said.
"If he keeps his eyes and ears open, he finds many
friends. I look forward to tonight when friend coyote
will serenade us with his lullaby."

"The Miwoks believe Coyote is the god who created
them," Wolf said. "And when he breathed life into
them, he cried out in joy."

Muir smiled. "In joy, yes. As he still does today.
Indians are closer to nature than we. They understand

we're but a link in the chain of life on earth. I wish I could infuse that knowledge into a few of those Washington politicians I try to deal with.''

''Sir?'' Wolf didn't quite understand.

Muir shook his head. ''Not sir, laddie. Call me Johnnie, for we're friends. Today's too fine to be blighted by speaking of politicians. Sometime I'll explain to you what it is I aim to do, but not now, not while we breathe this wonderful mountain air, not as we're about to come upon one of the most spectacular sights in nature.''

An hour or so later, they stood in a pine forest on the outer rim of a vast valley. Wolf drew in his breath as he gazed across at the opposite mountain wall rising into multiple flying turrets, which soared into the darkening blue of the evening sky. He'd never seen anything so breathtaking in his life.

In the next three days, Muir showed him not only the magnificence of the Sierras but how men were mistreating them by logging off the great trees and herding sheep to feed on the slopes and valleys, denuding them. Wolf learned of Muir's attempts to get Congress to set apart certain areas in California for ''a great national park or reservation.''

''The Sierras belong to us all,'' Muir insisted. ''Not for our selfish use but for us to preserve in their natural grandeur. We are a part of these mountains; we must not misuse them.''

The more he was in Muir's company, the more Wolf admired it. Muir said what Wolf had long felt deep in his heart but didn't know how to express. He and the wilderness were one.

''It's time to go back to civilization,'' Muir said at last. ''You're another like me, laddie. I've enjoyed your company, but I must bend to the yoke once more. I can use your help—will you join me? Someday we'll go to Washington to battle the politicians, but for now I need a helping hand on my ranch.''

By then Wolf was so reluctant to be separated from Muir that he would have followed him anywhere. ''A ranchhand's job suits me,'' he told Muir. ''I'll come with you.''

Ten-year-old Samara Volek ran down the school-house steps after her twin brother.

''Stefan, wait!'' she cried, hearing Druse echo her words behind her.

''Sammi, wait!''

But she couldn't wait for Druse; she had to catch up to Stefan before he got out of sight. Why did Mr. Mathewson always have to be so cross with Stefan? Her brother didn't like to study, but that didn't give their teacher the right to pick on him all the time.

What did it matter if Stefan forgot Grover Cleveland's name? Mr. Cleveland might be the President of the United States, but couldn't Mr. Mathewson see that Stefan didn't care who was President or what his name was?

Stefan hated the way Druse always trailed them; he'd be madder than he was already if she brought Druse along. Anyway, Druse had Tanya to walk with.

Leaving the log cabin schoolhouse behind, Samara ran as fast as her skirts would let her toward the big oaks, following her brother, knowing he was heading for their secret place. How she disliked having to wear a bustle! Boys were lucky.

By the time she reached the wall near the oaks, Stefan was nowhere in sight. Samara gathered up her skirts, dropped to her knees, and crawled behind the tangle of shrubs growing against the wall. Four months ago, Chung had killed a fox raiding the chicken coop. The boys—Arno, Ivan, and Stefan—had been sent with Chung to see if they could find a hole dug under the wall. But they hadn't, and so Grandfather finally decided the fox must have squeezed through the narrow opening between the iron bars in one of the gates.

Workmen had come that same week and welded crisscross bars to the gates.

About a week later, she'd accidentally found the hole when she'd crawled behind the bushes after Stefan had tossed Hortense Louise, her favorite doll, into them. Stefan was always getting mad and doing something hurtful. If he wasn't her twin brother, she'd never have forgiven him for being so mean to poor Hortense. But she had. She'd even told him about the hole she found instead of going directly to Grandfather.

Twigs caught in Samara's long braided hair as she eased her way along the wall to the hole. She never *had* told Grandfather because Stefan asked her not to. She hadn't liked agreeing, but after Stefan had blocked the inside of the hole with a rock, pointing out that no animal could get in so the chickens would be safe, she promised she wouldn't tell.

The rock was lying to the side of the hole now, so she knew Stefan was outside the wall. Where they weren't supposed to go. They were confined to the grounds at all times unless Grandmother or Grandfather was with them.

Much as she disliked getting dirty, she inched headfirst into the hole and wriggled through. Heaven only knew what trouble Stefan might get into if she wasn't with him.

When she caught up with her brother on the other side of the wall, he was racing around in circles shouting, "Free! Free! Free!" It took her almost an hour to persuade him to return.

"Someday I'm going to kill Mr. Thinks-he-knows-it-all," Stefan told her as they walked toward the hole. "Kill him, tear him in pieces and feed him to the coyotes."

"Aw, Mr. Mathewson's not *that* bad."

"I mean to do it. You wait and see."

Samara swallowed, fearing he really did mean it. Once in a while at night she'd wake as from a bad dream, sensing something dark and dangerous inside Stefan. Something that scared her. She'd never told anyone.

At the hole, Stefan went first, as he always did. Halfway through behind him, she froze. Was that Grandfather's voice?

Since she had no choice, Samara wriggled through to the inside of the wall. Her grandfather's frowning face was the first thing she saw when she emerged.

The bushes were gone, cut to the ground. Grandfather stood staring down at her, Stefan's arm gripped in his right hand. Chung, Ivan, Arno, and Druse hovered behind him.

Grandfather's left hand fastened on her wrist. "You boys get that hole filled in," he ordered.

He marched them both toward the house, Druse running along beside Samara.

"I'm sorry I told," Druse whispered to her. "I found your hair ribbon caught on that bush and I took it to Grandfather. I didn't know about the hole."

So Druse must have followed her, after all. Stefan wouldn't be happy about that.

Grandfather ushered the two of them into his study, closing the door on Druse. Making them stand in front of him, he leaned against the fireplace mantel and fixed them with a stern gaze.

"I hadn't planned to tell you two just yet, but I see I should have." He paused and took a deep breath. "Stefan, Samara, do you have any idea of what it means to be a Volek?"

Samara shook her head.

Stefan scowled at him. "If you're not grown up, it means you have to stay locked inside a wall."

Samara expected Grandfather to be angry. Instead, he looked sad as he asked, "Do you know why, Stefan?"

"No, but it's not fair."

"Maybe not, but there's a very good reason," Grandfather said. "The Voleks are not like other families. We have a dark and deadly secret, and because of this secret we have enemies—stalkers—who hunt us."

"What secret?" Stefan demanded.

"When Volek identical twin sons turn from boys into men, one of them inherits a terrible fate. Under a full moon he shapeshifts. He changes and becomes a beast. He rends and kills and, except for his twin, no one is safe from the beast.''

Samara stared at her grandfather, speechless with horror. Stalkers and beasts! She glanced at Stefan. He didn't seem a bit frightened.

After a moment, Stefan said, ''Ivan and Arno are identical. I'll bet it's Ivan. No, wait, Arno gets mad quicker.''

Grandfather shook his head. ''We won't know which twin will be the shifter until it happens.''

''But it'll be one of them?''

''I'm afraid so.''

Stefan's scowl grew darker. ''It's not fair,'' he said. ''Sammi's a girl.''

''She is, indeed,'' Grandfather said. ''So you two are not identical male twins.''

''Damn it to hell!'' Stefan cried, startling Samara. No one ever swore in front of Grandfather!

Stefan glared at her. ''Why'd you have to be a girl?'' he demanded. ''That means I won't ever get to turn into a beast.''

Chapter 6

Usually Samara liked the classes in the schoolroom, but today her stomach had begun to hurt after lunch. She'd told Tanya, who'd smirked at her.

"*I* know what's happening—don't you?" Tanya had said slyly.

Sometimes she positively hated Tanya. Just because Tanya had turned fourteen, while Samara and Stefan wouldn't be thirteen for another four months, didn't mean Tanya could lord it over her.

Samara crossed her arms over her stomach and tried to will her discomfort away before Mr. Mathewson finished quizzing Arno and Ivan about how congressmen were elected and began asking questions of Tanya and Stefan and her. She wasn't successful.

Luckily, though, the teacher was reviewing what they'd already learned. Stomach cramps or not, she was able to tell him the date California became a state—1850, the thirty-first state to be admitted to the Union.

Tanya was asked the next question.

"Wyoming was admitted to the Union just this month," Tanya said. "It's the forty-fourth state."

"Stefan," Mr. Mathewson said, "if I can have your attention, please."

Stefan was staring out the window, as usual. He turned and looked sullenly at the teacher.

"Stefan, who is the current President of the United States?" Mr. Mathewson asked.

"President Cleveland," Stefan said triumphantly.

"Wrong. Benjamin Harrison is our twenty-third President. Apparently you haven't either listened or studied the lessons this week."

"It was President Cleveland last year," Stefan objected. "How do you expect me to remember if they keep changing Presidents all the time?"

"They do not change, 'all the time'." Mr. Mathewson's voice rose. "The term for a President is four years, as you should know. You don't seem interested in learning, Stefan. Is there *anything* you're interested in?"

Stefan shrugged. "Hunting, I guess."

Mr. Mathewson's eyebrows rose and Samara winced, expecting him to launch into another lecture about the necessity of education and Stefan's ignorance. He didn't.

After a long silence, Mr. Mathewson said, "All right, Stefan. In an effort to interest you in studying, I'll assign you one wild animal per week. At the end of the week, you will turn in a paper on that animal, detailing its zoological classification, its habits, range, and physical characteristics. This week you will research the wolf. Do you understand?"

Stefan nodded, and Samara thought she detected a spark of enthusiasm in his eyes, encouraging her to believe he might actually do the assignment.

After school let out, Stefan hurried off with Arno and Ivan as he'd been doing lately, leaving her to walk with Tanya and Druse.

"Did you start?" Tanya asked as soon as they were away from the schoolhouse.

"Start what?" Samara asked.

"Bleeding."

Samara's eyes widened. It hadn't occurred to her that her stomach cramps could be related to what Liisi had told her happened to all girls when they were ready to become women. She bit her lip, not liking the idea one bit. She wasn't a woman yet—she wasn't even thirteen.

Tanya laughed. "You look scared to death. It's not so bad." She smiled condescendingly. "I ought to know. When we get to the house, I'll show you what to do."

Samara glared at her. "Liisi already showed me. And maybe it's not that."

But it was.

"It's time you and Stefan had separate bedrooms," Liisi decreed when Samara told her. "While boys and girls can share sleeping quarters, men and women do not. At least not until they marry."

"But we're twins," Samara wailed. "And Stefan isn't a man."

Liisi put an arm around her. "You're already becoming a woman—it won't be long before Stefan becomes a man."

"I've never slept alone in a room. I don't want to."

"You'll get used to it. You can have the room next to Druse and Tanya, if you like."

Samara realized it was useless to protest any further—Grandmother never changed her mind. "No," she said. "If I have to be by myself, I don't want to be next to anybody."

Stefan wasn't any happier about the move than she was. "They can't stop us from talking at night, just like always," he said belligerently.

Two nights later, Stefan startled her from sleep by shaking her shoulder. Samara sat up in bed.

"I didn't hear you come in," she whispered. "How late is it?"

"Nobody hears me when I don't want them to," he said smugly. "And it's not late; it's not even midnight. Come on." He tugged at her hand.

Samara, self-conscious about the sanitary apparatus under her nightgown, slid awkwardly from the bed. "Where to?"

"Don't you remember? The moon's full. It's a shifter's moon, and I think he's about ready."

Samara shuddered. For months after Grandfather had told them about Volek shapeshifters she'd been uneasy when she was near Ivan or Arno, but as time passed and nothing happened, her nervousness passed.

"How can you tell?" she demanded, fearing she wouldn't like what Stefan meant to do.

"They've both been acting different. Restless. Like I feel inside sometimes."

"It won't be both of them."

"Yeah, but you know how they've always been—what affects one bothers the other. The way I see it, they both feel the change coming. Only one'll change into a beast, but the other senses it. Like you sensed the stalker all those years ago."

Samara froze. She'd pushed that awful time from her mind, and she meant to keep it out. "I don't remember anything that happened—I was too little."

"I don't either, but I listen. Grandmother told Grandfather that she was sure you had a special talent for sensing stalkers. She said she'd like to develop your talent."

"I don't want to remember! I won't!"

"Ssh, keep your voice down. You can do whatever you want—*I* don't care. Only that kind of talent might come in handy sometime. Think about it. You ready?"

"Ready for what?" She was still upset and her voice shook.

"To go spy on Ivan and Arno, what else?"

She'd rather do practically anything else, but she'd always followed where Stefan led. "It could be dangerous," she reminded him. "Grandfather said only the beast's twin is safe."

"We'll be hidden. Come on."

Devoutly hoping this full moon wouldn't be the one to bring on the change, Samara trailed along the hall after Stefan in the dim light from the bulbs in the wall sconces. Last year, Grandfather had bought an electric generator and had the house wired for electricity. To her surprise, Stefan led her into his new bedroom.

"I picked this room 'cause it's next door to theirs," Stefan said, "and both rooms have closets, back to back." Instead of turning on the electric light, he lit a candle and, holding it, opened his closet door. *"Voila,"* he whispered.

At first she didn't see anything except his clothes hanging on the rod to either side with a space between. He pointed to the rear wall, holding the candle closer. Samara drew in her breath. Irregular lines showed where an opening had been cut in the wood of the wall.

"I borrowed the saw from Chung and cut it myself," Stefan said proudly. He eased the piece of wood from the opening, set it to one side, and she peered into darkness.

Putting his mouth close to her ear, Stefan whispered, "We can't talk after we crawl into their closet, okay?"

She nodded but immediately grabbed his shirt to hold him back. Leaning close, she whispered, "If you really think one twin will shift tonight, shouldn't we tell Grandfather?"

"It's only a guess. Anyway, he never goes to bed when the moon's full, didn't you know? If it happens, he'll find out soon enough."

Stefan blew out the candle and closed his closet door, shutting them into total darkness. She heard him wriggle through the opening. A sick excitement vied with apprehension as she followed. She wanted to see what would happen, and yet she didn't. When she was through the hole and inside Arno and Ivan's closet, she groped for Stefan's arm and clutched it nervously.

He eased her fingers off. So slowly she didn't at first realize what he was doing, Stefan inched the door open until a needle-thin ray of silver light filtered into the closet. Moonlight. Samara swallowed. The draperies in the twins' bedroom must be fully open. Perhaps the windows as well. Were Arno and Ivan inviting the shifting?

"My stomach hurts," one of them said. Since their voices were so similar, Samara couldn't tell which twin spoke. "How about yours?"

"Mine's okay, Arn."

So Arno was the one with the stomachache. It didn't seem very important to her, and she relaxed a little.

Stefan widened the crack of the door a bit, and she inched forward to look through it. One twin stood by the open window, looking into the night. She couldn't see the other. The twin in the moonlight stretched, raising his arms over his head.

"Let's go outside," he said.

"It's too late, Arn." Samara detected a touch of uneasiness in Ivan's voice. Though she still couldn't see him, she thought he stood near the bedroom door.

"I need to go outside. I need—" Arno broke off and suddenly stripped off his nightshirt. "I need to be free!" he cried as he tossed the shirt aside.

Samara clutched at Stefan again. Arno's voice was different—hoarse and sort of growly. She didn't like the sound. Arno turned from the window and she swallowed a gasp.

His face wasn't Arno's: it was changing, growing a muzzle.

"Blood. I smell blood." Arno's words were barely understandable.

She heard a door open. "Grandfather!" Ivan yelled. "Hurry!" The door slammed shut. "Arno?" Ivan's voice quivered.

The snouted beast that had been Arno raised its muzzle to sniff the air. Its glowing golden eyes fixed on the closet as it flexed taloned paws. Fangs gleamed when the mouth opened. A long, drawn-out howl chilled Samara's very bones.

"He's coming after us," she warned, yanking Stefan away from the twins' closet door and pulling it closed.

She scrambled through the opening, hearing Stefan behind her. They tumbled one after the other through his closet into his room. Stefan kicked the door shut. In the dark, she clung to his arm as they listened to a loud thud, then a scrabbling.

"He's trying to get into the closet," she whispered through trembling lips. "He knew we were there."

Remembering the last words Arno had said before he shifted completely, she shuddered. Blood, he'd smelled blood.

"What if he breaks through the closet door and finds that hole?" she asked fearfully.

Stefan pulled free of her. A moment later the hall door opened, and in the shaft of light she saw him peering into the hall. He turned to her. "Don't worry. Grandfather's coming. Grandmother, too."

If she hadn't seen the beast, his words might have reassured her. How could *anyone* challenge the beast and live?

"I'm scared," she whispered, fighting something inside her that wanted to scream and scream and never stop.

Stefan shut the hall door and turned on the electric light. His eyes gleamed with excitement. It shocked her to realize he wasn't frightened at all.

"I wish I was Arno," he said. "I'd jump from the window, scale the wall, and run into the hills. I'd run and run and never come back. Never change back."

She stared at him. "But—but you'd be a beast. A horrible beast. How could you ever want to be like that?"

Stefan examined his hands as though looking for talons. "I'd be a beast among beasts—bigger than a wolf, more ferocious than a mountain lion, more dangerous than a bear."

Samara shook her head, rejecting his words. What was wrong with Stefan? He sounded truly envious of Arno. She listened but heard no more howling, no sounds at all from the next room.

"What do you think's happening?" she asked.

"They're changing him back, I suppose."

"Grandfather and Grandmother? How can they?"

"Some *noita* spell, I guess. The twins weren't sure exactly what Grandma would do."

"You mean they told you about this?"

Stefan nodded. "Ivan and Arno know Grandfather explained to all of us about the shifting, so why shouldn't they talk about it? Whichever twin didn't shift was supposed to call Grandfather and then keep the shifter in the room until he got there. Now Arno has to be locked up for five days each month in a special cellar room with no windows. They won't let him out until he learns how to control himself so he doesn't shapeshift when the moon is full."

"What if he can't learn?"

Stefan shrugged. "I know one thing—they'll never lock *me* up, no matter what."

His words, his behavior troubled Samara. It was as though her familiar Stefan had been replaced by some sinister stranger.

"But why would they want to lock you up?" she asked at last.

He smiled slyly and didn't answer, disturbing her more than ever. Dear God, wouldn't this awful night ever come to an end?

Finally, someone tapped on the door and then Grandmother opened it. "It's safe to go back to your own room now," she said when she saw Samara. She turned cold gray eyes on Stefan. "As for you, young man, your grandfather will see you in the library before breakfast about that hole in the closet wall."

Safe or not, Samara was glad to have Grandmother's company on the way to her room.

"I suppose you both saw the shifting," Grandmother said when they were shut inside Samara's room.

Samara nodded. "It scared me."

"Was Stefan frightened?"

"No."

"I didn't think he would be." Grandmother urged Samara into her bed, then pulled up a chair and sat beside her. "You realize you both might have been killed, don't you? You, especially, were in terrible danger because you were bleeding. Blood excites the beast."

Samara swallowed.

"You mustn't blame poor Arno for anything the

beast tried to do,'' Liisi went on. "He has no control over and no memory of what the beast does.''

Grandfather had said the same thing. After watching the shapeshifting, Samara understood what they meant—the beast was *not* her cousin Arno. "Does it hurt him to change?'' she asked.

"It's painful, yes. We hope he'll soon learn to control the urge to shift.''

Samara raised up on one elbow. "You mean Arno *wants* to change into a beast?''

"He can't help the urge—until he learns control. And even then the urge never goes away entirely. The shifter chooses not to change.''

"But what if he learns control and doesn't choose to use it?''

"Then we'd have to keep him locked up when the moon was full. A shifter must never run as a beast—it's dangerous not only to him but to all Voleks. Terrible things would happen if a Volek shifter hunted in the hills. First of all, he'd frighten the neighboring ranchers. Sooner or later they'd form a posse and shoot him down. If that happened, when he died he'd return to human form, and they'd know who he was. Do you think we'd be welcome in this valley if our neighbors even suspected the Volek secret?''

Samara stared at her wide-eyed, finally shaking her head.

"The other danger is that a shifter running under the moon might attract the attention of a stalker. Stalkers not only try to kill the shifter but every one of his kin as well. We might all die.''

A silence fell while Samara considered such a terrible possibility. She didn't want to think about stalkers, but Grandmother was forcing her to. She sat up in bed and hugged herself. "A stalker came to Volek House once,'' she said, her words barely audible.

"Yes, when you were three. She killed Tanya's mother and Druse's mother and two of your Grandfather's friends who were staying here. She tried to kill Grandfather but failed, thank God.''

"She?" Samara asked in surprise.

"Stalkers can be men or women. Your screams warned us of danger—otherwise we might all have died. I know you don't want to remember the horrors of that night, but we need your help, Samara. We need your ability to sense stalkers. If you'll let me, I can train you to refine your talent. But it means going back into your childhood and reliving the night when so many died from the stalker's silver bullets."

Tremors shook Samara as the memory she'd held at bay for almost ten years surfaced. In all that time, she'd never allowed herself to say his name. "He's gone," she whispered. Tears rolled down her cheeks. "Wolf is gone."

Grandmother sat on the bed and held her close. "Wolf may be gone," she said, "but he's not dead. He blamed himself for letting the stalker into the house, and he was so distressed he ran away. We hope he'll come back to us someday."

Samara clung to Grandmother, sobbing, feeling as bereft as she had when she was three and first discovered that Wolf had left her.

Grandmother held her until she quieted, then stayed at her bedside until she fell asleep. Just before Samara drifted into slumber, she made up her mind that *she'd* never run away, no matter what. . . .

In the three years since Arno first shifted, things had changed at Volek House. He'd shifted only one more time before he mastered control, doing so well that he'd been able to go off to Stanford University with Ivan this past September. Samara missed them both more than she'd thought possible.

Grandfather decreed that whether Stefan intended to go to the university or not, until he was eighteen he had to attend Mr. Mathewson's classes in the schoolhouse on the grounds. The teacher and Stefan had finally reached an agreement—if Stefan did his assigned paper, the teacher didn't bother him.

Their grandparents took them on several trips after

Arno and Ivan were gone. Tanya still talked about the night they saw Cecelia Kellogg dance at the Baldwin Theater in San Francisco. Though Samara didn't remember Cecelia being at Volek House, Tanya claimed that *she* did.

"Cecelia used to talk French to me," Tanya said, "because I was the only one of us who could understand it. Arno and Ivan didn't know any. You and Stefan and Druse were too little to interest Cecelia anyway."

Samara didn't know whether to believe Tanya or not, but at the Baldwin she'd been wonderstruck watching Cecelia. Every seat in the theater was full, and the crowd clapped and cheered so much when the show was over that Cecelia came onto the stage again and danced one more number. She wore all black and her gown was tight rather than flowing like the others she'd worn.

The way she pranced and glided and leaped across the stage wove a spell around Samara. If she half closed her eyes, she could almost imagine Cecelia was a graceful and beautiful black cat.

Cecelia had supper with them at the Palace Hotel after the show, and Samara could hardly eat for watching her.

"We'd enjoy a visit from you," Grandfather said to her.

Cecelia smiled and shrugged. "I'm so busy. Perhaps next year."

Tanya thought she meant to visit them in the future, but somehow Samara knew that Cecelia had no intention of ever returning to Volek House.

For weeks after the trip, Tanya had sashayed around the house trying to imitate the way Cecelia walked. Though Tanya was pretty enough, and they both had dark hair and slim figures, she lacked Cecelia's grace and verve.

Samara didn't like Tanya very much. Of the two girls at Volek House, she preferred Druse. Though Druse might be a nuisance sometimes, trailing after her and

Stefan when they didn't want her, she was kind and sweet, while Tanya thought she was Miss Know-it-all and could be really nasty if proved wrong.

Like her or not, Samara was thrilled when Tanya invited her into her room, saying she needed some advice. Tanya locked the door and drew Samara to the window seat, where she pulled her down beside her.

Outside, a tule fog gathered, the usual boring November fog that no one enjoyed.

"Druse couldn't keep a secret if her life depended on it," Tanya said, "and I have to talk to someone or I'll go stark, raving mad. Promise me you won't tell a living soul—not even Stefan."

"Cross my heart and hope to die," Samara said, making an X over her heart.

Tanya took a deep breath. "You've met Rodney McQuade. What do you think of him?"

"He seems nice," Samara ventured cautiously, not sure what Tanya was leading up to. The McQuades had celebrated Rodney's twentieth birthday two months ago and invited all the Voleks to a party. Grandfather and Grandmother declined, as usual, but allowed her, Stefan, Druse, and Tanya to go, Grandfather driving them over in the buggy and picking them up later.

"Nice! Why, Rodney's wonderful!" Tanya clasped her hands together and gazed dreamily at the fog.

Samara eyed her in surprise. The McQuades had two boys. The elder, Richard, was married and lived in San Francisco where he looked after his father's interests in McDee Enterprises. The younger, Rodney, worked on the ranch. He looked a lot like his brother—they both were stocky and sandy-haired and had blue eyes.

"He's so handsome," Tanya crooned.

Samara raised her eyebrows. Pleasant looking, yes—but handsome? Arno and Ivan, dark and tall, with golden eyes, were her idea of handsome.

Tanya opened several buttons of her high-necked gown and drew out a gold chain. Threaded onto it was a ring with a sparkling blue stone set into it.

"A sapphire," Tanya said proudly, holding the ring in her hand. "Rodney bought it for me when he was in San Francisco visiting his brother."

Samara blinked. Tanya had drifted around in a trance lately, but she never dreamed the cause was a man— and certainly not Rodney McQuade, of all people.

"Is it supposed to be an engagement ring?" she asked bluntly.

Tanya blushed and nodded. "I don't dare wear it on my finger, though. Grandfather would have a fit."

"You mean he doesn't know?"

"Heavens, no! You're the only one I've breathed a word to."

"When are you going to tell him?"

"Never." Tanya's chin quivered as she blinked back tears. "He'd forbid me to marry Rodney."

Samara didn't understand. "But Mr. McQuade is Grandfather's partner. They're friends."

"Grandfather doesn't want any of us to marry. Ever. He as good as said so when I turned seventeen."

Samara knew Tanya had been called into the study on her last birthday, and she'd wondered what for. Tanya had never told her. Though she hadn't really thought about getting married herself, Tanya's words disturbed her.

"Why can't we marry?" she demanded.

"Because we're not supposed to have children. They might be shapeshifters because of our Volek blood."

It made sense to Samara. When you got married, you had children. Who'd want to bear a shifter? Heaven knows *she* wouldn't.

"Grandfather asked me," Tanya went on, "what I'd do if I got married and had twin boys. Whatever I told my husband, he couldn't be expected to understand the dangers. And when the one boy shifted, the beast would be uncontrollable, bringing disaster to everyone. If I didn't have twins, what would I tell the child I bore when it grew up and wanted to marry? Having Volek blood is dangerous, he said, and the shifting trait must not be passed on to another generation."

Samara didn't know what to say. Grandfather was surely right, but how could she comfort Tanya?

"I don't care what he says—he can't keep me from marrying Rodney!" Tanya's voice was fierce. "No one can!"

Startled, Samara gaped at her.

"The reason I'm telling you all this," Tanya continued, "is because I need your help. Rodney and I are eloping. Tonight."

Chapter 7

Late on the night of the planned elopement, Samara watched Grandmother lead a weeping Tanya into the study to wait for Grandfather. She feared Tanya would never forgive her, and she wondered if she'd be able to forgive herself.

Grandfather, she knew, was escorting Rodney back to the McQuades. Samara hadn't wanted to tell her grandparents about the elopement, but haunted by the specter of shifter babies being born to Rodney and Tanya, she'd gone to Grandmother at the last moment.

Aware she'd never be able to sleep, Samara climbed the stairs slowly, sighing as she sat down on the top step. No matter how long it took, she meant to stay there until her grandparents finished talking to Tanya and then apologize to her cousin.

Some time later, Druse eased down beside her. "I woke up and Tanya wasn't in her bed," Druse said. "Where is she?"

"In the study with Grandfather and Grandmother," Samara told her.

Druse drew in her breath. "What's she done?"

"She and Rodney McQuade tried to elope."

"Oh. Why'd they want to do that?"

Samara explained as best she could, and Druse was silent for long moments. "Grandmother makes a potion for not having babies," she said finally.

It was the first Samara had heard about it, but she wasn't too surprised that Druse knew. Druse had shown a talent for healing, and Grandmother was teaching her how to make and use various medicines.

"I like Rodney," Druse added. "He makes me laugh."

Samara put an arm around her. "I like him, too. But maybe he wouldn't want to marry Tanya if they could never have children."

"When I'm old enough, I'm going to marry Stefan," Druse announced.

"Does he know?"

"Sure he does—I told him. 'Course he said he wasn't never, ever going to marry anyone, but I didn't pay any attention. Boys his age don't think about marriage."

Samara hid her smile. Druse, at thirteen, was three years younger than Stefan, but at the moment she sounded years older.

"Grandfather won't care if I marry Stefan," Druse went on. "We won't be marrying outsiders—we're both Voleks."

Druse's relationship to her and Stefan was complicated. Samara thought of her as a cousin, but actually Druse was Wolf's daughter. Wolf was Grandfather's grandson by a woman in Russia. Grandfather also had had a son in California by another woman, and that son, now dead, was her and Stefan's father.

None of them, Samara decided, including Arno and Ivan, would have been born if someone had warned Grandfather about Volek blood when he was young. Someday she'd ask him why no one had.

"Who are you going to marry?" Druse asked.

"I haven't met anyone I want to marry. Maybe I never will."

"Cecelia Kellogg told Grandfather the same thing when we were in San Francisco—that she hadn't found anyone. He was talking to her about children carrying traits of their parents and grandparents. I wasn't supposed to hear, but I did."

Samara wondered why Grandfather would say such things to Cecelia, who wasn't a Volek. The sound of the back door opening and closing drove the thought from her mind. Grandfather had returned home. She shook her head. Poor Tanya—she was in for it now.

Druse, leaning against her, fell asleep before the study door opened, telling Samara that their grandparents were finished talking to Tanya. Samara shook Druse awake and, with an arm around her shoulders, helped the other girl back to bed. She returned to the hall and waited with a heavy heart for Tanya.

To her surprise, instead of dragging up the stairs, Tanya bounded up them. When she saw Samara, she flung her arms around her.

"I'm so happy!" Tanya cried.

Samara pulled back. "I thought you'd be mad at me."

Tanya beamed. "If you hadn't give us away to Grandmother, this never would have happened. Listen—Rodney and I are going to get married in a real wedding with everyone invited!"

Surprise made Samara temporarily speechless. Finding her voice, she asked, "When?"

"Sometime next spring."

"But what about the problem?"

Tanya shrugged. "We just won't have any children. Grandmother knows ways to prevent it." She smiled again, this time more slyly. "They had to agree. I told them if they didn't, I'd sneak off and marry Rodney anyway. And I would, too. He's the only man I'll ever love."

Tanya's wedding reception was held at the elegant new Citrus Hotel in Thompsonville. Everything about the wedding was beautiful, Samara thought, including the bride. Though Grandmother had one of her spells, falling into a trance, Mrs. McQuade managed to ease her away from the guests before anyone else noticed her odd behavior.

Mrs. McQuade, who'd known Liisi for over twenty years, didn't seem disturbed, but Samara knew both her grandparents were. She was herself after she heard

Grandmother whispering to Grandfather that she'd suddenly seen the bridal couple engulfed in flames—a frightening omen.

No one told the happy newlyweds that anything was amiss, and they left amid a shower of rice for an overnight stay in San Francisco. In the morning, they'd be getting on the train in Oakland to cross the country to spend their honeymoon in New York City. When they returned, they'd live in Thompsonville until their new house on McQuade property was finished.

Because she and Tanya had never been close, Samara was surprised to find that Volek House seemed emptier without her. Druse, with no Tanya for company, constantly tagged after her and Stefan.

"I expect to find Druse under my bed next," Stefan grumbled.

"She's planning to marry you," Samara warned him.

He rolled his eyes.

But in June it was Stefan who comforted Druse when the tiger-striped kitten she'd smuggled in from the barn clawed her face and neck in its frantic effort to escape.

"It wasn't you the kitten didn't like," he told Druse, dabbing away the blood with his handkerchief. "Grandfather doesn't take to cats, and I guess they don't like him, either. All cats seem to hate Volek House."

When Samara looked for the kitten later, wanting to be certain it wasn't still in the house, Stefan told her not to bother.

"It's gone for good," he said. "I killed it."

Samara drew in her breath in horror. "Why?"

He shrugged and walked away, leaving her deeply disturbed. More and more lately, he seemed to be turning into someone other than the Stefan she'd known since birth.

She was aware he could hardly wait until they turned eighteen so he could stop going to school.

"It's like I'm penned in the damn schoolhouse," he told her. "Did you notice the desperate eyes of the caged wolf we saw at the San Francisco Zoo? That's how I feel sometimes. Not only about school, but because I'm trapped here at Volek House. Once I'm eighteen I'm leaving, and no one's going to stop me.''

By the following June, Stefan had begun avoiding her. Samara tried not to care and sought Druse's company. More often than not, though, Druse was nowhere to be found, and Samara assumed she was in the tower room with Grandmother. Feeling left out, she was delighted when Tanya invited her to spend a weekend with them in their new house. Grandfather readily agreed.

On Saturday afternoon, Tanya served tea to Samara in the parlor after Rodney and his father had left for Thompsonville on business.

''You look so happy,'' Samara said, her tone tinged with envy.

''Being married to Rodney is more wonderful than I ever imagined. I've never felt so close to anyone before. At least not since my mother died—and I can hardly remember her.''

''He doesn't mind not ever having children?''

Tanya's smile faded. ''We don't discuss it.''

A sudden suspicion struck Samara. ''Surely you've told him you don't plan to have children.''

Tanya bit her lip. ''No. No, I haven't. He doesn't know the real reason I take Grandmother's potion—he thinks it's for my health.''

Samara bit back her impulse to say that was dishonest. It was none of her business what Tanya chose to do. But she wondered how Tanya could feel close to Rodney and at the same time conceal something so important from him.

When Grandfather came to get her on Sunday night, Samara almost brought up the matter on their way home but decided it wasn't her place to tell him.

''The moon's three days from full,'' Grandfather said.

He'd taught all of them the moon's phases when they

were so young that Samara couldn't recall a time when she didn't know exactly what phase the moon was in. She glanced from the buggy at the waxing moon, half-hidden by a passing cloud. Strange that the moon, so far from earth, could affect a Volek shapeshifter.

For some reason this reminded her of what Druse had overheard Grandfather say to Cecelia. Pondering his words, she asked, "Are there other shifters in the world besides Voleks?"

"I know of one. Dead now. There may be others—who can tell?"

"Did a stalker kill that other shifter?"

He sighed. "Yes. You're old enough to be told—the shifter was Cecelia's mother."

Samara's eyes widened. "A woman! I thought shifters were always men."

"That's true of Voleks."

After mulling it over, Samara said, "Then Cecelia shouldn't have children."

"That's right. She may pass on the trait."

They rode in silence for a time. "You've never asked questions about your mother," he said finally.

"Grandmother told me she was a Miwok and went back to her people because she wasn't happy at Volek House. I don't really remember her. Not like I do Wolf."

"You and Wolf had a special rapport." He sighed again. "I wish he'd come home."

Samara did, too. Especially now with Tanya gone, Druse busy with Grandmother, and Stefan wanting to be by himself.

Less than an hour later, she discovered just how wrong she was about Druse and Stefan. Grandfather stabled the horse and stayed talking to Chung while they unharnessed the animal from the buggy. Not wanting to wait, Samara walked to the house by herself. But she turned aside before she reached the back door, since the night was warm and the silver moonlight held a promise that entranced her.

She meandered along the brick path through the rose garden and, with the flowers' sweet scent drifting after

her, entered the grape arbor. There, where the vines'
thick foliage shut away the moonlight, she heard a girl
laugh and held still, listening.

The girl laughed again, low and intimate-sounding.
"Not *again*," she said softly in a voice Samara recognized.

Druse! What was she doing in the grape arbor? And
who was she talking to?

Without taking time to think, Samara edged quietly
ahead, alert for the slightest noise.

"Again and again and again." A man's voice this
time, and one Samara knew as well as she knew her
own. "You know you like it as well as I do."

Stefan. Druse was with Stefan. She stopped, suddenly not wanting to know why they were together.
But she was too late.

"You'll have to catch me first!" Druse cried.

Hidden by the shadows under the grape arbor, Samara watched as Druse, wearing not a stitch of clothing, darted out of the arbor and ran laughing over the
grass, only to be caught, tumbled to the ground and
embraced by an equally naked Stefan.

She'd never seen a man and woman mate, and she
didn't care to see it now. Samara closed her eyes, feeling betrayed without understanding why. No longer
worrying whether they heard her or not, she turned and
fled into the house, up the stairs, and into her bedroom.

No wonder I could never find Druse, she thought as
she paced up and down. She was with Stefan. Like
that. What's he thinking of? Druse is only fourteen!

Druse might have a woman's figure, but she was still
a child—Stefan should have more sense. She had to
talk to him. Tonight.

Knowing Druse and Stefan must come in soon because Grandfather barred the doors before he went to
bed, Samara marched down the hall to Stefan's room,
sat down, and waited in the dark with the door ajar.

When he finally pushed the door open and entered
his bedroom, Samara had her speech well planned.
But seeing him standing there staring at her, illumi-

nated by the dim hall light, a frisson of fear ran along her spine. Was that Stefan she saw? Her brother? Her twin? He looked different—his features somehow coarser. And when had his hair gotten so long?

"What're you doing in here?" His voice was hoarse. Growly.

Samara rose. "Stefan?" With dismay she heard a quaver in her voice.

"Who the hell else would it be?"

"You—you look strange."

He threw back his head and laughed. He sounded strange. Fierce. Samara struggled with an impulse to edge past him and flee to her room.

No! She'd come to have her say. Taking a deep breath, she opened her mouth to begin, then was horrified at what came out.

"Why did you kill that kitten last year?"

He didn't seem even slightly surprised by her question. "Because it hated me." He closed the door, strode past her, pushed the curtains open as far as they'd go, and opened both windows.

"That cat knew before I did," he said, his back to her as he stared from a window. The moonlight slanting into the room silvered his dark hair.

Samara hugged herself. "Knew what?"

"What I was. You sense it now, don't you?"

She bit her lip, uncertain what to say or do. "You're—different," she finally muttered.

"God, yes! It almost happened last month, this month it will. I'll be free!"

He turned and she gasped. His face was changing, altering. Like Arno's.

"Don't be scared." He growled rather than spoke. "I won't shift all the way. Not yet. The moon's rays aren't quite strong enough."

"But you can't! Not you. You're not a shifter."

His smile was grotesque. "You know better."

Gazing at his half-human, half-beast face, she couldn't deny the truth. Tears burned in her eyes, and one trickled down her cheek.

"Don't cry," he said. "This is what I've always wanted. I can hardly wait to shift all the way—to run, to be free."

She wiped her eyes with the back of her hand. "We'll have to tell Grandfather so—"

"No!" He took a step toward her, and she took a step back. "I want you to promise you won't tell him. Or anyone."

"But Stefan, you have to learn—"

"I won't be locked in that windowless room like Arno was. Never!" Stefan's eyes blazed at her. "I swear I'll kill myself if you tell." He raised his hand and made an X over his heart.

Seeing the sign, an echo of their childhood promises, brought a lump to her throat. They were no longer children, but Stefan was still her twin brother. She loved him despite everything. And she knew him better than anyone else in the world did. It was true that he might well kill himself if he was locked in that room. If she told Grandfather, she'd be murdering Stefan. She twisted her hands together, not seeing any alternative but to keep his secret.

"Does Druse know?" she asked.

"No. Why would she?"

"I saw her with you earlier. Oh, Stefan, she's so young."

"She was there—she's always there—and I can't control my urges. Not when the moon's near full. It's as if he—it—takes over my mind like it soon will my body."

Samara covered her mouth with her hands. "I'm afraid for you." Her voice was muffled.

"Don't be. Think of me as being free at last."

She shook her head. "He—it'll be free, not you. You're Stefan, but it's a beast. Grandfather told us you won't have any control over the beast or even know what it does."

"I'll know in my heart. The beast will be my true self."

"No! Never!"

"You can't understand. No one can. Except maybe Arno."

She raised her chin, pretending a bravery she didn't feel. "What about me? I'm your twin. Will I be safe from the beast? What if it turns on me? Kills me?"

He held out his hands. "I couldn't possibly hurt you. Ever."

"But does the beast feel the same? You don't know."

"Arno didn't harm Ivan."

"They're not us!" she cried. "We're not identical twins, so we've already broken one Volek rule about shifters. How can you be sure of anything? What if you shift into the beast and can't change back?"

"I'd be happy."

The tears she'd held back so long overcame her control and her chest heaved with sobs. Through the veil of tears, she saw the half-beast move toward her.

"Don't touch me!" she wailed, then turned and fled to her own room, locking the door behind her.

The next morning, Samara found a note from Stefan slipped under her door asking her to tell Grandfather he'd gone on a several-week camping trip into the mountains.

"I suppose I've been keeping too tight a rein on that boy," Grandfather remarked when she found him in his study and told him about Stefan's note. "God knows I don't want to lose him as we've lost Wolf. What do you think, Samara?"

Guilt hobbled her tongue. "Stefan doesn't like school," she managed to say.

"So Mr. Mathewson's been reporting for some years now. I understand from him that you're a good student—as bright as Arno or Ivan, in his opinion."

Samara felt guiltier than ever at the praise.

"What do you want from life, Samara?" Grandfather asked.

She didn't know, and she couldn't think what to say, so she merely shook her head.

"Do you dream of marrying, like Tanya?" he persisted.

"No. Who would I marry?"

He sighed. "I know I've restricted you. It's time I let you and Stefan go into the world. Would you be interested in attending Stanford University this fall? I'm sure Mr. Mathewson could make sure you'd be ready."

"Stefan wouldn't like the university. He hates being forced to learn."

Grandfather half smiled. "I can't imagine him being happy there. But you and Stefan aren't inseparable. Perhaps it's time you went your separate ways."

If only she could tell Grandfather the truth! Stefan was safe enough as long as it was daylight, but what would happen when the moon rose tonight? How she longed to share her fear for him. Her grandfather would know what to do.

Realizing she had to speak, she blurted the first thing that came into her head. "Druse wants to marry Stefan. I don't think that's a good idea."

Grandfather gazed at her a long time before he spoke. "What does Stefan think?"

"He says he'll never marry."

"Druse is far too young at the moment, but looking into the future a marriage between them isn't such a bad idea as you seem to think. They both understand the dangers of furthering the Volek line, and it would be two less outsiders joining the family."

She desperately wanted to cry that Stefan could never marry anyone because he was a shifter. She bit her lip to keep silent.

"Sit down here beside me, child," he said, patting the ottoman at the foot of his chair. "Good," he told her when she perched uneasily on the large footstool. "I well remember the night you and Stefan were born. I held you in my arms the next morning, and I named you for a Volek ancestor. You wailed when I called you Samara, and I decided then you had a mind of your own. You still do. I can see there's something troubling you, something you're reluctant to share. Believe me, I'd do anything in the world to help you."

She remained silent.

Grandfather sighed and smoothed her hair. "You resemble your blood grandmother," he told her. "She was a very pretty woman; a descendent of one of the old Spanish families who settled California long before the Americans came west. At the time I met her, I was a foolish and reckless young man who didn't realize what the future held. Otherwise—" He paused and smiled sadly. "If I had known about the Volek heritage, I'm afraid you and Stefan would never have been born."

Samara listened raptly, hoping he'd go on. Grandfather all too rarely spoke of the past.

"I want you to be happy," he said. "If you don't like the idea of the university, maybe a finishing school would suit you. I mustn't keep you hidden away at Volek House any longer."

She couldn't be sent away! What would happen to Stefan if there were no one here to look after him?

Before she could find a way to protest, Grandfather spoke again. "It was cruel of me to name you after the woman who brought the shapeshifting trait into the family hundreds of years ago. I hope you'll forgive me."

"Tell me about her," Samara begged, relieved to put off any more discussion about leaving as well as both thrilled and dismayed by what he'd said about her name.

"A very long time ago, when our forebears lived on the edge of the Russian forest," he began, "a pretty girl named Samara couldn't be stopped from wandering in the forest despite the danger of wolves. And of worse.

"The local Wise Woman warned Samara that the *lieshui*, the spirits of the forest, would ensorcel her, but the girl refused to listen. Samara had paid no attention to the village youths who came to court her, but one day she brought a stranger home with her: a yellow-eyed man dressed in silver-gray who wore a cloak of wolfskins. She said his name was Volek, and from then on she would look at no other man.

"Her family, along with the rest of the villagers, disliked and feared this man from the forest, but when it became clear Samara was with child, her father gave her to the stranger in marriage.

"On the night after the wedding, a full moon rose. It was then that the Wise Woman crept into the bedroom of Samara's father and woke him. 'Death rides the moon,' she hissed. 'You have welcomed a beast into your house; you have wedded your daughter to a son of the forest spirits, an *oborot* who is both man and beast. Rise and stab him with a silver knife while he sleeps, or he will kill you all and gobble your hearts before morning.'

"Samara's father roused his three sons, and armed with knives, they slipped into the bridal chamber and fell on the slumbering groom. The sons withdrew in terror when the stranger's flesh, penetrated by their steel knives, closed over immediately. But the father's silver knife rose and fell until blood stained the bedcovers and dripped onto the floor.

"The bridegroom howled and fell back on the bed. Though they believed he must be dead, when he began to change into a horrible beast the men took fright, gathered up the screaming Samara and ran from the room, carrying her to the Wise Woman.

"She forced infusions of herbs down the girl's throat to rid her of the child she carried. When the father and his sons returned to drag away the beast, he was gone. Neither he nor the stranger named Volek was ever seen again.

"Samara didn't miscarry despite all the potions she was fed. When she was finally brought to the birthing stool, she fell into a trance when the first child was born and died as the second child slipped from her womb. Her father meant to kill the babies, but when he saw how human they looked, identical twin boys who, except for their golden eyes, resembled his own sons when they had been babes, he hadn't the heart.

"The Old Wise Woman, who might have convinced him the twins must not live, was dead herself by this time, savaged by a wolf while she hunted for firewood in the forest. Or at least the villagers preferred to believe it was a wolf.

"Samara's twins grew to manhood, and the full moon rose and one of them—changed. The villagers waited and stabbed him through the heart with a silver dagger when he returned to human form. The other escaped, fleeing to a faraway city. There he took the name of Volek, which was his by right, and in due course luck brought him a wealthy wife who bore him nine children, none of them twins."

Grandfather paused for a moment and took a deep breath. "This is the story handed down from father to eldest son since that time with the admonition that if identical twin sons were born they must not be allowed to live. Unfortunately, my father couldn't bring himself to kill my brother and me. My twin, who was blameless, perished, but I survived. Years later, I returned to Russia where my father told me the story. I've repeated it to Wolf, to Arno and Ivan, a part of it to Tanya, and now I've told you."

Samara gazed at Grandfather, struck speechless by the terrible beauty of the tale.

"But I add a warning," he went on. "No more Voleks can be born. It's past time for the line, with its dismal shapeshifter heritage, to die."

Samara found her voice. "*You* were a twin?" she asked.

He nodded. "As I said, the wrong twin lived. I'm a shapeshifter. And, to my shame, I've fathered another. Luckily Arno, like me, prefers to remain human. He's learned to control the urge to shift. But we can take no more chances. No more Voleks will be born. No more!"

Samara swallowed. What would he do when he discovered he also had a shifter grandson? And worse, one who'd rather remain a beast?

Chapter 8

Samara peered from the music room window at the rain falling from dark clouds that didn't show any sign of dissipating. She sighed and returned to the piano bench to stare morosely at her book of musical exercises.

While she didn't hate practicing, her piano lessons had only been an excuse to persuade Grandfather not to send her to finishing school.

"Music," she'd told him. "I'm interested in music. I'll begin with the piano and see how I do. I can always go away later to learn more if I want to."

It was true that she enjoyed music, so it wasn't quite a lie.

Flexing her fingers, she set them onto the keys and began.

"Oh, no!" Druse spoke from the archway. "Not those tuneless exercises again. Why not play something with a melody?"

"Mrs. Arbuthnot says nimble fingers make the difference between a good and an indifferent pianist," Samara said, continuing to run up and down the scales.

Druse, carrying a newspaper, came to lean on the curve of the grand piano. "I can't bear this rain—three days already. Will it never end?"

Samara interpreted her words to mean that Druse was impatient for Stefan's return. Nothing she'd said had made the slightest impression on Druse or Stefan—they were still secret lovers, something Samara had not told her grandparents.

"I take Grandmother's potions," was Druse's answer to the possibility of conceiving a child.

"I don't put Druse at risk—I don't go near her when the moon's full," was all Stefan ever said.

Stefan's infrequent homecomings always coincided with Grandfather's equally infrequent absences. Grandfather had taken the train to Oakland yesterday and was due back tomorrow.

Samara knew Stefan was afraid Grandfather would somehow sense the difference in him and discover what he and Samara had kept hidden from everyone for almost a year—the fact that he was a shifter.

"Do stop banging on those keys for a minute," Druse begged. "I want to read you something from the San Francisco *Chronicle*."

Samara's fingers froze on the keys. She'd seen the *Chronicle* already, and she was afraid she knew what Druse intended to read to her.

" 'Spirit Wolves In Valley?' " Druse paused and looked over the top of the newspaper at her. "Are you listening?"

Samara nodded stiffly. Did Druse suspect?

" 'A San Francisco man,' " Druse read, " 'recently returned from a camping trip into the Sierras, tells a frightening tale of becoming separated from his companions and being chased by a fearsome beast. The beast pursued him and was about to overtake him when he was fortunate enough to find refuge in a foothills Indian village. The Miwok inhabitants of the village knew the beast well.

" 'The Miwoks claimed it was the second time this beast has roamed their territory. Some twenty years ago, the village chief told our hiker, what they called a Spirit Wolf was supposedly shot to death. Now he lives again, appearing when the moon is full, to terrorize the Indians.

" 'Our hiker, a business man of impeccable repute, insists the beast that chased him was not a wolf, spirit or otherwise, nor any other wild animal native to the mountains.

" 'If any of our readers has an idea what this mysterious beast could be, please write to this paper. Your intrepid journalist favors that most legendary of beasts, the werewolf, deep in his mountain fastness, emerging to hunt for prey only when the moon is full . . .' "

A silence fell after Druse finished. "Well?" she said finally, folding the newspaper.

"How should I know what the beast is?" Samara asked. "Likely it's a made-up story anyway."

"Stefan's cabin is in those foothills." Druse's gaze challenged her.

Samara stared back at her, willing her face to remain expressionless. Hearing the article aloud was even worse then seeing it the first time. How many people had read the article? Grandfather must have. What would he do?

At last Druse sighed and looked away. "I wish Stefan would come home," she said.

Stefan couldn't wait much longer, Samara knew, because the moon was waxing and would be full in less than a week. He never came near them during a full moon. Last week, she'd left a note in their secret hiding place to tell him of Grandfather's upcoming trip. If Stefan had gotten the note, why hadn't he returned to Volek House?

And, oh God, what if the story was true and he'd started hunting men?

Samara forced the morbid thought from her mind and looked determinedly at her music book. She could do nothing until she talked to her brother. But her heart wasn't in piano practice, and she couldn't make her fingers begin the scales again.

"I hate not being a twin!" Druse's voice was petulant. "Twins share secrets. Stefan only lets me share one thing with him, and you don't let me share anything with you." She flung herself away from the piano and stalked toward the archway.

Liisi, entering the music room, stopped her. Placing

an arm around Druse, she led her to the bay windows, motioning with her head for Samara to join them.

Liisi put her other arm around Samara and, pulling the two girls close, said in a low tone, "The stones warn me trouble is coming. Danger. Death. With your grandfather gone, we must prepare ourselves to withstand the peril without him."

Druse crumpled the newspaper in her hands.

Samara shivered. "What kind of trouble?"

"I wish I knew." Grandmother's voice was tense with worry. "We don't want the servants involved, so I've sent them home—except for Jose. Samara, you run and tell him to leave. And warn Chung to lock the gates and keep an eye out for strangers. Druse, you come with me."

While Chung was closing the back gate, Samara went around to the front with Jose to lock the front gate after she let him out. Gray clouds hovered overhead, but the rain was now more of a mist. As they reached the gate, she heard horse's hooves approaching. Hurriedly, she swung the gate open for Jose, hoping she could close and lock it before the rider appeared.

Misty rain or not, Jose, who was getting on toward sixty years, was in no hurry. *"Un cabellero,"* he said, stopping his horse halfway through the gate and craning his neck to look down the road where a man on a pinto rode toward them.

Warmth flooded through Samara, surprising her, making her glance overhead to see if by some miracle the sun had suddenly appeared. The day was still overcast.

"Hola!" Jose cried. *"Mi amigo!"* He kicked his old gray into a trot and rode toward the oncoming horseman.

Samara, about to swing the gate shut, held. The flow of warmth came from the rider, from the man on the pinto. She didn't recognize him, but somehow she felt she knew him.

Jose leaned from his horse to grasp the man's hand,

speaking Spanish so rapidly that Samara couldn't follow what he said. The man, answering him in the same tongue, reached around, lifted a bundle from his back, and showed it to Jose. Jose asked a question.

"Hawk," the man said.

After another rapid fire exchange in Spanish, Jose rode on, and the stranger came toward the gate. Alarmed, Samara started to close it.

"Wait!" he called. "I'm coming in."

She hurried all the faster.

"Samara?" he said. "Yes, it *is* you. Don't you know me?"

And then her mind, her entire body knew. "Wolf," she whispered, her relief so great she could hardly push the word out.

He rode through the gap she'd left open. Numbly she swung the gate closed and locked it. Wolf had come home!

He slid from his horse, still holding the bundle. "This is Hawk," he said, thrusting it at her.

Only when she took the bundle did she understand. Hawk was a baby! His dark eyes gazed solemnly at her from inside the wrapped blanket. His black hair grew straight up from his head, giving him the look of an Indian warrior. Samara looked at Wolf questioningly.

"My son," he said, "and Morning Quail's. He's your half-brother."

In her shock Samara almost lost her grip on the baby. "Where is my—my mother? she finally choked out.

"Dead." Wolf's voice was grim. He put an arm around her shoulders. "There's a shifter running in the hills again."

She couldn't control her gasp of horror as her mind conjured up a terrible picture of Stefan, changed completely into a beast.

Wolf's fingers dug into her shoulder. He stared into her eyes for what seemed like an eternity. At last he let her go. Clenching his fists, he raised his face to the falling rain and shouted, "Why?"

His rage frightened her, and she involuntarily tightened her grip on the baby, who began to wail.

The sound caught Wolf's attention. "Take him to the house," he ordered. "I'll see to my pinto."

Samara gathered her wits. "Chung will take care of your horse for you."

"Chung?"

She realized Wolf had never met him. "Chung lives in a cottage on the grounds. When Chung was a boy, Grandfather brought him home from San Francisco, and he's been here ever since. We—we trust Chung. Come to think of it, I'd better go with you and explain who you are because he's armed and wary of strangers."

Leaving Wolf with Chung, Samara, carrying the baby, hurried into the house through the back door, her mind in turmoil. The strange rapport she'd felt with Wolf alarmed her. Had he somehow sensed Stefan's secret? She was afraid to know.

In the kitchen, Grandmother lifted the baby from Samara's arms. "Welcome, little Hawk," she said, gazing down at him. "I hope you'll be safe here." She then handed him to Druse. "You'll take charge of him."

"But I don't know how to take care of babies," Druse protested, looking askance at the squirming bundle in her arms.

"You'll learn. Your healing talent will go a long way toward showing you what to do, and I'll help with the rest. First of all, he'll need milk and diapers." Grandmother turned to Samara. "Lock the house as soon as Wolf is inside. You stay with him. It's important that you do. Thank God he returned when we needed him the most."

Grandmother and Druse took Hawk up the back stairs just as Wolf entered the kitchen.

"Grandmother's happy you're home," Samara told him. "She gave Hawk to Druse to take care of and I'm supposed to stay with you, she says."

He smiled. "Orders already. How like her." His

smile faded as he looked at Samara. "Where is he?" he asked. "Where's Stefan?"

Samara eyed him, wondering how much he knew. She couldn't recall how Wolf had looked when he left Volek House, but the more she saw of him, the more familiar he seemed. He was half a head shorter than Grandfather, who was well over six feet, but they did resemble one another. Wolf was unmistakably a Volek for all that his eyes were brown, not golden, and his black hair straight rather than wavy. She didn't know if he'd had a mustache and beard when he left, but he did now.

"I'm not sure where Stefan is," she said finally.

"He's somewhere in the hills, though, isn't he?"

She nodded reluctantly.

"Does he ever come home?" Wolf persisted.

"Not often."

"And never when Grandfather's here, am I right?"

Again she nodded, almost certain now that she'd somehow given away Stefan without meaning to.

Wolf began to pace up and down in the kitchen. "Chung told me Grandfather will be home from San Francisco tomorrow. That means Stefan would have to come to Volek House today or tonight or miss his chance because he doesn't dare risk Grandfather sensing his shifter aura. How long since Stefan first shifted?"

Samara swallowed. "Almost a—a year." Relief combined with guilt ran through her once the words were out. "How did you know?"

He half smiled, a sad smile. "You showed me, just like you used to when you were little. Don't you remember how it is between us, Samara?"

To her embarrassment, tears flooded her eyes. "You left me," she whispered.

Wolf strode to her and wrapped his arms around her. "I'm sorry. But I had to go. You were too young to understand."

"Grandfather said he never blamed you." Her words

came through her sobs. "Grandmother doesn't either."

"That's why I had to leave. I knew they wouldn't blame me because they understand more than they should. But it *was* my fault, and I blame myself."

He held her away from him by her shoulders and gave her a slight shake. "Why haven't you told Grandfather about Stefan?"

"He said he'd kill himself if Grandfather locked him up. Stefan's my twin—how could I take the chance?"

"Last month the beast killed the woman who gave birth to the two of you. He killed Morning Quail—your mother and Stefan's. I don't assign blame, but who do you think is at fault? Stefan, because the beast he became killed her? Or yourself for keeping his shifting a secret?"

Her mother dead? Killed by the beast? She stared at him in horrified despair, her worst imaginings come true.

Wolf closed his heart to Samara's tear-stained cheeks and horror-struck expression. If anyone knew how she felt, he did. She'd blame herself for the rest of her life, just as he did. It couldn't be helped.

"Stefan can't be allowed to go on killing," he said.

"N-no," she quavered.

"What happened when Arno shifted?" he asked.

Samara told him, adding that the twins were at Stanford.

"So it's possible Stefan could learn to control his shifting," Wolf said.

"He doesn't want to. He—he *likes* being a beast."

Wolf clenched his fists. "He does, does he? Well, I mean to make sure he stops shifting once and for all. Who's at home?"

"Grandmother, Druse, you, me, and your baby. And Chung outside."

"Where's Tanya?"

"She married Rodney McQuade."

Wolf raised his eyebrows.

"They won't have children," she added.

"Whatever happened to Cecelia Kellogg?"

"She's a famous dancer in San Francisco. Haven't you heard of Cece?"

"Good God—that's her?" A picture flitted across Wolf's mind of a graceful young Cecelia in a filmy red dress dancing in the music room while her mother played the piano. And himself, a great lout entranced by her beauty, clumsily bumping into her. And discovering her terrible secret. . . .

He shook his head. He'd been right about Arno and Stefan, but apparently he'd been wrong about Cecelia; obviously she'd never shifted. At least not yet.

Bringing himself back to the present, Wolf said, "You must tell Grandmother and Druse about Stefan immediately."

"Not Druse!"

He stared at Samara, not understanding.

"She—they—they're lovers. Grandmother and Grandfather don't know."

Wolf raked his hand through his hair. "What else have you been hiding from them?"

"N-nothing." She looked ready to burst into tears again.

"Druse has to know for her own safety. I want Grandmother to take the three of you and lock you all up with her in the tower room when and if Stefan arrives. I'll confront him alone."

"No!" Samara cried. "I insist on being there when you and Stefan meet. It's my right. Besides, I'm the only one he ever listens to."

"He'll listen to me, all right." Wolf's tone was grim.

"Who'll listen to you?" Grandmother asked as she came into the kitchen. She crossed to Wolf and hugged him. "It's good to have you home. We need you here."

Grandmother Liisi had never been demonstrative, and Wolf was touched by her warm embrace. "I'm sorry to burden you with Hawk," he said, "but I had nowhere else to take him. Nowhere safe."

"If safe we are," Grandmother said. "The stones forecast peril and death."

Wolf tensed. Grandmother's predictions were true ones.

"Samara, don't just stand there," Grandmother ordered. "We must offer Wolf a meal and eat ourselves. While we have the chance."

Samara was setting the table when Druse came down with Hawk. Wolf hauled the old kitchen cradle in from the pantry and settled the baby into it, rocking the cradle back and forth with his foot.

"I can remember rocking you in this same cradle when you were a baby," he told Druse.

She slanted him a look. "I don't remember you. Not at all."

Wolf sighed. "I'm sorry to have deserted you, Druse. I don't expect you to forgive me."

"I lost my mother and my father at the same time," Druse said.

"Stop that!" Grandmother's tone was tart. "What's past is past. We've no time for recriminations. Druse, help Samara. Wolf, tell me what you've been doing all these years."

Wolf told her about his meeting with John Muir and how he'd helped Muir both at the ranch and in the older man's attempts to preserve the Sierras as a national park. "When I visited Washington, D.C., with him in '91," he finished, "I was able to meet President Harrison. His support helped push the park bill through Congress so that California now has three national parks in the Sierras—Yosemite, Sequoia, and General Grant."

"I've read about John Muir in the *Chronicle*," Liisi said. "Your time's been well spent in helping him prevent men from despoiling the wilderness. We *are* the earth, and if we kill it, we die."

Wolf nodded, pleased that Grandmother understood.

After they'd eaten, Wolf said, "We have no time to waste, Grandmother. As soon as I arrived at Volek

House, I found the bond Samara and I shared when she was a child was stronger than ever. Whether she willed the seeing or not, she showed me what Stefan has become.''

Druse dropped her fork and covered her ears with her hands. Grandmother reached over and pulled her hands down, saying sharply, ''You're too old to behave like a baby.''

''Samara told me Stefan shifted for the first time last year,'' Wolf went on. ''When word came to me that Morning Quail had died, I traveled to her Miwok foothills village. There I found Hawk. I don't deny he's my son—I know he must be. After my last visit to the village, she never sent word that she was with child, so discovering I had a three-month-old son was a shock. I'd sworn never to father another child.'' He offered Druse a sad smile.

''Hawk was a surprise, yes, but the real horror hit me when they told me about Morning Quail's death— her throat torn out by the 'Spirit Wolf,' a beast that couldn't be killed.

'' 'The Spirit Wolf has killed our game and terrorized the hunters,' the village medicine man told me. 'Morning Quail believed she could reason with the beast because she was its mother.' ''

Druse covered her face with her hands and moaned.

Wolf's pity for her didn't stop him from going on. ''The medicine man told me he thought the Spirit Wolf was living in an old cabin in the mountains, some miles from the Miwok village. I went there. The cabin was deserted, but I found evidence someone had been using it.'' He spread his hands. ''I may not believe in spirit wolves, but I'm a Volek so I believe in shape-shifters. When I left Volek House years ago, I knew of at least two potential shifters under this roof. Arno and Stefan.''

Samara drew in her breath, and Wolf glanced at her as he continued. ''I told Grandfather, but at the time neither of us were sure whether I had a true talent or not. I had to find out. After retrieving Hawk from the village, I rode here as fast as the pinto could travel. Samara let me through the gate, and when she showed me the picture in her mind, I knew my talent was true. Stefan was—Stefan is—a shifter. Arno, I'm told, learned to control his shifting well enough to enter the university. But what about Stefan?''

''We didn't realize Stefan was afflicted.'' Grandmother's voice shook. ''I would have helped him, if only—''

''He didn't want your help.'' Wolf spoke harshly. ''He prefers the beast state.'' He felt his words were arrows thrust into Samara's heart, but it couldn't be helped. She'd aided her twin in his perversity; she'd be hurt worse before this was over. ''Grandmother Liisi, the help we need from you now is silver bullets.''

Druse screamed and leaped to her feet, knocking over her chair and startling the baby. He began to wail. Grandmother rose and slapped Druse hard on each cheek.

''Whatever Stefan is to you,'' she said, ''no longer matters. He has deliberately violated our trust, and by doing so he has invited disaster into Volek House. Such evil behavior strips him of every right. He's not my grandson, not Samara's twin brother, not Druse's and Wolf's cousin. He's a vicious killer and a terrible danger to us all.''

Druse sank to the floor where she closed her eyes, wrapped her arms about her abdomen, and began rocking back and forth, moaning.

Grandmother reached down, grabbed an arm, and yanked her to her feet. ''I need your help melting silver,'' she snapped. ''Pull yourself together and come with me.'' She all but dragged Druse from the room.

A bell on the kitchen wall rang. Samara, who'd been trying to soothe Hawk, stared at the apparatus next to the bell, then at Wolf. ''That's Chung's cottage,'' she said. ''There's a connection between the house and cottage. You answer it.''

Wolf lifted the contraption and spoke into the mouthpiece. "Wolf here."

"Chung, sir. Master Stefan at back gate."

Wolf frowned, wondering why Chung hadn't simply unlocked the gate and let him in. Did the Chinese man sense something was wrong with Stefan?

"Stay in your cottage," Wolf ordered. "I'll let him in." He hung up and turned to Samara. "Take the baby to your grandmother and warn her that Stefan's at the gate."

Clutching the whimpering baby to her, Samara bit her lip. "What are you going to do?"

"Let him in."

Wolf strode down the path to the back gate, every muscle in his body taut with apprehension. Even though it was still early afternoon and the moon was five days from full, Wolf wasn't happy to see that the rain had stopped and the clouds were lifting. He'd prefer an overcast sky tonight—he was taking enough of a chance as it was.

If he didn't unlock the gate for Stefan, who could tell where Stefan might go? Or who might be his next victim? Stefan had to be stopped. Now. But God only knew if he was doing the right thing by admitting an uncontrolled shifter to Volek House.

For all he knew, he was dooming them all.

Chapter 9

Stefan's hackles rose as he watched the bearded man approach the gate. Where was Chung? What was this stranger doing on the grounds?

"I can see you don't remember me," the man said as he unlocked the gate. "I'm Wolf. I left Volek House when you were three."

The gate swung open. Enter or not? Stefan eyed Wolf uneasily. He didn't doubt the man's identity, but how could he trust someone he didn't remember? Still, he didn't recall his grandparents mentioning that Wolf had any particular talent, so likely it was safe enough.

He was inside before something Arno had once said came back to him: *"Grandfather told me Wolf predicted I'd be the shifter."*

Wolf slammed the gate and pocketed the key. Stefan shrugged—too late to retreat. But he feared no man. Except maybe Sergei.

"Grandfather still away?" he asked as casually as he could.

Wolf nodded. Without speaking, he led the way up the path to the house. In the kitchen, Stefan looked around. No pots bubbled on the stove—the place looked deserted.

"Where is everyone?" he demanded.

"Grandmother Liisi's stones foretold danger so she sent the servants home." Wolf's tone was terse.

"When did you get here?"

"A couple hours ago. I've brought bad news, Stefan."

"Oh?"

"Your mother's dead."

Stefan stared at him, wondering what Wolf expected. That he'd burst into tears? He couldn't even remember his mother's face. She'd been as good as dead to him from the moment she deserted him and Samara fifteen years ago.

"I'm sorry." His words were perfunctory, but he couldn't express an emotion he didn't feel. Noting muscles clench in Wolf's jaw, he wondered what bothered his cousin.

"She didn't deserve to die," Wolf said coldly.

"She wasn't much of a mother to Samara and me," Stefan told him. He considered that more than enough explanation for his lack of grief.

Being inside the house was making him edgy. His clothes felt heavy, even his skin seemed too tight. Best to eat quickly, grab a few essentials, and head for the safety of the hills. He started toward the pantry when footsteps on the uncarpeted back stairs made him whirl.

"Samara!" Wolf sounded upset. "I told you—" He broke off.

Stefan looked from one to the other. Samara wasn't herself; she eyed him like a frightened doe, taking care not to come near. What was up?

Every instinct told him to cut and run. But before he made up his mind to act, Wolf spoke.

"I told Samara how your mother died, Stefan. It's time you heard. The beast killed her."

A shock ran through Stefan. Not *a* beast but *the* beast. Wolf knew.

Tears glittered in his sister's eyes as she stared at him. "How could you?" she cried.

Useless to remind her that he had no memory of the beast's hunting.

"*You* killed her, tore out her heart, and ate it," Wolf added, his eyes as icy as his voice.

Stefan swallowed, willing himself to silence.

Samara took a long shuddering breath. "No more shifting, Stefan. No more."

His control broke. "No more? What right do you have to tell me what to do or to pass judgment on me?" He looked from her to Wolf. "You, who have no notion of what shifting's like."

"I know what the beast is like," Wolf said. "Unhuman. Evil."

Stefan's lips drew back over his teeth. "Damn you! If you think you're locking me in some windowless cell—"

"I'll kill you rather than let you shift again." Wolf's voice, low but vehement, was convincing.

Taken aback, Stefan recovered quickly. "Go ahead and try." He smiled. "I'm not easy to best, let alone kill."

With lightning speed Wolf bent, yanked a dagger from a boot sheath, and crouched. "Silver," he warned. "This knife belonged to a stalker. They know what kills shifters—and so do I."

"No, Wolf," Samara begged. "Please don't hurt him."

Silver. Hadn't Arno said something about silver being dangerous to shifters?

Stefan controlled his all but overwhelming impulse to leap at Wolf. In an unarmed fight, he was sure he could beat his cousin. But Wolf had the dagger. What if a wound made with a silver knife was poisonous? He couldn't take the chance.

"Please, Stefan, won't you at least try to learn control?" Samara pleaded.

Never! Not for her or anyone else. He had to be free. Calculating the distance to the back door against Wolf's possible quickness, he realized he couldn't make it. Out of the corner of his eye he located the nearest window. Plain glass, nothing fancy, because this was the kitchen.

"Warning me was your mistake," he snarled, diving for the window. He crashed through the glass, sprawled on the ground outside, and came up running.

He got no farther than the great oaks when he felt his gut wrench. He didn't know why he was shifting in the fading light of day with the moon still so far from full, but his heart leaped with surprised joy as he recognized the first sign of change. He'd soon be all but invulnerable.

Free! Raising his muzzle to the sky, the beast howled his defiance to all who might try to stop him. When his eyes fell on the great stone dwelling rising higher than the trees, the red bloodlust suffused him. He padded toward the building.

Silver. The word echoed in his mind, piercing through the crimson fury. He paused. Those inside the building meant to kill him with silver. Safer to satisfy his lust on the other side of the wall. In the house, they were ready and waiting for him. Sooner or later he'd drink their blood and gobble their hearts but better to return when they didn't expect him.

After one last angry glance at the house, he turned and ran toward the wall and the more helpless prey to be found on the other side.

Sergei, not far from Volek House, was riding along at an easy trot, thinking of Cump Sherman. General William Tecumseh Sherman. His old friend had died six years ago. It seemed only yesterday that he and Cump rode through the California hills together. So many good men from the old days were dead. Sitting Bull, too, shot down like a criminal by soldiers. Sergei had often wished he could have met the old medicine man in other circumstances than that fatal hill at Little Bighorn.

And Guy Kellogg. His death weighed on Sergei's mind most of all.

Somehow, by the grace of God, he still lived.

The chilling ululation took him by surprise. Before he had time to recover, his horse, a usually trustworthy black, shied so violently that Sergei was almost unseated. It took him long moments before he calmed the shivering animal enough to spur him into a gallop.

The black knew, as he did, what they'd heard sure as hell wasn't a coyote's call. Or a wolf's. It was a sound Sergei had hoped never to hear again.

There was only one explanation for that bone-zero howl. Unlikely as it seemed, a shifter was loose, running in the valley under the setting sun.

His heart contracted. Arno? Impossible. Early this very morning the twins had seen him onto the Oakland ferry when he left San Francisco.

Who then?

Not Cecelia. In the first place, she'd never shifted and he doubted she ever would. Besides, she'd taken the train for New York last week to perform at the Broadway Theater.

That left one more to consider—the third person Wolf had insisted was a potential shifter. Stefan. Stefan, who he hadn't seen in almost a year. Stefan, who came home at irregular intervals but never when Sergei was at Volek House.

He recalled the "Spirit Wolf" article he'd read in the *Chronicle* and grimaced in belated and dismayed recognition. Stefan! Hadn't the boy been camping in the hills all this time? And avoiding his grandfather?

Apprehension gripped him. Night hadn't yet fallen and the moon wasn't full. Why had the shifter changed at such an unusual time? And where was he?

The black pounded up to the front gate. Sergei, who carried an extra key, reined him in, ready to dismount and open the gate. To his dismay, he saw the gate was ajar. Urging his horse closer, he widened the opening, pushed through, slid from the saddle, and closed and locked the gate. Remounting, he advanced cautiously. When he reached the front of the house, he jumped down and eased open the front door.

Liisi and a bearded young man stood arguing in the foyer. The man whirled at his entry.

"Wolf!" Surprise and joy rang in Sergei's voice. He strode to his grandson and embraced him.

A moment later, Wolf pulled free. "Stefan's shifted," he said.

"I heard him," Sergei replied. "Where is he?"

"He escaped from the grounds. Over the wall, Chung thinks. Samara's missing, she must have gone after him."

That explained the front gate being open. "How long ago?" Sergei asked.

"Samara left about fifteen minutes ago," Liisi said. "Druse and I are trying to melt silver for bullets, but the fire isn't hot enough yet. What use is it for you to hunt him without silver bullets?"

Sergei stared at her. "Must we kill him?"

"Yes!" Wolf spoke emphatically. "Stefan refused control, he prefers his beast form."

Sergei shuddered, remembering all too clearly the seductive allure of bloodlust. "I may be able to salvage him," he said slowly. "I'm going to try."

"You mean to shift." Liisi spoke flatly. "Don't. The stones show death."

"He's a Volek," Sergei reminded her. "He's my grandson."

"He's a killer," Wolf said. "He tore out his own mother's throat."

Sergei grimaced in horror, then raised his head, listening. Could that be a baby's cry he heard?

"That's Hawk," Wolf said. "My son and hers."

Sergei sighed. Another Volek to carry the trait. "You wait for Liisi's bullets," he ordered Wolf. "I'll go after Stefan."

"I don't think he'll hurt Samara," Liisi said, "but if you shift, can you be sure *you* won't?"

He couldn't be. Hell, he wasn't even certain he could shift, given the years since he had, given the lack of the full moon's light.

"I'm coming with you," Wolf announced. "We both know you won't harm me, and I can protect Samara if I have to." He pulled a gleaming dagger from his boot. "And I've the stalker's silver knife to use against Stefan."

Liisi stepped to Sergei and put her arms around him. "You are my life," she whispered, and kissed him.

He held her close for a moment, unsettled by her embrace. It wasn't like her to be demonstrative. "And you, mine," he told her. When he stepped away from her, he saw tears gleaming in her gray eyes.

"I've warned Chung to stay inside his cottage," Wolf said when they reached the back gate.

Sergei unlocked it. After he'd relocked the gate from the outside, he handed his key to Wolf. Together they trotted northwest, toward the pine grove in the hills above the valley.

"The stalker's dagger," Sergei said after a time. "You've kept it all these years."

"To remind me to trust no one." Wolf glanced at him. "Except you. I've always trusted you. I always will."

Touched, Sergei gripped Wolf's upper arm for a moment. "I'm glad you came home," he said. "I've missed you."

"I didn't mean to have another child. The Miwoks have herbs to prevent babies, and I thought their potions would be as effective as Grandmother's. I should have known better."

"Never mind, Hawk is welcome. But thank God he isn't a twin."

"You think double births trigger the Volek shifting trait?" Wolf asked.

"Besides being Voleks, it's the one thing that Arno, Stefan, and I have in common. How long has Samara known about Stefan's shifting?"

"Since his first time. He swore he'd kill himself if she told you."

"Almost a year." Sergei shook his head. "Time for far too many to see or hear him. Already there's that article in the *Chronicle*. We must stop him before he attracts a stalker."

Wolf was silent a long time. They'd reached the

grove before he spoke. "I don't think Stefan can ever be controlled. In the long run, it would be kinder to kill him here and now."

Thinking of the tenacious hold of bloodlust, Sergei nodded. "Perhaps. But I have to try to save him."

"Why are we cursed?" The words burst from Wolf. "Why?"

"I believe the answer lies in the Russian forests. I'd always hoped to return there and search. Since Nicholas II has become the new czar, maybe Russia is once more safe for Voleks."

"We'll go!" Wolf cried. "After this is over, we'll sail for Russia, you and I."

Sergei took hope from the enthusiasm in Wolf's voice. But even as he considered the possibility, a chill crept over him, a certainty that he would never set foot on Russian soil again.

"If I can't go, you must," he said finally.

Wolf's answer was lost in the quavering howl arising from the depths of the pine grove.

The sound triggered a response within Sergei, a driving, pulsing need to answer the challenge. For the first time in over ten years, he felt the once familiar twisting of his guts that heralded a change. He tore at his clothes.

"It's happening," he told Wolf, his words already distorted. "Try to follow me."

"I always know where you are," Wolf assured him.

As Sergei's human reasoning faded, he remembered Wolf's special ability to track him whether he was man or beast.

Free! The beast, seeing the human near him, growled menacingly. The human didn't retreat. Still, the man held no visible weapon so he wasn't a threat. He wasn't prey. Nor was he the other, the challenger. Ignoring him, the beast loped away between the trees, alert for any sign of the interloper in his territory.

He picked up a faint scent. A male, as he'd suspected from the challenge. The scent, though, was mixed with traces of human smell, a complication that made the beast's hackles rise. He slowed his pace to consider how to cope with both the interloper and a possibly dangerous human.

Out of breath and near exhaustion, Samara stumbled into a clearing among the pines and stopped short. Twenty feet away an enormous, terrifying beast crouched over the bloody carcass of a deer. *The* beast. Stefan. His yellow eyes glared at her over the kill. He frightened her almost as much as the amorphous peril she sensed lurking somewhere among the pines.

After three tries, words pushed past the fear choking her. "It's Samara," she quavered. "You know me, Stefan. Your sister. Your twin."

The beast snarled, showing sharp, pointed teeth. Samara forced herself to take a step forward. "I won't hurt you, how can I? I only want to talk to you. Please, Stefan, change back before it's too late."

The beast rose to his hind feet, growling.

She froze. "Wolf hunts you!" she cried. "Hunts you with Grandmother's silver bullets. Another hunts you, too. Someone—something—dark and dangerous."

The beast circled around the kill and lunged toward her. Samara cried out, stepped backward, tripped over an unseen obstacle and fell sideways, her head smashing against the trunk of a pine. The last thing she heard as darkness wiped away the world was a hideous howl.

The brown-eyed man with the backpack halted, the howl ringing in his ears as it echoed from the hills. Close by. Though he'd never heard the sound before, he knew what it was. He'd been right to investigate.

This is your chance, he thought eagerly. This is what you were born for, what you've waited to do all your life.

He eased the pack from his shoulders to the ground, lifted off the new Krag-Jorgensen gun and smiled as he stroked its polished stock. With a five-round magazine rifle, how could he fail? He carefully removed the silver bullets from the container in his pocket, slid them one by one into the magazine opening and closed the gate. He sighted along the barrel and nodded. Dim as it was under the pines, there was still enough light to focus on a target.

Leaving the pack behind, he trotted in the direction of the howling. Minutes later, his heart began hammering against his ribs as he sensed the presence of his prey. At last! He slowed, moving cautiously toward his quarry, circling to keep down wind. Though it couldn't sense him, it might pick up his scent if he didn't take care.

There! He drew in his breath, paralyzed by the horrible sight, far worse than he'd imagined. The monster crouched over a deer kill, the fur of its muzzle wet with blood. Overcoming his momentary terror, he edged closer. Raising the rifle to his shoulder with a slow, deliberate movement he hoped wouldn't catch the beast's attention, he took aim.

As the hunter pulled the trigger the first time, the beast looked straight at him. Too late. The bullet smashed into its head. The hunter advanced and pumped two more bullets into the writhing, snarling shifter. Blood spurted from an eye socket. Though not quite dead, the beast was clearly finished. The hunter's mouth opened to shout his triumph when a slight noise to his left made the man slew around, his rifle ready.

A woman lay sprawled near the edge of the clearing. Finger on the trigger, he hesitated, his special sense telling him she wasn't a shifter. He lowered the rifle. To shoot a nonshifter would be murder. Unless she was shifter kin. He crossed to stare down at her. She twitched but didn't open her eyes. He dropped to one knee to examine her closer and saw that her dark hair was matted with blood.

Not shifter kin but shifter victim would be his guess. He lifted her to check for further wounds and found none, his hands lingering on the softness of her breasts. Her skirts, hiked above her knees, showed the ruffled edge of her white drawers. He couldn't take his gaze away from the tantalizing ruffle, and almost involuntarily his fingers followed his eyes, slipping under the loose edge of the drawers to stroke the smooth warmth of the bare skin underneath.

Aroused as much by his success in killing his first shifter as by the helplessness of the woman, he found himself throbbing with need. Why shouldn't he satisfy his desire? He was the victor, wasn't he? She'd be dead if he hadn't killed the beast before it finished her off. She owed him her life.

Quickly, his hands trembling with urgency, he stripped off her drawers, spread her legs and plunged into her. She screamed, moaning as he thrust violently within her until the convulsion of release left him gasping.

He stood and was rearranging his clothing when he suddenly sensed danger. He sprang for his rifle. He'd barely got it to his shoulder when a second beast leaped into the clearing and sprang at him. Shifter! He shot once before it reached him, and he pulled the trigger again reflexively as the beast's jaws fastened on his throat and tore his life from him.

Wolf raced into the clearing as the last shot was fired. Stefan, his face half shot away, lay dead across the carcass of a deer. Five feet away, a snapping, growling beast mauled a man. Grandfather!

Glancing hurriedly around the clearing in the near darkness, Wolf saw Samara lying on the ground, her skirts over her face and blood streaking her bare thighs. Her drawers were crumpled beside her, telling him what had been done to her.

Wolf ran to kneel beside Samara. When he pulled her skirts down she moaned and flinched away from him. Relieved to find her alive, he called her name.

"Samara, it's Wolf."

Her eyes fluttered open. "Dark. Hurt," she whispered.

When the beast howled, a long triumphant ululation, she clutched at Wolf, her face a mask of terror. He disengaged her fingers and leaped to his feet, whirling to face the beast, to stay between it and the helpless Samara.

As he watched uncomprehendingly, the beast slumped to the ground, groaning. Warily, Wolf approached. The stranger the beast had attacked was obviously dead, his rifle on the ground by his side. Wolf stared in dismay at two gaping, bleeding wounds in the beast's chest. Somehow he must try to staunch the blood. But how?

Before he could move, the beast convulsed, and before his eyes, began to shift.

"Grandfather, you're hurt!" he cried, falling to his knees as the beast muzzle flattened into a human face.

Sergei's eyes opened. He tried to raise his head and failed. "Stalker," he mumbled.

"You killed him," Wolf assured him.

"Stefan?"

"Dead," Wolf said. "Samara's alive." This was no time to mention she'd been raped.

"Stalker used silver bullets," Grandfather gasped. "I'm dying." He lifted a hand, feebly groping. "Wolf?"

Wolf grasped his hand, leaning close to hear his grandfather's barely audible words.

"Wolf, why. Find out why. . . ."

Chapter 10

Wolf laid the half-conscious Samara on the ground while he unlocked the back gate with Sergei's key. He leaned against the iron bars for a few moments of rest before lifting her into his arms again and carrying her through the gate and up the path to the house. He banged on the door.

"It's Wolf," he shouted. "Let me in."

Liisi opened the door. As he staggered in with Samara, Liisi looked past him. He shook his head.

"No one else left alive." His voice sounded as drained and empty as he felt. "Where do you want me to put Samara? I've got to go back."

As he carried Samara up the stairs, he told Liisi what had happened, using as few words as possible. It hurt to relive the horror.

He had no choice but to leave Samara with the shattered Liisi. Back in the kitchen, he remembered to pick up the speaker connected to Chung's cottage and tell the Chinese man it was safe to come out of his cottage. He asked Chung which horse would be least likely to balk at transporting dead men.

Chung met him in the stable, holding the reins of a dappled gray mare. "Czarina, she slow but she steady," Chung told him. "Master, he die?"

Wolf nodded.

Chung bowed his head. "He man with heart like dragon. He save me. Chung never forget. You need help?"

About to refuse, Wolf paused. Much as he wanted

to be alone with his dead, he realized he was close to
exhaustion. After Sergei and Stefan were brought back
to the house, he still would have the stalker's body to
dispose of.

"I need help," he admitted, and went to saddle his
pinto.

They rode in silence through the moonlit night. Far
off in the hills a coyote called, and Wolf winced at the
sound.

"Many howls tonight," Chung said.

Wolf didn't answer. He had no idea what Chung
knew or suspected, and he didn't want to find out.

Chung said nothing more until they reached the
bodies. Gesturing toward Stefan, he said, "That one
always reach for death."

The words rang so true that Wolf felt they should
be Stefan's epitaph.

Czarina proved to be as steady as Chung had
claimed, standing stoically as they lifted Stefan, then
Sergei, to lie across her back. Chung used several turns
of rope to tie the bodies in position. He asked no questions and made no comment whatsoever about the third
dead man.

"Last journey. Sad," Chung said as he led the bur-
dened Czarina away into the trees, leaving Wolf with
the stalker.

The pinto wanted no part of the dead man, shying
and snorting until Wolf finally gave up the attempt to
throw the body over the horse's back. Instead, he constructed a crude travois from pine boughs and rope,
lashing the stalker to it. When the pinto reluctantly
accepted the travois, all Wolf had left to do was decide
where to inter the body.

As he mounted the horse, the perfect place came to
him; a spot where the stalker wouldn't be discovered
for many years—if ever. The Miwok medicine man
had shown him an ancient secret burial cave in the
hills. Wolf had asked if the Miwok buried their dead
in the cave.

"These are not Miwok bones," Bear Claw had insisted. "We do not disturb the bones of the people from the morning of the world."

Wolf hoped the morning of the world people wouldn't be too upset to have the bones of a stalker lying among them. He'd make sure to apologize to the Old Ones for the intrusion when he reached the cave.

He didn't return to Volek House until dawn grayed the sky.

The next few days passed in a blur of grief. Ivan and Arno, summoned by Liisi's telegram, arrived and took charge—to Wolf's relief. Despite his grandfather's wish, he'd never wanted to head the Volek clan. Ivan and Arno, who already helped manage the various Volek business interests, were far more suited than he.

Samara worried him. Though her head wound proved superficial, and Liisi assured him there'd be no permanent physical damage from the rape by the stalker, Samara had retreated into herself. Her movements reminded him of a puppet's—jerky and unnatural. She didn't speak and she didn't eat unless ordered to by Liisi. Each mouthful had to be monitored or Samara stopped eating. No one else but Liisi could reach her through the wall she'd built. Whatever rapport he'd once had with Samara was gone.

Druse, after her initial hysterics, settled down and became engrossed with Hawk's care. Unless he was sleeping, the baby was rarely out of her arms. Wolf was pleased by his daughter's interest in her half-brother and relieved that his son was being well cared for.

They agreed to call the deaths "tragic hunting accidents." Whether the sheriff or anyone else believed their story, it was accepted, but Wolf knew there must be doubt. It would take time for local speculation to die down.

Two weeks after the funeral, Arno and Ivan invited Wolf into the study for a conference. "What are your plans?" Arno asked.

"Since Druse has agreed to assume full care of my son," he told them, "I want nothing more than to go

my way. If you need help, I'll stay on. Otherwise—''
He paused.

"We'd never push you aside," Arno said, "but if
you really aren't interested in McDee Enterprises,
we're willing to assume full responsibility. We thought
we'd alternate months in the San Francisco office—one
of us there and the other here at home to look after
the family."

Wolf smiled slightly. "Thank God there are two of
you. I'm no business man, nor am I suited to be head
of the household. But I'd stay on and do what I could
to help if it weren't for promises I must keep in the
East and also an urgent personal matter to attend to in
San Francisco. After that, I intend to carry out your
father's last request."

Arno and Ivan both leaned forward. "You didn't tell
us about any request," Arno said.

"Sergei and I had thought of traveling to Russia together, to the forests where our ancestors lived. For
answers. To find the reason why some of the Voleks
are shapeshifters. I know you've heard the story passed
down through the generations, the story that tells how
it happened—but not why. Your father was convinced
there was a reason he was a shapeshifter, and I believed him. With his last breath he urged me to find
the reason why."

Arno stared at him. "Yes, there *must* be a reason.
And a reason for the stalkers, too."

After a short silence, Ivan asked. "What about the
stalker who killed our father and Stefan? Do you think
another may come looking for him?"

"I don't know," Wolf said. "Before I interred him
where he'll never be found, I went through his pack
and his pockets, and there was nothing to identify him.
Except for the fact that he carried a clipping of the
Chronicle article, there was no clue as to where he
came from. The other two stalkers I've run across
worked alone—I hope this one was no exception."

"We'll stay alert," Arno promised.

"Yes," Wolf agreed. "Forever."

Before he left for San Francisco, Wolf had a private talk with Grandmother Liisi in her tower room.

"I was right about Arno and about Stefan," he reminded her. "Now I'm more convinced than ever that I'm right about Cecelia Kellogg being a potential shifter. I've got to warn her one more time."

"She refused to listen to any of Sergei's advice," Liisi said, ignoring the tears that came to her eyes when she mentioned his name.

Remembering the final parting between her and Grandfather, Wolf choked up. With Samara's infirmity and a baby in the household, Liisi hadn't had much time for mourning the man who was her life.

He said nothing of this to her, knowing she'd prefer he didn't. "Sooner or later Cecelia will shapeshift," he went on. "Do you have any charm I might give her that might help her control the shifting?"

"Since she's not of my blood or your grandfather's, I fear no charm of mine would be effective—as none were with her mother. But among her mother's effects was a silver buckle in the form of a cat's head. Because it was silver and belonged to her mother, and because the shifter trait was in Cecelia's blood, I set the buckle aside when we shipped the Kellogg's belongings back to New Orleans. In case it was needed. You might take the cat's head to her."

"Will the silver buckle prevent her from shifting?"

Liisi shrugged. "I can't answer that question. I'm afraid the buckle is all I can offer. You might try to teach her the charm that worked on your grandfather—" Liisi paused for a long moment before continuing. "I taught that charm to you, if you remember."

Wolf nodded. He'd never forget the dreadful night in the dark woods when he'd recited the Finnish words to help Grandfather change from his beast form so the hunting posse wouldn't discover what he was and kill him. It was the same night Samara and Stefan had been born.

"Do you think Samara will improve?" he asked.

"I wish I knew. Did she say anything at all to you when you found her?"

"Only two words. 'Dark. Hurt.' "

Liisi shook her head. "I think she sensed the stalker in the woods in much the same way she sensed the female stalker when she was a child of three—as a threatening monster. And this time the monster found her as she lay helpless and hurt her in the uniquely terrible way a man can harm a woman. She hasn't yet gotten over that. I can only hope she will. And that she isn't carrying a stalker child."

Wolf drew in his breath. "My God!"

"I've tried to take precautions. I've given her various potions to rid her of a possible baby, but she's vomited every one. I intend to keep trying."

A stalker born into the Volek family? Foreseeing the consequences, Wolf shuddered. "Do everything you can," he urged.

"I know the dangers as well as you." Liisi's tone was tart.

After she handed him the silver cat's head buckle, he got up to leave, but Liisi's hand on his arm stopped him.

"I noticed you stealing glimpses over your shoulder while we talked," she said. "Why?"

Wolf shrugged. "I don't like to look at that tapestry with the tree so I sat with my back to it. But not seeing was worse."

Liisi put a hand on either side of his face and stared into his eyes. Though her silver gaze daunted him, he tried not to glance away.

"Yes," she said finally, "the shaman power is still within you, unused."

"I'll never be a shaman!"

"Your mother's father was a shaman in Siberia, wasn't he?"

Wolf nodded reluctantly.

"Like shifting in the Volek line, shamanism runs in families. It's in your blood. Sooner or later you'll succumb."

She gestured at the tapestry. "That's the tree of life, with its crown in the upper world and its roots in the lower. Only the center of the tree is in this world we live in. To obtain knowledge, a shaman learns to climb and descend the tree, a dangerous journey, entering the higher and lower spirit worlds at will. The tree beckons you, Wolf; someday you'll find the call irresistible.''

Wolf left the ferry from Oakland carrying his new suitcase and hailed a cab. Liisi had insisted that Arno and Ivan see to it that he was completely outfitted before he left for the East, and under the circumstances, he hadn't liked to argue.

But in San Francisco he was on his own, and he was damned if he'd stay at the Palace Hotel just because the Voleks always did. He'd be far more at ease in a modest establishment away from the busy heart of the city.

"You'll find the Pine Cone Inn's just the ticket, sir,'' the cab driver said in answer to Wolf's question about hotels. At Wolf's nod, the driver turned his horse onto Van Ness.

"The city's sure growing,'' the driver, a grizzled older man, commented. "Weren't all that many years ago the cowboys used to drive cattle down this very street to the stockyards. Look at the fancy homes along here now. Beats all, don't it?''

"Do you know if Cece is performing in the city this week?'' Wolf asked.

"The dancer? That she is. In the ballroom at the St. Francis, if I ain't mistaken—and I ain't. Heard tell she knocked 'em dead in New York last month. Ever see her dance?''

"Once.'' Wolf didn't add that it was long before Cecelia became Cece.

"I'd like to myself, ' ut the St. Francis is a mite too rich for my blood. Only the toffs go there. Guess I'll have to stick with them French cancan girls at the Melodeon. Ever seen them go to it? They're—'' He broke off to swear at two men on bicycles who cut in front of the horse.

"Damn cyclists,'' he muttered. "Crazy as they

come. Never get me on one of them new-fangled contraptions."

The driver's nonstop conversation enlivened the ride to the outskirts of the city, where the Pine Cone Inn proved satisfactory to Wolf. He tipped the man generously. These days he had a bank account with more money in it than he needed or wanted.

Unknown to him, Grandfather had been depositing a monthly sum in his name from the time he'd first arrived at Volek House. The deposits had continued all the years he'd been gone, accruing interest. To Wolf, a man whose wants were few, the total amount seemed a fortune.

Grandfather had done the same for all the Volek children. And Grandmother Liisi had already transferred Stefan's unused savings into Hawk's name so the baby would be provided for.

Wolf settled into his room. When he registered at the desk, he'd noticed the inn had a telephone—like most businesses as well as many private homes in San Francisco. No doubt Thompsonville would soon have telephone service and then it could be extended to Volek House. Arno and Ivan would see to that.

He returned to the lobby and called the St. Francis to ask about seating for Cece's performance tonight.

"Sorry, sir, nothing is available. We're sold out."

"I'm a friend of Miss Kellogg's. Would you inform her that Mr. Volek is in town and would like to see her?"

"I will leave a message, sir." The clerk's tone held a hint of reproof, as though he considered Wolf's request improper.

After leaving the inn's name and his room number with the clerk, Wolf hung up. Since he hadn't had a full night's sleep in weeks, he returned to his room, removed his shoes, and stretched out on the bed. He promptly fell asleep, somehow more relaxed in this strange setting than within the familiar walls of home.

He woke with a start to a tapping on his door.

"Mr. Volek, there's a message for you at the desk," the maid's voice said.

"Thank you, I'll be right there."

Cecelia's reply, as relayed through the inn's desk clerk, was terse. "The St. Francis called and asked me to tell you that Miss Kellogg has reserved a table for you for tonight."

Later, walking through the crowded lobby of the St. Francis, he overheard one comment after another about Cece:

". . . flawless technique. She could have been a top ballerina . . ."

". . . the most sensuous dancer I ever saw . . ."

". . . scores of marriage proposals, but she always says no . . ."

The ballroom glittered with the electric lights that were reflected from the chandeliers by the long mirrors set between the panels of the mahogany walls. Jeweled, elegantly gowned women and men in formal dress sat at tables circling the dance floor.

The maître d' led Wolf to a front row table for two. "I am instructed to tell you that Mademoiselle will join you after the performance," the man announced after seating him.

Wolf's pulse speeded at the thought of Cecelia seated across the small table from him. Throughout the years, he'd never been able to put her completely from his mind. How could he forget her grace and beauty? Long ago she'd called him a clumsy boy—what would she think of the man he'd become?

His mind on Cecelia, he ordered the first thing he saw on the menu, then ate and drank with little awareness of what he swallowed. At last the lights were lowered, and without an announcement of any kind, without fanfare from the orchestra, in a whirl of red draperies, Cece twirled into the center of the large room.

She curtsied low, cymbals clanged, and then the music began, a Spanish melody Wolf half-recognized. Cece, castanets clicking, spun into a lively Spanish dance. He watched her, bemused by the flow of color as her skirts and petticoats, from the palest of pinks

to a deep crimson, floated and dipped as she twisted
and turned to the rhythm of the guitars.

The dance ended in another curtsy and enthusiastic
applause. Drums began beating, softly at first, then
louder, more insistent. A gasp went up as Cece
straightened, stepping out of the voluminous-skirted
gown and petticoats. She was now attired in a long,
slim black skirt and low-necked, form-fitting shirt-
waist that revealed the exciting curves of her body.

She kicked the discarded clothes to one side and
began to stretch, slowly and languorously, to the beat
of the drum. A flute joined in, then a guitar. Cece
began a prowling sinuous dance so mesmerizing Wolf
that after a time he imagined he was watching a black
panther stalking over the floor—a graceful, feral beast
hunting prey.

A blink of his eyes brought Cece back into focus but
now, for him, her dance held an edge of danger that
tingled along his nerves, tightening his muscles, up-
setting and arousing him at the same time.

He'd been Mima's lover, and he'd shared a blanket
with Morning Quail, but he'd never before felt such a
hungry rush of desire for any woman. He fought an
impulse to leap to his feet, toss her over his shoulder,
and carry her from the room, from the hotel, from the
city, carry her into the wilderness where they both
belonged and there mate with her, animal to animal.

Wolf shook his head to clear it, but her slow sensuous movements mixed with the passionate throb of
the drum kept him Cece's prisoner, trapped by her
allure. She danced closer and, as if she scented her
prey, stared directly into his eyes. Her green gaze
pierced through to brand his heart, rendering him
helpless. Her victim.

He raised a hand, palm outward, as though to ward
her off and Cece recoiled from him. She recovered
almost immediately, dancing away from him.

By the time her performance ended, Wolf had regained his wits, if not his equilibrium. When she appeared at his table, escorted by the maître d', he was

more or less prepared. She wore a white gown nipped in at the waist, its skirt trimmed with white ermine. Her only jewelry consisted of tiny pearl earrings. The low neck of the gown revealed enough to take his breath away. He got to his feet, unable for the moment to utter a word of greeting.

Once seated, instead of speaking, she reached for his hand and turned it over, staring at his palm. She took a deep breath and let it out slowly.

"What do you see?" he asked, puzzled.

"Nothing." Her voice was low, melodious.

"But you did see something when you were dancing," he persisted, uncertain he was right but needing to know everything he could about her.

"I thought I saw a star within a red circle on your palm," she murmured. "I must have been mistaken."

Looking at his hand, Wolf saw nothing of the sort. But then he hadn't expected to. "It's gone now," he agreed. "What does it mean?"

Cecelia swallowed. "I've seen the star within a circle before. Once. On another man's palm. I found out that it's called a pentagram. I don't know what it means, but I don't like it."

"What other man?" Wolf asked, a faint memory stirring. Hadn't Grandfather once mentioned pentagrams?

"You don't know him."

"Who is he?" Wolf persisted, searching his mind for what his grandfather might have told him.

Cecelia flushed. "My physician, Dr. Swanson."

If the man was merely her doctor, why the blush? Wolf fought his jealousy, knowing he couldn't ask.

"A pentagram," he said slowly, finally remembering. "My grandfather saw a pentagram on my grandmother's palm. And on the palms of two others."

She raised her eyebrows. "What does that have to do with me?"

"Grandfather's dead, you know."

Cecelia bit her lip. "The *Chronicle* carried his obituary. Sergei Volek was kind to me. I was sorry to read of his death, and I've been meaning to write his wife. . . ." Her words trailed off.

Wolf leaned closer. "The two men, the ones marked by the pentagram, died by his hand. My grandmother would have been killed, too, if she hadn't been a *noita.*"

Her green eyes widened and she shrank back in her chair. "I don't think I want to hear any more."

Wolf glanced around the crowded room. "I haven't finished. But I agree this is no place to talk. Where can we go?"

Cecelia eyed him dubiously. "I really didn't want to see you at all, much less talk to you. I invited you only because of your grandfather."

"I won't keep you long. We could take a walk. Or a drive. Do you have a wrap?"

In the end they walked from the hotel, turned onto Powell Street away from Union Square, and climbed the hill, pausing at the top to look down on the bay where tiny lights of ships winked lonesomely from the vast darkness of the water. No other pedestrians were in sight.

"We've come far enough," she said.

Inhaling her spicy, flowery scent, Wolf's resolve flickered. What he really wanted to do was wrap his arms around her and kiss her. Knowing she must be told, he sought for words to soften what he had to say and found none.

"My grandfather was a shapeshifter," he said bluntly. "He told me shifters see pentagrams on the palms of their victims."

Cecelia drew in her breath.

Aware she meant to protest, Wolf hurried on. "I'm sure you remember Stefan. He was a shifter, too, and he died, killed like your mother by a stalker—one of those who hunt and kill shifters."

"My mother wasn't—"

"She was," he cut in ruthlessly. "You haven't shifted yet, but seeing the pentagram is a warning that you eventually will." He pulled the silver buckle from his pocket and displayed it on his palm. The green stones of the cat's eyes gleamed in the dim light from a street lamp. "Liisi gave me this—it was your mother's. Because it's silver, the buckle may help you when—"

She slapped his hand, sending the silver cat's head flying. "No! I don't want it. I'm not what you say. I won't be. Never!" She whirled away from him.

Wolf caught her arm, turning her to face him again, holding her so she couldn't escape. "Listen to me! You can't control the shifting. I'm trying to help you—don't you understand?"

"Let me go!" She fought him, striking at his face with her fists and kicking at him.

Wolf yanked her against him, pinning her arms so she was helpless. "I don't want to see you die," he said. "Not only stalkers kill shifters. Men fear the beasts shifters become and hunt them down. I couldn't bear to have that happen to you."

Seeing her mouth open to scream, Wolf bent his head and covered her lips with his. For a heart-stopping second, he felt her respond to his violent kiss—and then she bit him. Hard.

He shoved her away and, freed, she ran down Powell toward the St. Francis. With the taste of his own blood warm and salty on his tongue, Wolf watched her go, making no attempt to follow. When she turned onto Clay, he sighed. He'd done his best and it hadn't been good enough. He dreaded what might happen to her but knew no way to prevent it. Cecelia would certainly never again agree to see him.

Sucking his throbbing, bleeding lip, Wolf hailed a cab. When he stepped off the curb, a glimmer of green winked at him—the buckle's cat's eye. He scooped it from the gutter and climbed into the cab with the buckle clutched in his hand. He was halfway back to his inn when he remembered that she'd seen a pentagram on his palm. Why had he thought they'd never meet again?

His hackles rose as he envisioned their next meeting. . . .

Chapter 11

Wolf wouldn't admit to being frightened, but New York City dazzled him. Drop him anywhere in the wilderness and he'd soon know exactly where he was, but the city confused him, interfering with his sense of direction. If he'd thought San Francisco noisy with its clanging cable cars, trolleys, and clattering cabs, New York was ten times worse.

"Come along, there's a good fellow," his companion called to him.

Wolf hurried to close the gap between them. If he lost sight of Muir's friend, he'd be on his own, and he didn't want that. He was a fast walker, but Theodore Roosevelt's normal stride was a lope.

He still wasn't exactly sure how he'd come to join Roosevelt's First United States Volunteer Cavalry.

"By George, you're exactly the man I want," Roosevelt had said when they met in April. "A man of the mountains, like Muir—a man I can trust." Roosevelt had the habit of biting off the end of each sentence, showing his teeth. "As soon as we declared war on Spain, I resigned as Secretary of the Navy to form this cavalry unit. I need you as my aide de camp. What do you say?"

With nothing to go home to, what could Wolf say but yes?

At first Roosevelt had seemed all teeth and eyes, because his teeth were big and square and because his eyes were magnified by thick glasses. He appeared to be a heavy, rather large man. It took some time for Wolf to realize that Roosevelt was actually fairly slender and no taller than he was. Even after he knew this, the earlier impression remained.

"I like big things," Roosevelt said to him as he caught up. "Big prairies, big forests and big mountains. But not big cities. Cities make me feel like a caged wolf—confined and hemmed in. Cuba, now, that'll be bully."

Wolf, never a master of geography, knew Cuba was an island but had only a vague idea of where it was, though he couldn't fail to be aware the battleship *Maine* had been sunk in the Havana harbor in February. According to the New York *Journal* headline: THE WARSHIP MAINE WAS SPLIT IN TWO BY AN ENEMY'S SECRET INFERNAL MACHINE.

Roosevelt clapped him on the shoulder. "We'll show those bastards they can't blow up an American ship, by George." He slowed his pace. "Here's the store, Volek—now to order the uniforms."

A week later, Wolf gazed at Colonel Roosevelt in admiration. His khaki riding pants were cinched at the waist by a belt whose large silver buckle was engraved with the head of a bear. His silver and gold-plate Colt, etched with scrolled designs, nestled in a hip holster, only its ivory handle with the buffalo head on one side and Roosevelt's initials on the other visible. A silver-plated bowie knife was sheathed on his other hip.

"Just in case, I've eleven extra pairs of eyeglasses stitched into my pockets," Roosevelt told him, "and one pair in the lining of my hat. Nothing like being prepared."

Wolf's uniform, though it fit well, had no extra embellishments except for the lieutenant's bars Roosevelt had wrangled for him. He still hadn't quite taken in the fact that in less than a month he'd be fighting Spaniards on the island of Cuba.

"*Cuba libre!*" was the Cuban rebels' slogan. Wolf supported the principle—all men should be free—but felt he was being pushed into this war without know-

ing all the whys and wherefores. What, after all, did
he have against Spain?

Once the troop transports from Florida landed at
Santiago in June, he found out. Men who shoot at you
very quickly become your enemy.

On July first, in relentless heat, Roosevelt's Rough
Riders, many of them horseless by now, charged up
Kettle Hill near Santiago in the face of heavy fire from
Spanish soldiers. Roosevelt pounded ahead of his men,
and Wolf was hard put to keep up with his colonel.
He finally pulled abreast, bullets zinging past.

Roosevelt glanced at him and smiled. "Bully!" he
shouted over the boom and crackle of gunfire.

Wolf, inspired by Roosevelt's enthusiasm and bravery, suddenly felt invincible. Neither of them would
die today on this hot and dusty hill; they'd not only
win, they'd come out unscathed.

He'd no more than thought this when a Spanish cav-
alryman drove his horse over the crest of the hill toward them, his rifle aimed at the colonel. Sighting
quickly, Wolf fired. The man dropped his rifle, swayed
and slid from his saddle to tumble onto the ground.
His horse galloped past them, riderless.

"Tally up another mount for our men," Roosevelt
said.

Wolf was content to leave it at that, but in the evening as they counted their losses—a third of the unit
dead or wounded—Roosevelt drew him aside.

"There's no way I can repay you," he said. "But
I'll never forget. You know where to find me if you
ever need me."

The next month, back in New York with the war
won, Wolf read an account in the *Journal* of the Rough
Riders' victory at San Juan Hill and smiled wryly. According to the Cuban rebels who'd been their allies,
Kettle Hill was what they'd won—San Juan Hill was
some miles away from where they'd fought.

The *Journal* might be close to the truth but, like the
Chronicle's account about the Spirit Wolf, the story
wasn't correct. Wolf wondered if newspapers ever re-

ported real truths. Then he wondered how many of those who read the papers wanted the truth.

Though Roosevelt had mentioned finding a position on his staff for him, Wolf knew he couldn't stand working indoors. He craved the freedom and solitude of the California mountains. It was time to go home.

Yet a sense of something left unfinished dogged Wolf, keeping him in the city even though he longed to leave. What, he didn't know. The voice in his mind whispered too low to be understood.

On the last day of September, he dreamed of Grandfather. . . .

While lightning streaked the night sky, Sergei lay injured on a battlefield with dead men all around. Because he was a shifter, Sergei's wounds healed rapidly. Wolf, both a watcher and a part of Sergei, felt strength return. Rising to his feet, Sergei cocked his head as though listening to a summons. Wolf could hear nothing, but he felt the surge of compulsion that jolted through Sergei and forced him across the dark and wasted ground into a meadow of tall grass.

SHE was there. Wolf couldn't see anyone, but he sensed her presence in Sergei's mind and smelled the musk of a woman. He knew her hair was red, her eyes green as the July grass. He knew Sergei both feared her and lusted after her.

Sergei wasn't aware Wolf was a part of him but she was, and it was him she spoke to, not Sergei.

"Blood of his blood." Her whisper was both smooth and rough, like a snake's scales, and it set Wolf's teeth on edge. "Blood of his blood, you are bound to me and my blood. There is no escape. . . ."

On October first, he met Willa Gebhardt.

The Rough Riders had been an odd mix of cowboys, wealthy polo players and ex-convicts, with few ordinary men. Some of the survivors lived in New York. Larry Cardiff, who'd been a polo player before his leg wound made playing impossible, had befriended Wolf.

Larry, cynical and sophisticated, was totally unlike

anyone Wolf had ever known. If they hadn't fought together, Wolf might have shunned his company. But the war, short as it was, had forged a bond he couldn't deny. Larry, wracked with guilt over the death of a cavalry comrade, needed him, and so he stayed on. He'd been a guest at Larry's Park Avenue apartment for the month of September.

"You ought to reconsider Roosevelt's offer," Larry said over what was his breakfast but Wolf's lunch. "He'll be our next governor, you know. And it wouldn't surprise me to wake up some morning and find he's been elected President."

"I'm not much for politics," Wolf said.

Larry poured himself another cup of coffee. "A wise man." He took a couple of sips and set the cup down. "Ever been to a seance?"

"No," Wolf told him, somewhat surprised at the abrupt change of subject.

"Then you must come along tonight. It's an experience every man should suffer through at least once."

Wolf pondered Larry's choice of words. Suffer through? "I don't think—"

"Be a sport. They need seven live bodies, I'm told, or the spirits refuse to be summoned. You're the seventh."

Wolf moved his shoulders uneasily, last night's dream still vivid in his mind. Shamans believed in true dreaming and, while he wasn't a shaman, hadn't Liisi insisted the trait was in his blood? Reminded of the dream woman's words, he grimaced.

"No need to make faces, old chap," Larry said. "It's all quite painless, I assure you. You'll thank me for taking you when you set eyes on the medium—she's a stunner. Her husband's a helpless invalid, or so I'm told. More than one of my friends has tried their luck with her, but she's apparently resigned to being a virtuous wife. Perhaps you'll change her mind."

Wolf didn't bother to tell Larry that he'd never try to seduce another man's wife. But, in the end, since he was accepting Larry's hospitality, Wolf felt obliged to go to the seance.

They walked to the medium's brownstone—Larry was supposed to exercise his leg in moderation. A chill October breeze toyed with fallen leaves along the evening streets, reminding Wolf that summer was over. A sense of impending doom as thick and gray as a tule fog settled over him, making him glance over his shoulder.

"No hoodlums in these parts," Larry assured him with a wave of his cane.

Wolf didn't reply. Nothing so tangible as hoodlums haunted him. A stalker? he asked himself, and almost immediately dismissed the idea. Since he wasn't a shifter, he wouldn't attract a stalker. What, then?

"Ah, here we are," Larry said. He'd fortified himself with several stiff drinks before they left, but Wolf had refused even one. An occasional glass of wine with meals was all he allowed himself. He'd listened to enough drunken men baring their souls to realize the risk of being overwhelmed by drink. He had too many secrets to keep.

As they climbed the steps to the front door, Larry added, "I can only pray Mrs. Gebhardt won't call up Aunt Hildegarde's spirit from the great beyond—Auntie was a fire-breathing dragon if ever there was one."

Shamans dealt with spirits. Wolf shied away from dealings with shamans. Why in hell had he agreed to come?

Larry clapped him on the shoulder. "Melissa Weidman swears by her, but I'll give you ten to one this medium's a fraud like all the others."

Fervently hoping Larry's prediction would be the truth, Wolf let Larry precede him when the door opened and an elderly female servant in black stood aside, wordlessly inviting them to enter.

Leaving their hats on a long table in the walnut-paneled foyer, they followed the servant into a parlor, well-furnished but quite ordinary looking except for the round rosewood table in the room's center. Seven chairs surrounded the table. Red shades on the lamps lent a not altogether flattering crimson glow to those present—one other man and three women.

"Darling!" A blond woman Wolf recognized as Melissa Weidman launched herself at Larry and embraced him. "How sweet of you to come."

Larry disengaged himself and introduced Wolf to the others—Melissa's mother, a friend of Melissa's named Olive Whitcomb and Olive's friend, Allan Adams.

They all had what Wolf thought of as the monied look, but being around Larry for a month had gotten him used to such people. There was nothing about any one of them to make him nervous, so why was the back of his neck prickling with unease?

He grew so uncomfortable that he finally turned.

A woman dressed in brilliant green stood just inside a door on the far side of the room. She'd entered so silently he hadn't heard a sound. They looked at one another for a moment that stretched longer than time. Then her eyes flicked away from his, and with a provocative rustle of her gown, she drifted slowly across the room toward the table. Ignoring the exclamations of the others, he crossed to her and bowed slightly.

"Wolf Volek," he said, surprised to hear the words emerge as more of a challenge than an introduction.

Her only response was a slight smile. Eyes not quite green, not quite brown, gazed into his. She wore no jewelry other than earrings—large circles of gold that set off her long white neck and her honey-colored hair twisted into an intricate knot at the back of her head. Her features were too strong for her to be called pretty, but she was damned attractive.

With the others crowding around the table, he had no further chance to speak to her. It wasn't necessary. Something had already passed between them. A challenge and its acceptance? He wasn't quite sure.

"For those of you who haven't met me," she said, "I am Willa Gebhardt. I will sit here." Her voice was low and slightly hoarse, and he felt it sink into his bones. "Mr. Volek will sit on my left. The rest of you may choose your seats."

How old was she? he wondered. She was not at all girlish—had she ever been? Her secret smile hinted of forbidden pleasures, a smile that made a man lust to have her teach him what she knew. Was she thirty? Forty? It was impossible to tell.

"To my left, Mr. Volek," she repeated, and he realized everyone else had sat down.

When they all were in place, Willa ordered them to put their hands palm down on the table and link their little fingers. When Wolf's finger touched hers, heat sizzled through him, warning him of the intensity of his attraction to her.

"The lights, Una," Willa ordered.

The elderly servant turned off the lamps and shuffled from the room, closing the door behind her. The only remaining light was a tiny candle in a red votive holder set directly in front of Willa, its minimal flicker giving her a macabre, sinister appearance.

"We are seven," she intoned. "One by one we clear our minds, the better to concentrate on those who have gone before. One by one we choose who to remember and who to forget, until at last only the strongest memory can remain in each mind. Seven we are, each with a secret, a desire, a need and a regret. Seven. We are seven. Seven made one by the linkage."

She fell silent. Wolf no longer looked at her, he was too preoccupied with the shifting images in his mind, faces he only vaguely recognized—was that his mother?—and others he'd hoped never to see again. At last all vanished except one.

Wolf saw Sergei Volek as clearly as though his grandfather stood before him. He realized with a jolt of apprehension that Grandfather had become a part of him in the same way he'd felt a part of Sergei in last night's dream. Not as an advisor but as watcher. And participant.

Intent on what was happening to him, at first the voices were only a background murmur to Wolf. Until he heard someone he knew.

"Come off it, Diff," a man's gruff voice commanded.

A chill snaked along Wolf's spine. That was Curly speaking. Curly, bald as the granite dome at Yosemite. Curly, a cowpoke from Texas who'd been Larry's buddy in Cuba. Curly, who was prone to nicknames and who'd dubbed Larry "Diff." Curly, who'd died at the battle the *Journal* called San Juan Hill.

"Ain't doing no good to me nor you," Curly went on, "to keep blaming yourself. Fact is, that bullet had my name writ all over it, clear as snake piss."

It was Curly speaking, but the voice came from Willa's lips. Wolf swallowed.

"I could have stopped—" Larry began.

"Naw. Weren't enough time and you know it. Makes me mad as hell to watch you wallow in guilt like a pig in a mud hole. Come off it, or I might just take to haunting you—if'n I kin get the hang of it. Fact is, you're alive and I'm dead. Ain't a damn thing you could've done to make it come out different. You hear me, Diff?"

"I hear you." Larry's voice quavered.

Another silence stretched into infinity. A cold draft eddied around Wolf's ankles, rising to wrap around him like an icy rope. The candle in the red glass wavered and snuffed out. One of the women gasped.

"Mother! No!" Willa cried, her voice shrill with terror.

A short silence, then another voice spoke, a woman's, low and seductive. "I sense your presence, Sergei," she said. "Were you foolish enough to believe death would break the bond?"

Through his shock and dismay, Wolf was aware the voice came from the woman seated next to him, the woman whose little finger was entwined with his. From Willa. Yet the voice was not hers any more than Curly's voice had been.

"I drew you here just as I did in the past, Sergei," the voice said. "There's no escape. Not for you, not for me, not for those of our blood."

Wolf, more frightened than he'd ever been in his life, told himself he'd jerk his hand away from Willa's, rise and stride from the room. From the house. Get away from the voice who spoke to his grandfather. Never return.

He couldn't move.

"The rest of you are dismissed," the voice continued. "Go from here. Go quickly. You will not speak, nor will you come back this night."

Wolf felt the person on his left disengage her finger from his, he heard chairs scrape and the rustle of clothing as the others rose from the table. Willa's finger remained intertwined with his. He wondered if she was as unwilling a participant as he was—a reluctant player in a game of someone else's devising. Or was it some*thing* else?

His grandfather was still there, still a part of him, but unreachable. He tried but found he couldn't communicate in any way with Sergei. Or with Sergei's spirit. Or whatever it was. Wolf shuddered, feeling invaded. Helpless.

The door opened, and he realized the others were leaving the parlor. In the dim light slanting briefly into the room, Wolf saw that Willa's eyes were open and glazed, her expression a rictus of terror. Any doubt fled that she was as much a victim as he. The door closed them into darkness once again. The two of them. With whatever else held them prisoner.

Willa's hand trembled, moved and tightened convulsively over his. "Come with me," the voice commanded.

He rose as though drawn up by invisible strings. Holding his hand, Willa pulled him with her, and he was compelled to follow. He wasn't certain if or when they left the parlor, but he found himself descending stairs. Into a cellar?

She opened a door and drew him through it after her. A moment later, a light flared—a match—and Willa lit a black candle. She released his hand, returned to the door, and locked it.

Though he couldn't move his feet, he could turn his head. He examined his surroundings. Shadows leaped and danced in the corners of the small, paneled room. There were no windows. Cupboards ranged along the rear wall, one with a long countertop. Near him was a wide sofa upholstered in green velvet with a white bearskin rug thrown over it so the bear's head snarled from one arm.

The room smelled very faintly of decay, the scent overlain with a heavy musk that seemed to enter his brain, making him dizzy.

Willa turned to him. Slowly she raised her arms to unpin her hair. He held his breath, his gaze fixed on her. Down tumbled the soft strands, curling over her breasts, beckoning him. He took a step forward.

She reached to him and unbuttoned his suit coat. "Do you remember the last time, Sergei?" the voice purred.

Not Willa. And yet it was Willa's fingers undressing him, caressing him. When she slipped free of her gown, it was Willa's naked body that pressed against his, urging him down onto the tickling softness of the bearskin.

Her smooth curves enticed him; his blood ran hot; he was rigid with lust; he would have this woman or die. Though he knew with one small sane part of him that it wasn't Willa seducing Wolf, he was so consumed by desire for her that he didn't care. About anything.

When he entered her, suddenly everything turned as red as her hair winding around him. He possessed her in a crimson hell of burning, seething passion. Hate, not love, drove him. Sergei's hate, transformed through him into unremitting lust for the woman whose voice spoke through Willa. It was really Sergei and that woman writhing and spasming, traveling together into fiery depths with Wolf and Willa their helpless pawns.

He wished he could free himself, and at the same time he desperately wanted the embrace to last forever, to never end.

Chapter 12

Wolf took the next train to California, unashamedly fleeing from Willa Gebhardt. He was certain that if he didn't put thousands of miles between them, he couldn't stay away from her. No matter how strong his own will might be, whoever or whatever controlled Willa was beyond his power to resist.

As it was, she haunted his dreams so that he fought sleep and arrived in Oakland tired to the bone. He was unable to forget the bright red hair he'd plucked from his jacket the morning after the seance. Willa's hair was honey-colored, not red—Larry had confirmed that—and neither Melissa Weidman nor Olive had red hair. Wolf shied away from speculation, doing his best to eradicate every memory of what had happened in that shadowed basement room.

He felt sure the episode had to do with Sergei's past, arising from something his grandfather had never told him; he was convinced that even Liisi didn't know the details. At the same time, he feared his grandmother would sense he was somehow different. He flinched at the idea of being questioned in Liisi's tower room, so he decided not to go home immediately but to visit Muir in Monterey. If Muir wasn't at the ranch, Wolf made up his mind he'd tramp into the mountains by himself. He craved the simplicity of the wilderness, where things were what they seemed to be.

* * *

On a drizzly June morning in 1899, a baby girl was born in a midwife's cottage on the Hudson River in Tarrytown near the ferry docks. A solitary crow cawed from a tulip tree outside the window during the birth, an omen that disturbed the midwife—one crow meant sorrow. Immediately after pushing out the afterbirth, the infant's mother insisted on being helped to her waiting carriage without even looking at the child she'd delivered.

"Leaving the poor mite with you, is she?" the midwife said to the woman who'd accompanied the mother on arrival.

Yuba Steinmetz clutched the swaddled newborn infant to her breast, gazing tenderly at the red fuzz covering the tiny head. "She's mine! Jael's mine."

The midwife, tidying up after the birth, shrugged. The way she'd heard it, the mother had an elderly and impotent—but wealthy—husband, so was forced to conceal her love child or be cast out. It wouldn't be the first time she'd brought such a child into the world.

"No one will ever take Jael from me." The Steinmetz woman's voice was high and fierce. "Never!"

"Likely no one will try," the midwife said soothingly. At least, that had been her experience—the sinning wives were only too glad to be rid of the results of their indiscretions.

Yuba Steinmetz's smile as she gathered her long cloak about both herself and the child was cunning and secret. She opened the door to leave, then looked back over her shoulder at the midwife. "They won't ever find me or Jael."

Wolf, caught up in Muir's plans to save the Yosemite Valley from further destruction at the hands of timber thieves, stayed on through '99 and into '01 to work with the older man. He was with Muir on September 6 when the news came that President McKinley had been shot by an assassin in Buffalo. McKinley died eight days later.

Overriding Wolf's shock about McKinley was the

stunning realization that his friend, the man he'd fought with in Cuba, was now the President.

"President Theodore Roosevelt," he said aloud, testing the sound of the words.

Muir, writing at the desk in his study, turned to look at Wolf. "This is our chance. We've got to get him to visit Yosemite before I sail for Europe."

Wolf nodded. *If you ever need me,* Roosevelt had once said to him. "I'll send a telegram," he told Muir.

On May 14 of the following year, President Roosevelt arrived in San Francisco. On the next night, he, Wolf, and Muir camped under the giant sequoias in Mariposa Grove. In the morning, they mounted horses and took the trail to Glacier Point.

"Who needs tents?" Roosevelt demanded that evening as they cooked thick steaks over an open fire in the meadow behind the Point. "This is the bulliest ever!"

After dark, as Wolf and Roosevelt sat around the embers of the campfire drinking coffee and reminiscing about the Rough Riders, Wolf suddenly realized Muir was missing. Moments later, a tower of flame shot into the sky and Wolf grinned, knowing Muir had fired one of the huge dead pines they'd passed.

Roosevelt cheered. "A five-hundred-year-old candle—hurrah for Yosemite!"

On returning, Muir directed the conversation, doing his best to convince the President of the necessity to protect Yosemite Valley by making it a part of Yosemite Park.

"People aren't meant to be ravishers and despoilers of earth," Muir insisted. "We're stewards, all of us, with a divine command to obey—to cherish and preserve the earth we live upon."

His words rose gooseflesh on Wolf's arms. *A divine command.* Yes, he told himself. Yes!

Listening to Roosevelt's favorable comments, Wolf knew the President was impressed and felt sure Muir's pet project was due to succeed. At the same time, he sensed a dormancy inside himself had been awakened by Muir's impassioned words. An urgency possessed him, driving him to his feet. He'd been created for a single purpose; there was something he must set right; he must hurry or it would be too late. He strode away from the fire and stopped, bewildered. What was it he must do? He didn't know and there was no one to tell him.

Because of the inexplicable compulsion, Wolf had difficulty falling asleep. In the morning, he woke to find his blanket covered by several inches of snow. Roosevelt romped through the snow like a boy. "The grandest day of my life!" he crowed.

Watching him, Wolf realized that nothing would ever change the energetic enthusiast Roosevelt was—not even the presidency.

Two days later, after Roosevelt had gone on with his entourage to Sacramento, Wolf said good-bye to Muir and set off, at long last, for home. Maybe at Volek House he could come to terms with what he was destined to do.

Though he could have telephoned Ivan or Arno in San Francisco at any time during these past three years in California, he had not. He wasn't sure whether it had been a reluctance to be drawn into family business, or whether he'd needed the time to renew himself after the fighting in Cuba and his strange experience at the New York seance. Even now he had nightmares about red-haired witches.

He found a telephone-like device installed at the front gate and was about to ring the house when he saw Grandmother Liisi making her way slowly down the drive toward him. He smiled wryly, prepared for her greeting.

"Welcome home, Wolf," she said as she unlocked the gate. "I knew you were coming, so I decided to meet you."

"I didn't mean to stay away so long," he said, dismounting and leading his horse so he could walk with her.

"Ivan and Arno thought perhaps you'd sailed for Russia, but I didn't believe you had."

"Not yet. I intend to soon. I hope all's well here."

Liisi shrugged. "There are more of us."

His heart sank as he recalled Samara's rape by the stalker. "Samara had a baby?"

"Yes. Melanie's four." She slanted him a look. "Leo and Quincy are also four—making you a grandfather."

He stared at her in consternation. "Druse?" he stammered. "Druse had twins? Who did she marry?"

Liisi sighed. "I'm afraid Stefan was their father."

"My God!"

Giving him no time to recover, she said, "Tanya and Rodney McQuade have also added to the clan. Last year Tanya bore twin girls, Jennifer and Lily." She frowned. "I'm uneasy about those girls. I wish Tanya had remembered how dangerous it is to pass on Volek blood."

Another with Volek blood was his son, Hawk, now five. If Grandfather were alive, he'd be appalled at the increase in Voleks. The night with Willa Gebhardt crossed Wolf's mind. What if—? He shook his head as though to dislodge even the thought of such a possibility.

"Druse didn't tell me until she began to show," Liisi went on. "Then she refused to take my potions; she was determined to bear Stefan's child—children, as it turned out."

His grandsons were male twins. With Volek blood on both Druse's side and Stefan's. He grimaced. One was bound to be a shifter when he became a man. They were already four years old.

"I should have come home before now," he said.

"You couldn't have prevented any of the children from being born. Actually, having to take care of Melanie has been good for Samara—though she's far from her old self. And we've hired a nursemaid—Jose's granddaughter Maria comes in during the day to help with the children."

Chung came hurrying up to take Wolf's horse. "Good you home," he said. "We miss."

Wolf clapped him on the shoulder, feeling a bond with the man who'd proved to be a staunch ally on the terrible night Sergei and Stefan had died.

As Chung walked off with the horse, Liisi caught Wolf's arm, stopping him before they reached the steps. "Look at me," she ordered.

He had no choice but to obey. Since he hadn't taken a good look at her, he was startled to see that her hair had turned completely silver with no trace of blondness left. New age lines showed around her eyes and mouth, yet even at seventy-one her pale gray eyes held their power of command.

Shaman's eyes.

As he watched her pupils widen and then contract, he willed himself to remain calm. Shaman or not, what had he to fear from Grandmother Liisi?

"Yes," she murmured at last, turning away. "She left a mark. But I don't see any permanent harm."

Since Liisi spoke to herself, he said nothing, even though her words made him uneasy. He dare not ask questions, since that might lead to questions from her that he didn't want to answer.

"You'll let me know what you sense about Druse's twins," she said, leading the way up the steps. "And Samara's Melanie. She frowned again. "I doubt if you'll sense anything amiss with the McQuade twins, but I'm afraid no good will come of their birth."

Wolf nodded, agreeing to do what he could to help, not relishing what he might find.

In less than a week, Wolf had settled into the household routine so thoroughly that he could almost believe he'd never been away. After a day or two of wariness, Druse's natural warmth reemerged, and he started making friends with the daughter he hardly knew.

His grandsons were lighter skinned than their mother, with very curly dark hair and the golden eyes of Volek twins. Neither Leo nor Quincy were shy of him but his son, Hawk, stood apart, staring, unable to decide whether he liked this strange father or not.

When Samara spoke to Wolf, she seemed distracted, as though only part of her attention was on the outer world. She never smiled, and he found no trace of the bond they'd once shared.

Wolf told Liisi immediately that Quincy was the shifter, but he waited a full week before bringing up the subject with Druse. They were alone in the morning room having coffee.

"I know how you predicted Arno would be affected," she said. "And Stefan, too." She paused, waiting.

"It's Quincy." He spoke as gently as he could, being careful, as she'd been, not to use the word shifter in case there were any servants within earshot.

"You're positive?"

He nodded.

Druse sighed. "I hoped against hope they'd escape the problem."

"They're Voleks."

"What about Melanie?" Druse glanced over her shoulder at the open door and lowered her voice. "Her father—will she take after him?"

"I have no way to tell. I can't sense—them."

"Samara worries about it. We all do. I think poor little Melanie feels how uneasy we are about her. At least Hawk's all right. Isn't he?"

Wolf nodded. "I wish I knew how to make friends with him."

"Take him for a walk in the woods," Druse suggested. "Just the two of you. Tell him about being a soldier in Cuba."

"Would he be interested?"

"He's a boy, isn't he? Try it."

On their walk, Wolf did everything he could think of to prod Hawk into speech, but the boy said as little as possible and then only if asked a direct question.

Finally, in desperation, Wolf began to talk about his son's mother. ". . . and so, because that was the first thing she saw on the morning of your birth," he finished, "she named you Takenya. In the Miwok tongue that means Hawk-Swooping-Down-On-Prey."

Hawk stared at him for a long moment. "I like my name," he said at last. "I wish I was a really truly hawk so I could fly."

"I've seen men travel through the air in baskets under giant balloons," Wolf said. "Maybe someday you and I can take a ride in one."

Hawk's slightly slanted black eyes widened in pleased surprise. "What do those balloons look like?" he demanded. "How do they stay up?"

"I'm no expert, but we'll find pictures in some of the books in the library with explanations of why—"

Hawk grasped his hand, pulling him toward the house. "Let's hurry!"

The day before Christmas, Hawk broke his collarbone leaping from the barn roof while holding onto a makeshift flying contraption. While Druse and Liisi strapped the broken bone into place, Wolf retrieved what he realized was Hawk's attempt at constructing his own balloon.

"Next time, tell a grownup before you try flying," he advised his son.

Rodney and Tanya brought their twin daughters to Volek House on Christmas Day. As casually as he could, Wolf picked up Lily, then Jennifer. Though he hadn't seriously expected to find that either of the babies was a potential shifter, he was relieved to be right. Taking Tanya aside, he told her the good news.

"Well, of course not!" she exclaimed. "They're completely normal. Why, they don't even look like Voleks. They're McQuades, through and through."

He was tempted to remind her that their sandy hair and blue eyes didn't mean the girls couldn't pass on the shifter trait, but he knew she wouldn't listen to even the slightest hint her babies weren't perfect.

Rodney was as enthralled with the twins as Tanya. "We were beginning to think we weren't ever going to have a child," he said to Wolf in private. "It was sort of strange how it came about. My wife got all upset because I accidentally broke the last two bottles of that special health tonic Mrs. Volek makes up for her and what happened?'' He winked at Wolf. ''We wound up with twins.''

Rodney was no fool, Wolf thought. Had he deliberately broken the bottles, suspecting a connection between the tonic and a barren wife?

As the new year passed from January to February and then March, Wolf told himself he should be planning his Russian trip. But he enjoyed his son's company so much he found it hard to leave. Then Ivan and Arno took advantage of Wolf's presence at the house to both stay in San Francisco for the month of April, explaining that they were looking into making an investment in the new automobile industry and wanted to be sure it wasn't too much of a risk.

From the way all the boys, Leo and Quincy as well as Hawk, followed him around, it was clear to Wolf that they needed a father. He tried to do his best. Even with Melanie.

She was a very pretty little girl, with brown curly hair and brown eyes. But she held aloof from everyone as though sensing their doubts about her. Wolf felt sorry for her and agreed with Liisi—the child should never have been born.

If only they knew more about stalkers. Was it a trait that emerged at puberty, like shifting? Or were stalkers formed in the womb and born already able to sense shifters? Would a stalker raised with a potential shifter like Quincy try to kill him after his first shifting?

It could be that the stalker trait didn't necessarily manifest itself in each child and little Melanie was absolutely normal. But he felt certain she could pass the trait on so, one way or another, Melanie posed a danger to the clan.

On the other hand, Melanie's birth into the family was a chance to learn more about stalkers.

Liisi's continuing worry about the McQuade twins disturbed Wolf, and he visited Tanya often, hoping to ease Liisi's mind by his reports on the normal development of the little girls. He taught his son and grandsons how to shoot with a bow and arrows as well as with a gun. With him remaining at home, Arno and Ivan were able to spend more time together in San Francisco. He knew he contributed to the welfare of the household.

Though glad to do his part, his continuing need to discover his purpose in life kept him restless. He finally decided that the answer might lie in Russia, in the forests of the Volek ancestors. Hadn't Grandfather urged him to go there?

By the time he made up his mind to set sail for Russia it was February of 1904. Before he could announce his plans, the conflict between Japan and Russia over trade in Korea and Manchuria blossomed into a full-scale war between the two countries. Wolf postponed the journey.

In the early spring, he planned a camping trip into the foothills with the three boys. The night before they were to leave, he was downstairs making last-minute preparations before going to bed when the phone rang. After midnight—who'd be calling? He hurried to the special cubicle constructed to hold the instrument and lifted the receiver.

"Volek House, Wolf," he said.

"Get over here at fast as you can!" Rodney McQuade shouted frantically. "Bring Druse." He broke the connection.

Wolf ran up the stairs, woke Druse, and told her about the call. When he came out of her room, Liisi stood in the corridor.

"I heard the phone ring, and I overheard what you said to Druse," Liisi told him. "It'll be a fire, connected in some way to the twins. I knew the flames I saw at the wedding boded ill."

Liisi was right, though the fire was out by the time Wolf and Druse pounded up on their horses. Rodney, his father, Paul, and two nearby ranchers sloshed water from buckets on the smoldering remains of the south wing of the house. Tanya crouched in a wagon, a lantern by her side, one whimpering twin bundled in her arms. The other twin sprawled motionless on the wagon floor.

Wolf had to shout at Tanya to make her notice him. "Are the twins hurt?" he demanded, climbing into the wagon.

Tanya prodded the motionless one with her toe. "Take her away," she said, her voice low and toneless. "I never want to see Jennifer again."

Wolf crouched to examine the girl and found to his relief that she was breathing. Druse, standing beside the wagon, reached for Lily.

"Give her to me, Tanya," she said firmly. "I'll help her." When Tanya didn't respond, she repeated her words.

Slowly, as though each movement was an extreme effort, Tanya held out the whimpering bundle to Druse. "Don't let Jennifer near her," she begged. "Don't even put them in the same house."

Druse turned back the blanket to look at Lily and drew in her breath. "Oh my God," she whispered.

Wolf leaned over to look and wished he hadn't. On the left side, the skin of Lily's face and chest was blistered and blackened—not simply burned but charred.

Tanya pushed at Jennifer with her foot. "Take her," she cried, her voice rising. "If you don't, I swear I'll kill her."

Wolf gathered the unconscious Jennifer into his arms and jumped down from the wagon.

"Wait!" Tanya shrieked. "Bring Lily to Mother McQuade's, not to Volek House. Take Jennifer to Liisi. Tell her—" Tanya's voice faltered "—tell her Jennifer starts fires. With her mind. And don't ever, ever bring Jennifer back. Not after what she did to her own twin."

Wolf started home with Jennifer while Druse went on to the senior McQuade's house with the badly burned Lily, leaving Tanya with her husband. Jennifer still hadn't roused when he carried her into Volek House. Liisi was waiting, Samara with her.

Still holding Jennifer, Wolf told them what Tanya had said.

"A fire-starter," Liisi whispered, shaking her head. "I should have guessed."

Samara blinked, staring at Jennifer.

"Bring Jennifer up to the tower room," Liisi ordered, "where I can set a guarding spell on her so she won't burn the place down when she wakes. Other than that—" She shook her head. "I've never dealt with a fire-starter."

Samara trailed after them, muttering, as they climbed the stairs. "Red," Wolf thought she said. "Angry red."

"Jennifer's not quite four—too young to set her own controls," Liisi said when they were all inside the tower room. "She doesn't realize she can maim and kill. I'll have to try to find a way to shut down her fire-making. If I can."

Wolf lay Jennifer on the blue silk rug in the center of the room, noticing for the first time the dark bruise over her right forehead and temple.

"Someone hit her," Samara said.

"And a good thing," Liisi put in. "If she hadn't been knocked unconscious, they'd all be dead. We'll have to tie her within the circle I make."

Near dawn Jennifer roused. She whimpered and tried to reach a hand to her head before opening her eyes. When she discovered she couldn't move, she began crying for Lily.

"Jennifer," Liisi said. "Lily's not here. You're at Volek House because you burned your sister."

"Didn't," Jennifer sobbed, staring at Liisi through her tears.

"We know you can set fires," Liisi said. "It's dangerous, so we can't let you do it—that's why you're tied."

Something sizzled between Jennifer and the edge of the circle enclosing her. Wolf swallowed, realizing she'd tried to burn Liisi.

"We can't keep her tied!" Samara protested. "The poor little thing doesn't understand."

"The poor little thing will burn the house down around our ears if I release her," Liisi said tartly.

"There must be something else you can do," Samara said.

Liisi eased down onto a three-legged stool. "I don't like tying her any better than you do." She put a hand over her eyes. "I'm so tired, so very tired. And I don't know enough about fire-starters to stop Jennifer."

Never before had Wolf heard his grandmother admit to any weakness.

Liisi glanced at him as if in warning, then fastened her gaze on Samara. "What will become of the poor child? If she isn't controlled, every time she gets the least bit angry, everyone around her will be in danger. Not just Voleks but others. Sooner or later, someone will kill her to stop her. I'm afraid the best all-round solution would be to do away with her here and now."

Samara balled her fists. "No!"

Liisi opened her eyes wide. "Do you have a solution?"

Samara didn't answer the question directly. "I can feel red inside her," she said slowly.

"Like you felt darkness inside the stalker." Liisi spoke softly, carefully, her expression reminding Wolf of a stalking cat readying itself to pounce on a mouse.

Samara, intent on the sobbing, struggling Jennifer, nodded.

"You controlled the stalker," Liisi said. "You paralyzed her and you were only three. You're a grown woman now—you're stronger."

The night of the stalker came back to Wolf with such disturbing clarity his heart began to pound. Samara *had* stopped the stalker from shooting. He recalled being frozen into position himself. Only Mima, badly wounded as she was, had been able to move, to retrieve the dropped gun. To kill . . .

"Why wasn't Mima affected?" he asked without thinking.

Liisi answered. "Because she was dying. Those near to death can't be easily controlled."

"I'm afraid," Samara whispered.

Liisi sighed. "Then there's no hope for Jennifer."

Unable to bear the look of anguish on Samara's face, Wolf put his arm around her. She stiffened, but when he spoke soothingly, she gradually relaxed.

Like the tentative brush of an evening breeze after a hot afternoon, he felt something inside him. A moment later, his world turned a fiery, raging red. Startled, he almost released Samara before he realized she'd linked with him as she had when she was a child.

He was looking inside Jennifer.

Involuntarily, his mind filled with the cooling image of mountain snow-melt pouring over high rocks and falling hundreds of feet into Yosemite Valley.

"Water," Samara whispered.

"Yes," Liisi agreed.

Liisi opened a tiny crack in the warding circle and Samara poured Wolf's image of the mountain falls through the opening and into Jennifer. He didn't know how she did it, though he was aware his presence lent Samara strength.

After a few moments, the child's sobs cut off and she stopped struggling, fixing her gaze on Samara.

"The fire's out, Jenny," Samara said. "The fire's out and the water won't let you start another. No more fire." Liisi handed Samara a pair of scissors, and she reached into the circle, cut the ties binding Jennifer, and lifted the girl into her arms.

Quivering from head to toe, Jennifer buried her face in Samara's shoulder. Wolf, discovering there was no longer even a trace of the angry red that had clouded his vision, glanced at Liisi. She smiled reassuringly as she rose from the stool.

"Jennifer's controlled," Liisi said. "But we'll have to keep her here at Volek House with Samara, just in case."

Wolf's shoulders sagged in relief. Not only was Jennifer rendered harmless but in helping the child Samara seemed to have helped heal herself.

His elation was short-lived when he remembered Lily's charred face. Poor Lily had to pay the price of her twin's fire-starting. If she survived, she'd be scarred for life.

Chapter 13

Key in hand, Wolf turned away from the Palace Hotel desk, resigned to spending the night. There wasn't much about the city he cared for. Except for the greenery in Golden Gate Park, April in San Francisco lacked the color and scent and the spring promise of the San Joaquin Valley.

He crossed to the elevators and waited for a car. He'd have chosen another hotel, but Ivan and Arno had insisted he must use the suite reserved for McDee Industries at the Palace and there was no point in being churlish about it. Besides, it was just for one night.

Tomorrow morning he'd be sailing for Russia at last! Excitement pounded through him, making him less aware of the crowded elevator car.

God knows it had taken him long enough. How many years had it been since he promised Grandfather to go? He'd been thirty-two then; he was almost forty-two now. It was past time to honor his vow, past time to search for his personal destiny as well; a destiny he believed was linked with his Volek heritage.

"I've never seen the hotel so jam-packed," a middle-aged woman said to the younger woman next to her.

"Everyone's in town to hear Caruso tonight," the second woman replied. "He sings so divinely. Don't you just love *Carmen*? It's my favorite opera."

Wolf listened to their conversation with half his attention until the women got off. Since the McDee suite was at the top, he was the last to leave.

The older he became, the less he tolerated crowds. Even in the privacy of the McDee suite he felt hemmed in and uneasy, sensing the mass of people in the city. He began to pace, scarcely noticing the luxury of the three rooms.

Enough! he warned himself after a time. You've only tonight to get through. Relax. Taking a deep breath, he let it out slowly. He picked up the complimentary copy of the *Chronicle* from a table and sat in one of the upholstered chairs to glance at the morning headlines for April 17, 1906.

SUPREME COURT INVALIDATES DIVORCES

ENRICO CARUSO TO SING AT METROPOLITAN OPERA

VESUVIUS FUND TO AID VICTIMS OF ERUPTION TOPS $20,000

DANCER CECE WEDS SOCIETY DOCTOR

Wolf went rigid, staring at the last headline, reading it over and over again before he numbly went on to the story.

Thomas H. Swanson, M.D. was described as a distinguished fifty-year-old physician who treated some of the city's wealthiest families. The marriage was to have taken place this morning at the chapel of Mission Dolores; the reception was being held in the Garden Court of the Palace Hotel in the afternoon. This afternoon.

Wolf glanced at his watch. Just after three. He rose and took two steps toward the door. Paused. Shook his head. Started to turn away. Stopped again.

Damn it, why shouldn't he go down to the Garden Court? Why shouldn't he have a look at Cecelia and her new husband? Unable to think of a reason not to, he strode to the door.

After edging through the throng of wedding guests until he was close to the bridal couple, Wolf deliberately looked at the groom first. Dr. Swanson's fair hair was as yet untouched by gray. He had a blond mustache, a hearty manner, laughed frequently, and looked younger than his fifty years. Though well-built, he was half a head shorter than most of the men at the reception.

Cecelia, Wolf knew, would be close to forty-three. Had she waited this long to marry to avoid bearing a child? Not that she was too old yet—but it would be less likely to happen. Bracing himself, at last he looked at her.

For a moment, his eyes stung with unshed tears. Maturity had made her more beautiful than ever; in her long pearl-white gown she seemed as lustrous as the moon. And about as approachable. Even though he knew she'd never been meant for him, he envied Thomas Swanson as he'd never envied another man.

He was about to leave when her gaze crossed his. She held for a moment, her green eyes widening, then bit her lip and quickly glanced away. Not wishing to spoil her wedding day by reminding her of the unpleasant past, Wolf retreated to his rooms.

He stood by the windows of the suite's sitting room looking down on the city while turning the silver cat's head buckle over and over in his hands. He never traveled without the buckle. The bustle on the streets below, noisier than ever now that automobiles had joined the trolleys and horse-drawn cabs, was overlaid with the images in his mind: Cecelia dancing in the music room of Volek House; Cece's erotic dance at the St. Francis Hotel; Cecelia in his arms on the crest of Powell Street. . . .

Apparently he'd been wrong about Cecelia being a potential shifter. If she hadn't shapechanged in forty some years, it was unlikely she ever would. He was certain she never *had* shifted, because otherwise she surely wouldn't take the chance of marrying Swanson.

I'm glad I was wrong, he told himself firmly. Shifting is a terrible curse. Cecelia's lucky to be normal; she deserves to be happy.

But a tiny mouse of doubt nibbled away at his reassurances. Even though she was over forty, how could she be certain she would never shapeshift? He thought of his grandfather—Sergei could control his shifting, and after General Custer's death, he'd vowed never to shapechange again. He'd broken that vow. In the California foothills, when Wolf was not yet a man, he'd seen his grandfather become a beast in a time of peril. He'd watched the awful transformation again when the stalker threatened Stefan. What if some vast and overwhelming danger confronted Cecelia? Was it possible a great shock could trigger her into shapeshifting?

He turned from the window, upset by his musings and tormented by the knowledge she was another man's wife. He'd heard one of the wedding guests remark that the newlyweds planned to spend the night at the hotel before embarking in the doctor's new Packard touring car for a honeymoon at a seaside hotel in Monterey. Why should he bother going to bed when it wasn't likely he'd sleep tonight?

By four-thirty, when false dawn began to lighten the night sky, Wolf could no longer stand being confined inside the suite. The city streets wouldn't be a great improvement, but at least they'd be nearly deserted this early in the morning.

As he walked away from the Palace down Market Street toward the Ferry Building, Wolf noted that the ubiquitous morning mist was thinning; no doubt the sun would soon disperse it. It would be a fine day to sail through the Golden Gate bound for Russia. Unfortunately, the earliest he could board his ship was noon. He'd have to fill the hours somehow.

Here and there a man stood on a corner waiting for a trolley car. A laborer, dressed in overalls and carrying a dinner pail, crossed the street ahead of Wolf. There was little noise except for an occasional milk or newspaper wagon clattering by.

The rising sun brightened the mist, poking its golden light through rapidly widening gaps in the grayness. Somewhere in the distance a dog began to howl. A dray horse turning onto Market off Fremont Street suddenly threw up its head, whinnied shrilly, and began to struggle in the traces. Wolf stopped to watch while the driver fought to control the frightened animal. Looking around he could see nothing to upset the horse—especially since it wore blinkers.

Then the earth under Wolf's feet seemed to slip away, sending him reeling and staggering. As he tried to regain his balance, he realized what was happening—an earthquake. Since it wasn't by any means his first experience with a California temblor, he didn't take undue alarm until he found himself thrown flat on his face in the street.

Stay down, ride it out, he told himself, not even trying to regain his feet. A low rumbling began, growing louder and louder until it reverberated in his very bones. On the street ahead of him the horse, dray wagon and driver disappeared in a shower of dust and debris as a great crack opened and swallowed them up.

Shocked, Wolf struggled to sit up. Failed. Above him, the tall buildings swayed in a macabre dance. Bricks and chunks of masonry shot through the air like cannon balls, slamming onto the street so close to him that chips from them stung his face.

The poor doomed horse had sensed the quake before it started, he thought. Most animals could. Shifters, too. He remembered how Grandfather always knew a quake was coming before the shaking began. Arno had inherited the same ability.

Would Cecelia know? The thought of her at the hotel, helpless and injured—or worse—drove him to his knees. He began to crawl over the shuddering ground toward the Palace.

In the bridal suite on the fifth floor of the Palace Hotel, Cecelia woke abruptly and sat up in bed, screaming.

"What's wrong?" Thomas demanded, startled from sleep.

She was too frightened to answer; she couldn't stop screaming. He tried to take her in his arms, but she fought him.

"My dear, be still!" he ordered. "Nothing's wrong—you've had a bad dream, that's all."

The nightmare hadn't been in her sleep, it was now—didn't he understand? She tried to gasp out that something dreadful was about to happen, but the words were choked off by her terror.

He succeeded in wrapping his arms around her, holding her close despite her struggles to free herself.

"No," she managed to cry. "No!" But he wouldn't let her go.

All her senses screamed *Danger!* Her heart fluttered in her chest like a bird struggling in a hunter's net; she gasped for breath. Her stomach wrenched in painful spasms.

"Let me go," she begged, hearing the growl in her voice with amazed horror.

"What in hell's wrong with you, Cece?" Thomas sounded exasperated, holding her away to look at her in the dim light of early morning. She had no time to worry about his feelings, convulsed as she was by the struggle going on inside her.

"Jesus Christ, look at you!" Tom's shocked voice was shrill in her ears as he abruptly released her.

The bed began to quiver, to shake. The overhead light fixture swayed like a pendulum. Earthquake! But the knowledge didn't alarm her nearly as much as what was happening to her. After one final terrible inner wrench that twisted agonizingly through her body, Cecelia's surroundings began to fade. Her last conscious thought was of Wolf and his final warning to her all those years ago on Powell Street.

The beast, immediately aware of threat, spent little time reveling in her freedom. The human was close. Too close. His yells hurt her ears and his fear was rank in her nostrils. She snarled a warning, and he flung himself away from her, falling to the floor. She leaped over the end of the bed. A part of her knew she was in a room, a room that made her feel trapped, caged.

The floor rocked sickeningly under her feet; the roar

outside was deafening. Plaster fell off the ceiling; unseen objects thudded from tabletops onto the floor.
From the other side of the door she heard humans calling in alarm. The man shut in with her shrieked as he
scrabbled away from her. Whatever the danger outside, she couldn't bear being confined in this room.

She had to get out! But how? Her taloned paws
weren't capable of opening a door.

The human could. If he would. As she tried to keep
her balance in the violently shaking room, she kept a
wary eye on him. He stopped screaming. Pulling himself to his feet by clinging to a dresser near the window, with one hand he pawed through objects, his
breath rasping harshly. When the shaking eased, he
swung around, pointing something at her. A gun.

He meant to kill her! Rage rippled through the beast.
She crouched and sprang. The gun roared. Something
struck her in the shoulder, scarcely slowing her. Her
claws raked down his right side, and she breathed in
the exciting tang of blood.

He cried out and flung himself sideways. Glass shattered; he disappeared and damp air laden with scores
of strange and unpleasant scents flowed around her.
The beast padded to the broken window and looked
out. The man sprawled motionless on the pavement
below. Too far for her to safely jump. But the alternative was being trapped in the room.

She crouched and leaped through the jagged hole in
the glass.

The landing, on all four feet, jarred through her,
robbing her momentarily of breath. When she was able
to move, her first step shot pain along her right front
leg. She kept on despite the pain, instinct warning her
to seek a hiding place. She needed trees, bushes, a
jungle—there she'd find sanctuary. And prey.

She raised her head to catch scents and detected a
trace of greenery to the west. Limping, skirting debris, keeping close to buildings when she could, the
beast trotted westward past occasional moving humans. Others lay dead like the man who'd tried to kill

her. At times the earth trembled beneath her feet, up-setting her balance, but she went on as soon as the tremors stopped.

A wailing, as of many human voices, came faintly from the south, along with the stench of smoke. Water flooded some of the streets, but she was afraid to risk stopping for a drink—there were too many humans about. She knew some of them saw her because they shouted and pointed, but so far no one had threatened her.

Sensing their danger, she avoided the tangles of wires in the streets that wriggled while emitting blue sparks. Always she followed the scent of trees, diffi-cult as it was to pick out of the myriad of other odors—some so strong and vile they turned her stomach. Her front leg gradually stopped throbbing and the small wound in her shoulder no longer bled, enabling her to quicken her pace to a lope.

At last she saw the trees. As she raced toward them, she noticed, to her dismay, a thin line of humans strag-gling in the same direction. With no other place to go, she plunged between flowering bushes, searching for a substantial stand of trees. When she found a small grove, she paused beside a pond and lapped water, then chose a tree and climbed it. Stretching out on a broad branch, she rested while keeping alert for any sign of danger. So far, her senses told her no human had penetrated into the woods, but she'd take no chances. Her hunger could wait until she was certain it was safe to hunt.

Her eyes half closed and a rumbling began deep in her furred chest, a sound of satisfaction. After all these years, she was finally free.

She meant to stay free.

As Wolf stumbled toward the Palace, he saw a man plunge from the fifth floor of the hotel to the street below. Moments later, Wolf gasped as a great black beast leaped from the same broken window and landed on all fours next to the dead man.

About the size of a large mountain lion, the beast didn't resemble any animal he'd ever seen. Though it seemed more feline than anything else, the taloned, fanged beast was a fearsome mixture. He knew immediately what it was, who it was.

"Cecelia!" he cried.

The beast paid him no heed, limping rapidly westward. Heading for Golden Gate Park? Wolf wondered. The woods of the Presidio? He paused a moment to drop to one knee beside the dead man and grimaced at the deep and bloody gouges in Dr. Swanson's side. Those wounds didn't come from the five-story fall: they were claw marks.

Wolf knew he must stop Cecelia before the beast she'd become killed others. He trailed her along debris-strewn sidewalks, passing street car tracks torn up and bent as though by a malevolent giant. Electric wires, tangled and sputtering, lay among the piles of bricks and mortar. Smoke, blowing from the south, stung his nostrils.

A faint cry for help stopped him. Glancing around, he noticed a woman crouched in the recessed doorway of a dry goods store. Other earthquake survivors passed her by without looking at her. He hesitated, then climbed toward her over a mound of crumbled stone that had fallen from the building's facade. She stared up at him with frightened eyes.

"My baby's coming," she gasped, clutching at his arm. "Please help me get to a hospital."

Wolf scanned the surroundings, hoping to see some kind of conveyance. A dead horse lay in the street, still hitched to the overturned wagon; otherwise, there was nothing.

"Ohh!" the woman wailed, letting go of Wolf and sinking to the cement floor of the entryway. "It's coming now!"

He gaped at her, then tried the door of the building. Locked. Not knowing what else to do, he knelt beside her. She lay on her back, knees bent and legs apart, alternately gasping and moaning.

Another woman might know what to do, but there wasn't a woman in sight. Gritting his teeth, he gingerly lifted her long skirt. Blood stained her underclothes. Though he'd never watched the birth of a baby, he'd seen animals born, and it occurred to him he'd have to remove her drawers to make room for the emerging infant.

He explained this to her as he fumbled with the ties to the drawers and clumsily pulled the underpants down and off, laying them on the cement between her legs. Her face red with exertion as she strained, she didn't object, didn't say anything. Sweat beaded her forehead.

Yellowish fluid gushed from the birth canal opening, followed by more blood. The woman grunted, obviously pushing down, exactly as animals did. The top of the baby's head appeared, and Wolf held his breath until the head emerged completely. He reached down to prevent the baby's face from scraping against the cement. The shoulders appeared, then suddenly the entire body slipped free, and he was left holding a wailing newborn.

Realizing there'd be an afterbirth, he laid the child on her mother's abdomen. "It's a little girl," he said. "She's fine. Don't move yet."

When the afterbirth slid out, Wolf took his pocketknife and cut a strip from the woman's drawers to tie the umbilical cord before severing it. He removed his jacket and wrapped the little girl in it before showing the child to her mother. He remembered Druse as a newborn, and he knew this baby was much tinier.

The woman smiled and touched the baby's cheek. "She looks like her father."

Balancing the infant in one arm, he helped the woman to her feet with the other.

"I hope you can walk, ma'am," he said.

"I'll try," she quavered. "How can I ever thank you?"

As they stepped from the entry, the ground undulated under their feet and more of the facade broke

away from the building to crash around them. Wolf
hustled mother and child into the middle of the street.

"Where do you live?" he asked.

She shook her head, biting her lip. "My boarding
house is in ruins. I'm afraid I'm the only one who got
out. It was because my pains started. A month early.
I was frightened, so I came downstairs to knock on
the landlady's door. Before I could, everything started
shaking so I ran outside. I tried to get to the hospital
but . . ." Her words trailed off.

"Your husband?"

"He's a sailor—his ship's not due in till next
month."

"Any other family?"

"I have an aunt and uncle in Oakland."

Wolf considered whether he ought to look for a hospital and decided against it. For all he knew, any hospital might be as badly damaged as the buildings
around them. And if not damaged, extremely busy. He
had no idea if Oakland had suffered as much from the
quake as San Francisco, but at least she had relatives
there. "I'll get you to the ferry," he told her, turning
back in the direction he'd come.

By the time they reached the Ferry Building, other
refugees from the quake were thronging on the docks,
eager to leave the city by ferry. Wolf managed to find
an older couple who agreed to watch over the mother
and child and help them to their Oakland destination.

He started off again for Golden Gate Park, eyeing
with dismay the smoke rising ominously from different
sections of the city. San Francisco might have a magnificent fire department, but he recalled the flooded
streets he'd passed and shook his head. The quake must
have ruptured the water lines. Firefighters, no matter
how skillful and dedicated, couldn't combat flames
without water.

His delay couldn't have been avoided—how could
he have left that poor woman alone?—but he worried
over what the beast might have done and what might
have happened to her since he'd last seen her. He'd

heard rumors that armed soldiers from Fort Mason had been ordered into action, and that meant men trained to shoot first and ask questions later. Though their guns weren't loaded with silver bullets, if enough soldiers shot the beast at once, she'd be doomed.

The other grim possibility was that the beast, having had a taste of blood, was now hunting for prey—human prey.

The beast, half dozing on the tree branch, came alert when a new scent mingled with the smell of rabbits, mice, and birds. Prey! Luck was with her; she was downwind from it. Moving cautiously and quietly, she gathered herself for an attack. Soon she heard the prey approaching, drawn, she knew, by the water in the pond.

When the prey passed under the branch she sprang, landed on its back, and severed its spinal cord with one crunch of her powerful jaws. Blood, hot and salt-sweet filled her mouth.

As she feasted on its flesh, the part of her that knew about rooms, doors, and guns told her what she'd killed was a horse. She hadn't yet eaten her fill when another scent made the fur ruffle along her back. She raised her head and growled, knowing a human was near and coming closer. Humans weren't prey, but they were dangerous. They carried guns. Guns could kill her. Humans were her enemies.

The beast rose from her crouch and snarled, showing her fangs, torn between defending her kill and slipping between the trees to circle back and stalk the approaching human. Deciding on stealth, she reluctantly abandoned the carcass of the horse for the dubious safety of the sparse woods.

As soon as the human saw the dead horse, his shriek made her ears ache. She was in a good position to spring at him and finish him off, but scenting other humans, the beast abandoned her quarry and hid deeper within the small grove, fearfully aware that if the humans spotted her and surrounded the grove, she'd be trapped.

She dare not remain here; she must search for a denser woods. She preferred a jungle, but the part of her that knew about human things warned her there were no jungles nearby.

Cautiously, she loped away from the smell of humans to the far edge of the trees. There she paused and sniffed the air, smelling smoke. Mingled with the smoke was a faint scent of pines to the north. The beast eyed the open space she must cross with dismay. Who knew how far away the forest was? Other stands of trees, no larger than the one she was in, beckoned. The open space between her and the nearest was dotted with bushes, offering some cover. Giving up on the pine scent for the moment, she plunged from the first grove and ran toward the next.

Once among the trees, she discovered a place where greenery grew over piled rocks. Between the rocks and hidden by large flowering bushes, a skunk had fashioned a den, now abandoned. Wrinkling her nose against the odor, the beast dug into the earth between the rocks until the hole was large enough for her to hide in.

Leaving her bolt hole, she searched for water but didn't find any. Climbing a tree, she eased onto a limb and waited. Her hunger hadn't been satisfied, and now she was thirsty as well. But the faint odor of humans disturbed her. Though not close, they were in the area. She'd have to be very, very careful.

Unhappy, hungry and thirsty, she pulled her lips back to show her teeth. Humans were the enemy. She must kill them before they killed her.

Wolf stood beside the mutilated horse. The beast's kill, he was sure. As soon as he'd reached the park, now thronged with people who didn't know where else to go, he'd heard about the wild animal running loose.

"Killed a horse and ate the whole critter—nothing but bones left," one old man told him.

"One of them catamints," another offered.

"I heard 'twas a wolf," a third insisted, and then pointed the way toward the woods where the dead horse lay.

All the activity would have driven off the beast, Wolf felt. As far as he could determine, no one had actually seen her. But with the fires raging in the city, more and more people would pour into the park. Sooner or later she'd be spotted. And then—?

Wolf took a deep breath. He must find her first. What he'd do then he didn't know. She was dangerous and unpredictable. He recalled the long-ago night at the St. Francis when she'd not only seen a red pentacle on his palm but admitted she'd seen one on another man's hand as well. Thought she hadn't known what it meant, he had. The circle within the star marked victims of a shifter.

She'd told him the other man was her doctor. Swanson. Yet, disregarding the warning, she'd finally married him. If she hadn't killed the poor bastard outright, fear of the beast had driven Swanson to jump to his death. Wolf Volek was the next scheduled victim.

How the hell am I supposed to save her, he asked himself, without her killing me first?

Chapter 14

As evening darkened the sky, the beast watched from her tree branch as a man edged cautiously into the small grove. By the way he acted, she decided he was searching for something or someone. For her? He hadn't glanced up yet, so she fought her urge to growl, aware any sound could give her away.

Even though he didn't carry a gun he was a human, and therefore an enemy. Men had driven her from her prey before her hunger was slaked. If this one came close enough, she'd leap from the branch and kill him. Men weren't her legitimate prey, but the lust for blood thrummed within her, demanding to be satisfied. Blood was blood and meat was meat. She flexed her claws, anticipating how she'd sink them into his flesh as her jaws closed on his unprotected neck.

A flicker of movement at the far edge of the grove caught her attention. Its scent wasn't human but animal. Though she couldn't put a name to the smell, when the animal came closer, she recognized it as a dog. The dog trotted along, nose close to the ground, stopping when its path intersected the man's.

He stopped, too, and spoke to the dog. Its tail wagged briefly before it resumed tracking. Tracking her. The beast gathered herself, waiting.

The dog halted again near the tree and circled, sniffing the ground, obviously searching for her tracks. Finding none, the animal raised its head, looked at her branch, and barked. The beast leaped. The force her of jump pinned the dog beneath her, and she sank her teeth into its throat, savoring the taste of blood for an instant before she released the dead animal to stare at the man.

He didn't move. When he spoke to her, his words hissed into her ears like snakes. She snarled and took a step toward him. Men's shouts in the distance made her hold, listening. Coming this way? She couldn't take the chance. Whirling, she ran into the trees toward the rocky refuge she'd ferreted out earlier.

When he was certain she was gone, Wolf dragged the dog's body into a nearby clump of hibiscus bushes and hid it among the foliage.

"Thank you, brother, for giving your life for mine," he murmured before turning away.

Finding the beast Cecelia had become was his responsibility. He didn't want others discovering the dead dog and forming a hunting party—which they might very well do if they connected the dog's death with the horse's.

He had no illusions—if he came within her reach, she'd kill him as quickly as she had the dog. All he had for protection was the Finnish changer's chant Liisi had taught him and the silver cat's head buckle that had belonged to Cecelia's mother. He had no idea if either would be effective. Taking a deep breath, he clutched the silver buckle in his hand and began the chant as he followed the beast's spoor into the gathering darkness, well aware that danger haunted every step he took.

"Dark spirit," he intoned, "Do not ride the night . . ." Unexpectedly, the memory of a long ago nightmare sprang into his head, threatening his concentration on the words of the chant. He was sixteen, asleep in his bed at Volek House and yet he wasn't there at all.

He ran along a street, the paving cracked and rubble-strewn, toward a forest of greenery. Among the trees and bushes death waited. The metallic taste of

fear fouled his mouth, terror clouded his mind, but he
ran on.

Ahead, the dark spirit hidden in the greenery
screamed a challenge; a caterwauling cry more chill-
ing than any cougar's. He longed to stop, to turn back.
He could not. All he could do was race toward his
doom. . . .

He'd thought it a nightmare then. But instead, as
Liisi would have told him, the dream had been a shaman's vision of the future.

Wolf swallowed, mastering his terror, and forced
himself to go on. When he stepped into a tiny clearing
by a rocky hillside, he resumed the chant. ''Dark
spirit, remain in Tuonela's midnight depths where you
belong. Evil one, seek not the light of this world. You
of the dark, remain in darkness. . . .''

He froze as a caterwaul rose from the rocks ahead
of him, rising and falling in an eerie pitch that made
the hair bristle on his nape. He'd tracked Cecelia's
dark spirit to its lair.

For long and terrible moments he forgot every Finnish word he'd ever learned. Gradually his mind cleared,
but his voice was hoarse and halting as he took up the
chant again. He thrust the silver cat's head before him
like a talisman as he edged forward.

The beast shook her head, but the man's words continued to buzz in her ears like troublesome gnats.
Though she didn't understand the words they clouded
her senses, making her uneasy. And angry. She fought
their effect.

He was her enemy. Death to enemies. Kill first, before the enemy strikes.

He came closer to the tall bushes that hid her rocky
den. And still closer. His hated scent made her ears
flatten. A low growl rumbled in her throat. Through
the leaves she saw something gleam in his hand. A
gun? No, worse. She might survive bullets, but she
sensed her death lay within that gleam.

The beast burst from her den, smashed through the

bushes and, talons searching, fangs thirsting for blood, pounced on the enemy.

Wolf, knocked onto his back by the beast's attack, screamed as her claws raked down his face and left shoulder. Her breath was hot and rank in his nostrils, and he caught a blurred glimpse of ferocious green eyes as he brought up his uninjured arm and thrust the silver buckle into her open mouth. Her fangs bit down on his hand, crushing it. Faint with pain, he was only able to moan before darkness overtook him.

He floated in the darkness for eons before a voice, faint and dreamlike, called to him. "Wolf, you must hear me. Wolf, Wolf, hear me."

A woman's voice, sounding strangely blurred. If he made the effort would he remember whose? It was far easier to keep on drifting.

Another woman's voice spoke. A stranger's. He could make no sense of the words.

Was he in Tuonela, the Finnish realm of the dead, with Tuoni's daughter calling to him? Death's daughter calling him to hell?

Disconnected shards of memory drifted in his mind. In Finland, dead men walked the earth as wolves. On the first new moon in March, would he return to life as the animal he was named for?

"Wolf, don't die!"

The words jolted through him, piercing the darkness. He recognized the voice. Not Death's daughter. Cecelia. He struggled to open his eyes.

His right eye stared into near darkness. Something was wrong with the left. He tried to lift his left hand to discover what, but cold fingers closed around his.

"Wolf! Oh, thank God!" Cecelia's words were slurred, barely understandable. The dim blur of her face hovered above him. "Stay still. You're—" Her voice faltered. "You're hurt."

He grew conscious that he lay on his back on the ground and that another person besides Cecelia knelt beside him.

"Gei and I will help you," Cecelia said.

Who was Gei? And what was wrong with Cecelia's voice?

"Blood, he stop." The woman's words had the same sing-song lilt as Chung's. A Chinese woman?

Did she mean he'd been bleeding? He felt as weak and helpless as a newly hatched bird fallen from the nest. What had happened? He couldn't remember. He tried to sit up and pain laced through him, making him groan.

"No move," Gei ordered. "You drink." She held a cup to his lips.

He struggled to swallow the bitter liquid. As it went down, he suddenly recalled where he was. San Francisco. Earthquake. Had he been hurt in the quake? He tried to bring back more, but his thoughts were fuzzy.

"Home," he mumbled. "Go home to Volek House."

"Yes," Cecelia said and he heard tears in her voice. "I'll take you home."

Gei stared at the dark-haired woman called Cecelia. While she was hiding her cart, she'd heard weeping and, venturing to look, discovered a naked woman kneeling beside an injured man. Even though numbed by her own circumstances, the woman's lack of clothes had surprised Gei. After covering the dazed Cecelia with her fur-trimmed satin cloak, Gei, who had nowhere else to go, remained with her.

Now she wondered where the man's home was and how Cecelia expected to get him there with the city burning all around them. Even if it were possible, it was doubtful the man called Wolf would live long enough to go home.

The left side of his face, shoulder, and arm were a bloody ruin, and his right hand was badly mangled. He possessed a dragon's heart to have survived his deadly injuries this long, but he'd soon succumb. She was glad she'd stolen enough opium to ease his pain for the short while he'd live.

"It's all my fault," Cecelia mumbled.

"No talk," Gei advised. She was surprised the woman could, considering the open, bleeding sores on her lips and tongue. From the difficulty Cecelia had speaking, Gei thought her throat must be blistered as well.

Cecelia paid no attention. "Volek House is in the foothills of the mountains," she said. "The Sierras. I must get him home."

Gei blinked. The mountains called the Sierras were far from San Francisco, she knew. Far from the tongs and the revenge that was sure to catch up with her if she remained anywhere near the city. Unlikely as it was that the man would live through any journey, much less a long one, it was clear the gods who'd sent the earthquake were offering her a further chance for escape.

"Me help," she told Cecelia. "You wait. Me go, come back."

Hidden in the bushes no more than forty paces away was the cart she'd brought with her when she'd bolted from Wu Pei's glittering mansion deep within the Chinese quarter—the mansion that had been her prison.

When she was ten, Wu Pei's men had bought her from her mother, a widowed vegetable seller in China. The Yankee captain of the ship that had brought her to California had taken a fancy to her because he had a daughter about her age. Despite the efforts of Wu Pei's men to keep her locked in a cabin with the other women slaves, Captain Hames had insisted she be allowed the run of the ship and had become her friend. From him she'd learned enough English words to understand and speak the language.

Wu Pei had found such a talent useful, and her face and form attractive, so he'd kept her for his own use instead of letting her be locked like the others into the cribs of Chinatown. Though she'd come to hate her master with all her heart and soul, Gei knew she was fortunate. Wu Pei's prostitutes, like all Chinese prostitutes, were slaves and considered expendable. Not only were they forced to accept every customer, even those visibly diseased, but if and when they became too ill or too old to service men, they were locked in a room without food or water and left to die.

Gei was as much Wu Pei's slave as any of the prostitutes but, repulsive as he'd been, at least she'd had only him to satisfy. Until last month, when he grew tired of her and gave her to his head hatchet man—a merciless brute who'd hurt her cruelly. Sooner or later, she knew, he'd scar her badly enough to ruin what looks she had left. Then she'd be sent to the cribs. She'd decided to kill herself first and had been secreting stolen opium for that purpose.

The earthquake had changed her mind. Finding the brutish hatchet man pinned under a fallen chimney, she'd taken great pleasure in slitting his throat with his own dagger. When she discovered Wu Pei was trapped in an upper room, she'd loaded a vegetable cart with jewels, food, fine fabrics, and her hoard of opium before she set the house on fire and fled.

Even in the confusion and terror following the quake, she knew Chinese eyes would see her, would know what she'd done. She'd never be safe among her people again.

As she pulled the cart into the clearing where the dying man lay, Gei assured herself it mattered little that he'd bleed all over the brocades and silken tapestries she'd stolen. The man was her ticket to safety, and with care, the blood would eventually wash out.

After insisting Cecelia put on one of the brocade robes from the cart, Gei took back her cloak. Knowing they wouldn't get far with Cecelia barefoot, Gei removed the man's shoes and stuffed the toes with silk scarves before handing them to Cecelia.

It took their combined strength to maneuver Wolf into the cart. Gei covered him with a tapestry, and with both women pulling the shaft, they dragged the cart from the woods onto one of the park roads and joined the refugees thronging toward the Ferry Building.

* * *

Wolf lay on a sealskin robe in an underground yurt. He knew he was dead because the wrinkled old man with the piercing black eyes told him so. Though the ancient one didn't reveal his name, Wolf recognized him as his shaman grandfather, Gray Seal, a man long dead, a man he'd never seen in his life.

"Are you worth bringing back?" Gray Seal asked.

Wolf had no answer.

"My blood is in you," the shaman said. "My blood mingled with the tainted blood of a shapeshifter."

"I'm not a shifter."

"Are you a shaman?"

About to say no, Wolf suddenly understood such a reply would doom him. "I've been told by a shaman woman that I am," he answered cautiously.

Gray Seal stared into his eyes for time unending, his dark gaze seeing what was inside as well as outside. At last the blue shimmer around the old man arced across the space separating them and danced over Wolf's naked body. He writhed in agony as fire shot through him, consuming him.

When nothing remained of his body except a pile of bones, Gray Seal crouched beside the bones and began counting them.

Wolf, no longer inside his body but hovering in the air near the smokehole of the yurt, watched as four shadow-shapes—a bear, a wolf, a seal and a raven—surrounded Gray Seal.

The raven flew up to perch on top of the ladder leading to the smoke hole, its bright eyes studying the shadow that was Wolf.

Kut, he thought, the raven creator, the Kamchadal trickster. Kut the spirit-raven sees my *haamu*. The word was Finnish, but he didn't know the Kamchadal equivalent of shadow-soul.

"Is there an extra bone?" Gray Seal asked the three animals beside him when he finished counting.

"No," grunted the bear.

"No," barked the seal.

"Yes," said the wolf. "My brother has one extra bone."

Kut flew down to perch on Gray Seal's shoulder.

"What says Kut?" the shaman asked.

Kut squawked so loud the yurt shuddered with the sound. The seal and the bear disappeared. The wolf sat back on his haunches and howled in chorus with the raven's raucous cries.

"We will boil the bones to purify them," Gray Seal announced when he could be heard. "If the extra bone remains, we can be sure there's no illusion."

Wolf watched as the three dropped his bones, one by one, into a black iron kettle set on a tripod over the fire. With dismay, he saw Kut pick up the last tiny bone in his beak and fly up toward the smoke hole. If the raven left the yurt with the extra bone, Wolf's *haamu* could never join with Wolf's body again. In desperation, Wolf's shadow-soul blocked the exit.

Kut flapped his powerful wings in an effort to blow Wolf away from the hole. He clawed at Wolf's eyes. Though Wolf threw up one hand to shield his eyes, pain blinded his *haamu*. Still he clung determinedly to the smoke hole. Finally Kut's beak stabbed through Wolf's heart, bleeding the life from the shadow-soul, and Wolf felt himself shrinking to nothing. But before he was completely diminished, he caught a glimpse of the stolen bone falling, falling, dropped from Kut's beak when he stabbed into Wolf's heart. The bone splashed into the boiling water of the kettle.

As Kut settled onto the top rung of the ladder with a derisive squawk, Wolf's *haamu* stopped dwindling and reformed. Not completely. As a result of his battle with Kut his face was scarred, his left eye was missing and his right hand badly mauled.

Below, the shaman, watched closely by the spirit wolf, chanted over the steaming kettle for hours on end. Or perhaps days, weeks or months—in this yurt there was no measure of time.

Finally the wolf rose onto his hind legs and blew into the kettle. The steam dissipated. The shaman reached inside and brought out the bones, one by one, laying them on the sealskin robe to form a man's skeleton. When it was complete, Gray Seal shook his head.

"The extra bone is not here," he declared. "It was an illusion."

Kut flew down to the shaman's shoulder. The wolf spirit wavered, beginning to disappear. Wolf despaired.

"Look again in the kettle, old man," a woman's voice ordered.

Obviously taken aback, Gray Seal stared at the shimmering silver shadow forming beside the wolf. Unlike Gray Seal, a long silver cord extended from her up through the smoke hole of the yurt. Because she was alive in the middle world, Wolf realized. With a leap of his heart, he recognized Grandmother Liisi.

Gray Seal glowered at her.

"Well?" she demanded.

Slowly, reluctantly, the old shaman peered into the kettle. Reaching in, he pulled out the tiny bone Kut had tried to steal.

"You see?" Liisi asked, her gaze fixed on Gray Seal. "You cannot deny he is a shaman." She put an arm around the neck of the spirit wolf, and Wolf's *haamu* felt warmed by the embrace.

"Why do you care, Woman of the Finns?" Gray Seal demanded. "He is not of your blood."

"He is of my spirit, which is an even stronger bond. Complete what you've begun, Kamchadal. Put the flesh back onto your grandson's bones and declare him a shaman."

Wolf opened his eyes. His eye. He'd lost the left one to Kut in the yurt. Sunlight flooded the room. His old room at Volek House. A woman bent over him.

"Grandmother," he whispered.

"You're finally awake," she said.

Had he dreamed everything?

"The yurt?" he faltered.

She smiled. "You remember that."

He didn't know whether to be relieved or frightened. Reaching up to feel his face with his left hand, he found it difficult to move his bandaged arm.

"Your left eye is gone; there was no way to save it." Liisi's voice was matter-of-fact. "Druse did what she could for your right hand, but it won't be what it was. Your left arm will be stiff, but you'll be able to use it once the wounds heal. And, of course, you'll be scarred for the rest of your life. Do you know how you came by your injuries?"

Wolf ran his tongue over dry lips. Kut, he started to say but stopped before the word emerged. Before Kut, before the yurt, there'd been something else— something dark and terrible.

Liisi held a glass to his lips, and he raised his head enough to swallow the slightly tart liquid. The effort exhausted him.

"I've kept her out of your room," Liisi said as she set down the glass.

Her?

As if he'd spoken aloud, Liisi answered. "Cecelia. Her scars are not as deep as yours and will improve with time."

"Scars?" he managed to ask, unsure what Cecelia had to do with Kut and the yurt.

Liisi sat once again on the chair beside his bed and took his left hand in hers. At the contact, strength seemed to flow into him. "Three weeks ago, on April seventeenth," she said, "you set off for San Francisco to sail for Russia. Early on the morning of the eighteenth, an earthquake struck. Many died in the quake and the fire that burned most of the city." She paused, watching him.

San Francisco. The Palace Hotel. Cecelia's wedding reception. Like the Edison moving pictures he'd seen in New York, one scene after another flashed across his mind.

The woman having her baby in the ruins. Golden Gate Park. The beast. . . .

"I see by your face you've remembered," Liisi said, rising. "Now I can let Cecelia in."

No! Wolf wanted to call after her. No, I'm not ready. He remained silent, watching Liisi go out, leaving the door open. After a time Cecelia entered the room, closing the door behind her. She stood for a long moment looking at him, her green eyes glittering with tears.

For an instant, he saw those eyes set in the face of the great black beast that had attacked him and he recoiled. She winced and started to turn away.

Wondering if, when he looked at her, he'd always see the beast that was a part of her, Wolf, with a mighty effort, forced himself to whisper, "Stay."

Chapter 15

Wolf sat on the top rung of the corral fence, the September sun warm on his shoulders. Across the corral, Chung was training a new colt to the halter and Wolf watched wistfully.

He'd grown used to the black patch covering the scarred socket of his left eye, but the limited use of his right hand still troubled him. He flexed his stiff fingers—only the third was whole—and suppressed a sigh.

"You lucky you alive." Gei's voice, coming from behind him, made him start. Along with his physical injuries, he seemed to have lost his special warning sense.

He didn't want to talk to Gei. Or to anyone. He merely wished to be left alone—especially by Cecelia. He could scarcely bear to be in the same room with her.

He grunted a noncommittal response. How he felt was none of Gei's business.

Gei, wearing her Chinese tunic and trousers, climbed onto the fence and sat beside him. "Why you no like Cecelia?" she asked. "You be dead if she no save you."

Besides himself, no one but Liisi and Cecelia knew the truth. Or ever would. He didn't reply, hoping she'd go away.

"She sad," Gei persisted. "She cry."

Cecelia hadn't shifted again—not yet. Liisi had put

together an apparently successful binding charm for her, using the cat's head buckle. Because of a shifter's unusual healing power, the scars around Cecelia's mouth had already faded to faint lines. Her beauty was practically unmarred—she could resume her dancing career if she chose. Why did she stay on at Volek House, a place she once claimed she hated?

As if in answer, Gei said, "She try be nice to you. You mean to her."

Wolf gritted his teeth.

"Cecelia my friend," Gei went on. "She pretty woman. You no look pretty no more. She no care; she want to be your woman. Why you no let her?"

Wolf, fuming, turned to face Gei. "I'll ask *you* a few questions. Why do you avoid Chung? He's obviously smitten with you and he's a fine man. He's my friend. Why don't you like him?"

Gei pursed her mouth and started to climb down from the fence. Wolf clamped his left hand on her arm, holding her in place. "Chung thinks you despise him because you're from a higher caste. Is that the reason?"

Gei ducked her head to avoid looking at him. "My mother sell vegetables," she muttered.

"So did his parents." Wolf glanced at Chung, out of earshot at the far end of the corral. "Did he ever tell you how and why he came to Volek House?"

"No tell."

"My grandfather rescued him in San Francisco. From the police. It all started when Chung's parents refused to sell his sister to a wealthy Chinese merchant who wanted her for his—I guess the word is concubine. You understand?"

Gei drew in her breath and nodded.

"The merchant had his men abduct the girl and burn the parents' house. They were both killed. Twelve-year-old Chung escaped with his father's old pistol and tried to rescue his sister. He found and shot at the kidnappers. They shot back. One bullet killed his sister; another killed a bystander. A white man. The Chinese witnesses swore Chung had the only gun."

"Sister better off dead," Gei muttered.

"Grandfather didn't believe Chung should be strung up for a killing he might not be guilty of, so he brought him home to Volek House. For good. Chung doesn't dare ever return to San Francisco."

Gei raised her head and her dark eyes stared at Wolf. "You say true? He never go back there?" She seemed relieved, though he didn't understand why.

"I heard the story from my grandfather and from Chung." Wolf took a deep breath and let it out slowly. "Given the right circumstances, any man is capable of killing—I'm no exception. But there's a difference between me and a man who's a killer at heart. Whether Chung fired the fatal bullet or not, I don't think he's a killer."

Gei was silent a long time. "Women, they kill, too," she said at last, so softly he hardly made out her words.

Wolf, remembering the female stalker, nodded grimly. He released his grip on Gei's arm.

She touched the back of his hand with her long fingernails. "You, me, we make bargain. Me be nice to Chung. You be nice to Cecelia."

Wolf raised his eyebrows. He opened his mouth to refuse and paused. For months Chung had been gazing at Gei with a desperate longing that was painful to see. God knows he was indebted to Chung for his help on that dreadful night when Grandfather died. Yet how was he to rid himself of his bone-deep aversion to Cecelia?

"I'll try," he said reluctantly.

"Good. You make Cecelia happy." She gazed across the corral at Chung. "He strong man. Make good lover."

Wolf stared at her. She smiled. "You no sick no more. You go try." She patted his arm, climbed down from the fence inside the corral, and trotted across the dirt to where Chung worked with the colt.

As the sense of her words penetrated, Wolf shook his head in disbelief. Make love to Cecelia? To his shock, instead of revulsion, a perverse excitement flared inside him.

If you take Gei's advice, you've got less sense than Hawk had when he jumped off the barn roof, Wolf warned himself. At least Hawk thought his flying contraption would save him. You *know* it's not safe to get involved with Cecelia. Taking her to bed might trigger another shifting—who can tell?

But the possible danger fueled Wolf's excitement rather than cooling it. He slid down from the rail and walked slowly toward the house. Toward Cecelia.

He couldn't find her. Encountering Liisi near the tower stairs, he asked her if she'd seen Cecelia. His grandmother's silver gaze froze him where he stood.

"You've fought hard and long against the fate decreed for you," she said. "It was difficult for you to accept that a man born to become a shaman must yield or die. Only when faced with death did you choose shamanism. I'm thankful you didn't need another catastrophe to finally understand that Cecelia was the woman meant for you from the beginning."

"I'm not sure I believe that."

Liisi shrugged. "You do; I see it in your eyes. But before you're free to pursue her, you must agree to help me." She reached up and pressed the palm of her right hand onto his chest, over his heart. "You live because of my intervention. Is that the truth?"

Once again Wolf saw her shimmering silver shadow-soul hovering beside Gray Seal in the underground yurt, heard her demand that the old shaman reach once more into the cauldron, heard her insist that Wolf might not be of her blood but he was of her spirit.

"It is the truth," Wolf agreed.

Liisi took her hand from his chest and, with a flick of her head, directed him up the tower stairs. When they were safely shut inside her tower room she said, "At initiation, all shamans need both an animal and a human sponsor. At yours, a spirit wolf was the animal; I was the human. I have foreseen that in your time you will sponsor another of our line—one greater than either of us.''

"Who?"

Liisi half smiled. "Visions are never as clear as we'd like. For all I know this one of our blood or of our spirit may not yet be born. But be sure it will come to pass. At the moment, I need your help with another of us. With Jennifer.''

Wolf blinked. "I thought Samara had her under control."

"If you mean Samara prevents Jennifer from fire-starting, yes. The world is safe from Jennifer as long as she remains at Volek House and providing Samara's health holds up. Controlling the girl puts tremendous strain on Samara, though, and she can't go on much longer. At five the child is not yet old enough to be trusted to control herself. We need your help.''

He spread his hands. "How? I have no talent for control.''

"As a shaman, you can find the help you need in worlds other than this one. I dare not make another trip to the worlds below or above ours—I'm getting too old. You are younger and stronger and have a powerful spirit-animal to aid you when you reach your destination.''

Wolf gaped at her. "You want me to make a shaman's journey when I have no idea of how to go about it?''

Liisi's smile was pitiless. "I intend to teach you. To survive the journey you must remember every word I say—and I'll be imparting to you all the knowledge I've acquired in my lifetime. If you'd had the sense to agree to your fate earlier, you'd have less to learn all at once. The first lesson will be here and now.''

Hours later, Wolf descended the tower steps with his mind roiling in confusion, convinced he'd never master the lore he'd need to journey between the worlds.

I didn't want to become a shaman, he thought angrily. It was thrust on me.

He stomped down the stairs to the first floor, stopping abruptly when he heard the piano. Someone in the music room played the lively Spanish dance tune he remembered from those long-ago days when he was young and entranced by the grace and beauty of a green-eyed girl who despised him.

He was no longer the clumsy boy she'd called him. She was no longer an innocent young girl who yearned to be a great dancer.

Slowly, quietly, he entered the music room. Samara sat at the piano, her fingers dancing over the keys while Cecelia, dressed in a long, flowing black gown, twirled and pirouetted around the room. Little Jennifer McQuade watched from a red velvet settee near the archway.

Wolf slipped into the room and eased down beside Jennifer. He'd paid little attention to the child since that frantic night when she'd set fire to her parents' house and all but killed her twin sister. Lily had survived but was scarred for life.

Jennifer glanced at him and then ducked her head, reminding him of the way Gei sought not to be noticed. He wondered what she made of all that had happened. Did she blame herself, as her mother blamed her? Deliberately, he put his arm around Jennifer's shoulders and gave her a hug. Jennifer stiffened at first, then gradually relaxed until she leaned against him. The feel of her tiny, fragile bones under his hand moved him. How helpless she was.

He felt that Jennifer's spirit might be as badly scarred as her twin's skin. If he could help her, he would.

Since he couldn't bear to watch Cecelia dance, not yet, he closed his eye. In the darkness, his tenuous bond with Samara enabled him to sense how taut and driven she was. He sighed, aware that he was the only one who could help both her and Jennifer.

Throughout his convalescence, he'd kept the vision of traveling to Russia at the back of his mind, telling himself that someday . . .

He knew now he'd never make that trip, knew he

must pass on the need to go to Arno and Ivan. They, not he, were the ones who'd fulfill Sergei's last request.

His only traveling would be between the worlds. Was it remotely possible his shaman journey might offer a clue as to why there were Volek shifters? Wolf shook his head, doubting that he'd dare to take enough time to investigate. From the little he'd already learned from Liisi, it was clear that journeys to the upper or lower worlds were so perilous the smallest error meant death. He not only had the dangers of the journey to overcome, but he must also master every nuance of shamanism in order to know how to bring back help for Jennifer.

"Cousin Wolf," Jennifer whispered, poking him with her elbow. "Wake up. She's looking at you."

He opened his eye, belatedly aware Samara was now playing a waltz. Cecelia, standing in front of him, swayed to its rhythm, her green gaze fixed on him. When their eyes met, she held out her arms in a mute invitation to dance.

Wolf, feeling as awkward as he'd been at sixteen, stumbled to his feet, drawn to her by his mounting desire to hold her in his arms. When he touched Cecelia's hand, her skin felt clammy and a chill ran along his spine.

Cold as death.

He'd danced with the Miwok men in hunting ceremonies, but he'd never mastered the intricate steps of a waltz. With Cecelia guiding him, Wolf discovered he could follow the cadence of the piano as easily as he'd followed the beating of a drum. Waltzing with a woman in his arms, though, was not the same as dancing around an open fire with Miwok hunters. And waltzing with this particular woman was like nothing else in any world.

She smelled of secret night-blooming flowers, exotic and lush. Strands of her dark hair floated up to touch his lips and cling caressingly. Her supple body, moving under his maimed hand, pressed lightly, insistently, against his. He felt invaded by her. Surrounded. And aroused beyond all reason.

He whirled her through the archway and across the foyer to the foot of the staircase. With one arm still around her, he held her away, searching her face.

Her eyes, now cloudy as jade, revealed nothing, but he felt her tense. Grasping her hand, he urged her up the stairs. Did she come reluctantly? He wasn't sure. God knows he had reservations as well. But it was too late for either of them to turn back.

There was no tenderness in their lovemaking. By rights, so violent a coming together should have happened under the trees and in darkness rather than in his bed with sunlight pouring in through the open window. She was the night—she was darkness, wild and dangerous—and she met the fierceness of his taking with a feral passion that left him spent. When he regained enough strength to move, he raised on one elbow and looked down at her.

Cecelia smiled lazily, her half-closed eyes sated. For an instant Wolf recalled another time of passion when the woman's eyes had suddenly changed from hazel to blazing green. He drew in his breath. He'd hoped that memory had been locked away permanently.

Cecelia's hair was black, not red. Whatever she was, she'd come to him openly, not taking the guise of another woman as the one in New York had done. Her fire had been natural, like the lightning, not the choking heat of hell-flames.

She reached up and touched his scarred face with the tips of her fingers. "I don't remember hurting you," she said softly, her eyes sad.

"Grandfather told me a shifter's beast never shares its memories with its human half."

She bit her lip. "It's hard for me to believe such a vicious animal is a part of me." Tears spilled down her cheeks. "I'd rather die than ever shift again."

Though he'd never expected to feel tenderness for Cecelia, it flooded through him with her words. He lowered his head and kissed her gently. She wasn't the beast who'd attacked him; she was Cecelia, and she feared that beast as much as he did.

"You're safe with me," he said, holding her close. It wasn't the truth; she'd never be safe again and they both knew it, but saying the words comforted him. When she sighed and snuggled even closer, he understood he'd reassured her as well.

We'll get married, he told himself. Cecelia will be my wife. But we'll have no children. Hawk was my last mistake.

In March of 1908, Nicholas was born to Wolf and Cecelia Volek.

"At least he's not a shifter," Wolf said as he cradled his newborn son in his arms after the doctor had left.

Cecelia sighed in relief. "I took Liisi's potions faithfully," she said. "I don't know why they failed—but now that you've told me our son won't suffer my affliction, I'm glad we have him."

In 1910, in January, the Wolf Month of the Kamchadals, Reynolds was born to Wolf and Cecelia Volek after a long and difficult labor.

"I stopped taking the potions because I thought I was too old to have any more babies," Cecelia said, exhausted by her travail.

"You *are* too old," Wolf told her. "You damn near died bearing this one." He nodded at the child nestled at her breast. Glancing around to make certain they were alone, he knelt beside the bed and took her hand. "And I'm afraid our luck ran out."

Cecelia winced and briefly closed her eyes. "Is he—?"

"Yes."

Later that morning, Wolf took Hawk for a walk through the woods. At thirteen, Hawk showed promise of being taller than his father. His Miwok and Kamchadal blood showed in his brown skin, straight black hair, and slightly slanted obsidian eyes. But his eager enthusiasm was all his own.

"Maybe you can convince Ivan and Arno, Papa," Hawk said as they left the house. "If they bought an aeroplane, it really would be a faster trip between here and San Francisco. It'd be easy to make an airstrip in one of the fields and—"

"Everyone's not as interested in flying as you are," Wolf put in. "Some people insist that if God had intended man to fly, we'd have been born with wings."

Hawk's scowl showed what he thought of that. "Ivan said he and Arno decided to buy stock in a new plant being built to make aeroplanes," he went on. "If we're investing money in them, why not own one?"

Wolf smiled at him. "Have patience. Sooner or later we will."

Hawk sighed. "It's hard to wait. Baby Reynolds will probably be practically grown by the time Ivan and Arno make up their minds. Why don't *you* buy an aeroplane, Papa?"

"What do you think of your new brother?" Wolf asked instead of answering the question.

"I'm glad he's a boy instead of a girl. But babies sure can't do much. Nick's almost two and he's still in diapers. I'll be an old man before they can go camping with me."

Wolf chuckled, pleasantly distracted by Hawk's impatience. He ruffled his son's hair. "If Arno and Ivan don't buy an aeroplane in the next five years, I promise I will."

"Five years!" All during their hike across the hills to the pine grove, Hawk bombarded his father with air records set by various pilots in different countries and the merits of one type of aeroplane compared to another.

Wolf listened with half an ear, his mind reverting to why he'd brought Hawk on this walk. The boy seemed so young, but in truth he was older than Wolf himself had been when Sergei told him about his Volek heritage.

As soon as they stepped under the trees, Wolf held

up a hand. "No more talking until I make certain no one else is anywhere near us."

Hawk's eyes widened and he instantly fell silent. When Wolf was sure they wouldn't be overheard, he sat under one of the big pines, motioning Hawk to sit next to him.

"You're a Volek, son," he began. "You're one of the lucky Voleks, like Leo and Nick. Quincy and Reynolds are not so fortunate. You're old enough to understand that what I'm going to tell you is not to be repeated to anyone outside the family. Not anyone at all. And within the family, not to any of the children younger than you."

Staring wide-eyed at Wolf, Hawk nodded. His eyes grew wider yet and his mouth dropped open as Wolf repeated the Volek legend handed down from father to son over the centuries, finishing with the history of the American Voleks and how two of the family shifters had died.

"I knew we were different," Hawk said after a moment. "I mean, other kids get to go to school in town or to boarding school. But shapeshifting! I guess I understand about shifters—but where do stalkers come from?"

Wolf shrugged. "I wish I knew. It was one of things I hoped to learn by making a trip to Russia. Maybe one day you'll go there in my place and discover why the Voleks breed shapeshifters and for what purpose." He looked blankly at Hawk, seeing instead the dying Sergei. "There must be a reason."

"Ivan said he and Arno were going to Russia sometime."

"I hope so. One of the Voleks must trace our roots back to the forests where our ancestors came from."

"I will, Papa. Maybe by the time I'm old enough to go they'll have aeroplanes that can fly all the way from California to Russia without stopping."

"Maybe. But in the meantime, remember what I said about shifters. Quincy and Leo are twelve, so it may be six years before Quincy shifts for the first time—or it may be only one. I'm leaving it up to Arno to explain the Volek problem to the twins, because Arno can prepare Quincy better than I can. As for your brother, Reynolds, he has many years ahead of him to enjoy before—'' Wolf broke off, shaking his head.

''Doesn't Arno ever change into a beast anymore?''

''No. Grandmother Liisi showed him how to control his shifting. She'll do the same for Quincy when he needs to learn.''

Hawk pondered this for a while. ''What does it feel like to turn into a beast?'' he asked.

''My grandfather, who was a shifter, told me it was the most horrible thing that could ever happen to a man.''

Hawk made a face. ''I guess I wouldn't like it then. Besides, a man could never be a pilot if he was a shifter, 'cause what if he changed while he was up in the air? A beast couldn't fly the plane and it'd crash.'' His eyes widened. ''Is that why Arno doesn't want to fly?''

''Could be.''

''You explained about shifters, but what about Jennifer? She isn't a shapeshifter, is she?''

''No.''

''Okay, but there's something wrong with her, isn't there? Otherwise, she'd have lessons at our schoolhouse with me and the twins and Melanie. And why does she live with us when she's got a mother and father? Her twin sister lives with them—why doesn't she?''

Wolf told him.

''Did that happen to her because she's a Volek?'' Hawk demanded.

''Grandmother Liisi and I both think so. Just because a Volek is lucky enough not to be a shifter doesn't mean he or she can't pass that trait on to their children. My grandfather never mentioned fire-starting in the Volek line, so either Jennifer's the first or—'' he hesitated, then decided Hawk must face up to the worst ''—or the first to survive. If any were born in the past, they might have died young.

''Think about it. Think how dangerous a baby fire-starter would be. Nick, for example. You've seen him fly into a tantrum when he gets upset. What if he started a fire instead? Burned the people he was angry with? If a baby fire-starter can't be controlled, he or she would have to be killed for the safety of everyone else.''

Hawk swallowed ''Who controls Jennifer?''

''Samara. It's an ability she has.'' Wolf didn't mention how he'd tried to make a shaman's journey to bring back help for Jennifer and failed. Hawk had enough to digest without knowing his father and his grandmother Liisi were shamans.

Now that Reynolds had been born, as soon as Cecelia regained her strength, Wolf would be making the journey again. Or trying to. Which was one of the reasons he'd told Hawk about his heritage.

''Remember, son,'' he said, ''if anything happens to me, you must watch over your two little brothers. Especially Reynolds. And don't forget what I said about Russia.''

''I won't forget, Papa. But you're not awfully old—you'll live for a long time yet. Won't you?''

Hawk looked so anxious that Wolf smiled reassuringly as he rose. ''I'll do my best.''

Hawk got to his feet slowly, his expression troubled. ''You said Samara has an ability. And Druse has got one 'cause she's a healer. Grandmother Liisi foresees things. Quincy and Reynolds are going to turn into shifters. How about Leo? And Melanie? And Nick? How about me?''

Because he didn't want to get into the problem of Melanie—he hadn't told Hawk her father was a stalker—Wolf spoke lightly. ''You were born to be a flyer. Your mother must have known that when she named you. I like to think aeroplanes were invented just so you could fly when you got old enough.''

Hawk's face lighted up. ''I'm going to!'' he cried.

"I will. And in case Leo and Nick don't have any abilities, I'll teach them to be pilots, too." He frowned. "Maybe even Melanie. Girls can learn to fly, can't they?"

"As far as I'm concerned, they can."

Together they walked deeper into the woods, the soughing of the wind in the pine boughs relaxing Wolf as it always did. The woods and Hawk's cheerful company made him forget for the moment that not only was he guilty of adding another Volek to the clan, and a shifter at that, but that he was forty-eight years old and no nearer to discovering the reason for Volek shifters than he had been at thirteen.

Chapter 16

Wolf could no longer feel the deerskin of his shaman drum under his fingers, but he heard the beat, alternating with the throb of Liisi's drum. He'd made the drum under her guidance from the skin of a buck stretched over a wooden frame formed from the wood of a lightning-struck tree. He'd killed the mule deer himself, and Bear Claw, the Miwok medicine man, had overseen the tanning of the hide.

Wolf had painted his chosen symbols around the sides—symbols only he knew the meaning of. The tin cross hanging from the drum had been Morning Quail's, given to her by her dead shifter husband who'd had it fastened around his neck when the Miwoks found him as a newborn. Grandfather had recognized the cross as one he'd given to a Californio woman as a token of love. Now the cross belonged to Wolf—a remembrance of his grandfather that Liisi told him was his amulet from a friend.

Hanging from the drum's other side was the shriveled, mummified little finger of the female stalker. Unnoticed by anyone, Liisi had cut the finger off the dead body and preserved it.

"Your amulet from an enemy," she'd called it when she gave the grisly relic to Wolf.

The beat of his drum followed his *haamu* through the shadow-hole and into the darkness between the worlds; he'd ride the beat to his destination. Behind him stretched the silver cord tethering his shadow-soul to his living body: a body that would remain in Liisi's tower room until his *haamu* returned to animate it once more.

His destination was Tuonela, realm of the dead. He used the Finnish name because it described the nether world better than the English word hell. His first journey there had failed when the maiden of Tuoni refused to ferry him across the River of the Dead because he misspoke the crossing charm.

This time he'd cross Tuonela's river on his own.

Liisi had warned him no two shamans experienced the realm of the dead in the same way. To Wolf it was cavernous and gloomy, lit by too few ill-burning torches. Monstrous shadows lurked in rocky recesses ready to pounce on the unwary.

When he came upon the black, foul-smelling river, he began to chant a snake spell under his breath. While in his body he was unable to shift his shape, but a shaman's *haamu* had powers beyond the body. And so his shadow-soul flowed and lengthened, changing into a powerful water snake. As the snake, he plunged into the icy water of the river and began swimming to the far side.

Other snakes glided closed to him, hissing, "Stranger, where do you go?"

He knew better than to answer. In Tuonela, you replied to no questions, ate no food nor drank any liquids if you wished to ever leave again.

A bright red snake with green eyes struck at him with poisonous fangs, but the fangs grated on metal instead of penetrating his *haamu* and the venom dissipated in the water, burning along his scales without seriously poisoning him. Grandfather's tin cross, he knew, had saved him.

"This is the time of *Kekri*," the red snake hissed before gliding away.

Kekri, the time of sacrifice at the end of October.

In the middle world it was not October but the end of January, with a gray tule fog blanketing Volek

House. Tuonela, though, was not ruled by the middle world's time, weather, or customs.

A boat glided near him, and Wolf slid deeper into the murky waters as the daughter of death struck at him with an oar. He was obviously not a welcome visitor.

"Kekritar," she called to him, her voice mocking.

Sacrifice? Not him! They'd have to find some soul more willing. Or one unable to fight.

He reached the other side of Tuonela's river and slithered onto the rocky bank. One word of power was all it took to shed the snake-shape.

"Find Tuoni's inner chambers," Liisi had told him, "but avoid Death himself. In his chambers will be the charm against fire-starting. It's up to you to recognize what you need and to bring it back."

Wolf turned away from the river and scanned the three shadowy caverns before him. He bent, picked up three stones, and said a separate spell over each. Because the middle stone glowed for a moment, he chose the middle cavern. Just inside its entrance, a warty gray frog the size of an elephant materialized to block his way.

"Stranger, you cannot pass," the frog croaked.

"I am no stranger for I have faced death before," he said.

The frog flicked out its long, sticky tongue at him, but Wolf leaped aside, tossing the middle stone onto the tongue. The frog swallowed the stone and disappeared in a flash of flame. Wolf passed into the cavern and entered a tunnel. Soon the dank gray walls changed to shiny black obsidian, reflecting and enhancing the meager light. Grotesque birchbark masks hung along the walls, grinning evilly.

"Kekritar," they whispered as he passed.

The light ahead grew redder, the air warmer. The tunnel ended in an arch whose opening was obscured by a crimson mist. Feeling a warning tingle at the base of his spine, Wolf stopped short of the mist, aware it could kill. After a moment's thought, he began to whistle.

Long and long he whistled, coaxing, until at last a wild ocean wind from the chill waters of the Baltic Sea blasted through the tunnel and blew away the toxic mist. Wolf passed under the arch and into a vast chamber. Before he had a chance to notice anything more than a large iron chest with its lid open, two giant archers sprang at him, arrows nocked and ready.

He flung his two remaining stones into the air, one to either side; the archers loosed their missiles, and the arrows flew after the stones, piercing them. Laden with the stones, the arrows reversed their flight and buried themselves in the archers' breasts. Arrows, archers, and stones dissolved into a red mist that disappeared.

Wolf surveyed the chamber and tensed. He relaxed slightly when he realized what he'd at first taken for scores of men and women were merely statues. He circled the room, studying them. Some were metal— gold, silver, copper, iron. Others were of stone—jade, crystal, turquoise, obsidian. There were wooden statues, too—mahogany, ash, oak, pine. One, a woman's, was a smoky red, of some substance he couldn't identify. Her emerald eyes seemed to follow him as he walked past, making him uneasy. Though she didn't move, menace pulsated from her.

Each statue held an offering in an outstretched hand. One of these offerings, Wolf sensed, was the charm he sought for Jennifer. And he feared he knew which statue held the charm he needed—the malevolent one with the emerald eyes.

"You are right." Her words crawled into his ears like garden slugs. "Come and take what you want—if you dare."

Wolf approached her warily. Her fingers were curled around the tiny ruby salamander in her left hand in such a way that it was impossible to reach the charm without touching her. To touch her courted death.

"You fear me rightly, Sergei Volek's grandson," she

said, "for I am your enemy. Our paths have crossed before—do you not remember?"

Red and green. The venomous snake in the river.

"And before that." Her voice left a slime trail in his head.

Red hair, green eyes. . . .

Her laugh rang through the chamber, echoing from the walls until the entire room shuddered with mocking laughter.

"The woman was my daughter," she told him. "Her body took your seed, but I was the one you coupled with."

Her daughter Willa, of the honey-colored hair and hazel eyes, had been as much a victim as he, just as Wolf had thought at the time. Who was this hellspawned woman? Without a doubt she was dead, for no life cord trailed from the statue. If it was a statue.

Liisi had prepared him for every peril she could conceive he might encounter, but because he'd never told her about the seance in New York, nothing she'd taught him was of any use in outfacing this evil spirit. He was on his own. Unfortunately, he didn't have the slightest idea what to do.

Still, he was damned if he'd made this abominable journey merely to give up when success was within his grasp. This time he was determined not to return to Volek House empty-handed.

"Shall we embrace once more?" she asked lasciviously, suddenly opening her arms wide and reaching for him.

Making up his mind quickly, Wolf drew his lips back to show his teeth and a took a step toward her.

She faltered for a moment, obviously taken aback. Wolf, who'd been hoping to surprise her, snatched the ruby salamander from her hand and whirled to flee only to be held back by her grip on his little finger. As he struggled to free himself, fiery pain shot along his hand and coiled inside him, draining his power.

When he finally yanked his hand away, she gave a

shout of triumph. "I have your finger! You're mine forever."

Since it felt as though his little finger had been jerked from its socket, he believed her. His heart sank. A shaman was doomed to stay in the nether world if he left anything of himself there. Wolf glanced at his hand as he fled. Seeing his finger still attached, he belatedly understood the finger she crowed over was the stalker's. His enemy amulet.

Almost immediately she realized she'd been tricked, and her heavy tread thudded behind him. A quick look over his shoulder showed her gaining. She'd be on him before he reached the arch, and once she caught him he was doomed. The iron chest loomed before him, lid raised, inside nothing but darkness.

Liisi had told him shadow-holes existed in all the worlds, warning that unlike the holes created by a shaman drum, these could be dangerous, leading into the past lives of those who dropped through them. Did the chest contain a shadow-hole? If so, it offered escape. Into what, he had no way of knowing.

Since he had no choice, Wolf leaped into the iron chest. As he dropped into oblivion, he heard the lid clang shut.

When he came to awareness, he found he'd catapulated into his worst nightmare. He was a child again, his naked body emaciated and chilled as he huddled in the Kamchadal animal pen, a pit dug deep into the earth with wooden bars set close together, rising six feet up from ground level. There was no way for him to escape. He had nothing but the ruby salamander clutched tightly in one maimed hand.

"No!" he howled in anguish. The word emerged in a weak, high-pitched whine.

No matter that the knowledge of his forty-eight years lay within his head, his starved child's body had no strength, no powers. He was helpless.

A raven flapped down and perched on a spindly alder sapling, cocked its head to look at him and cawed mockingly. *Kekritar, kekritar,* the raven seemed to say,

making Wolf realize that's exactly what he was—a sacrifice. A sacrifice to the superstitious ways of his people.

And this time there'd be no Grandfather to rescue
him.

Despairing, he began to cry.

Fool! Liisi's voice echoed in his mind. *You are still
a shaman, no matter what body you wear.*

Wolf's tears ceased as he realized the truth in her
words. He closed his eye and sought to find his inner
center where no cold or hunger existed. But barks and
howls of approaching dogs distracted him. The noise
of the dogs meant the men were returning to the village from the hunt.

Men who believed he was a wolf in human form.
Men who'd throw stones to torment him, laughing
when he tried to dodge. How he wished he really was
a wolf.

"I am here." The voice was in his head. Whose?

A vision of a gigantic gray wolf appeared before
him. His spirit-brother!

"Help me," he answered in his squeaky child's
voice. "Help me, brother wolf."

The vision took on solidity and became a huge gray
wolf beside him in the pen.

"Climb on my back, brother," the wolf said.

He scrambled to obey. Placing the salamander between his teeth, he dug his fingers into the wolf's fur
as his spirit-brother, with a mighty leap from the pit,
cleared the bars of the pen, raced through the village
and into a sparse stand of spruce. There they stopped.
Spirit-brother looked up, so Wolf did, too. High on
the trunk of a tree, a drum hung on a snag.

A shaman's drum, Wolf knew. Gray Seal's drum,
hung there by the Kamchadals when he died to keep
his soul from returning to the village as a malevolent
ghost. Still on the wolf's back, he removed the salamander from his mouth and held up his arms.

"Blood calls to blood," he chanted. "Gray Seal is
not dead; he cannot die while his blood runs in my

veins. By blood his drum is mine, by right his drum is mine. Blood claim, drum claim. Mine.''

The tree shook violently, tossing the drum off the snag. It fell end over end and landed in Wolf's outstretched arms. The sealskin cover was torn, but when he held the drum to his spirit-brother's mouth, one lick of the wolf's tongue and the cover became whole once more.

Sliding to the ground, he placed the drum on the frozen earth and, crouching, began to thrum it with his good hand, intoning the shaman's chant for home-going while his spirit-brother howled an eerie accompaniment.

When the earth opened beneath him, Wolf was no more aware of falling into the hole than he was of the excited cries of men and the warning barks of dogs as they neared the spruce grove.

He was no longer part of their world.

Wolf opened his eye to find Liisi bending over him in the tower room.

''You've been gone two days,'' she said.

Wordlessly he opened his maimed hand. The ruby salamander gleamed in the lamplight. Liisi plucked it from his hand, closed her eyes, and pressed it against her forehead.

He sat up, watching her, his stomach rumbling with hunger.

''Yes,'' she said finally. ''Yes, this fire lizard is what we need.''

Until then, he hadn't realized he was holding his breath.

Liisi brought him a peeled orange, a chunk of cheese, several slices of bread, and a glass of pale yellow liquid he knew contained one of her tonics. When he finished the meal, he got to his feet.

''Did Sergei have an enemy—a woman with red hair and green eyes?'' he asked.

Liisi frowned. ''Why do you ask?''

''Because I had to take the ruby salamander from her and she damn near killed me.''

''She's a witch.'' Liisi spat the words out.

"I agree. She may be dead, but she's sure as hell still a witch."

"She had a daughter." Liisi spoke reluctantly. "Sergei's daughter. Not by his choice."

"Oh my God."

Liisi's silver eyes bored into his. "So you've met the daughter. Where?"

Wolf told her, confessing what had happened. "Not by *my* choice either," he finished.

Liisi sighed. "I wish you'd told me sooner."

He nodded. Keeping it a secret had nearly cost him his life.

"What does she expect to gain by forcing her daughter to bear your child?" Liisi demanded.

Wolf had no answer. Until this moment, he hadn't allowed himself to think there might be a baby. Now he was as sure as Liisi that there was one, but he had no clue as to why the witch would want such a child to be born.

"I don't doubt we'll find out someday," Liisi said. "A witch makes a resourceful enemy. Keep that in mind, Wolf, because I won't live forever."

He took her hand. "I'm not capable of replacing you."

"No one is asking you to," she said tartly. "You're a shaman, that much is true, but you're no *noita*. When I die, someone will come, either a man or a woman. That person will be a Finn, like me. You must convince the others to accept whoever it is because the Voleks will be his or her family to look after, as I have."

"You've made such an arrangement?"

"Not in writing, not on the telephone. But you can be sure the chosen one will know when I'm dying and will be here for my funeral." She drew her hand away from his and touched his scarred cheek. "Because you made the journey, Jennifer has the chance to lead a more normal life. Thank God you're a resourceful survivor like your grandfather."

Once Liisi used the salamander to create a lasting

control charm for Jennifer, Samara was released from responsibility and Wolf felt he'd done his duty. He'd earned the right to relax and enjoy his baby sons.

In 1915, he took all the children to the Panama-Pacific International Exposition in San Francisco—the city celebration of the opening of the Panama Canal. The exposition was a fantasia of color and light and exotic sights: the Tower of Jewels, the Court of the Seasons, the Court of Flowers, and the statues of the Rising and the Setting Sun.

Hawk, at eighteen, was hardly a child. He soon discovered the exposition offered aeroplane rides, and after his first flight over the city, he could think and talk of nothing else. He found a pilot willing to teach him to fly and lost no time reminding Wolf of his promise to buy an aeroplane.

By the end of the year, Hawk had made his first solo flight and had overseen the construction of a landing field, complete with hangar and windsock, outside the gates of Volek House. He flew Ivan to San Francisco in early May of the following year, returning the same afternoon.

Wolf watched the aeroplane swoop over the field and circle to land into the wind, torn between pride in his son and the fear that one of these days that damn contraption of wood and metal was going to come crashing down, just as Hawk's childhood flying invention had done. Hawk had survived the fall from the barn roof, but if the aeroplane failed, he sure as hell wouldn't live to walk away.

The aeroplane settled onto the ground and bumped toward the hangar where Wolf waited. It stopped; Hawk climbed out and leaped to the ground. Wolf trotted over to him.

Hawk grinned as he came up. "She flew like a dream," he said. "Ivan was impressed."

Wolf helped him push the machine into the hangar. As they walked toward the house, Hawk said, "In the city, everyone's talking about the war in Europe. Before I took off to fly home, I listened to a couple of pilots discussing how the side with the most and the best aeroplanes is going to win. Seems to me they're right."

Wolf listened to him list the reasons why and nodded, thinking that in '98 aeroplanes might have made a difference in Cuba.

"The pilots think the French Nieuports outfly the German Fokkers and are superior in every way to our Curtiss JN-2's," Hawk went on. "The Jennies are the ones the U.S. Army used in Mexico against Pancho Villa." He glanced at his father. "I'd sure like to get in the cockpit of a Nieuport and try her out."

"I promised to buy one aeroplane," Wolf said, "not a squadron."

"You couldn't buy a Nieuport anyway. The French Army gets them all for the Lafayette Escadrille." Hawk's eyes took on a faraway look that unsettled Wolf.

America wasn't involved in the European war, and President Wilson had once promised they wouldn't be. But look what had happened since. First there'd been the German U-boat attacking and sinking the British liner *Lusitania* off the Irish coast, killing over a hundred Americans. Later came the news that German saboteurs were active in the United States itself—that explosion in the Du Pont powder plant in Delaware was one example. Most ominous was Wilson's recommendations to Congress to increase the standing army.

All in all, it looked to Wolf as though America would be drawn into the war pretty damn soon. Flying was risky enough as far as he was concerned—he hated to think of Hawk not only aloft in a flimsy aeroplane but being shot at by the enemy besides. He told Hawk so.

"With luck the war will end before we get into it," he added.

Hawk didn't reply.

A month later he left in the night and, the next Wolf heard, had joined the Escadrille Americaine, attached to the Lafayette Escadrille. By the end of June, Hawk was in Verdun, France. Wolf could only hope Nieuports *were* superior to Fokkers.

In April of the following year, President Wilson asked Congress for a declaration of war against Germany. Two days after the declaration, Ivan and Arno took Wolf into the study.

"We're going to enlist," Arno said.

Wolf stared at them, aghast. "But you're forty-one years old! The army wants younger men—like the President told Teddy Roosevelt when he asked permission to raise a volunteer company the way he did in '98. Besides, Arno, you're a shifter. Don't you remember your father's warning that battle triggers the bloodlust?"

Arno nodded. "I won't risk it because I won't be fighting. I plan to volunteer for the Ambulance Corps."

"We've contributed generously to political candidates' campaigns," Ivan put in. "Some of the men are in Congress now. I doubt that I'll have any trouble getting an Army commission, forty-one or not."

"How about McDee Enterprises?" Wolf protested. "I'm no businessman."

"We've hired capable executives." Arno smiled at Wolf. "And you know our mother usually makes most of the major decisions anyway. Is Liisi ever wrong?"

Wolf sighed, defeated. "I know why Hawk went to war—his craze for flying drove him. But I don't understand why you're doing this."

"For the same reason you charged up San Juan Hill with the Rough Riders in '98," Ivan said. "It's our country and we mean to fight for it, each in our own way."

Arno's golden eyes held Wolf's. "You've had your share of excitement," he said, "while Ivan and I have stayed home and been good boys all our lives. Don't you think we deserve at least one great adventure?"

Chapter 17

Near dawn on September 12, 1918, Captain Ivan Volek glanced at the gray skies, sneezing as he cursed the rain. With visibility so poor, the landmark rise of Montsec, the thousand or more foot butte the U.S. First Army had advanced toward for two days, was hidden. As he listened to the booming of the artillery, Ivan checked his watch. Almost time.

The St. Mihiel salient was mostly rough and broken country, easy to lose your bearing in. Salient was a word he'd never used until he landed in France as a green first lieutenant. He'd soon learned, among other battle terminology, that it meant the projection of the army toward enemy lines. This salient was particularly nasty in wet weather, when the low spots became mucky swamps, difficult to cross and breeding squadrons of mosquitos.

Ivan knew General Pershing was determined that this all-American offensive would succeed, not only to push the Boche back into Germany, but to justify Blackjack's insistence that U.S. troops be allowed to go into battle as a unit. Up until now they'd been spread among the other armies.

As soon as they pushed on this morning, Blackjack promised air cover—French and British as well as American. Ivan wondered if Hawk would be up there—the kid was already an ace, racking up six victories over the Hun, the last he'd heard. He was proud of Hawk, but he didn't envy him. While it was true there was no mud, mosquitos, or poison gas up in the air, Ivan preferred keeping both feet on the ground.

Another glance at his watch brought him to full attention. Five-thirty. Time to jump, thank God. Waiting while listening to that buster of artillery fire was worse than fighting.

In the gray dawn, in the seconds before he led his men from the trenches, a surge of fear mixed with anticipation flooded through him. Would he live to see another dawn? His unit advanced along what he'd been told was the southern face of the salient, through mud and barbed wire. Enemy rifle fire was sporadic, and he didn't see a single live target. He was beginning to wonder if the Boche had retreated when the crack of rifles increased, accompanied by the tac-tac-tac of a machine gun. They'd reached the enemy's front line.

Unlike Belleau Wood, where the Germans had fought doggedly, refusing to give an inch, enemy soldiers began pouring out of their trenches in swarms, hands in the air.

By evening, Ivan's division had captured three wartorn villages and mopped up most of the remaining pockets of resistance with a minimum of casualties. As they bivouacked for the night, Ivan, sneezing, his throat raw, head throbbing, told himself he'd feel better in the morning.

An explosion woke him from feverish dreams. He sprang to his feet, head swimming. "What is it?" he demanded.

"Damn Boche tossed a fucking potato masher into camp, sir," Sergeant Prater told him. "Sentry nailed him, but the grenade got a couple of the men. They need help bad."

Ivan took one glance at the mangled soldiers and nodded. The nearest advanced dressing station was over a mile away, in a hamlet near Thiancourt, one of the captured villages. "Get a truck started," he ordered, "I'll drive them over."

"Begging the captain's pardon," Sergeant Prater said, "but you look like hell. Sir."

Ivan nodded. He felt like hell. "Maybe the medics can fix me up while they're at it."

"In that case, sir, I'll get the truck."

The two men were loaded into the back of the truck with a young corporal to watch over them. Or, more likely, Ivan decided, to keep an eye on him—no doubt on the sergeant's orders. Prater was a good man.

By the time he reached the dressing station, Ivan was glad the corporal was along because he wasn't too sure he'd be able to drive the truck back. The injured soldiers were unloaded and carried into the church, one of the few buildings still standing in the tiny village. Ivan slumped into a pew and waited to speak to the harried doctor.

"You've got influenza," the doctor said when he finally got around to taking a look at Ivan. "Better stay here—you won't be any use to your unit for a week or so. I'll give you a couple of aspirin for the fever—not much else we can do for the flu."

The corporal drove off, leaving Ivan wrapped in a blanket and stretched out on one of the pews, alternately shivering and burning up with fever.

We look alike, Arno and I, but we're not, he thought. If I was Arno, I wouldn't be sick. Shifters throw off illness as easily as a lady shrugs off her evening cape at the opera. Shifters heal faster than anyone else besides being able to influence men and attract women. No one ever sees me first or talks to me first—it's always Arno. I love him, he's my twin, but sometimes I wish I'd been the shifter.

How is he? I haven't heard from him since I landed in France. We've never been apart this long in all our lives. God how I miss him. . . .

He walked through a forest of burned and broken trees, trees destroyed by war. Dead men lay rotting among the ruined trees and Ivan paused by each, fearing to see a familiar face. He found no one he knew. The dead grew fewer and then there were none, but the blackened trees went on and on.

No birds sang, no squirrels leaped, chattering, from

*tree to tree. This was a silent woods, a dead woods.
War had killed it. Men had killed it. What did trees
matter when there were kingdoms to be won?*

*He was lost in the dead forest and he knew there
was no way out, that he was doomed to wander through
the shattered trees forever.*

*His destiny was the forest's destiny—unless he could
bring life back to the forest, he was doomed. There
was a way he could save himself and the trees as well,
but he couldn't do it without Arno. He needed his twin.*

"Arno!" he called. "Arno, where are you?"

No one answered.

He must find his brother. Now. . . .

Ivan struggled to his feet, almost falling as they tangled in the blanket. Stumbling, lurching, he staggered past the altar and through the door behind the nave into the dark and rainy night.

Griselda Dachen rose from the cot where she'd tried unsuccessfully to sleep and walked through the darkness to the table that contained one of the few possessions from her past. Thank God her mother's stepsister had taught her the French tongue as a child, otherwise she might well be dead by now—a despised German in a country at war with Germans.

A hated Boche. She, who was only half-German. Her mother had been half-French, half-Gypsy, which accounted for Griselda's dark complexion and hair. Her eyes, though, were blue—a legacy from her despised father. She'd never gotten on well with him, and the situation grew worse after her mother died. She'd left home at sixteen and made her own way in the world.

She'd been doing quite well telling fortunes in one of the better Paris cafes when the war broke out. Unfortunately, she'd been using her own unmistakably German name—Dachen. The proprietor had all but thrown her out. She'd left the city, hoping to stay with her aunt, but the aunt had sailed to Montreal to live with friends in Canada until the war was over.

Griselda, abandoning her last name, had tried her

luck in small towns, making enough to get by. It hadn't been too bad until she was suddenly caught in the fighting. At the moment, it seemed impossible to escape from the war zone.

Sitting by the table in the darkness, she felt for the silk velvet cover of the crystal ball that had been her mother's—her most precious possession. It was after midnight; today was the thirteenth of September. Her birthday. Should she look?

Griselda smiled wryly. All day the big guns had boomed, men had died, armies had advanced and retreated. This village, in German hands yesterday morning, was now occupied by American soldiers. Who knew whether she'd be alive or dead by the time this new day was ended?

How ridiculous it seemed to scan the crystal ball to try to see the face of her true love.

"Each year on the morning of your birthday," her mother had told her when she was thirteen, "in the darkness before the sun rises, you must look into the crystal ball. Each year, until a man's face appears. This man will be your true love."

Her mother had died the following summer. Since then, Griselda had never missed a year. First from curiosity, later because it was a way to remember her mother. War or no war, why should she miss this year?

She lifted the silk cover from the crystal and gently caressed its cool roundness. Taking her hands away, she stared into the darkness toward the ball, unable to see even its outline in the pitch black. If this were like every other year, nothing would happen. She sighed. Twenty-seven years old, many men, but no true love.

Still, as the fighting today in and about what remained of the village reminded her, there were worse things in life than not finding one's true love.

A faint glow in the darkness startled her. For a moment she didn't realize it was the crystal, and when she did, she was wonderstruck. Though during the day she sometimes saw what was to come within the crystal, never before had it glowed in the dark.

A face swam hazily into view, a man's face—no, two men's faces—no, one. Griselda blinked, trying to clear her vision. A man's face. Dark wavy hair. Eyes the color of amber. Bold features. But the face kept blurring into two. Before fading entirely away, the eyes seemed to change, to grow feral, and then even the glow disappeared.

Shaken, she clutched the edge of the table. Her true love? Closing her eyes, she sought her inner center where peace always reigned. Finally calm, she covered the crystal and rose from the chair, only to grab onto its back as pain stabbed into her chest.

Hurts to breathe. Dizzy. Can't go on. Must. Where is he? Must find him. . . .

Griselda fought the feelings and thoughts pouring into her mind and her body. This hadn't happened to her in years, not since her mother lay dying and she'd suddenly felt every painful breath her mother took and knew how bitterly her mother resented being ill. It had been a terrible experience, one she never wanted to repeat.

Somehow she knew that this time it was a man who forced her to feel what he felt. Who was he? Where was he?

As if compelled by a power outside herself, Griselda groped her way toward the door and unbolted it, passed through a hall to a back door that hung askew. Leaving the safety of her room with soldiers nearby was dangerous, and she hesitated at the door before going on. A misty rain slicked the stone doorstep, cool under her bare feet.

The darkness outside wasn't quite as intense as that inside her room. Something lay sprawled in the mud near her door. A man. The one she'd felt in her mind?

Taking a deep breath, Griselda edged toward him and crouched to gingerly touch his head. Fiery hot. Feverish. He might die if she left him here. So many soldiers had died—what was one more? He was none of her concern.

"Mama, I'm sick," he mumbled.

She'd learned enough English to understand what he said, and his words disarmed her completely.

She shook his shoulder. "Get up," she ordered. "Up!"

"Can't."

"Yes, you can. I'll help you."

With agonizing slowness, he managed to push himself onto his hands and knees. Urging him along, half dragging him when he stopped crawling, Griselda hauled him into the room she'd taken over as hers, in a house left vacant by the fighting. He collapsed on the floor and she locked the door again.

Lighting her precious stub of a candle, she looked him over. A big man, bearded, wearing a wet and muddy captain's uniform. Kneeling, with great effort she rolled him onto his back and began undressing him. Whatever his sickness, wet clothes would surely make him worse. As she struggled to get his jacket off, he opened dazed eyes. She gasped and rocked back on her heels. Amber eyes.

Was he the man she'd seen in her crystal ball? With the beard covering much of his face she wasn't completely certain, but she thought it likely.

"You're sick," she told him.

"Flu," he mumbled as his eyes drooped shut.

She'd had the flu last month when the epidemic swept through the Lorraine Valley. She might have died of starvation if an old farm woman hadn't nursed her. Later the poor old lady had been killed when a mortar shell demolished her cottage.

His undergarments felt fairly dry so she left them on. Covering him with her extra blanket, she slid her one and only pillow under his head. The floor was no hospital bed, but she'd do the best she could for him. Griselda smiled wryly. For her true love. Such as he was.

When it grew light, she thought of going to the church and telling the medics at the dressing station that he was in her room. After consideration, she changed her mind. He needed rest and someone to dribble soup and fluids down his throat—she had nothing else to do but take care of him while the medics at the dressing station were understaffed and overworked. If she told them the captain was here, they'd insist on taking him away. She felt a certain proprietary interest in him.

Hadn't she seen him in the crystal ball? Hadn't she rescued him? So, she'd nurse him until he was well enough to return to war.

On the following day she learned his name was Ivan. By the third day he was lucid enough to remember her name. Four days later, he was able to sit up and feed himself, though still too weak to walk alone to the shattered room of the house that they used for a latrine.

Sickness didn't destroy his natural attractiveness nor his inherent cheerfulness and courtesy. Griselda quite liked him. In no way did he resemble her despised father, who'd also been a soldier. Still was one, as far as she knew, unless he'd died in the fighting.

When talking to each other, they spoke a mixture of English and French—his French on a par with her limited English.

"I've been a lot of trouble to you," he told her on the evening of the fifth day. "I've taken all your time, used up most of your food—"

"I'm glad to share. As for my time—" She shrugged. "In war, what is time?"

"Time given freely to another is always a gracious gift. I appreciate yours."

Griselda smiled. "I've no one else to donate my time to. Besides, who else could take care of you?"

"Tomorrow I'll be strong enough to find my unit and rustle up some supplies for you."

She shook her head. "You need a few more days to recuperate. And your unit is gone with the rest of the American soldiers. They moved out two days ago. Only a few French *poilus* remain to occupy the village."

Ivan surged to his feet. "Gone?" He started for the

door, staggered and leaned against the wall to keep from falling. He was surprised they'd left without him. On second thought, he realized why he hadn't been missed. Sergeant Prater must have believed he was with the medics, while the medics would think he'd rejoined his unit.

"See how weak you are?" Griselda scolded. "Come, rest."

"Where did the Americans go?" He slid down the wall until he sat on the floor.

"To the Argonne, is the rumor. And it is almost certainly true. You aren't yet strong enough to fight."

Ivan frowned. He'd been sure Pershing would drive on east toward Metz. Instead, he'd shifted his troops to the north. The Argonne terrain was far nastier than here, and the German fortifications there were formidable. It would be Belleau Wood all over again, only worse. Griselda was right: a man whose head spun every time he stood on his feet was in no shape to face the enemy. At the moment he couldn't even get to the Argonne, much less fight.

It was another week before he'd regained enough strength to feel confident he wouldn't collapse unexpectedly. By then, he'd come to realize Griselda was not only attractive but she was the woman he'd always wanted and never found. Most of the women he'd met preferred Arno, and he was damned if he'd settle for being second choice. He didn't exactly blame his twin—Arno couldn't help his attraction for women any more than he could help being a shifter—but he resented it.

"Don't you have anyone in France?" he asked Griselda on the evening before he planned to leave. The persistent cold rain kept them inside the house, but they'd gone into what had been the main living room of the house, lit a fire in the fireplace, and sat side by side on a blanket in a sheltered inglenook where the roof didn't leak too badly.

She shook her head. "No one."

"You've spoken of an aunt in Montreal," he persisted. "Are there no other relatives?"

"I have a father," she admitted. "If he still lives. I really don't care whether he's alive or dead." When he didn't immediately respond, she added, "I suppose you think that's heartless."

"*You're* not heartless."

"My father is. Have you ever read Nietzsche?"

"I recognize the name, but I'm no philosopher."

"My father loves to quote him. 'Man is created for war, and women for the pleasure of the warrior,' is one of his favorites." Her voice was laced with scorn.

Ivan, who'd been about to put an arm around her shoulders, held. "I, uh, can't say I agree," he mumbled.

"Oh, you're nothing like my father. Nothing at all. Otherwise I wouldn't have taken care of you."

"But how do you survive all alone in this war-torn countryside?"

Griselda slanted him a secret smile. "Among other things, I tell fortunes," she said. "Give me your hand; I'll tell yours."

Ivan held out his right hand; she took it and turned the palm up. Examining his palm in the firelight took her so much time he began to fidget. Close as she was, her woman's scent tantalized him. Didn't she realize how difficult it was to keep from pulling her into his arms and kissing her?

"I'm confused," she confessed. "Your lines all seem to be doubled."

Ivan chuckled. "You *are* good at fortunes. I have a twin."

Griselda's eyes widened. "Two of you." She spoke as though to herself. "Two. Ah, I see." She looked at him. "Where is your twin?"

"I wish I knew. Somewhere in France—Arno's in the Ambulance Corps." Damn it, he'd had enough of talk—he needed to hold her. Turning his hand so he grasped hers, he pulled her closer and kissed her.

Her lips were warm under his, her body soft when

he wrapped his arms around her. She didn't stiffen in his embrace or reject his kiss, but she didn't respond, either. For long moments, caught in his own desire, he paid no attention. Finally becoming aware of her lack of passion, he released her reluctantly.

Placing a hand to either side of her face, he looked into her eyes, their blue reflecting the fire's flames.

"I'm in love with you," he said softly.

"No. You want me, perhaps, but wanting isn't love."

"And you?"

"I like you." Her warm breath caressed his face. "I am not in love."

Ivan dropped his hands and took a deep breath, trying to conceal his disappointment. "I won't ask if you want me because I can tell you don't."

She shrugged. "I've never wanted a man in the way you mean."

"When I have more time, I'll do my best to change your mind."

"I didn't refuse, you know."

Mere accommodation wouldn't satisfy him. Nor did he care that she'd likely had men before him—she'd as good as said she cared for none of them. How else would a woman alone survive in such desperate times? What he needed from her was eager response, a passion that drove her as urgently as it did him. He knew he wouldn't get it. Not now. She'd need to be courted.

"I don't just want you," he told her. "I meant what I said—I love you. As soon as I can, I'll be back for you, Griselda, and we'll go to Paris. Have you ever been there?"

"Possibly."

"Possibly you've been to Paris or possibly you'll go there with me?"

She bent and kissed him gently and quickly on the lips. "Ivan Volek, you are a sweet man. I can't think of anyone I'd rather see Paris with."

* * *

In early November, near the Côtes-De-Meuse, in an evening hell of whining shells lit by the arcing flight of tracer bullets, Arno and another medic took on a mercy mission to retrieve a wounded *poilu* lying in the no-man's land between trenches. They were cutting through barbed wire when a burst of machine gun fire sent them diving onto their bellies—too late for Luke, his companion.

Luke, his jugular and carotid severed, fell on top of Arno, drenching him with blood. While the tac-tac-tac of the machine gun persisted, Arno didn't dare to move. Luke's blood spurted over his body and face until he could taste its warm saltiness on his tongue.

Moments later he felt his gut wrench, something that hadn't happened to him in years. But he damn well knew what it meant. The taste of blood had triggered his long-buried urge to shift.

His scalp tightened with dread. As a man he had little enough chance to survive in the front lines, but as a beast he'd have no chance. One sight of the beast and both sides would try their damnedest to kill him. He'd never survive the onslaught of bullets.

With Luke's body still covering him for protection, Arno wriggled forward on his stomach, searching desperately for a trench, feeling the dead man jerk as bullets slammed into the body. Just as he thought it was hopeless, he all but fell into a hole. Heaving Luke's body from his back, he slithered into the one-man dugout, thankful the soldier who'd scooped away the dirt had left.

Arno saw with dismay that his fingernails had lengthened and thickened to talons. He tore open his shirt and grabbed the amulet he wore around his neck along with his identification tag, the talons scratching his increasingly hairy chest. Clutching the flattened steel oval with its incised rune, *Elhaz,* symbolizing a splayed hand, Arno intoned the charm against changing. Over and over he mumbled the powerful words, fighting the beast's fierce urge to be free.

Since his uniform was blood-soaked, the feel, taste

and scent of blood clogged the dugout, fueling the bloodlust Arno had once thought he'd never experience again.

Hold the rune in your mind as well as your hand, his mother had told him when she taught him how to thwart the beast within. *Make* Elhaz *a part of you.*

Closing his eyes, Arno evoked the shape of the rune, struggling to etch it into his mind as indelibly as it was incised in the steel. *Elhaz,* the symbol of protection,↑, enabling the possessor to face temptation without succumbing. In addition to *Elhaz,* locked within the steel was a fragment of the *noita* charm that his shifter father had worn.

His mother, his father, and *Elhaz* protected him. He would not change. He refused to change. He was a man, not a beast. A man!

Overhead, gun flashes lit up the sky, and above their boom came the throb of the night bombers. War raged around him and within him.

The changing slowed, stopped. But, ominously, did not reverse. His nails were still talons, his teeth fangs. Keeping the runic image bright in his mind, Arno continued to chant. As the hours passed, the beast slowly retreated. But if Arno faltered, the beast advanced until he fancied he breathed in its hot and fetid breath.

As night crawled on, the fear and wonder of his first shifting haunted Arno. He hadn't fought the change then; he'd welcomed it. Gloried in it. Why fight the beast now?

Visions of what he'd seen in the past year clotted in his mind—ruined villages, dead animals, gutted fields, and blackened, broken trees. And the men, oh God, the broken men. Some in bloody fragments, some dead and bloated, some so maimed—with blood and guts and brains spilling out—that they'd be better off dead. Men did this to men. Why, then, consider the beast evil?

He growled, deep in his throat.

No! He must not change. If this was no-man's land, it was that much more so for the beast. To shift was to die. Hastily, Arno began the chant again, trying to feel each word as he spoke it, concentrating on the meaning behind the words, blotting everything else from his mind.

By the heart of my father, whose blood created me, by the breasts of my mother, whose milk nurtured me, by the Holy Three, who know my soul, I belong to the human race. I am a man. . . .

At dawn, in a driving rain, Arno climbed warily from the muddy dugout where he'd spent the worst night of his life. Crouching, he broke into a stumbling run toward the safety of the French lines.

The supervisor at the advanced dressing station goggled at him when he dragged in. "We gave you up for dead."

"Luke's dead." Arno could scarcely get the words out. "I found a hole to hide in."

The supervisor looked long and critically at Arno as he stood dripping rainwater mixed with Luke's blood onto the wooden floor. "You've consistently refused leave, so I'm not recommending it now," he said. "I'm *ordering* you to take two weeks. In Paris."

Exhausted, physically and mentally battered, Arno only vaguely experienced the trip west to Paris. It wasn't until he climbed into a Paris cab and found himself unable to give an address that he realized how fatigued he was. "Drive until I make up my mind," he told the man.

He'd been to Paris when he first arrived in France, but he didn't recognize anything he saw until he caught a glimpse from the cab window of the statues in the Jardin des Tuileries. He then recalled the garden was near the Ritz Hotel, and that triggered the memory of the pact he'd made with Ivan before they left California.

If one of us gets leave, he'll go to Paris and deposit a note at the the Ritz desk for the other.

"Place Vendome, driver," Arno ordered. "The Ritz."

The hotel was full; no rooms available. When Arno

gave his name, though, the clerk handed him an envelope, telling him it had been left for monsieur this very morning.

Tearing open the envelope, Arno pulled out the paper inside, his fingers clumsy with eagerness. It seemed like ten years since he'd last seen his twin. If this damn war ever ended, they planned to travel to Russia together in a search for the Volek past. But for now just being with Ivan was enough, was what he needed.

"I'm in Room 51 until Sunday, November 10," Ivan wrote.

Arno smiled for the first time in weeks as he asked the clerk to please ring Room 51.

There was no answer. The clerk, who'd been casting increasingly perplexed glances at Arno, said, "Does monsieur perhaps have a twin?" At Arno's nod, the clerk added, "I believe I observed monsieur's brother entering our dining room." He gestured.

Arno strode into the dining room and almost immediately spotted Ivan leaning across a table. Arno's gaze shifted to his brother's companion and he held. God, what a stunning woman! Her tan skin stood in vivid contrast to the brilliant blue suit she wore, and her long dark hair rippled down her back in defiance of fashion.

As if sensing his intent stare, she turned and looked at him with eyes as blue as her dress. A frisson of excitement rippled through him. Whoever she was, he wanted her. Had to have her. Meant to have her no matter who she belonged to.

Only then did he remember she was with the person he loved most in the world. His twin.

Chapter 18

Wolf shifted the knapsack on his back as they threaded through the pines. He'd packed it with no more camping supplies than usual, but it felt heavier than it should and, despite the cool December breeze, sweat ran down his face.

Leo, directly behind him, said, "Quincy and I can set the pace for a while, if you like."

They think I'm getting old, Wolf told himself. Damn it, I may be one-eyed, but I'm as good a man as ever. "Thanks, but you two set a mean pace. We're not soldiers charging the enemy, you know."

"Too bad the war ended before we had our chance to get into it," Quincy grumbled.

In September, Leo and Quincy, almost twenty, had registered for the draft. Luckily, they hadn't been called before the November Armistice. Even though Quincy had never shifted, Wolf dreaded to think what might have happened if he'd been drafted.

"If the war is over, why doesn't Hawk come home?" Leo asked. "And Arno and Ivan?"

"It takes time to ship troops across the Atlantic."

"I'll bet Hawk wishes he could fly across," Quincy put in.

Wolf nodded. No doubt Hawk would try something like that if he had the chance. He was proud of his son—a war hero, a flying ace like Rickenbacker.

The uncertainty of whether or not they'd be drafted had kept Leo and Quincy undecided about going to the university. Or, to be exact, the draft coupled with Quincy's disinterest in further schooling. Quincy didn't seem to have much interest in anything except hunting and fishing. And where Quincy led, Leo followed.

This camping trip was long overdue. It was too late in the season to venture into the high mountains, but he didn't expect snow in the foothills where they'd be camping. Wolf planned to swing by the Miwok village on the way home. He liked to keep in touch with his Miwok friends, and the twins had been there often enough with Hawk and with him so they felt at ease with the Indians.

Not that they were entirely accepted by the villagers, mainly because the Miwoks regarded twins as half-finished, believing they shared one spirit between two bodies.

"Sometimes the spirit lives in one, sometimes in the other," old Bear Claw, the medicine man, had explained. "When a man's body is empty, without a spirit, evil seeks to enter. When this happens the man becomes a beast and must be killed."

Shaken by Bear Claw's words, Wolf hadn't agreed or disagreed. He'd said nothing. How could he when he knew Quincy was a shifter?

"Looks like rain later," Leo said, bringing Wolf back to the present. "We may have to build a brush shelter."

Wolf remembered the night he and Muir and Teddy Roosevelt had camped in Yosemite and how snow had covered their blankets during the night, delighting Roosevelt. Teddy had died in January, Muir four years before, on Christmas Eve. Wolf shook his head. It was hard to believe men as full as life as Muir and Roosevelt were gone.

"We can make a brush lean-to," he told the twins, "or we can change our plans, push on to the Miwok village, stay there tonight, and head into the hills tomorrow."

"I vote for the lean-to," Quincy said. Wolf nodded even before Leo chimed in to agree.

The clouds lowered until in mid-afternoon the sky grew dark and heavy with moisture. Wolf had begun to scout for a good campsite when Quincy said, "Look!" and pointed.

Wolf stared in dismay at the ancient, rotting, plank cabin in a small clearing overgrown with brush and saplings. A chill ran along his spine. For years he'd avoided taking the boys past this place, but lately he'd all but forgotten about Stefan's hidey-hole.

"There's no door but the roof doesn't look too bad," Quincy said. "Why don't we spend the night here?"

Before Wolf could say a word, Quincy trotted off to examine the cabin. Wolf hurried after him. "Wait!" he called. Quincy paid no attention.

"Something wrong with the place?" Leo asked, loping alongside Wolf.

"Yes." Wolf wanted no part of that cabin.

"Hey, Quince! Wait for me," Leo shouted, speeding up.

Before either of them reached him, Quincy ducked inside the cabin. A moment later, he yelled something incoherent and rushed back out, brushing furiously at the sides of his head. "It bit me!" he cried. "A god-damn bat bit my ear."

Leo noticed Wolf's shudder and shot him a puzzled glance before he turned his attention to his twin's injured ear.

I should have kept Quincy out of that damned place, Wolf told himself. He remembered Muir telling him that he suspected bats, like mad dogs, could carry hydrophobia and infect humans with a bite.

"He got bit, all right," Leo said. "I can see the fang marks."

"You're sure it was a bat?" Wolf asked.

"Hell, there must've been a dozen of the ugly little buggers hanging upside down off a rafter," Quincy said. "A couple of them flew at me and one got me. Hurts like the devil."

As Wolf painted the bite with tincture of iodine from the first aid kit, a sense of foreboding as dark as the clouds overhead settled onto him. From bitter experience he knew better than to dismiss the feeling. Thank God he'd ignored his sons' pleas to come along on this trip, promising them a later camp-out. At least Nicholas and Reynolds were safe at Volek House with their mother.

"We'll go on to the Miwok village," he said. When neither twin objected, he wondered if they, too, felt uneasy.

The rain began before they reached the village. Sporadic at first, it soon settled into a steady downpour that soaked them through by the time they saw the first of the round bark-and-brush dwellings of the Miwoks.

Bear Claw welcomed them into his lodge. "I dreamed you would visit," he told Wolf as the three peeled off their outer garments and wrapped themselves in blankets provided by Bear Claw's aged wife.

Wolf wasn't surprised, for he knew Bear Claw was a true dreamer, as Indian medicine men often were. He emptied his pack and offered the old man the gifts he'd brought—canned fish, tobacco, and coffee.

Later that night, after they'd eaten and the twins had fallen asleep, Bear Claw expanded on his dream.

"I saw suffering in your stone dwelling," he said. "I saw these half-souls who lie sleeping in my lodge. I saw the disease of one become the disease of the other until they were both afflicted. I saw the elder will never be cured. I saw other twins of your blood riven apart. And you, my friend—" Bear Claw paused, his dark eyes sad. "You I saw with your head bowed in mourning for one who was not there."

Wolf sat in silence, pondering Bear Claw's gloomy foreseeing. "Can you tell me the name of the one who wasn't there?" he asked at last.

"I cannot."

Or would not.

"Let us smoke and then we'll speak of other matters," Bear Claw said.

After the pipe had been used and put away, Wolf told the old man about the bats in the deserted cabin and how one had bitten Quincy. He'd barely finished when Bear Claw's wife shuffled over to stand beside her husband.

"That one—" she pointed, "he burns with fever."

Quincy. Wolf rose and edged around the fire to kneel beside him and found Quincy's forehead was hot, confirming the old woman's words.

Quincy half-opened his eyes. "Hurts to breathe," he muttered.

The bat bite? Wolf asked himself. Did hydrophobia develop this quickly? He glanced at Bear Claw and the wise dark eyes met his gravely.

By morning Quincy was delirious, thrashing and moaning, with a hacking cough. Eyes glazed with fever, he recognized no one, fighting off Wolf when he tried to coax him to drink Bear Claw's fever potion.

"Let me try," Leo insisted, taking the metal cup from Wolf.

He bent over his brother. "It's me, Quince," he said softly, putting one hand behind his twin's head and holding the cup to his lips with the other. "It's Leo. Come on, drink up."

Quincy flung out his arm, knocking the cup from Leo's hand. At the same time, he turned his head and sunk his teeth into his brother's forearm.

Leo yelled in pain, jerked away, and sprang to his feet, cursing. Blood ran down his arm and dripped onto the earthen floor of the lodge. "What's the matter with him?" Leo demanded, tears in his eyes.

Wolf, horrified, couldn't answer. Mad dogs bit as Quincy had done.

Bear Claw, who'd been sitting across the fire from Quincy, rose slowly. "With no spirit inside him," he said, "a man behaves like an animal. Sick animals turn on those who try to help them. You—" he pointed at Leo "—lie beside your twin but do not touch him in any way."

Leo glanced at Wolf who nodded, aware Bear Claw planned to coax what he believed was the one spirit the twins shared from Leo's body into Quincy's. He didn't hold to this Miwok belief but said nothing, well aware he didn't know everything. If Bear Claw's medicine-making didn't help, it could do no harm.

Fetching his blanket, Leo stretched out on the floor next to his brother. Bear Claw hobbled to the far end of the lodge and took down a fur-and-feather head-dress, a deerskin pouch, and a small drum. He donned the headdress and seated himself beside Leo.

"Close your eyes and don't move," he ordered as he opened the pouch.

Wolf watched as the chanting Bear Claw sprinkled dried leaves onto Leo's chest, then threw others into the fire. As a blinding, pungent smoke arose, the medicine man began beating the drum. His eyes stinging from the smoke, Wolf felt the rhythmic beats throb through him, reminding him of shadow-holes that led to other worlds, and he wondered if Bear Claw, in his way, traveled elsewhere.

When at last the smoke dispersed, a drum beats slowed and stopped. Leo and Quincy both lay motionless. With a bone spoon, Bear Claw stirred a liquid in the metal cup. He rose and crouched at Quincy's head. With his thumb, he pushed down on the sick man's chin, forcing his mouth open. Little by little, he drizzled the potion into Quincy's mouth until the cup was empty.

Neither Leo nor Quincy roused for some time. Leo woke first, yawning. He sat up, glanced at Quincy, then got to his feet and walked to where Wolf sat.

"Is Quince better?" Leo asked.

Wolf replied cautiously. "He's no worse. Let's see your arm—I'll put some iodine on that bite."

When Quincy finally opened his eyes, he gazed blearily around the lodge. "I feel like hell," he said hoarsely. "All my bones ache, my throat's sore, my chest hurts."

"Sounds like what I had three weeks ago," Leo said, relief in his voice. "Druse said it was influenza."

Flu? Not hydrophobia? There'd been an epidemic of

influenza in the country. Wolf decided Leo might well be right. Thank God.

Four days later, Quincy was well enough to begin the hike back home, the bat's bite on his ear no longer visible. But Leo's arm, though the bite hadn't become purulent, still bore the circular imprint of Quincy's teeth. Though the mark wasn't the same, Wolf was unpleasantly reminded of the pentagram a shifter saw on his victim's palm.

As Ivan stopped his Mercer Runabout at the gates of Volek House, he saw his mother standing just inside the iron bars, the setting sun touching her silver hair with crimson. Despite his bitterness, he couldn't help being glad she'd come to meet him. She—and possibly Wolf, whose emotions were difficult to probe—was the only living person who didn't favor Arno. Liisi treated him exactly the same as she did his twin.

The gates swung open and Ivan drove the car through, stopped, and jumped out to hug his mother.

"I knew you'd be here today," she said. "Just you."

Ivan smiled wryly. If she was ever wrong, he'd never found her out. He closed and locked the gates, then helped her into the car to drive with him to the house.

"I still prefer horses," she said tartly. Almost immediately, she reached over and laid a hand on his. "We'll talk later, when there'll be no interruptions."

Ivan didn't reply, his heart sinking. She already knew something was wrong, and she wouldn't rest until she had the truth from him.

He managed to get through the ritual of greeting everyone—thank God the twins and Wolf were on a camping trip, cutting the number down—and made a pretense of eating dinner. As the coffee was served, he thought longingly of escape—but his escape had been to come home, and now there was no place else to go.

When his mother rose from the table, he gritted his teeth and got up, too.

"Ivan and I will be in the study," Liisi said to the others.

Inside the study, seeing a fire crackling in the grate, Ivan shut off the lights. "I prefer firelight," he told her.

She nodded. "A fire warms the spirit." She sat in the platform rocker that no one but Liisi ever used.

Ivan stood by the mantel.

"Sit down," Liisi said, not quite an order but more than a suggestion. "Where I can see you."

He didn't want to sit, but he didn't care to oppose his mother, so he chose one of the leather chairs opposite hers.

"What went wrong between you and Arno?" she asked.

Though he'd thought he was braced for the question, the words seemed to pierce his heart. Taking a deep breath, he said, "Arno eloped with the woman I loved." His mouth twisted. "They were kind enough to leave me a note. As if anything could explain such a betrayal."

Never mind that he'd seen the truth in Griselda's eyes even before Arno reached their table at the Ritz—Griselda would never have gone away with Arno if he hadn't bedazzled her, hadn't urged her to marry him. Arno, who could have any woman he desired, had taken away the one woman Ivan had ever loved.

"I suspected a woman was at the bottom of it," Liisi said. "Who is she?"

Haltingly, he told her about Griselda.

"Part Gypsy, is she?" his mother said when he finished. "No wonder Arno couldn't help himself."

Ivan stared at her, shocked. How could she defend what his twin had done?

"Did she say she loved you?" Liisi asked. "Make you feel you were the most important man in the world?"

Ivan shook his head.

"Then how did she delude you?"

"She would've come to love me in time. She'd have married me."

"Sooner or later Griselda and Arno would have met.

It's fortunate for all three of you that they met before you convinced her to marry you." Liisi leaned forward. "Don't you understand? Arno would never willingly hurt you any more than you'd hurt him. The truth is that he and Griselda were destined for one another and he couldn't help himself. Neither could she. I know you're deeply wounded, but don't bear a grudge against your twin, Ivan. That's like hating yourself."

He flung himself to his feet. "I never want to see either of them again!" Stalking to the door, he yanked it open and left without looking back.

No one understands, he thought bitterly as he grabbed a bottle from the liquor cabinet without so much as glancing at the label. He stomped up the stairs to his room and slammed the door behind him.

Tomorrow morning I'll go into the hills, he told himself as he swallowed the fiery liquid—brandy, by the taste. I'll camp by myself. Just me and the trees. I've forgotten how a woods should look, should smell. A woods of living trees, not dead and broken ones.

But when he woke in the morning with one hell of a headache, he saw the grayness pressing against his window and groaned. Tule fog. He was trapped inside the house.

Late that night, he came downstairs and, sitting on the piano bench, morosely picked out the tune to "Mademoiselle From Armentières" with one finger, a glass of whiskey—not his first—in his other hand. Hearing a noise, Ivan looked up to find Samara standing in the archway in a white nightgown, her feet bare. He said nothing, hoping she'd go away. Instead, she marched into the music room and over to the piano, where she stood beside the bench, glaring down at him.

"So you think you're an outcast." Her voice was sharp, antagonistic. "You're feeling pretty damn sorry for yourself, aren't you?"

His eyes widened. What in hell was she up to?

"What've you got to be sorry about?" she demanded. "Did you watch your twin slaughtered before your very eyes? Killed by a stalker? Were you raped by that same vile stalker? Did you bear his child—a child everyone fears? A child who's truly an outcast? Do you wake screaming at night from dreams of suffocation while some faceless monster pierces you with hideous pain?''

"No, Samara," he stammered, aghast at her attack but too befuddled by the whiskey to defend himself.

She reached down and took the glass from his hand. "Can you escape what's in your head with this? If so, maybe I should try it." She lifted the glass to her lips and downed its contents, staring at him defiantly when she finished.

"That's right, look at me," she said. "Take a good look at this thirty-nine-year-old woman whose father was a beast and whose mother deserted her. A woman who's never been held lovingly by any man. What man would want me?"

"I—I find you attractive," he managed to say. And damned if she wasn't at the moment, her dark eyes blazing, her face flushed with emotion, her hair unbraided and cascading over her shoulders. The nightgown, though not revealing, hung from a yoke above full breasts that pressed against the white cloth.

The sudden realization that she quite probably wore nothing under the gown quickened his breath.

"*You* find me attractive? I don't believe you."

"But you are." Ivan rose from the bench and put his hands on her shoulders. She felt warm and solid under his fingers and she smelled of lavender. And of woman.

She blinked up at him. "Do you mean it?" Her words slurred slightly.

Ivan let one hand slide to her waist. With the other he waved expansively. "Prettiest thirty-nine-year-old woman I ever saw." He knew he was feeling the whiskey, but what the hell did it matter? Samara *was* pretty, by God.

Samara giggled.

"Ssh," he warned. "Wake everyone up." He urged

her toward the stairs. "Brandy in my room. We'll have another drink."

She leaned against him. "I don't drink."

Maybe not, but she'd finished off his whiskey like a trooper. He led her up the stairs, down the hall, and into his room, excited by the feel of her softness pressing against his side.

She sat on his bed. "I've never been in your room—not when you were in it."

He eased down beside her and put an arm around her shoulders, drawing her closer. She didn't resist. A tiny voice in his mind warned him he was drunker than he realized, but he paid no attention.

"I'm forty-three," he confided. "Never had a woman love me."

She stroked his cheek. "Poor Ivan."

"They all loved Arno."

"*I* don't."

He kissed her, finding her lips warm and willing, if inexperienced. When he touched her breasts, he knew he was right—she wore nothing under the gown. Desire flamed like a torch.

"What are you doing?" she asked when he shifted her so she lay on the bed.

"Won't hurt you—want to hold you in love."

"Love," she echoed as he stretched out beside her and gathered her into his arms.

Ivan woke to the second day of fog with another headache. He groaned, turned over and froze. Samara, her dark hair spread over a pillow, lay next to him, asleep. What in hell was she doing in his bed?

Fragments of the night before drifted within reach and he tried to put them together. Samara in her nightgown, haranguing him. The two of them climbing the stairs together, his arm around her. The soft weight of her bare breasts in his hands. . . .

Though he couldn't remember the details, he must have made love to her. To his niece. Good God! He groaned again and she opened her eyes, blinked, and then stared at him with mixed apprehension and interest.

Not knowing what to say, Ivan smiled weakly. Actually she was only his half-niece, since he and her dead father had been half, not full, brothers. No more whiskey, he vowed. No more liquor of any kind.

Someone tapped at the door. Ivan tensed. "Who is it?" he asked.

"It's Liisi," she called through the door. "I'm worried. Samara seems to have disappeared. Her bed hasn't been slept in and—"

"I'm here," Samara said before Ivan could stop her.

Liisi opened the door. As she stepped into the room, Ivan resisted the urge to bury his head under the covers. No explanation he could make would excuse his behavior. The silence lasted for what seemed an hour.

"Well," Liisi said finally, "I see I was wrong when I thought I was too old to be surprised by anything. Shall we have the wedding before or after Christmas?"

Ivan was too stunned to speak. Wedding? Jesus, what next? He expected Samara to laugh, to protest. She did neither. After one swift glance at him, she turned to Liisi.

"I think that's up to Ivan," she said calmly.

"Very well." Liisi brandished the yellow paper she held in her hand. "A telegram arrived early this morning. From New York. Arno and his new bride will be home for Christmas."

Damn them both to everlasting hell. Rage ripped through Ivan, shattering every other emotion. He started to spring from the bed, recalled at the last moment he was naked, and had to content himself with sitting up.

"Samara and I will marry as soon as possible." He spoke through his teeth. "Certainly before Christmas."

"A wise choice," his mother told him, her silver eyes enigmatic.

It took him until the following day to realize how

neatly she'd manipulated him. Manipulated Samara, too, for all he knew, into accosting him in the music room. Had it been Liisi's plan all along to marry them off to one another? If so, she'd never admit it.

Frustrated and angry though the thought made him, he said nothing. He wanted his own wife by his side when Arno and Griselda walked into Volek House. And Samara would suit as well as anyone.

During the hurried flurry of preparations, Wolf returned from the camping trip with the twins. The three of them took the news so calmly that Ivan wondered at times if everyone had been in on the conspiracy.

Only Melanie looked at him askance. "You really *are* going to marry my mother, aren't you?" she asked the day before the wedding.

"It looks that way," Ivan told her.

"Then I guess you'll be my stepfather as well as my great uncle." Her dark eyes regarded him dubiously.

She looked so forlorn that Ivan impulsively put an arm around her shoulders and hugged her. An outcast, Samara had labeled the poor kid. If her appearance wasn't so woebegone, she'd be a pretty girl.

"You can go on calling me Ivan if you want. Or you can call me Papa, because that's what I'll be."

She smiled hesitantly. "I never had a father."

"You will after tomorrow."

He'd try to be a father to the girl, he vowed. Just as he'd try to be a decent husband to Samara. They might deserve a more loving father and husband, but he was what they were going to get, so it was up to him to do his best.

On the morning of the wedding, Liisi didn't come down to breakfast. When Ivan, concerned, went to her room, he found her dressed but resting on the chaise longue. He knelt by her side, alarmed by her pallor and the dark circles under her eyes.

"Are you all right, Mama?"

Liisi sighed and rested a hand on his shoulder. "I

had a vision during the night." She took her hand
away and edged over. "Sit next to me, son."

Ivan obeyed. His mother smelled faintly of cloves,
and when he held her hand between his, he found it
cold as a Sierra glacier.

"Czar Nicholas II," she said. "Russia."

Ivan waited, but when she didn't go on, he said
gently, "The czar and all of his family were killed by
the revolutionaries in July, if you recall."

"Of course I remember. Do you think I'm growing
senile?" Her tartness reassured him. "But it wasn't
Nicholas himself who appeared in my vision; it was
Rasputin, the Holy Fool, the man who dominated the
czar's court. Do you know what a Holy Fool is?"

"I've heard Rasputin called everything from mystic
to charlatan."

"He was both. And, as are most Holy Fools, he
was also mad. In my vision, his ghost stood between
you and Samara at your wedding, separating and yet
joining you, one to the other. He laid a bony hand on
Samara's abdomen and at the same time, with his other
hand, touched your genitals.

" 'From these will come one greater than I,' he said,
and laughed. Crazy, lunatic laughter I could hear in
my head long after the vision faded."

Ivan stared at her. "We don't plan—that is, Samara
and I—well, we don't want a child. She already has
Melanie."

Liisi sniffed. "Melanie is a grown woman in years if
not in spirit. And, remember, I foresee what is true."

"I won't argue. But why should that vision upset
you? It seems harmless enough."

"That was the first vision. The second was a shaman, Indian by the look of him, old, wearing a neck-
lace of bear claws. 'Darkness gathers,' he warned.
'See the stones fall.' "

"The Miwok medicine man is named Bear Claw,"
Ivan said.

She waved that aside as of little import. "Do you
realize what he meant?" she demanded.

Ivan shrugged. "Volek House is built of stone."

Liisi frowned. "You don't take this vision seriously enough."

"Mama, I'm getting married today. I'm not altogether sure it's the right thing to do, and I'm nervous as the devil. Forgive me if I'm preoccupied."

"If Rasputin himself assures you the marriage was meant to be, I'd say you could stop worrying." Again she spoke tartly.

How could he reply to that?

"I had a third vision." Her voice grew somber. "One I can't reveal. Not to anyone. After I—" She paused and began again. "After the wedding, you must tell Wolf that I had three visions in the night. Promise me you won't tell him until then."

Her request seemed harmless enough. Actually he was pleased that she spoke to him of her visions rather than to Wolf. "I promise, Mama."

"Good. Now leave me. I'm tired from being awake most of the night and must rest so I can enjoy the wedding."

She looked old, older than he'd ever seen her. And frail. Ivan bent to kiss her cheek. "You're sure you're feeling all right?"

"If I wasn't, I'd send for Druse. Run along and do your worrying elsewhere."

He left her room, descended the stairs, and opened the front door to test the weather. The fog was definitely lifting, the day promised to be pleasant. He'd taken one step onto the porch when something large and white startled him by swooping out of the mist and flapping past on soundless wings before disappearing once more into the thinning fog.

An owl, he realized belatedly. A great snowy owl. A night hunter. Never before had he seen one fly during the day. He stared at the concealing mist, shaken. Much as he resisted belief in omens, he couldn't help but wonder if seeing the bird at such an unusual time meant bad luck.

Chapter 19

The wedding at St. Catherine's Church in Thompsonville passed in a blur for Ivan. He must have given the
right responses because the ceremony went off without
a hitch. The guests were to motor to Volek House for
the reception. He and Samara ran the gamut of rice-
throwing, climbing into his open Mercer runabout to
lead the way. As he accelerated onto the road, Samara
clutched at her headdress, laughing, as her veil blew
behind her in the wind.

He smiled at her, thinking he could have done worse
than to marry Samara. His good spirits lasted until he
saw the low-slung roadster pulled up outside the gates.
It could, of course, be a guest's car, but somehow he
knew it wasn't. As if sharing his premonition, Samara
laid her hand over his on the steering wheel.

Without a key there was no way to get in, since
Chung was chauffeuring the family Dusenberg, Gei with
him, and the day servants, busy in the house, had been
given no instructions to open the gates.

As they pulled alongside the roadster, Arno got out
and came over to the driver's side of the Mercer. He
started to offer his hand, apparently thought the better
of it, and drew it back. "Hello, Ivan," he said. "Samara. We heard about the wedding when we passed
through Thompsonville. Congratulations." He didn't
quite meet Ivan's eyes.

"I'm glad you've come home safely, Arno," Samara
said.

Ivan found himself unable to greet his twin. Without speaking he held out the key, never once glancing at the passenger in the roadster.

Arno opened the gate and waved the Mercer past.

"You didn't even say hello," Samara said as she and Ivan entered the house.

Ivan didn't reply. What was between his twin and him was his private affair, and he had no intention of discussing it, not even with his wife. He deliberately turned his back when Arno and Griselda came in the door, ignoring them as they climbed to the second floor—though he heard every footstep. A persistently honking horn announced the first of the cavalcade of guests—or so Ivan thought, glad he'd be distracted by the reception. Not until Druse burst through the door did he find he was mistaken.

"It's your mother!" she cried. "Come quickly, Ivan."

He ran through the open door and down the steps to the Dusenberg. Gei stepped aside to let him get into the back seat where Liisi rested in Wolf's arms.

"Is she all right?" Ivan demanded.

"She's dead." Wolf's voice quivered with suppressed emotion.

Tears welled in Ivan's eyes as the meaning of his mother's third vision dawned on him. "She foresaw her death," he whispered. "I wish I'd understood earlier that was what she wanted me to tell you."

"I can't stop death." Wolf's voice was sad. "No one can." He turned to Chung. "Please let the guests know the reception is canceled—catch them at the gate, if you can."

"I'll carry my mother," Ivan said.

Without a word, Wolf placed Liisi's slight body in Ivan's arms, preceding him up the steps and into the house. Arno and Griselda, halfway down the flight of stairs from the second floor, stopped, staring at Ivan and his burden.

"Is she—?" Arno asked, his voice breaking before he finished.

Wolf nodded. Ivan said nothing as he eased past the pair without pausing.

"Damn it, Ivan!" Arno cried, slamming his fist on the banister rail. "She's my mother, too."

From the foyer, Leo watched the undertakers carry Grandmother Liisi's black coffin from the parlor, where she'd been lying for a day and a night, to the hearse that would take the coffin to the church for the funeral. The stranger who'd suddenly appeared at the gate last night followed close behind the coffin, dressed all in black, like some kind of priest or minister, except he didn't wear a clerical collar. Waino Waisenen was a Finn like grandmother—her cousin, he claimed.

Though Waino's hair was snow-white, Leo couldn't tell how old he was—maybe forty. His skin was as white as his hair and his eyes so pale they seemed no-color, like an icicle. Most of the time he wore dark glasses, even in the house. Ivan hadn't wanted to let him through the gate but Wolf insisted, claiming Grandmother had told him of Waino's coming.

Wolf usually let Ivan and Arno run things, he never said much, but when he did no one contradicted him. Even Wolf seemed a bit put off by Waino's oddness, though. Druse didn't. She said he looked the way he did because he was an albino. Once Leo had seen a white fawn with reddish eyes, and Wolf had told him the fawn was an albino and that albino mule deer were defective, lacking the normal brown pigment of their species. Up until now, he hadn't realized people could be albinos—was Waino defective in other ways, too?

It used to be Arno who took charge, but since the two of them had come back from the war, Arno left the decisions up to Ivan. Maybe it had something to do with the fact they didn't speak to one another. Their estrangement made everyone in the house uncomfortable.

A lump rose in Leo's throat as the coffin disappeared through the front door. Grandmother was gone forever. The house would never be the same. He looked around, wanting to share his sorrow with Quince, but his twin had slipped away. He went to look for him.

The trouble between Arno and Ivan bothered Leo. He couldn't imagine not speaking to Quince. Not that they didn't get into scraps, but that was different. Twins might disagree, but they weren't meant to be cold to each other. If you were around Ivan and Arno these days, you could catch pneumonia from the chill.

He found Quince under the piano in the music room. When they were kids, they used to drape the paisley shawl over one end of the grand piano and pretend the space underneath was their secret cave. Hell, they hadn't done that in more than ten years—what was old Quince up to?

"Just felt like it," was all Leo could get out of him.

Leo shrugged and crawled underneath to join him. Quince was the leader, he had been since they were babies, like Arno had led Ivan until lately. Leo wondered if it would ever switch around between him and Quince and shook his head. He couldn't imagine Quince ever doing what he said. Absently he rubbed the bite mark on his left arm. Though it had healed, the mark was still red and sometimes itched.

Arno was the shifter and so was Quince. Except Quince had never shifted. Arno and Ivan had talked to them so many times about what to watch for and what to do when it happened that it got boring. He'd begun to hope they were wrong and Quince wasn't what they said.

"I wish Hawk would get back." Quince's voice sounded different, hoarse and sort of growly. "Wolf's getting too cautious. Hawk's different. He'd go with us bow hunting in the mountains; we'd track deer through the snow—" His voice trailed off. "Did you ever notice how much redder blood looks against the snow?"

"Never thought about it," Leo said.

"I think about things like that a lot lately."

Leo glanced at him, started to ask "How come?" and stopped before the words came out. He blinked, staring at his twin's hand, at nails as long and sharp as talons. "Jesus," he muttered, swallowing.

"Quince," he said urgently. "Damned if it isn't happening. I better go get—"

"No!" The taloned hand clutched Leo's arm. "They'll stop me."

"That's the idea. We promised—"

"*You* did. I never promised anything except to Grandmother—and she's dead. Come on, let's get out of here before it's too late." Leo could hardly understand his twin's last few words; they were more of a growl than speech.

He followed Quince, crawling from under the piano, and gasped when he saw his brother in the full light of day. Quince's face was elongated, hair grew thickly on his arms and face, and his teeth were fangs. He looked hideous.

"Can't stand these clothes," Quince growled, shedding them as he hurried toward the front door. "Open it—I can't," he ordered.

Leo obeyed. The hearse was gone; no one was in sight. Quince loped toward the thick stand of oaks at the side of the house and Leo ran after him, his mind in a whirlwind of confusion. It was broad daylight. Why was Quince shifting when there wasn't a full moon? When there wasn't danger threatening? Arno had stressed that those were the two main reasons for a shifter's change.

What should he do? Part of him longed for the security of having Arno and Wolf stand by to help, but his loyalty to his twin kept him from turning back.

"Quince, wait up," he shouted at the hairy back plunging into the trees. He scratched at the bite mark as he ran because it had started to itch and burn like fury.

Come to think of it, he didn't feel right. His gut ached, the collar around his neck was suddenly too tight, and his shoes hurt his feet. Frightened, he threaded between the trees, calling to his twin, the strangely hoarse sound of his own voice panicking him.

Quince was the shifter, not him!

Then why was he kicking off his shoes, flinging off his clothes? Why were his hands changing, where was all the hair coming from? What was this terrible wrenching inside him?

"Wolf!" he screamed in desperation, and was appalled to hear himself howl instead. The answering howl was the last thing he remembered.

Free? The beast glanced around warily, remembering walls and gates. What should he do? Then his brother beast loped toward him from the shadows under the trees and his uncertainty faded. He'd follow his brother.

Wolf was talking to his two young sons as he dressed for the funeral. He stopped in mid-sentence when he heard the first howl.

By the time the second howl sent the hair on his nape prickling, he'd already shoved Reynolds and Nicholas through the dressing room door into the bedroom he shared with Cecelia. She stared at him, her expression horrified.

"Is it Quincy?"

"I'm afraid so. Lock the boys in here with you and don't open the door for anyone but me or Druse."

"Don't go out," she begged. "Stay with us."

He paid no attention. She knew as well as he did that with Liisi gone there was no one else who knew the shifter charm as well as he did. For five years now he'd carried with him the amulet Liisi had fashioned for Quincy.

As he raced down the stairs, he thought that Arno might be of help—but the fact Arno was a shifter himself made Wolf uneasy. Grandfather had warned him how tempting it was for one shifter to change into a beast to join another already shifted.

Waino Waisenen stood waiting in the foyer. "I'll come with you," he said calmly, his dark glasses hiding his expression.

Wolf shook his head. "Too dangerous." Even if it

wasn't, he dared not expose the Volek secret to the stranger.

Waino paid no heed, following him out the door. "I know words of protection against shapechangers; you'll need my help."

His words jolted Wolf. But he had no time to worry about what Waino did or did not know, or even about his safety. To be fair, he gave him one last warning. "You'll be facing death."

"I've done so before and still I live."

They ran side by side toward the grove of live oaks in the side yard, plunged into the trees, and neared the wall just in time to see the beast top it and leap to the ground on the other side.

Wolf ground his teeth. Damn, Quincy'd gotten away. In daylight. Even in this sparsely settled valley, someone was sure to spot him. He'd have to go after him. Turning away from the wall, he was about to speak to Waino when he noticed the man staring intently at a large clump of camellia bushes between the trees and the wall.

"He's gone," Wolf said.

Waino gestured toward the bushes with his head.

Maybe Leo was hiding in them, Wolf thought. He'd probably trailed Quincy after the shifting. "Leo, we know you're in there," he called, striding toward the bushes.

A low growl halted him in his tracks even before Waino shouted, "Stop!"

"Leo?" Wolf said.

The menacing growl came again.

"There are two," Waino said from behind him.

Two beasts? He'd seen one go over the wall. Had Leo shifted as well as Quincy? Wolf stared at the bushes. He'd never once felt the telltale shifter emanations from Leo. But who else could the second beast be?

Making up his mind, Wolf took the amulet from his pocket and began chanting the shifter charm, not surprised when Waino joined him, their voices intoning the ancient Finnish words together. Slowly Wolf inched forward, still chanting, the amulet on its leather thong held in both hands. The rune *Mannaz*, ᛗ, was inscribed on the steel charm. *Mannaz*, symbol of the divine within each person, could also mean a linking of two—had Liisi sensed what would happen?

Waino's words changed, became a coaxing croon. With a snarl, the beast thrust through an opening in the bushes. As it sprang, Wolf tossed the thong over its head, at the same time leaping aside. With a strangled cry, half-shout, half-howl, the beast began to change.

Moments later, Wolf stared at the naked Leo. "What happened?" he demanded.

As the dazed Leo fumbled to explain, Waino handed him the clothes he'd discarded. When Leo reached for them, Waino caught his arm and stared at the fiery red circle on his skin.

"Who bit you?" he asked.

Wolf answered. "His brother."

"Ah. I have heard—" Waino paused, gazing uncertainly from Wolf to Leo as though wondering whether to go on. "You're not happy that I know about Volek shifters," he said, speaking directly to Wolf. "When she realized death waited on the threshold, Cousin Liisi shared your secret with me. I understand it will be hard for you to trust me as she did, but surely you're aware I've come to stay."

"We'll talk about that later," Wolf said. "I want to know what happened here."

Waino shrugged. "It's obvious. When his brother bit him, the shifter saliva activated a latent tendency in Leo to shapeshift."

Both Wolf and Leo stared at him. "The bite mark *did* start to burn and itch just before I—I—changed," Leo said. "After Quince turned into a—a beast."

"Let's get you back to the house." Wolf urged Leo along even though he was only half-dressed.

Once inside, he hustled Leo to the bedroom he shared with Quincy. "For safety's sake, I have to lock

you in," he told him. "Quincy's still loose. I'm going
after him and I don't want to worry about what you're
doing while I'm gone."

Leo fingered the amulet. "This is supposed to be
Quince's, isn't it? You'll need it." He started to lift
the thong from his neck.

"Don't touch that!" Wolf ordered. "Until we can
sort this out, the amulet stays around your neck to
prevent another shifting. The beast has no conscience
and you're inside Volek House. Those in the house
with you need to be protected from you—do you understand?"

Leo swallowed and nodded. "Maybe if I came with
you, I could help," he suggested hesitantly. "Quince
won't hurt me and—"

"No! If he's near you, whatever influence that bite
gave him over you might make you shift despite the
amulet. We can't take any chances."

"Then you believe what Waino said about the bite?"

"It's as good an explanation as any."

Once Wolf locked Leo's door and pocketed the key,
he hurried to his own room and told Cecelia what had
happened while he took down an old wooden chest
from the closet shelf and removed a sheathed silver
dagger.

Cecelia's eyes widened. "That's not enough; he'll
kill you. What about a gun?"

"What good is a gun without silver bullets? Liisi
may have some stashed away in the tower room. I'll
have Druse look for them, but I can't wait—I have to
go after the beast before he's seen. Don't let anyone
go outside until I come back."

"Liisi's funeral—?"

"Call and tell them we have an emergency and must
postpone the funeral."

"The day servants?"

"Tell them whatever you can think of that will keep
them in the house.'

When Wolf ran down the stairs, he found Waino
waiting once more in the foyer. Realizing the man

meant to go with him no matter what argument he might put forth, Wolf merely said, "I have no amulet for this one."

Waino patted a bulging pocket. "Don't worry."

Wolf eyed him uneasily. He had only Waino's word that he was Liisi's cousin. True, he was Finnish, but what if Waino was something or someone other than he said? Something that also knew about shifters? It wouldn't be the first time Wolf had inadvertently welcomed a stalker into Volek House.

He motioned with his head toward the door, and Waino donned the wide-brimmed black hat he wore to protect himself from the sun. Once they were outside and the door was closed, Wolf slid his hand under his coat and gripped the hilt of the silver dagger.

"Guns are useless against the beast," he said, probing, waiting tensely for Waino's reply. Would he admit he had silver bullets? What then?

"I'm not carrying a gun," Waino said. "I couldn't shoot straight to save my life. Besides, he's a Volek. I know you don't want to kill him."

Wolf hesitated, all but convinced by Waino's words. If the man was a stalker, wouldn't he have killed them all by now? And wasn't it true Liisi had warned him to expect a relative to arrive after she died? Still . . .

"Which gate?" Waino asked.

Without speaking, Wolf led the way toward the back gate. When they were outside the walls, trotting toward the pine grove, Waino said, "Interesting that Quincy's beast didn't wait for the moon to rise—almost as though the change was long overdue. I wonder if Liisi, even after she died, was in some way responsible for keeping him from shifting. After all, he didn't change until her coffin left the house."

A memory came to Wolf of Liisi once telling him that when Quincy was twelve she'd shown him the amulet and explained its purpose.

"I won't need it, Grandmother," Quincy had insisted. "Honest. I promise you I won't shapeshift." He'd laid a hand on his heart. "I promise."

"He promised he wouldn't shift," Wolf said to Waino.

"Ah. Liisi must have been powerful enough to bind him to a freely given promise, forcing him to keep it." Waino shook his head admiringly. "I wish I could have met her in person." He smiled. "You have a fascinating family, fascinating. Especially your daughter. Her healing skills are remarkable."

Wolf shot Waino a considering glance. He hadn't realized the man had so much as said two words to Druse. Changing the subject abruptly, he said, "I think I know where the beast is heading. He may have shifted during the day, but he's a night hunter and he'll want to den up until it's dark. There's an old cabin a few miles from here. . . ."

In the late afternoon, a Miwok hunter carrying a bow and quiver of arrows intercepted Wolf and Waino before they reached the cabin. As he introduced Waino to the Indian, Wolf noted with alarm that two of the arrows were silver-tipped.

"Bear Claw said you would come," Sitting Fox said. "As he said the spirit wolf would return."

"Is he—the spirit wolf—in the cabin?" Wolf asked.

"He is. Three of us watch and wait."

"I'm going to try to take him alive," Wolf warned.

Sitting Fox said, "I'll tell the others. But we shoot if we must. Shoot to kill." He slipped into the trees and disappeared.

"I assume they're good shots," Waino said. "So we'd best get closer to the cabin to give ourselves better odds of hauling home a live beast."

With the cabin in view, Waino somehow, imperceptibly, assumed charge of the hunt. He started a tiny blaze and threw on dried leaves while he chanted. He captured some of the aromatic smoke in a black rubber balloon which he then inflated to the size of a muskmelon before he sealed the end of the balloon.

He tied a steel knife to the balloon with black ribbon, spit on the knife blade and, followed by Wolf, crept from tree to tree until he was opposite the cabin.

With the ease Wolf knew could come only from long practice, Waino balanced the knife in his hand and threw it.

The knife sailed through the air, slowed by the attached balloon, and thudded into the wooden threshold of the doorway with an audible thwack. The balloon deflated on impact. Inside, the beast snarled.

"The windows, I think, are too small for him to get through?" Waino asked.

Wolf nodded.

"Good. So he can't leave the cabin without passing by or over the knife. We wait, now, until moonrise lures him to the hunt."

"He must sense we're near."

"Of course. But bloodlust overrides caution. He must hunt."

Sergei had told Wolf much the same. Caught in bloodlust, a beast loses all fear of danger.

The beast padded back and forth on the earthen floor of the cabin, keeping away from the stink at the door. He'd already measured himself against the windows and knew he was too large. To leave, he had to pass the knife in the doorway and its unpleasant smell.

And he must leave, must run under the moon, run down his prey and drink its hot blood, sink his fangs into its red heart. . . .

He growled low in his throat. Men waited in the trees beyond the cabin. Men had sent the knife and the stink to plague him. Did they have guns? He'd wait until dark settled over the clearing, slip out and be away before they could shoot. Though men weren't the prey he craved, if any of them tried to stop him, he'd kill.

His brother hadn't followed him. Why? Where was he? Trapped? Locked away? His hackles rose.

Slowly, slowly, the sky darkened. Through the window came the faint scent of deer and his muzzle rose, savoring the smell. Soon, very soon, he'd trace that scent to its source.

At last stars gleamed in the dark sky and the beast

sensed rather than saw the faint light of a rising moon. Time!

He trotted to the doorway, keeping to one side, sickened by the stench there. With a rush, he bounded over the knife and made for the shelter of the bushes growing near the doorway. Before he reached them, he staggered and slowed and his vision dimmed. Knowing he must find cover, he struggled on.

Suddenly metal wrapped around him, blinding and burning. Choking. He snarled and snapped and fought. To no avail. The hated scent of man thickened around him, but he lay bound and helpless and in pain, barely able to breathe.

Wolf stared down at the giant beast, almost pitying him. He'd seen cowboys who were experts with a lariat, men who could rope anything, in motion or not. But never before had he watched a man use a silver chain as though it were a rope. Waino's finesse and accuracy had stunned him.

"He should be changing back to human," Waino muttered. "Let's chant the shifter charm together."

They did. The beast remained a beast, the moon shining down on his bound form.

"Beast or not, we've got to get him home," Wolf was saying as three dark figures materialized around them. The Miwoks.

With the help of the Indians, they fashioned a crude bark sled that could be pulled by leather thongs. Using tree branches, they levered the beast onto it.

"If he comes again, we will kill him," Sitting Fox warned.

"I hear you," Wolf told him.

With Waino pulling on one of the thongs and Wolf on the other, they began the long journey home through the night with the helpless beast.

"What will you do with him when we get to Volek House?" Waino asked.

"Lock him in the special cellar room until he shifts back."

"And what if he doesn't?"

Wolf hadn't considered such a terrible possibility. "He's sure to eventually."

"Maybe. But he hasn't yet. We can't leave the chain on once we get him there—the silver will poison him fatally. He'll be sick from it as it is—but he's young and healthy, he'll recover. When he does, you'd better make damn sure that cellar room has a stout door and walls." He glanced over his shoulder at the sled. "I know the binding strength of blood ties, but I have a premonition that this one—and the family—would be better off if you'd let him die with a Miwok silver-tipped arrow in his heart."

Chapter 20

Melanie Volek sighed as Hawk sent his biplane gliding downward to circle the airstrip before landing. Her first flight had been glorious, so wonderful she wanted to remain up in the air forever. She'd felt as free as a bird under the bright blue of the May sky with misty white clouds as her companions.

They'd left everything behind—the troubles, the quarrels, the past. In the sky was freedom, on the ground the gray pile of Volek House with all of its miseries.

Hawk had flown in from New York last month, the returning war hero, tall and handsome in his pilot's gear. She'd grown up with Hawk, but this self-assured man seemed far removed from the diffident boy she'd known. The only similarity was his enthusiasm for airplanes.

I wish we could fly away right now, she thought as the airplane wheels touched the ground. Just Hawk and me. Fly away into tomorrow and never come back.

When the plane bumped to a stop, Hawk sprang up and helped her out of the cockpit. "How did you like it?" he asked.

"Flying's better than going to heaven—you don't have to die first."

He grinned and, as he lifted her down to the ground, hugged her. "I can see you're a gal after my own heart. Next time we won't just circle over the valley, we'll pick a destination."

As she waited for him to secure the plane, she thrilled to think there'd be another time. He actually approved of her! Who'd ever think Hawk would grow up to be so dashing and sophisticated? He'd probably left dozens of French girls weeping when he came back to the States.

Melanie tucked stray wisps of dark hair loosened by the wind under the thick braids that wound around her head and sighed. She was anything but dashing. No man ever looked at her twice—not that she often went anyplace where men were.

Hawk sauntered over to her, stopped in front of her, cocked his head, and studied her for so long that she began to fidget.

"You know," he said at last, tugging at one of her braids, "if you cut your hair short and bought the right kind of clothes you'd be smashing. As chic as any Parisienne."

Chic? Her? "Nice girls don't bob their hair," she said primly.

He laughed. "Who said you had to be nice? Is being nice any fun?"

Melanie was more delighted than shocked by his words. "Now that you mention it, I don't have much fun," she said in what she hoped was a saucy manner.

He put an arm around her shoulders and hugged her again. "Old Hawk's here now—we'll see what we can do to change things."

Could he? She longed for a change. Not that she expected him to be able to help poor Quincy, not after Wolf and Waino and Leo had all tried and failed. Just thinking about him still locked away in the secret cellar room depressed her.

"It's like a dungeon," she said aloud.

"What—Volek House?" Hawk asked. "Can't disagree with that. But don't despair, I'll help you escape."

"Where to?"

"Does it matter?"

She stared into his eyes, black and shiny as jet. "Really escape, so I never have to come back?"

"If that's what you want."

His arm around her shoulders, his nearness, made her breath come short and she licked suddenly dry lips. Without warning, his head dipped and his tongue touched hers, sending a frisson along her spine. He straightened without actually kissing her, but she was sure what he'd done was more potent than any kiss.

"First order of the day," he told her, "is a haircut for you. Then clothes. We'll fly to San Francisco and do both. Tomorrow."

"But—"

"No arguments. I'm running this affair."

Affair? But of course he didn't mean a *real* affair between a man and a woman. After all, they were related after a fashion, like most everyone else at Volek House. On the other hand, so were her mother and Ivan, and they'd gotten married.

"Meanwhile," he went on, "back to the dungeon and its gloomy inhabitants."

Though she tried to suppress it, Melanie couldn't help her giggle.

Late the next afternoon, going up in the elevator at the Mark Hopkins Hotel, Melanie fingered the bobbed ends of her hair uncertainly. Never had her head felt so light and free, but how did she look? She glanced at Hawk and found him watching her.

Leaning close, he whispered, "You're gorgeous."

He ushered her from the elevator and toward the McDee suite. While it wasn't the first time she'd been to the suite, she'd never before been here with one man, just the two of them.

He unlocked the door and opened it with a flourish. "After you, mademoiselle."

Giggling is *not* sophisticated, she reminded herself. Instead, she gave him what she hoped was an insouciant smile, covering her acute attack of nerves.

"*Très bien,* the champagne awaits," he said, motioning to a low table in front of a couch done in Chinese brocade.

Sliding her new sable stole from her shoulders, she walked slowly across the room to where a bottle of Dom Perignon cooled in an ice bucket.

"God, you're graceful," he said. "I've never seen you make an awkward move."

It was on the tip of her tongue to tell him any grace she had was probably the result of the dance training Cecelia had given her. No, she thought, accept the compliment as though you hear wonderful things about yourself every day.

She eased down onto the couch and he sat beside her. After popping the cork, he poured the bubbling wine into two stemmed glasses and offered her one.

"To San Francisco," he said, raising his glass to touch hers. "The American Paris."

She sipped the pale liquid and set down her glass. "Is it really?" she asked.

He shrugged. "Nothing is like Paris, but this is as close as you can come in the States."

He told her stories of Paris while they drank champagne. As bemused by him as she was by the wine, she made no protest when he drew her close and kissed her. Nor did she object when, later, he scooped her into his arms and carried her into one of the bedrooms where, she noted, both their overnight cases rested on a luggage rack.

She'd never been made love to, but so far she'd enjoyed every kiss and caress, and she looked forward to what was to come. She didn't dislike what happened, but afterwards, when he rolled away and she lay staring at the ceiling, she tried to tell herself she wasn't disappointed, tried to ignore the question threading insistently through her mind—*Is this all there is?*

Early the next morning, after two more episodes of lovemaking, Hawk propped himself onto his elbow and looked down at her. "I can tell it's not working for you."

She couldn't manage a lie, but she made an attempt to evade a direct answer. "I like you very much, Hawk."

His smile was wry. "Damned by faint praise."

"I—I don't think it's you."

He shrugged. "Don't blame yourself. Sometimes the spark between two people just isn't there. I wish it had been."

A month later, Ivan told Melanie that he and Samara had decided to move to San Francisco. "I hope you'll choose to come with us," Ivan added with a smile.

Melanie agreed with relief. After the fiasco with Hawk, it was difficult for her to sit at the dinner table with him at Volek House and even harder to speak to him as though nothing had ever happened between them. Especially since, no matter what he said, she knew the problem lay with her.

Ever since she'd been a tiny girl, her relatives, no matter how much they tried to conceal it, had given her one clear message: you aren't like everyone else; you're not like us. You're an outsider and you'll always be one. Even her mother had never fussed over her the way she later did over Jennifer McQuade when Jenny came to live at Volek House.

Melanie didn't expect the situation to change with the move to San Francisco, but at least she'd be away from Hawk. And from poor Quincy suffering in his locked room. And she'd be free of the smoldering anger between her stepfather and his twin, Arno—an anger that infected all of Volek House.

Though she wasn't sure, she suspected that anger had something to do with Arno's French wife, Griselda. She couldn't help but wonder if the fact that Griselda was going to have a baby had anything to do with Ivan's sudden decision to move.

Curtis Volek was born to Griselda and Arno on August 15, 1919. Wolf assured the parents that the boy was not a shifter.

One month later, Waino Waisenen married Druse Volek.

On August 15, 1920, Beth Volek was born in San Francisco to Samara and Ivan. Despite Liisi's strange vision of Rasputin, to Ivan the little girl seemed perfectly normal.

On January 27, 1921, Marti was born to Waino and Druse. Marti was not a shifter, but she wasn't normal either.

In Berkeley that September, Jennifer and Lily McQuade, after seventeen years apart, insisted on sharing an apartment while attending the university.

Since her mother refused to allow her to return home, Jennifer had left Volek House for boarding school when she was ten. Lily had been kept at home until she was twelve, then sent to a different private girls' school than the one Jennifer attended.

Because of her stay at Volek House, Jennifer understood Grandmother Liisi, Cousin Wolf, and Cousin Samara had special talents, but neither twin knew the Volek secret because Tanya McQuade hadn't yet told them.

Lily stared long and hard at her scarred face in the entry mirror. Over the years, the angry red had faded to a shiny pink over her left temple, ear and cheek. Her clothes hid the scars on her left shoulder and upper arm. Was it possible Rolfe Utmeyer could overlook such terrible disfigurement? Apart from the fact that she helped him with chemistry, he really seemed to like her.

Jenny didn't think much of Rolfe, calling him a good-time-Charlie and claiming he drank too much, but it was precisely his boisterous, joking manner that didn't distinguish between her and anyone else that attracted Lily to him. All too often people were either put off by her scars, treating her as though she was somehow defective, or else were extra-nice to her. Rolfe behaved as though she was normal.

The hell with what Jenny believed about him. Her

twin, with her perfect, if lightly freckled, complexion, could have any man in their class if she wanted. Jenny didn't bear any scars at all—Jenny gave them.

Lily shook her head and turned away from the mirror to look from the window at the street below. Jenny had been three when it happened, too young to know better—it was wrong to blame her for the burn scars. Besides, down deep she loved her twin more than anyone else in the world, more than their parents who'd kept them apart for so long. Mama seemed afraid to have Jenny come home. Or be with Lily. Mama didn't seem to understand. She and Jenny were twins; they belonged together.

Outside, wisps of fog floated past, pale and gauzy in the dim evening light. Bay fogs were not depressing thick gray blankets like Valley tule fogs. In the Bay area, the sun always broke through before the day was out.

"Lily?" Jenny called from her bedroom. "Are you going to get dressed for the Halloween party or not?"

Lily drifted toward the bedrooms. There were two, but she and Jenny shared one and used the other for a study. After years of feeling like half a person—a feeling Jenny claimed she'd had as well—they savored their renewed closeness.

This was Lily's favorite kind of party—costume. With her disfigured face hidden behind a mask, she could behave as if she was as pretty as any of the other girls. She'd chosen to be a princess in a full-skirted white gown and a wig with golden curls to hide her own pale red hair. Atop the curls, she'd wear a sparkling rhinestone tiara. Her mask was a frothy affair decorated with lace and sequins that hid all but her mouth.

Jenny was already in costume. In her long black gown, black fright wig, conical hat, and green-skinned witch mask, she was a truly hideous sight and Lily told her so.

Jenny's sinister witch's cackle was in keeping with

the costume. Then she slid the mask up as she watched
Lily dress, spoiling the effect.

"Remember what I told you about frat parties," she
warned. "Never go upstairs."

"I'm not two years old, you know!"

Jenny smiled. "If you were, none of the guys would
try to lure you to your doom."

"What a way to put it. As if a little petting is
doom."

"Who said it was? But you get in one of those bedrooms with some guy who's been guzzling hooch until
he's ossified, and believe me, it's doom."

Lily shot her an angry look. "You mean Rolfe, don't
you? Why do you always pick on him? Are you jealous
because he pays attention to me?"

Jenny sighed. "I didn't mean Rolfe in particular."

But Lily knew she was lying. She nursed her anger
until Jenny parked their yellow roadster in back of the
frat house and they heard, from the open windows, a
banjo and voices singing "You'd Be Surprised." The
lively music coaxed Lily into a party mood, and she
was smiling by the time they walked through the door
into the smoky, jack-o-lantern-lit room.

It seemed as though half the college was at the
party—already the room was too crowded to dance.
When Lily tasted the punch, she could tell it was
spiked and she hesitated. As Jenny kept reminding her,
you had to be careful what you drank—some of the
homemade booze was lethal. After a moment, she
shrugged and finished the glass. A girl had to take a
few chances, and she needed the light-headed,
nothing-mattered feeling alcohol brought.

To hell with those old men in Washington who
passed laws like Prohibition, trying to keep people
from having fun. She drank a second glass of punch.

When she was half finished with the third, a Roman
gladiator offered her a Pall Mall and Lily, not wanting
anyone to suspect who she was, took the cigarette,
turning quickly away before he could offer to light it.
Try as she might to get over her fear, fire anywhere

near her—even a match—could panic her. She didn't, couldn't, smoke for that reason and unobtrusively disposed of the cigarette.

She'd already identified Rolfe as the pirate with a patch over his eye, but since he had an arm around a girl dressed as a Theda Bara vamp, she didn't go near him until the spiked punch gave her the courage.

"Why dally with commoners," she asked him haughtily, disguising her voice as best she could, "when a princess stands before you?"

Rolfe gave a whoop of laughter, let go of the dark-haired vamp, and caught Lily around the waist. "And what's your name, princess?" he demanded.

"My royal heritage forbids me to tell."

"Just how royal are you?"

"That's for you to find out," she said, greatly daring.

He laughed again, squeezed her waist, and led her into a corner. "Do princesses drink?" he asked, pulling out a silver flask, unscrewing the top and offering the flask to her.

"Do birds fly?" she replied pertly, and put the flask to her lips, thankful the mask hid her involuntary grimace as the fiery liquor scalded her throat. Rolfe took back the flask and took several healthy swigs.

"Hey, hey," he said. "This bird is damn close to flying right now." Handing her the flask again, he urged, "Come on, princess, catch up so we can fly together."

Her head already whirling from her previous drinks, she made a pretense of swallowing.

"Atta girl." He lowered his mouth to hers and kissed her.

It wasn't at all what she imagined a lover's kiss would be; his mouth was open and he shoved his tongue between her lips, invading her mouth. He tasted of the liquor in the flask, making her stomach churn unpleasantly. She struggled away from him and fled, desperately seeking fresh air.

The room spun dizzily, the crowd hemmed her in,

trapping her. Grinning malevolently, the jack-o-lanterns stared at her from smoky yellow eyes. Her tiara was knocked askew by a Viking's hand and she swayed, whimpering, feeling more and more nauseated. Where was Jenny, why didn't she come to her rescue?

Suddenly a black-gloved hand grasped hers; a man's strong arm supported her. She leaned against his black-clad shoulder gratefully, not looking at him, not caring for the moment who her rescuer was.

"I'm going to be sick," she moaned.

He scooped her into his arms and carried her through the crowd, upstairs, and eased her onto a bed. When she tried to look at him—was he actually wearing a cape?—everything blurred, so she closed her eyes, gratefully descending into a spinning darkness.

Something kept pulling up her skirt, forcing her from the dark refuge. "Don't," she begged, opening her eyes reluctantly.

Terror stopped her breath as, in the dim light from a window, she stared into the fanged face of a man dressed all in black. He sat on the bed beside her, his hand under her dress.

"No," she moaned.

"Too late, pretty lady," he said in a sepulchral voice, his words slurred. "You're the vampire's victim." He laughed hollowly. "Vampires drink blood."

He must be wearing a mask. Lily tried to force herself to reach up, grab the mask from his face, and push him away. But fear paralyzed her. What if she touched him and it really was his face?

She couldn't move or speak. When the ghastly face lowered to hers, she tried to scream, but the sound died in her throat.

Jenny turned from the group she'd been talking to and scanned the room. Where was Lily? With that glittering tiara she'd been easy to spot, but now there was no sign of her. The last Jenny had seen her was in a corner with Rolfe the pirate. Now she couldn't find him, either.

She tried to watch over Lily despite her sister's resentment because Lily was so naive. Surely Lily, after she'd been warned, had enough sense not to let Rolfe take her upstairs. Or did she? Jenny began tunneling through the crowd toward the door.

When she reached it, to her surprise she found Rolfe sitting on the floor with a dark-haired girl in his lap.

"Where's Lily?" she asked. "The princess."

He looked up, his eyes glazed, and shrugged.

Jenny went into the foyer and paused, wondering where to look next—the powder room?

From upstairs, faint and muted, came a scream. Without stopping to wonder if it was her sister, Jenny hiked up her witch's skirt and hurriedly climbed the stairs, calling Lily's name.

There was no answer. On the second floor some doors were open, some closed. The rooms with open doors were empty. The first closed door she tried was locked.

"Lily?" she called, rattling the knob.

"Not in here," a man's voice said.

About to turn away, Jenny held, an image forming in her mind of long white fangs. Fear that was not her own spiked through her, convincing Jenny that her sister was in that room, helpless and afraid.

Heat burned below her throat—the salamander she always wore around her neck on a gold chain warning her not to lose control. She grasped the charm in one hand, easing it from under the witch's dress. The salamander was hot to the touch.

She'd never fire-started since Grandmother Liisi fastened the charm around her neck and taught her the control words. First because she couldn't, and then because she wouldn't. She'd learned not to be tempted to fire-start. In the past few years, she couldn't recall the salamander ever growing warm.

Damn it, she had to get inside that room. Jenny closed her eyes and broke through her control, letting the image of fire build in her mind. Fire burning through the lock of the door, a flame hot enough to melt the metal.

Inside the room a man yelled in pain. The smell of charred wood filled the air. As she opened her eyes, the door swung open. Inside a man, his clothes in flames, rolled on the floor, screaming. Lily lay sprawled across the bed.

Jenny bypassed the burning man, rushed to Lily, yanked her from the bed, pulled her bodily across the room, and thrust her into the hall. Then she plunged back into the smoke and grabbed a blanket from the bed, throwing it over the thrashing man, wrapping him in the blanket to kill the flames. From the top of a dresser, an unlit jack-o-lantern grinned evilly at her. Flames licked up the legs of the dresser.

Choking from the smoke and the sickening stench of burned flesh, Jenny struggled to drag the blanketed man from the room. Someone, alerted by the noise, arrived to help her. As soon as the burned man was safely into the hall with others to see to him, Jenny hurried to her sister and, with an arm around her waist, guided Lily down the stairs and out of the house.

Lily didn't say a word until they got in the car. "You burned him," she whispered, staring at her sister. "You burned him just like you did me."

Guilt twisted in Jenny's gut. She'd meant the fire to melt the lock and not touch anything else. Certainly not a human, not again. She listened to the wail of a fire siren and shuddered.

"I don't care!" Lily cried. "He wasn't human; he was a vampire, he deserved to be burned."

Jenny's hands tightened on the wheel. "He was a man. Vampires don't exist."

"He *was* one!" Lily's voice rose hysterically.

"We were at a costume party. The man wore a vampire mask."

"But he said he was going to drink my blood!"

"He had something quite different in mind. Something a damn sight more human.'' Exasperation mixed with Jenny's guilt.

"Did you see a mask?'' Lily demanded.

"For heaven's sake! There are no vampires. And if there were, I doubt very much if I could set one on fire. He was a man and I burned him. Damn it, Lily, I shouldn't have fire-started. I shouldn't have broken my word to Grandmother.''

"Don't worry,'' Lily said. "Why, with all those jack-o-lanterns burning it's a wonder a fire didn't start sooner. No one will ever suspect you.''

Tears rolled down Jenny's cheeks, blurring her vision until she pulled the car to the curb. Even her twin didn't understand how she felt. Weeping, pounding on the wheel, she cried, "*I* know what I did. And I swear I'll never do it again. I'll never fire-start, no matter what. Never!''

Chapter 21

In the new home her mother and stepfather had bought in Pacific Heights, Melanie stared down at her half-sister, doubting if she'd been even one-tenth as cute as a baby. She couldn't blame Samara for doting on little Beth—she was so sweet with her dark curls and big yellow-green eyes. And, of course, Beth was Ivan's first child.

I was Samara's, Melanie thought. I was her first child but I was unwanted. Unlike Beth.

Melanie had never fathomed the mystery of her father. Samara refused to speak of him at all. She'd learned from a reluctant Druse that her mother hadn't been married to him and he'd died before Melanie was born. But Druse claimed she didn't know his name or anything else about him.

Maybe, if he'd lived, her father would have loved her. It was clear no one else did or ever would. She'd tried college and hated it because she didn't fit in. But then, she never had. No one would ever miss her if she didn't exist.

Wandering away from the sleeping Beth, Melanie drifted to the window. The November sun bathed the city in golden warmth for everyone to enjoy. Only inside her was it as heavy and chill and gray as tule fog.

I don't belong in this family, she told herself. Nor in this city or even Volek House. I don't belong anywhere.

If only her father were alive—but he wasn't. From something Druse had once said, Melanie believed

Samara had met him in the mountains. Another time she'd accidentally overheard Chung telling Gei about someone who'd been buried in the mountains. From his words, she'd thought Chung meant her father, but when she confronted him and pressed him to tell her more, he pretended not to understand and started speaking Chinese.

The sun sparkling on the waters of the bay and the busy purpose of the boats and ships, all going somewhere, annoyed her. She had no purpose and nowhere to go.

Unless—was it possible she might find her father's grave? Surely no one would be buried without some kind of marker and a headstone would give his name, at least. She had no idea where to look, but that didn't matter. She could go on searching for the rest of her days—they'd all be glad to be rid of her.

At last she had a purpose in life. For the first time in months, Melanie smiled.

Ivan stopped his new Packard in front of the gates at Volek house but made no attempt to get out and open them with his key. Going in meant facing Arno. He'd thought he was ready, but when push came to shove . . .

Damn it, he had no choice. Wolf could have helped, but Wolf wasn't home. Since Hawk had returned, he'd been flying his father all over the country so that Wolf could meet the medicine men of various Indian tribes. They'd flown into the wilds of Mexico two weeks ago to talk to some Yaqui mystic and there was no way to contact them.

Arno was the only one left to ask for help. God, how he hated to. Taking a deep breath, Ivan opened the Packard door.

He took two steps toward the gate and halted. Inside the gate, his brother strode down the drive toward him. For long moments they stared through the bars at one another.

"What do you think?" Arno asked at last. "Has Melanie turned stalker or not?" He swung the gate open as he spoke.

From his words, Ivan realized Samara must have called Arno. He wasn't sure if he was relieved or annoyed.

"All the note said was she'd gone to find her father," Ivan replied.

Arno nodded. "So your wife said."

Your wife. Samara. As Griselda was Arno's. For a moment, Ivan was back at the Ritz in Paris, reading another note. How could he ever forget their betrayal?

"Hasn't anyone ever told Melanie that her father's dead?" Arno asked.

Ivan gritted his teeth, aware he had to swallow his rage. At least until Melanie was found. "Samara couldn't bring herself to ever speak of him to anyone, even Melanie, but she thinks Druse did."

"Then we'll ask Druse how much Melanie knows and start from there."

Arno was taking over as he'd always done in the past, Ivan realized, and was surprised at his lift of spirits. Damn it, did he want his brother in charge?

Without another word, he slid back into the Packard and drove through the gates, stopping to wait while Arno locked them again and got into the car. When a man comes asking for help as I am, Ivan told himself, he'd damn well better be polite.

Druse looked from Ivan to Arno. "All I said to Melanie when she asked about her father was that he hadn't been married to her mother and that he was dead. But from something Melanie said to me once, I think someone must have told her he was buried in the mountains."

Ivan exchanged a glance with his brother. The mountains!

"Wolf never told anyone where he buried the stalker," Druse went on. "Chung went with him to bring Grandfather and Stefan home, but I don't believe even Chung knows."

Chung confirmed this. "My wife, she speak Mandarin, don't understand good when I talk Chinee. Better we talk English. Melanie, she hear when I say to Gei how hunter die and be buried in mountains. She ask me more. I no tell no more. Wolf, he never say what he do with evil hunter. I no want to know."

"I wish to hell the Miwoks hadn't up and decamped," Arno said as they walked back to the house. "They're the best mountain guides around."

Ivan was aware the Miwok village had moved far to the north after Quincy's first shifting, evidently preferring not to take any more chances of encountering spirit wolves. He couldn't blame them. Quincy frightened him in a way Arno, when shifted, never had, even though both had turned into rapacious beasts.

"Having a tracker would help," Ivan said. "Winter's a bad time to tackle the mountains, even for an experienced hiker. Melanie . . ." His words trailed off. Arno knew as well as he that Melanie had never joined in the camping trips.

"A tracker," Arno echoed. He stopped and turned to face Ivan. "I could find her."

Ivan recoiled as Arno's meaning sunk in. The beast was a superb tracker. "God, no! You'd kill her."

"Not if you were with me to prevent it."

"How the hell am I supposed to do that?"

Arno smiled one-sidedly. "We'll take along father's old Colt. When he went through Liisi's tower room, Waino found silver bullets—some fit the Colt. Wound the beast with one of those, and he'll shift back and be harmless."

Ivan stared at his brother. The way he felt about Arno, his brother was a fool to trust him with a gun loaded with silver bullets. "No," he said involuntarily. "I might kill you."

"That's the chance we have to take." Arno's golden gaze met his. "Don't we, brother?"

Ivan would have given anything to avoid Griselda before he and Arno left for the mountains, but she came into the kitchen with little Curtis as the twins were selecting food for their knapsacks.

"Ivan," she said. "How are you?"

He looked at her glossy black hair worn long in defiance of fashion, golden hoops dangling Gypsy-like from the lobes of her ears, looked at the face he'd never forgotten, would never forget, at the blue of her eyes—the blue of French skies—and for a moment he couldn't speak.

"Never better," he managed to mumble at last, and quickly turned to the child who was examining him curiously with the same bright blue eyes. "Hello, Curtis," he said.

The boy stuck his thumb into his mouth, glancing at his father, than back at Ivan.

"He's confused because there are two of you," she said.

Like you were? Ivan was tempted to say. Except she hadn't been too confused to choose the twin she preferred.

"My crystal ball showed two faces," Griselda went on. "As well as—" She paused. "Wolf says Curtis is all right."

Ivan was suddenly reminded that Wolf hadn't visited them in their San Francisco home since Beth was born, so he'd never seen her. But, of course, she wouldn't be a shifter. Though it was true that Cecelia Kellogg and her mother were shapeshifters, Volek women had never been. Beth was in no danger.

"I'm glad Curtis is—safe," Ivan said. He spoke the truth. He wouldn't wish shapeshifting on anyone.

Curtis took his thumb from his mouth. "Two daddies," he said clearly, smiling delightedly. "One mama, two daddies."

"No, dear, he's your Uncle Ivan," Griselda corrected.

Curtis thrust out his lower lip. "Is not."

Griselda scooped him into her arms. "Be careful," she said to the men. "Both of you." She kissed Arno quickly and left the kitchen with the little boy chanting, "Is not, is not, is not."

"He's recently discovered the power of saying no," Arno said. "I guess your daughter is a little too young yet."

Ivan murmured something noncommittal. He loved Beth; she was the sweetest little girl in the world, and he'd grown fond of Samara, but they both seemed very far away now that he was near Griselda. . . .

He was jerked from his reverie by the strangest sensation he'd ever had—the awful feeling that something was crawling through his mind. He whirled around. Druse had come into the kitchen, a baby in her arms. He'd all but forgotten she and Waino had a daughter.

Not Druse in his head. The baby? He peered at the child, startled by how her silver-gray eyes resembled his mother's. Damned if the baby didn't have Liisi's eyes. The pale eyes and the fair hair were particularly striking because the little girl had an only slightly lighter version of Druse's dark skin.

"Marti wanted to meet you," Druse said.

"How do you do, Marti?" Ivan said formally, thinking it was an odd way to put it. The baby was too young to care whether she met anyone or not.

Marti didn't smile.

The unpleasant feeling in his head was fading, thank God. "How have you been?" he asked Druse. She looked tired and more careworn than he'd ever seen her.

"I'm feeling older," she said. "I miss you, Ivan. And I miss Samara."

"She often speaks of you."

"I hope you find poor Melanie." With that, Druse drifted from the room, carrying the baby away with her.

Because of what Arno planned to do, they couldn't risk taking horses, so the brothers set off on foot across the field to the pine grove. At first Ivan was overly conscious of the holstered Colt he wore on his right hip, but as they fell into a steady pace, he forgot the revolver.

"You never really answered my question," Arno said. "Is Melanie a stalker?"

Ivan shrugged. "I don't know. She seemed a bit down the week before she left but nothing unusual. Melanie's never been Little Miss Sunshine."

"You don't think she's using this disappearance of hers as a ruse?"

"Why should she? Melanie has free access to Volek House anytime she wishes."

"From what I've heard, she has no idea of what her father was. But she *does* know about stalkers. And shifters. Knows I'm one. And Quincy and Leo. Cecelia, too, for that matter. She's even aware Wolf's son Reynolds is a potential shifter."

"We know so little about stalkers," Ivan said. "Maybe someone has to teach them what they are and what they must do."

"And maybe not. But you have a point. Even if Melanie has changed into what her father was, she may be too confused to turn on us."

If she is a stalker, Ivan thought, and you shift to track her, won't that trigger her? Put you in danger? He shook his head. Melanie might remember that silver was poisonous to shifters, but she'd never shot a gun in her life. Even if she had, where would she get silver bullets?

As if following Ivan's thoughts, Arno said, "Wolf taught all the kids to use bows and arrows, Melanie included."

Was it possible—? Ivan shook his head but couldn't escape his uneasiness. Wanting to change the subject, he asked, "Is something wrong with Marti?"

Arno glanced at him. "So she got inside your head, too, did she?"

Ivan hadn't quite believed it was the baby until now. He nodded. "Felt like a snake in my mind."

"She hasn't done any real harm—we're hoping she can't. Druse keeps her as far away from Quincy as possible, though, because we've discovered Marti can make him worse."

"Can't he be let out at all?"

Arno shook his head. "He shifts back and forth so randomly we don't dare. Leo brings him food and clean clothes—things like that. It's hard on the poor kid, but he insists on doing what he can for his twin. He does seem to have a calming effect on Quincy. That's why

Wolf is making all these trips—he's hoping some sha-man somewhere will know of a way to help Quincy.''

"What do you think?''

Arno didn't answer for so long Ivan didn't believe he meant to. "I've never told anyone what happened to me in a trench in France,'' Arno said at last, and launched into the story of his struggle to keep from shifting in the middle of a war.

"The urge is strong, Ivan, even in me,'' he finished. "Stronger than you can imagine. Luckily Leo doesn't have the irresistible need to set the beast in himself free that his brother does. Or even my less violent urge. In fact, I don't think Leo would ever shift again if Quincy were to die.''

Ivan looked at him. "Then you believe death is the the only solution for Quincy.''

"I hope not, but I'm afraid it is.''

"But who—?'' Ivan broke off.

"Who'd shoot the silver bullet into his heart?'' Arno asked. "None of us Voleks. Unlike Father, there's not one of us who could bear the guilt of killing our own.''

Don't be too sure, brother, Ivan said to himself, once again aware of the Colt at his hip.

They hiked on in silence, saving their breath as they climbed steadily until, near sunset, they finally reached ground covered with a light dusting of snow and Arno called a halt. His breath puffed white into the chill air when he spoke.

"As near as I can figure, we're close to the place where Father died. Neither Wolf nor Chung like to talk about that night, but over the years I've pieced to-gether enough to make a good guess.''

Ivan looked around at typical high foothill coun-try—pines, rocky outcroppings, hillsides dropping into small valleys—uninhabited by humans. "So the stalker must be buried around here?''

"Wolf wouldn't have carried him far.''

"But why would Melanie come here? She doesn't know the truth about her father.''

"Don't you remember Father's Russian saying about blood calling to blood?"

Looking into Arno's golden eyes, Ivan saw his reflection. Arno sees himself in my eyes, too, Ivan thought, feeling for a moment they were united as they used to be, one instead of two. Not only of the same blood but the same person, split in twain before birth. He blinked and the spell was broken.

"Besides," Arno pointed out, "we have to start somewhere."

After examining animal and bird tracks in the snow, they agreed the fall was no more than a day old. For all their scouting they found no trace of human footprints.

"There's no use putting it off any longer," Arno said at last. "I hope to hell I can manage without the moon. And that when I do change I can remember to hunt for Melanie."

A chill colder than the December wind settled around Ivan's heart. He wasn't afraid of Arno's beast, it would never harm him. What he feared was himself.

Arno lifted off the amulet with the *Elhaz* rune, handed it to Ivan, leaned against a pine trunk, and closed his eyes. For a long time nothing happened. Ivan, watching, was lulled into the belief that Arno had failed, when suddenly his brother straightened and clawed at his jacket, moaning. Ivan tensed.

Off came Arno's clothes. By the time he was naked, the change was well along. Dark hair covered his body in a thick coat, his face had elongated, his teeth were fangs. Tension knotted Ivan's gut as the beast fixed feral eyes on him and snarled.

Free! The beast growled a warning at the human not to come closer, even though he knew this was one human he wouldn't harm, even though the human carried a gun. Couldn't harm because blood linked them in some strange way.

The human called to him, the same sound, over and

over, almost like a bird's cry: Mel-an-ee, mel-an-ee, mel-an-ee.

The beast ignored him, raising his muzzle to test the scents carried on the evening breeze. Birds. Small gatherers of nuts. Fox. A sickening trace of skunk. None of these were fit prey. He trotted between the pines, seeking deep cover, then stopped to sniff the air again, aware the human trailed him. It didn't matter; he'd soon outdistance him.

The scent of deer mixed with the tang of blood excited him. Prey! Already wounded, the easier to bring down. But he detected human scent as well, scent other than the one who followed him. The beast hesitated. Danger came with humans.

The injured deer was close enough to tempt him. If he controlled his hunt lust, he could creep up on the prey, at the same time pinpointing the other human's position. If he saw danger, he'd hunt somewhere else.

Resisting the urge to howl, the beast loped on, circling to arrive upwind of the deer. The unknown human didn't matter—humans had no sense of smell.

To his satisfaction, the darkness under the trees deepened. Night was his time, even without the moon. As the deer scent grew stronger, he slowed, sliding cautiously from one tree to the next. The unknown human was also near by, close enough to raise his hackles.

When he finally spotted the deer lying on the ground, struggling feebly, the scent of blood had grown so overpowering it was all he could do to hold back, fighting the bloodlust that threatened to overwhelm him.

The deer was caught in a human's steel trap, helpless, its leg broken. Though the human wasn't visible, the strong scent warned the beast to remain cautious. He scanned the trees and the ground around the deer, his gaze finally stopping at a broken wall of rock rising just beyond the trapped prey. Rocks meant dens, meant caves—it was there the human hid.

With a gun?

The beast tried to make sense of what lay before

him—the deer in the trap, the human lurking in a hole in the rock wall. Why? Waiting for him?

The deer sensed him and its struggles grew frantic. The tang of fresh blood clotted the air, pulsing redly in the beast's head until he lost control. He leaped. The deer bleated in terror as he sprang for its throat.

Warm blood flowed satisfyingly over his tongue and down his throat as he tore at the prey's flesh, making him forget everything else.

Until the denned human screamed.

The beast's head came up. A woman. Standing near the rocks staring at him. He saw no gun, but she angered him, interrupting him at the kill. He rose, snarling, her shrill screams hurting his ears.

Ivan ran frantically through the darkness toward the sound of screaming, terrified that he'd be too late to save Melanie. It must be Melanie—what other woman would be in this desolate place on a December night?

When he heard snarls, the hair prickled on his nape. He stumbled over a mangled deer, recovered his footing, and saw them in the pale light from the rising moon—Melanie cringed against a rock wall, the beast advancing on her.

"No, Arno, no!" Ivan yelled. "No, don't, that's Melanie!" At the same time, his hand gripped the hilt of the Colt and yanked it from the holster.

The beast turned his head, looked at Ivan and froze. Blood stained the fur around the muzzle, making him more fearsome than ever. Ivan took careful aim at the beast's heart.

The Army had taught him sharpshooting; at this distance he couldn't miss. As he began to tighten his finger on the trigger, the beast threw up his head and howled, the sound laced with agony.

Ivan shuddered, aimed again, and fired.

Chapter 22

"The deer," Melanie cried. "The deer!"

Samara, bending over her daughter in the bedroom at Volek House, grasped Melanie's shoulders and shook her gently. "Wake up," she ordered. "Wake up, Melanie. You're having a nightmare."

Melanie's eyes opened. For a moment, she stared at her mother without seeming to recognize her, then her face crumpled and she began to weep. "Mama, I couldn't open the trap. I tried, but I couldn't. And then the beast—"

"I know, dear, I know." Samara sat on the bed and smoothed strands of hair from Melanie's forehead. "But that was months ago. You're safe now."

Melanie sat up, hugging herself. "*I'm* safe. But the poor deer died. And Arno—" Melanie shuddered. "I can't stand to look at him."

Samara frowned. "You knew he was a shifter."

"Then why isn't he locked in the cellar like Quincy?"

"Because Arno controls his beast." Samara stood up. "Just remember, you wouldn't be alive if it hadn't been for him."

Melanie grimaced. "I'm sure no one will let me forget it."

Samara sighed. Moving back to Volek House hadn't been easy for the girl, but as Ivan had pointed out, they belonged here. Uniting with Arno to find and rescue Melanie had changed Ivan's attitude toward his brother. They were once again as close as ever. As they should be.

"You'll never know how close I came to killing him," Ivan had admitted to Samara. "Killing my twin. And the beast knew it. Yet he didn't attack; he waited to die. At the last moment, thank God I had enough sense to shift my aim so the silver bullet merely glanced off his shoulder." Ivan shook his head. "At that, I scarred him for life."

"I hate this place!" Melanie cried, bringing Samara's attention back to her.

"You have nothing to complain about," Samara said firmly. "Everyone's gone out of their way to try to help you."

"If you mean the screen test Hawk arranged through one of his old flying buddies, what makes you think that helped me? You forced me into going through with it, but why would anyone in their right mind want to put *me* in a movie?"

Samara held onto her fraying patience. "I suggest you wait for the results before despairing."

"Despair! What do you know about despair?"

God grant you never know as much about despair as I do, Samara said to herself. . . .

Melanie's screams had roused Wolf from an uneasy sleep. He'd opened his door, ready to go to her, when he saw Samara slipping into her daughter's room. Another nightmare, he supposed. Now thoroughly awake, he walked along the hall, pausing at Melanie's door to listen to the murmur of voices inside. Reassured, he continued on, his thoughts reverting to the troubling problem of Quincy.

Though the shamans and medicine men he'd visited had offered many remedies for controlling shapeshifters, not one had helped Quincy. Much as he dreaded the journey, there was but one avenue left to explore.

He tapped lightly at Waino's door—since Marti's birth Waino and Druse no longer shared a bedroom. Marti was proving to be another troublesome enigma, but so far she was more annoying than anything else. She'd never harmed anyone. Quincy was a killer.

Waino answered so quickly that Wolf suspected he'd been awake before the knock. "Ah, Wolf. Shall we go to the tower room?"

Waino's disconcerting faculty of always being one step ahead had ceased to bother Wolf. God knows he needed an able ally.

The tower room was no longer the same as when Liisi was alive. Waino had removed Liisi's tapestries and her blue silk rug but had done nothing to add his stamp to the room.

"It remains a place of power," Waino had explained, "but not mine. I dare not interfere."

The one thing of Liisi's he did use was the bone kantele. He removed it from the wall now, his fingers idly caressing the instrument while Wolf took down his shaman drum and seated himself, Indian fashion, in the center of the room where the silk rug once lay.

"I will give you a word," Waino told him, "and the word is *hiisi*."

Hair rose on Wolf's nape. Evil spirit. Demon.

"If the need arises," Waino continued, "you will return the word to me."

Endeavoring to calm himself, Wolf turned inward, seeking the peace of nothingness that lies within every individual—though few ever find it. Only when both spirit and body were serene did he begin to tap the drum and chant, hearing the strings of the kantele weave a minor-keyed melody around and through his words and the drumbeats.

After a time, he heard neither kantele nor drum. Whether he still chanted, he did not know because the shadow-hole between the worlds had opened to his spirit. Down he plunged into darkness, the only light the silver gleam of the cord attaching him to life.

"I have been waiting," a voice whispered from the dark. "Long and long have I waited."

Before Wolf had time to think, something thick and scaly coiled twice about his waist, halting his passage.

"You are mine," the voice said. "You have always been mine."

The reddish glow from the coils showed him the head of a giant serpent hovering in front of his face. Wolf fought his terror. Had he encountered the Monster Between the Worlds?

The snake hissed with laughter. "You know me, Volek spawn, and that is not my name." Another coil slipped around Wolf's legs, then one about his chest. He couldn't move.

Horror gripped him tighter than the coils. The witch!

"It was meant for us to become one." The snake's mouth opened wide, forked tongue darting between the fangs. With fascinated dread, Wolf watched the jaws unhinge until the passage was wide enough to encompass him.

He writhed, struggling to back away from the slow advance of the snake's head, but her coils held him fast. A drop of red venom struck his chest, burning its way toward his heart.

"Hiisi!" he gasped.

The snake's head plunged down over him and he fell into a burning hell.

The strains of a song called to him, faint and far away from the terrible world of pain that stabbed at his heart and crushed his bones.

"Come, come," the song urged. "Come this way, come to me."

Through his tears of agony he saw a dancing blue light beckoning him, showing him the way of the song. With the last of his strength, Wolf flung himself at the light. Soothing blue wrapped around him, cooling, mending as he drifted. . . .

He opened his eye. Around him rose the stones of Volek House. Waino's white face hovered above him.

"You've made your last shaman journey," Waino said.

Wolf sat up, his head swimming with weakness. "The eternal enemy of all Voleks was waiting for me."

"Never have I fought such a powerful foe. Death,

hideous and evil, awaits if you ever attempt the passage between the worlds again.''

Wolf sighed, aware Waino was right. "Is there to be no solution for Quincy?''

Waino waved a hand. "This room of power must be his home.''

Wolf, startled, looked around at the stone walls of the tower. Secure. Isolated from the rest of the house. High, inaccessible slits for windows. With the addition of a stronger, steel reinforced door and massive bolts, it would be a veritable prison.

"Quincy can't be loose,'' Waino said. "Since he must be kept caged, this room will at least have a more soothing effect on him than the cellar where he now languishes.''

Depressed and saddened, Wolf nodded slowly. "I'll see to having a new door put on and some amenities added.''

"Mind you, I haven't altered my belief he'd be better off dead.''

"I can't disagree. But he's a Volek, and we Voleks don't kill our own.''

Grandfather did, Wolf thought as his words echoed in his mind. Grandfather killed the shifter who was his own son. But he shot the silver bullet before he knew the truth.

No one was more surprised than Melanie when Granville Darcy of Darcy-Goldfarb Studios called to offer her a screen contract. Her surprise didn't prevent her from accepting. In July, she left for Los Angeles with a firm resolve never, no matter what, to return to Volek House.

By July of '23 she'd been renamed Melda Vance, her dark and sultry beauty had caught the public's fancy and she was well on her way to stardom.

By July of '23, Marti Waisenen was two and a half years old. Though her physical development seemed normal, mentally she remained an enigma.

* * *

Marti lay in her bed, a thin sliver of moonlight falling across the safety rail, and watched the shadow pictures parade inside her head. On this floor, everyone was asleep except her. No one was in the room high in the tower or on the first floor. Way down underneath the ground, the unhappy wild one paced and fretted.

Feeling her touch, he reared up and started to howl, but she shushed him. How could she help him if he made noise? She would have helped him before, but she'd been too small. Even when she finally learned how to climb stairs she wasn't strong enough to work locks. But she'd gotten bigger and she'd learned.

He wanted to run free. Why didn't they let him? He hated his cage so violently that his misery made Marti's head hurt.

They were afraid of him. All except Leo. She knew everyone by name. In her head. The others spoke words but she didn't know how, and so some of them thought she was defective. Curtis called her "Dummy" if none of the big people were around.

Nobody liked her except her mother. Her mother loved her, but she wasn't sure if her daddy did. Even though she tried not to, she made her daddy uneasy.

The beast had a name for his other self—Quincy. He wasn't the only person in the house who had a beast self. Arno did. And Cecelia. Leo's beast wasn't as strong as the others. Beth didn't have a beast, but something inside her was shadowed and beyond Marti's reach. Wolf was different from the rest. He didn't have a beast, but like her daddy and Beth, there were parts of him she couldn't crawl into.

She'd tried to make Leo set the Quincy beast free. He wanted to, but he wouldn't. Nothing she tried worked on him. Out of everyone in the house, only the beast heard her and paid attention. He was her friend and she was going to help him. Tonight, while the moon shone. He liked moonlight.

Marti sat up and very carefully climbed over the guard rail and slid to the floor. She didn't want to fall and hurt herself—that would wake her mother and ruin everything. She was big enough to reach the doorknob now, and she quietly opened the door, let herself out, and closed the door behind her.

Going down the stairs took time, but at last she was at the bottom and she padded into the kitchen in her bare feet. There, she picked up the little wooden chair that was hers and carried it with her into the study. climbing on it, she pressed the third wolf's head on the carving that decorated the panel beside the fireplace.

A section of the paneling slid sideways, leaving an opening. Marti lugged the chair to the opening, climbed on it, and pushed the light button inside. Now she could see the stairs going down under the ground. None of the servants who worked in the house during the day knew about this part of the basement. Beth didn't know and neither did Curtis. They didn't even know about the Quincy beast. But she did because she found out things by crawling inside people's heads.

She didn't climb down the stairs right away. Instead, she toted the chair to the front door and climbed on it to unbolt the door. Then she opened it, leaving the way clear for the beast.

The stairs down to the beast were steeper and harder to go down than the staircase to the second floor. It took her a long time to descend because she had to drag her chair along with her.

The Quincy beast got so excited by her coming that she had to warn him that if he howled she wouldn't let him out. Lugging the chair to the heavy bolted door, she sent pictures to him showing the way out of the house.

It took all her strength to shove back the massive bolts. She climbed down from the chair, pushed it aside, and told the Quincy beast the door was unlocked.

Even before she completed the mind picture, he rammed against the door. Once, twice, three times. The door gave, slamming open, and she blinked up at him. He snarled, showing his fangs, but she knew he wouldn't hurt her so she wasn't really scared.

He bounded up the stairs and disappeared. Marti climbed back to the study and then realized she'd left the chair behind so she couldn't reach the wolf's head on the carving. Yawning, she stared up at it. All those stairs had been harder than she'd expected and she was too tired to go down and retrieve the chair. Now that the Quincy beast wasn't making her head hurt, she found herself too tired to even climb the stairs to her room.

She pulled herself onto the leather couch and curled up. As she dropped into sleep, she heard the beast, free at last, howl. She smiled.

Free! The beast loped into the night. Near the trees he stopped, howled his elation to the full moon and waited for an answer. None came. Where was his brother? The beast howled again, demanding, coaxing.

His need to have his brother join him warred with his longing to leap the wall and hunt in the hills for prey—and for a mate.

Then, among the other human scents from the house and the caretaker's quarters, he sensed one closer. Hunting him? His hackles rose. He'd never be caged again! He'd started to circle toward the wall when he saw the human. A woman. She had no gun; he wasn't in danger from her.

Instead of loping past her and on to the wall, he paused, her disturbing female scent strong in his nostrils. Suddenly the need to mate grew imperative, overriding his urge to hunt. She wasn't a proper mate, but she was female.

She hadn't seen him yet, but she was afraid; he could almost savor the taste of her terror on his tongue as she hurried through the trees. Her fear combined with her female smell excited him past caution. He sprang from cover.

She screamed once before he overtook her and bore her to the ground, clawing away the clothes that covered her body and gouging bloody furrows through her flesh. He yanked her into position, ignoring her shrieks of pain when he forced himself inside her. His fangs sank into her neck to hold her in place while they mated. He lapped at her blood in his lust-induced frenzy.

Suddenly something sharp stabbed at his back, piercing through fur and flesh. Human scent surrounded him.

Before the beast could withdraw from the woman to confront his attacker, something metal-hard slammed across his head. Stunned, the beast pulled free of the woman and, snarling, flung himself on the man.

A gun roared. Before the man could pull the trigger again, the beast's fangs met in the human's throat, relishing the taste of an enemy's blood. He savaged the man until the body lay in tatters. The woman, covered in blood, twitched and moaned. He growled at her but decided she offered no threat.

Sensing two more humans approaching, the beast turned toward the wall. Before he could flee, a noose settled over his head, tightening around his neck, burning, hurting, choking him until he could see nothing, not even the bright gleam of the moon. . . .

Wolf and Waino dragged the beast's limp body to the back door. Once they were in the kitchen, Wolf ordered Arno and Ivan to attend to Chung and Gei. Hawk and Leo helped carry the beast up the many stairs to the tower room, where he was shoved inside. Waino loosened the silver noose, pulled it off the beast and left the room, closing the door behind him. He bolted it and then locked the double locks, keeping one key and handing the other to Wolf.

"You can't just leave him," Leo protested. "He's hurt."

"A pitchfork can't do much harm to a beast," Wolf said. "And Chung's shot missed him."

"Worse luck," Waino added. "Chung had two silver bullets for that rifle. If he hadn't been afraid of hitting his wife, he could have killed the beast then and there." He shook his head. "God knows she'd be better off dead. As would Quincy."

Wolf glanced at the steel-reinforced door. "He's in forever this time."

As they started down the stairs, Hawk said, "I still don't understand how a little kid like Marti could have set him loose from the cellar. She wasn't even supposed to know he was down there."

"My daughter surprised even me," Waino said. "Why the beast didn't kill her is another mystery."

In the kitchen, Chung's dead and mangled body lay on the floor, covered by a blanket. Druse looked up from where she knelt beside Gei.

"She's bleeding from everywhere," Druse said. "We can't save her. The baby doesn't seem to be harmed but—" Druse paused, biting her lip.

Wolf winced and glanced away from Gei's maimed, blood-stained body. If she died, the baby was doomed.

"Poor Gei." Samara's voice was hoarse with tears. "She told me walking in the moonlight calmed the baby when it grew restless and kicked too much. If only she hadn't—" Samara began to weep.

Waino reached into his jacket pocket and pulled out the long, slim ivory handle that concealed his wickedly sharp Finnish blade. He knelt beside Gei and felt for the pulse in her throat, shook his head, and chanted a few words under his breath.

He slid the knife from concealment, clicked the blade into place and put the tip of the blade under Gei's navel. Wolf bit back a startled oath as Waino slit her abdomen open. He fully expected to see blood pour out, but the bleeding was slight and sluggish, indicating Gei was all but exsanguinated.

Using the knife rapidly but delicately, Waino sliced through what Wolf took to be the muscle of the womb, enlarged the opening, and set the knife down. Reaching inside the womb with both hands, he lifted out the infant, still encased in its birthsack, and handed the child to Druse. A boy, Wolf noted.

Fluid gushed when she used the knife to pierce the

caul and pull the membranes from the baby's head. She wiped its face with a towel, tipped its head down, and began to breathe into its mouth and nose.

Waino tied the infant's umbilical cord with a piece of string hastily handed to him by Samara and then severed the cord. "Gei's dead," he said.

At that moment the baby choked, gasped, and began to wail. Tears filled Wolf's eyes, drying in startlement when a voice whispered in his head.

"His name is Bren," Wolf muttered when he could speak, the name Chung's spirit had whispered to him. "Bren Volek," he added, "because he is one of us. A Volek orphaned him; Voleks must now be his mother, father, brothers and sisters."

Chapter 23

"The sheriff's satisfied," Hawk told Wolf in the study a week after the night of horror. "Or at least he pretends to be. He won't bother us further about the deaths, anyway. He doesn't think much of Chinese—'Chinks,' he called them."

Wolf nodded. Waino had suggested letting Hawk, famous locally as the area's war hero, be the family spokesman. A savage dog, gone mad and since destroyed, had been the cover-up story of Chung and Gei's death.

"I thought I'd seen death in all its gory aspects," Hawk went on, "but what happened to them was worse than anything I saw in France. Damned if I mean to sit around and let such godawful tragedies go on year after year. I've made up my mind to fly to Russia as soon as I can. Sergei Volek told us the answer might be there, and I mean to do my best to find out why Voleks are shifters." He stared at his father. "There has to be a reason, a meaning for this suffering."

"I agree," Wolf said slowly, a chill foreboding raising the hair on his arms. "We must know. But about flying—the Pacific's a long way across. I don't believe—"

Hawk grinned. "Do you think I'm still five years old and about to jump off the barn roof? Russia's not so far away as you think. Look at a map—Alaska's only a few miles from Russian territory. I'll fly to Alaska first and go on from there."

Wolf smiled back at Hawk, trying to ignore the presentiment that still prickled through him. No, Hawk wasn't five any longer, but there were times he wished his oldest son was still a boy, like Nicholas and Reynolds—a boy he could keep from harm.

On the day Hawk left on his Russian journey, Wolf flew to San Francisco with him to say good-bye there. He returned by train to Thompsonville the following afternoon and arrived home to find the household in turmoil.

"Marti's missing," Druse told him, her eyes swollen from crying. "We can't find her anywhere in the house or on the grounds." She flung herself in Wolf's arms and sobbed. "Oh, Papa, where's my baby?"

Waino, anxious and disturbed, told Wolf what had happened. "Samara tried to keep an eye on Marti, but Bren's only two months old so he takes a lot of her time. I'll admit I should have been more vigilant but—" he turned his hands palms upward "—I had no idea she'd wander off like this."

"How could she have gotten through the gates?" Wolf asked.

Waino shook his head. "We don't know. Actually, I don't think she did."

"Perhaps not. Just how well have you searched the grounds?"

"Besides us here at Volek House, the McQuades sent fifteen of their field workers to comb the grounds, and they did a thorough job. Didn't find anything. Rodney came over with his rabbit hound—she's an excellent tracker. We let her smell a nightgown Marti had worn but—" He shook his head.

"The dog found no trail?"

"At first we thought she had, but after a bit she began running in ever narrowing circles and then stopped as if she'd come to the end of the trail even though there was nothing to see. Marti would have to have flown away like a bird. Or been taken away." The fear in his eyes penetrated coldly into Wolf's mind.

They both knew concentric circles could be powerful charms.

Witchcraft? Wolf didn't like to even think the word.

"I found no trace of outside influence," Waino added, as though Wolf had spoken aloud.

"Where was this circle?"

"I'll show you."

As they walked toward the grove of live oaks, Wolf said, "Exactly how long has Marti been gone?"

Waino passed a hand over his face, almost dislodging his dark glasses. "Since the time we were saying good-bye to Hawk."

Wolf tried to recall who'd come to the airstrip to wave them off and who'd remained inside the gates. Hawk had taken off at sunrise—about six-thirty. The day servants hadn't yet arrived. Samara had stayed behind to look after Bren and Marti; Cecelia had remained in bed with a headache. All the others had been at the strip—except, of course, for Quincy, locked in the tower.

"Quincy?" Wolf asked.

"I remembered how Marti set him free once before. Even though I was certain she couldn't do that again, I checked the tower room as soon as we realized she was missing. Quincy was himself, for a wonder. I've had this hunch he communicates telepathically with Marti, and so I asked him if he knew anything of her whereabouts. I got no answer—he'll speak only to Leo.

"Later, when Leo asked him the same question, Quincy said, 'Marti went away. She'll be back.' Leo couldn't get any more from him."

A shadow-hole? Wolf asked himself and shook his head. Marti might have some powers they didn't yet understand, but he was almost sure her talent wasn't developed enough for her to make a shaman's journey.

Still, where was she?

"The day servants?" he asked Waino.

"They came to work about the time we missed Marti. I don't see how any of them could be involved."

"No strangers about?"

"Not within the gates."

"Damn it, Waino, there must be some clue. Can't you think of anything odd or unusual that's happened in the past few days?"

Waino frowned. "A white owl has taken up residence in the tallest of the pines. The owl seemed to disturb Ivan for some reason not connected to Marti's disappearance. I hadn't made any connection until you asked."

Wolf blinked. An owl? Some of the medicine men he'd met believed owls were death birds. Most agreed they were birds of power. "I'll take a look at that owl after you show me the spot where the hound lost Marti's scent."

Wolf saw nothing to distinguish the place where Marti apparently had disappeared except the stick Waino had thrust into the ground there to mark the spot. They went onto the small stand of pines. As they approached, Wolf noted that no owl was visible among the dark green of the branches.

"The owl chose the tallest tree." Waino pointed. They walked between the trees, looking up into the greenery. "That one," Waino said.

There was no sign of a white owl. Wolf dropped his gaze and froze, staring. A small form lay crumpled under the tree. Marti? He plunged forward and dropped to his knees beside her. She didn't move.

"No!" Waino cried as he knelt next to Wolf. He touched her neck gently and smiled in relief. "She's alive!"

A brief examination didn't show any obvious injuries, but Marti remained limp and unresponsive as her father gathered her into his arms.

When the little girl was safely in bed, Samara sat by her side, begging her to wake up. Neither her words nor anything else roused Marti.

She didn't open her eyes for two days. When she did, she seemed unchanged from the Marti they'd grown used to. Because she didn't talk, she couldn't tell what had happened to her. Samara decided Marti had just been lost on the grounds and been overcome by exhaustion.

Wolf didn't believe it, but since he had no better explanation, he said nothing to contradict Samara.

"We have to think about hiring someone to keep an eye on Marti," he told Samara and Waino a few days later. "Druse has too many other responsibilities. We need someone who has no other duties, who's with her day and night."

"Bring a stranger into Volek House?" Samara's voice was shocked.

"Not *any* stranger," Wolf said. "We'd be careful. We'd screen the person carefully and, if possible, let Marti meet her before she comes here."

"Marti?" Samara frowned. "She wouldn't know a stalker any more than the rest of us."

"But," Waino objected, "didn't you once tell me that you and Wolf sensed the last two stalkers?"

"Too late," Samara said sadly. "And only as danger, not as stalkers."

"I wasn't worried about stalkers," Wolf said. "What I meant was Marti would have to approve of anyone who came to look after her. Otherwise the person might not stay because Marti has the ability to make her life miserable."

"I don't like the idea," Samara said. "I'm against it. Voleks have too much to hide to allow a stranger free access to the house."

"We'll consider your suggestion," Waino said.

Wolf dropped the subject but decided he'd begin looking for possible candidates anyway, since sooner or later Samara was going to realize Marti needed full time watching. Full time protection. At least until she got older. Like Jennifer, who'd nearly destroyed her twin before she learned to control her bizarre talent, Marti was too young to understand the power she commanded. Without protection, she might not have the chance to grow older and learn.

Or, alternatively, without help, she might destroy them all.

While he didn't have his father's special ability to sense auras, Wolf had learned the hard way to screen out liars and opportunists. And, since he'd become a shaman, he recognized power, no matter how intensely a person tried to conceal it. Marti needed a caretaker, someone to concentrate on her and her alone, and he meant to find one before it was too late.

A week after Marti's strange disappearance and recovery, news came from Alaska.

Aleut fishermen had recovered airplane parts they'd found floating in the Bering Straits between Alaska and Siberia. The plane had been positively identified as the one piloted by Hawk Volek. There was no trace of the pilot.

For Hawk, the roof had proved too high after all.

Wolf packed and went alone into the mountains to grieve. He recalled old Bear Claw's long ago vision that saw him mourning the one who was no longer there—a true dream. Though Druse held a special place in his heart as his firstborn, Hawk had been the child of his spirit. His death saddened Wolf's soul.

There was little use in trying to console himself with the knowledge that Volek House was as secure as it had ever been, that even with their unresolved problems, the clan was safe for the time being. Not when Hawk was gone forever.

Wolf had been camping at different sites for ten days when he woke before dawn one morning, every sense in his body alert. He sat up and looked around.

A blue haze shimmered at the foot of his bedroll. He tensed, waiting.

"You know me." The voice spoke in his head.

He did. Bear Claw.

"Your shadow-soul has come far to seek me," he replied in the same fashion. "To console me."

"No, Wolf-Shaman, my spirit-soul has come. To warn, not console."

Then Wolf knew Bear Claw was dead.

"I have delayed my journey along the Path of Spirits to bring you my final vision," Bear Claw told him. "The one you seek is not far. She waits, blind to her power and bereft of knowledge, in the golden city by the bay. You must rescue her to save yourself and those of your blood. If you fail, your enemy will destroy you all."

As the shimmer faded and disappeared, Wolf called after Bear Claw, "May your journey be swift and your path smooth."

Wolf rose and packed his belongings, regretting the days he must travel to reach home. Who the enemy Bear Claw spoke of was he didn't know. Another stalker? The demon-witch? In any case, it was imperative he begin his search as soon as possible for the woman he must rescue in order that she might rescue them.

But go home first he must—the delay was inevitable. All journeys held peril. Before he started on his next one, to find the woman of Bear Claw's vision, he must first prepare his surviving sons in case he didn't return.

Hawk had died trying. Now Nicholas and Reynolds must fulfill the vow made to Sergei. It was up to them to search out and decipher the past—beginning in Russia.

All my life, Wolf thought, I've tried to protect the wilderness around me. Is this our family's purpose?

Whether it was or not, Voleks needed purpose in their lives to offset the disasters brought about by the sinister legacy they carried. Whether he lived to see their return or not, he knew what Nicholas and Reynolds must bring back from their journey.

Clan safety wasn't enough. His sons must bring back hope. Or else the Voleks would perish.